PRAISE F(

"Lyrical, vibrant, imaginativ   al voice
will draw you into a mesmerizing world."
                          —Emma Raveling, author of the Ondine Quartet

"E. J. is one of those authors who deserve to be immortal just to
continue writing mind-blowing novels for their readers."
                                                      —*Book Vogue*

"It's so easy to lose yourself in Mellow's evocative and engaging prose."
                       —Charlie Holmberg, author of *The Paper Magician*

SYMPHONY
FOR A
DEADLY
THRONE

SYMPHONY
FOR A
DEADLY
THRONE

E.J. MELLOW

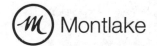

Text copyright © 2023 by E. J. Mellow
All rights reserved.

No part of this book may be reproduced, or stored in a retrieval system, or transmitted in any form or by any means, electronic, mechanical, photocopying, recording, or otherwise, without express written permission of the publisher.

Published by Montlake, Seattle

www.apub.com

Amazon, the Amazon logo, and Montlake are trademarks of Amazon.com, Inc., or its affiliates.

ISBN-13: 9781662500985 (paperback)
ISBN-13: 9781662500992 (digital)

Cover illustration and design by Micaela Alcaino
Cover image: © Egor Shilov / Shutterstock; © paprika / Shutterstock

Printed in the United States of America

For Alexandra,
my selfless sister,
who would give up her heart
if it kept another's beating

Born on a moonless night, the eldest of three,
Her hands hold the key to her power;
Music is her catalyst for control
To awaken magic set to devour

If you listen to her symphony play
If you listen to her symphony play

She conducts with poise and calm,
the sister to shoulder all ire,
But a storm she will quickly awaken
Upon any who threaten her king's desire

If you listen to her symphony play
If you listen to her symphony play

So take care, my child, if wrapped in her song,
If swaying too close to her band;
You may think your actions your own,
But your will is now hers to command

When you listen to her symphony play
When you listen to her symphony play

—A verse from Achak's Mousai song

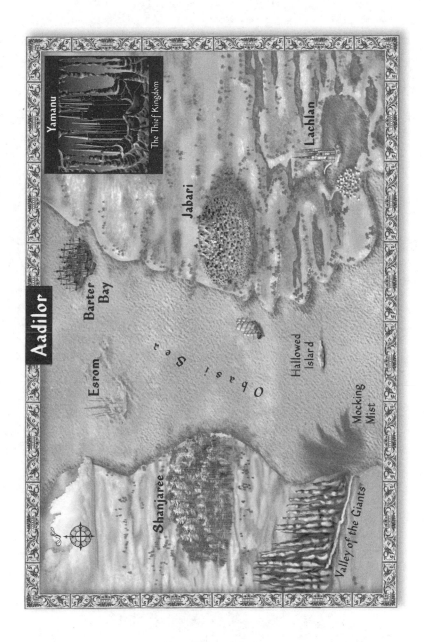

PROLOGUE

$\mathcal{T}$he night Zimri D'Enieu became an orphan, he was told he would be living with a king.

As he walked down the glistening onyx hall, he did not know how his limbs were moving, so heavy were they. He did not understand how his breaths came one after another; all his air had been taken, drowned with his parents. And though his mother had taught him tears changed naught, Zimri, at nine years of age, could do nothing to stop the ones streaming down his face from beneath his mask.

Both lost at sea.

Both. Lost.

Lost. Both.

These were the last words he had comprehended until a tall figure, whose violet eyes held stars, came to take him away.

Achak, they had called themselves. A face unburdened by a mask with skin as black as Zimri's, but glossy and made of different material than that of this world. They had a form constantly morphing from woman to man. A shape-shifting that was as fluid as a breeze rippling over a midnight pond.

Achak was brother and sister with two minds sharing one body.

Zimri absorbed this information as he did all things, quickly and quietly.

When growing up within the Thief Kingdom, one learned that reality rarely existed. His childhood was made up of impossibilities and contradictions.

Like now.

He had gone to bed with his life full to awaken to find it empty.

As Zimri brushed away new falling tears from under his velvet eye mask, he observed the large hall. Every few paces the smooth floors would be interrupted with rising sharp obsidian, which was pinched between similar jagged formations protruding from the ceiling. He'd later learn that the interior of the palace mimicked the outside cave kingdom, where stalagmites and stalactites rose and fell. Out there disguised citizens oozed from cracks to peer skeptically at those who walked by.

What are you hiding? What can I take?

While here, masked courtiers slid from shadowed corners to watch him being shepherded through.

How do you know our king? How can I take?

Teeth, talons, jewels, feathers, and carved bone were woven into the masses, all accents to gowns and robes and suits, who turned to regard their procession. Their stares seemed to hang longer on the maskless creature leading the way than on a young child present in the palace. Achak, it appeared, did not fear their identity being known in this kingdom of chaos and debauchery. A choice reserved only for the most reckless or foolish. Though Zimri could sense Achak was neither. The emotion exuding from the twins was that of dangerous confidence. They appeared to walk uncovered because they had nothing to hide from this hidden world.

There is no wickedness here we have not already seen and done, said the twin's disinterested gaze.

Zimri shivered behind his guide, easily picking up the tangy scent of their otherworldly power. It was evident Achak was known in this court, and while so were the D'Enieus, like most noble thief houses, their faces were not.

A person's reputation and identity are priceless commodities in our kingdom, my son, Zimri's father had once told him as he tucked him into bed, *and often mutually exclusive. But the best part is that with a switch of a disguise, we can be reborn. Tomorrow you could be someone else entirely than who you are tonight.*

At the time it had sounded wonderful and exciting, but now as Zimri trailed the twins and ran his gaze over the hungrily observing crowd, strangers in a strange place, he wished nothing more than for today to have remained yesterday so he could be the boy who still had parents.

"What a delicious little fish," said the high-pitched voice of a courtier who bent to peer at Zimri from beneath their beaded headdress, only green eyes visible.

"Is he here for our entertainment, Achak?" asked another, their long pointed nails reaching to run along Zimri's shoulder. Their excited curiosity wafted from their form: sweet and sour, causing his muscles to tense. While still naive in his magic, Zimri was blessed with the lost gods' gift of reading people's emotions. Feelings came to him in odors and scents; sadness and anger were always more rotten, while happiness and hope held floral fragrances.

"He is here for the king," said Achak, not breaking their pace. "So best not touch what is not yours."

The duo recoiled, a quick shot of fear—meat souring—as they bowed along with their apologies. Achak's warning only added to the collective court's intrigue, however. Murmurs spread through the hall like fire to dry brush. The crowd's attention now fell exclusively to him; it was a room of pungent intrigue.

But while most children might be seized in terror by such beastly surroundings, Zimri was all too familiar. Similar patrons flooded the lower floors of his home daily.

At the reminder of his parents and their club, a deep ache squeezed between his ribs, more suffocating pain. *Lost. Both lost.* Zimri lowered his gaze from the watching court, staring instead at his moving feet, to the black floor beneath them and a rippling reflection of a boy now orphaned.

What will become of Macabris? he thought, eyes welling with more tears.

Could it disappear as easily as his parents?

Yes, his magic softly wept inside him. *Just as easily as us.*

Yes, Zimri silently agreed, grief rising, *just as easily as me.*

So lost in his mourning and unknown future, he did not look up until Achak guided them through large heavy doors flanked by two massive stone guardians to enter the throne room.

Oppressive heat gripped him through his coat in the same grain fall he shivered from the ancient magic pooling in the cavernous room. Lava snaked orange fire on either side of a long walkway that became thinner the more closely they approached the throne: a squeezing of doubt in the mind. *Are you sure you want to be here?*

No, thought Zimri. *I want to be home.*

Though he'd spent many sand falls studying the fang-tipped palace from his bedroom's window, wondering of the king inside, Zimri's curiosity was dried up this night. He merely wished for the impossible—to be back in his family's sitting room, beside his father and mother, listening to their many conversations regarding that night's take at Macabris. The notorious guests in attendance, the debts they now held at their fingertips. At least then they'd still be alive.

But they weren't.

And never would be. The Fade was selfish and would not easily part with the dead.

"Step closer." A booming voice tangled with a dozen others pulled Zimri back to the throne room. Achak had moved from his side, leaving him exposed before the Thief King.

Blazing fear shot through Zimri as he stared at the ruler of his home for the first time. Many stories surrounded the king, most ruthless, terrifying aplenty, but his origin was lost to the No More. Swallowed up by the abyss that collected stories no longer told. And yet his history did not seem to matter to his people. Especially not to Zimri's parents, who had spoken only in reverence of their ruler. It appeared the only concern the citizens of his kingdom had was that it remained as it always was: welcoming of every creature, depravity, desire, sin, and lost gods' gift Aadilor had to offer.

Our kingdom exists to hold the chaos from spilling into the rest of Aadilor, his mother had said during one of her many teachings regarding their home. *If ever you venture beyond our hidden caved city, you will most assuredly hear foul, unkind words spoken about the Thief Kingdom. While most have never visited here nor ever will, they still hate us. That is the nature of people when they do not understand a thing, when they fear what is not like them. Little do they know their lives are as they are because of our kingdom, because of our king. He rules over a world too wild for the rest of Aadilor to appreciate.*

And that very king had ordered Zimri to step closer.

With the sliver of his remaining strength, he shuffled forward, keeping his attention on the pulsing cloud of smoke that hid his ruler from his view. This he had been told about by his mother as well.

Did you know our king sits mostly in smoke, my darling? she had asked him as he sat atop her bed watching her lady's maid cinch and clasp her gown into place. His parents had been preparing for a grand soiree at the palace. Zimri had thought his mother looked like Yuza then, the lost goddess of strength, with her black skin shimmering with a gold dusting while her headdress fanned out in sharp points above her head—the sun at dusk. *He only reveals his disguised form to those trusted few.* Her chest had puffed in pride. *One day, my son, I know you will see him as your father and I do.*

Zimri would later wonder what his mother would say to how much their king would end up revealing to him.

Currently, he could not make out an edge of his crown or arm or shoulder within the dark cloud. Only the king's consuming power slid down from the dais, and with Zimri's Sight—his ability to see magic because he held magic—he saw the silver threads curl forward. His king's shimmering ribbons stroked along his arm, coming to circle his neck. A kiss of cold sensing, feeling what power might live inside Zimri's heart. In response his own magic squirmed through his veins with unease. *Hide,* it whimpered. *We must hide.*

But while only nine, Zimri knew there would be no hiding while in his king's domain.

Gathering every bit of courage, he did his best to ignore the probing magic and remained still. It felt like a lifetime until the silver fingers retreated, affording him a gentle exhale, one that was quickly robbed as his king spoke words that sliced open his chest.

"You have lost your parents this night." A sentence holding no feeling, no mercy, only fact.

You have lost your parents this night.

No! A rush of anger erupted in Zimri, his hands curling into fists. *It is a lie. You speak lies!*

"It is a hard reality to take in for one so young," continued his king, as if he, too, held gifts similar to Zimri's and knew his heart. "And even for those very old, but it does not change circumstances. It is a great loss to have them enter the Fade."

Zimri bit his lower lip to keep it from wobbling, the realities of his life once again slamming down. How quickly his rage returned to exhausting grief.

"Your parents were confidants of mine." The cloud of smoke pulsed with each of the king's words. "Briella and Halson did important work for this kingdom through Macabris." A pause to allow this information to settle, their known names to echo in the soaring hall. "Given you have grown up here, you no doubt understand the value of secrets and what it means to hold someone's true identity in your hands. Zimri D'Enieu of the second noble thief house, your parents held many of their patrons. It was the demanded trade for guests who wanted a heavy debt dropped or punishment for those who dared steal or cheat in Macabris. A very clever business model and how they came to be my closest advisers. A king must know what goes on in his kingdom, you see, so I collect those who do."

Despite the circumstances, Zimri greedily took in every word. His parents had been His Grace's eyes and ears beyond his palace. At least one set of them.

Furtively, Zimri glanced to where Achak stood behind him. Catching Zimri's stare, Achak's grin flashed sharp, as if saying, *Yes, we see and know what goes on in this kingdom, too, and more.*

"You are no doubt wondering why I share all this with a child," said the king, returning Zimri's attention to the hovering black cloud. "But before I answer your questions, you must answer three of mine. Are you willing to enter this trade?"

Zimri's magic prickled with anticipation in his veins. Though just a boy, he sensed this was one of those grain falls that would reweave his future, just as the loss of his parents had.

He hung suspended in the room for two breaths; his years of lessons and study—both from books and from his mother and father—flooded through him. The pieces of his mother's *senseer* gifts that had passed to him at birth. The history of the D'Enieu name in this kingdom, what he had been taught it stood for: poised, powerful, perceptive. What he needed to uphold. *Proud. I must make my family proud.*

So he did this the only way he currently knew how; he used his gifts. *Find truth,* he silently asked of his magic as he pushed it from where it swam warm in his blood to test the air. It was a gentle gold exhale from his skin, a light cloud moving toward dark smoke. He attempted to collect what His Grace might be feeling, desiring him to do, as his mother had begun to teach him. *You will be able to mold them one day,* his mother had explained. *After more practice, you will be able to manipulate the emotions others feel just as I can with their thoughts. You will be able to coax the deepest, darkest confessions. Oh, my darling, you will be the collector of so many secrets, and we shall be so proud the day you rule Macabris in our stead.*

He did not yet know these nuanced abilities of manipulation, however, so his magic hit clumsily upon thick, impenetrable power, nothing subtle in his searching.

A husky laugh filtered from the King of Thieves. "I commend you on your boldness, my child," he said. "And I am pleased to see you have potential with your gifts, but you are naive to think your magic is any match against this throne's."

Zimri snapped back his gifts, sensing the blush on his cheeks. *Naive.*

"I take your actions as intrigue, however," the king continued. "So I shall begin our trade in questions, if you agree?"

With a swallow, he nodded. "Yes, my king. I agree."

"Very good. Do you, Zimri D'Enieu, desire to hold your family's place in my court?"

Zimri's heart raced, as he hadn't expected this to be the subject of his king's inquiry. Yet he hardly had to think before responding, "I do."

"Do you wish to grow into filling Briella's and Halson's positions as my closest confidant?"

He felt weightless, out of body. "I do."

"Will you swear your loyalty to this throne and the secrets it will reveal?"

A pause, heartbeat stampeding against Zimri's ribs as the words of his mother surrounded him once more. *One day, my son, I know you will see him as your father and I do.*

"I will swear it," he said.

As if a breeze blew through the throne room, the thick smoke surrounding the Thief King evaporated, revealing a resplendent-in-white figure.

Zimri's mouth hung agape as he took in the blinding creature sitting on his onyx throne. He was draped in pearl, ivory, and alabaster detailing, the color of his skin nonexistent beneath his opulent disguise. His headdress was a study in ornamentation as it braided and camouflaged whatever hue his beard had held before the mask twisted into sharp, curling horns atop his head. And there, in the center of his plated chest, nestled a white skull with black teeth. Teeth that matched the shrouded eyes peering down at Zimri. "Then swear it with blood," ordered the King of Thieves.

In an instant Achak was beside Zimri again and, with a click, produced an intricately carved silver cylinder. "Place your finger at the glowing tip, my child," they instructed.

As Zimri did, a sharp prick befell his finger, and he sucked in a breath, pulling back his hand to see crimson gathering at the top. Blood.

"A Secret Stealer," Achak quietly explained as they pocketed the item. "What you have seen of our king you will not be able to repeat even if you tried."

Zimri opened his mouth to attempt just that, but his tongue froze, his mind going blank. Even though he could plainly see his king in all his glory, he could not utter the words to explain what he saw.

With unease, Zimri cradled his smarting hand to his chest.

"Best get used to the pain, young one," said Achak. "There will no doubt be more secrets to steal by morning."

Zimri's magic twisted uncomfortably in his gut along with his growing fear. *What other secrets? And do I really want to know them?*

"You have pleased this throne tonight," said the king, the detailing of his costume shifting like fish scales as he leaned into his sharp, high-backed chair, "and no doubt have pleased your parents where they rest in the Fade. Now that you have honored your part of our trade, I shall honor mine. You have been called here tonight, Zimri D'Enieu, because the loss of your parents has left a much-needed hole to fill. One which you have stated desire to one day occupy. Advantageous, given that, per your parents' will, if they should perish, Macabris will be yours once you come of age."

The room fell away as Zimri's magic thrummed along with his quickening pulse. *Macabris will be yours.* The smallest grain of hope awoke in his chest. Not all was yet lost of his parents, of his home. *Macabris will be yours . . . once you come of age.* Hope was quickly replaced by doubt. *Ten years. I will need to wait ten years.*

"What will become of it in the meantime, Your Grace?" he dared ask.

"Its assets will be run by your parents' bank, Stockpiled Treasure," said the king, gloved fingers rapping along on his armrest. "But you should understand, the falling sands rarely keep people or places as they once were. A decade is a long while for Macabris to stand without a master. Part of the club will likely be sold to one who can run it in your stead. When you return, if you wish to, it assuredly will not be the same as when you left. But do not fret; there are many paths you can walk to become one of my confidants, if it is not destined to be through Macabris. Your gifts certainly have promise for such a task."

It must have been a sight to watch a small boy pull his shoulders back with such determination before a mighty king. "I *will* reclaim my parents' home, Your Grace," said Zimri, desperate to believe his own words, "and when I do, I will ensure Macabris is as my parents had always wished: ruled by a D'Enieu."

His king regarded him, shrouded gaze measuring, before he gave a nod. "I look forward to the day, child, but tonight you shan't return to Macabris at all. You will come to live with me."

Zimri blinked, his mind flooding with confusion. "But . . . why?" An improper response, but orphans were not ushered to live with kings. Least of all the Thief King.

"When you hold something of value, you take care of it," he explained. "And while I sit before you the King of Thieves, you may come to learn that I am also made of a different kind of skin and bone." His horned head tilted. "Unless, of course, you wish to take your chances on our kingdom's streets?"

Panic settled fast within Zimri. "I—no, I do not, Your Grace."

"Then I suggest you do as I bid and follow Achak. They will take you to a private chamber for you to sleep. There's much more to come on the morrow."

"Thank you, Your Grace." Zimri's thoughts whirled as he bowed low before following Achak through a hidden door that slid open from the rock wall at the back of the throne room. The air was more breathable here, cooler as he walked the shadowed hall. Still it did nothing to calm his racing mind.

Despite exhaustion bearing down, burning and begging his eyes to close, there was no way he'd be sleeping this night. Even as Achak left him alone in a large bedroom where a crackling fire's warmth bathed a thick rug and plush bed, everything inviting him to lie down—he could not.

He paced, replaying the events of today over and over and over, his magic swirling dizzily in his blood with his growing panic.

How am I to live here? he thought. *In the palace of the Thief King?* Were children even meant to be inside these walls? Surely not, given the stories of the screams filling the lower dungeons. *And what of my possessions sitting in my room at home?* Or could Zimri no longer call Macabris home now that it was in the hands of his parents' bank? By the stars and sea, he wanted his parents!

The threat of those blasted tears returned, blurring Zimri's vision, but now alone, he felt he could finally collapse into his grief. Sinking into a nearby armchair, he tore off his mask, throwing it to the floor, and set loose the sobs fighting their way up his throat. With shoulders shaking and head in hands, he cried from the thought of never hugging his father again, never curling beside his mother, never smelling her perfume or his cigars. He cried from the thought of not telling them he loved them before they had left and for not being able to recall the last time they had whispered the words in return. Zimri wept, filling the room with a heavy gold cloud of his heartache: fruit spoiled. It wasn't until the light filtering of piano music slithered into his room that he slowly stopped. Wiping his running nose on the back of his coat's sleeve, Zimri glanced up.

He was surprised to find his door had been left ajar, welcoming in the soft, lulling song.

Though he had assuredly never heard it before, it felt familiar. The notes spoke to his melancholy, a whispering of loneliness or perhaps merely being alone.

As if in a trance Zimri stood, brushing away the last of his tears from his cheeks to follow the melody out of his chamber and down a shadowed hall to the left. Only a few sconces along the walls lit his way before he was brought to the door to another chamber. It was just as dark in here, save for a bubble of violet light surrounding a girl who sat playing a piano in the center. Her fingers flowed like water over the keys, her magic pouring from her to illuminate her ivory nightgown and long braided hair that was as black as the night itself. Her eyes were closed, her white skin and delicate features not hidden behind any mask but exposed, relaxed as her body swayed ever so softly to the song she produced. Zimri was so unaccustomed to seeing another, especially a child, without a disguise that he momentarily forgot how he had left his own mask in his rooms.

While no music book sat before the girl, no notes for her to follow, she played as though she had awoken this story many times prior. The song blazed from her hands. Until her eyes opened, locking to his, and she stopped.

Zimri's heart lurched, the instinct to flee seizing him, but for some reason he did not. He stood rooted as he and the girl wrapped in purple light drank in each other's features.

She was perhaps the same age as he, with a slightly pointed chin and small nose. But her eyes—this was where he could read her emotions, despite his gifts—so big and blue and expressive.

Distrust, they said.

"You are in my family's private chambers," came a voice, surprisingly commanding from one so young and delicate seeming.

"Achak showed me in," said Zimri, his voice hoarse from crying. "My room is just down the hall to this one."

"Your room." It was not a question but a digestion of his words as she assessed what he had shared. "You look sad," she eventually said.

"I am sad," Zimri answered as only one so young could: candidly. "My parents entered the Fade today." As the truth fell from his lips, a wave of nausea washed over him, haunting reality pouring into his gut. *My parents entered the Fade today.*

The girl took a moment to churn over this piece of information, her gaze remaining stoically connected to his. "My mother is there," she said after a beat. "So they are in good company."

The tension in Zimri's shoulders eased ever so slightly when he heard that another as old as he might know of the sorrow he felt coursing through his broken heart. And though he and the girl knew nothing else of each other, Zimri held a decided sense that if they had, they'd share much of the same. It was a Knowing. One that came from two souls touching and finding they were made up of similar threads, similar dust and bones.

"Would you like to sit and listen?" she asked next, tinkling the keys to send a small sliver of her purple magic to illuminate a nearby armchair that had been covered in shadows.

After a moment of hesitation, Zimri approached, crossing the dark to make his way toward her light.

"Can you tell me your name?" the girl inquired as he took a seat.

Zimri knew he ought not answer such a question, but she had already seen his face and much had happened tonight that ought not have, so he found himself saying, "Zimri."

"Zimri," she echoed. "That is a beautiful name."

He felt his cheeks reddening. No one said that about his name, not that many knew it. He was merely the son of the D'Enieus. The child of Macabris.

Your name will be shared with the kingdom when it means something, my son, and even then, his father had once told him, *it might not end up being the name we gave you at birth.*

"I'm Arabessa," said the girl.

"Arabessa," he repeated, excitement racing down his spine. His childhood had not been filled with meeting many other children. "That's also a pretty name."

"I know," she said, turning back to her piano.

Neither of them spoke again as she set loose her fingers to dance over the keys.

It was mesmerizing, like staring at a fire in a hearth. What appeared as random movements were in fact purposeful. A reaction. A prediction. Zimri couldn't turn away. Her magic jumped from her hands, shades of purple as she awoke note after note from the piano.

He had never felt such kinship while listening to music. What Arabessa played captured everything he was feeling. All his sadness and loneliness and grief. All that he had lost today. Would be living through tomorrow. Alone.

Yet now, with her melody surrounding him, this girl and her warm violet gifts touching the edges of where he sat, Zimri didn't feel lonely. For the first time since learning of his parents' death, he felt seen. Seen by a girl whose eyes were now closed, who existed somewhere else.

A place Zimri also wanted to be.

So he closed his eyes and fell away too.

When Zimri opened them again, he would be tucked into the bed in the room he had first been shown, wondering if the girl who had played him to sleep was merely a dream amid his nightmares.

Arabessa.

He would soon learn that she was more than real. She was another secret to steal: the eldest daughter of the Thief King.

And he would come to love her.

Years later,
when falling sands demand change

CHAPTER ONE

*A*rabessa Bassette knew the uselessness of screams.

She knew because howls of agony she had extracted from many. Never would they curb the pain or restrain the tormentor from prying them free.

Still, knowing this did nothing to lessen her current urge to roar at the crowd in her path.

"Excuse me," she said through gritted teeth as she twisted past yet another masked party ogling a shop window and clogging the dark sidewalk. "Please, do step aside," she tried again. Not a one budged; they merely kept pointing in shared disgusted delight at what was on display. "*Move*, you rodents!" Arabessa's patience had finally snapped. "Or I shall add your fingernails to the ones hanging before you."

With squeaks of terror and flashes of wide eyes through disguises, they fled, leaving a momentary space in her path.

"*Tourists,*" Arabessa grumbled, glaring through her own eye mask as she charged forward. Her outburst did not relieve her frustration even a hair. If anything, she now felt mildly embarrassed.

Arabessa was not one to make a scene with her impatience.

That was saved for her younger sister Niya.

But with the approaching Star Eclipse, the Thief Kingdom was flooded with visitors.

And while this celebration, which occurred only every nine years, usually lightened Arabessa's spirits, when in a hurry, maneuvering through busy streets filled with obtuse pedestrians did not a good mood make.

She had somewhere to be, but somewhere else to be before that.

And Arabessa was not one to be late.

That was saved for her youngest sister, Larkyra.

Allowing the cool caved air to fill her lungs, she attempted to calm her pricks of irritation as she squeezed by yet another group of slow-footed sightseers.

By the Fade, is this kingdom no longer hidden? thought Arabessa sourly as she rounded a corner.

She was used to the wave of old residents visiting for the next month of heightened debauchery, but this was madness. For those not familiar, it was a pricey endeavor to find the Thief Kingdom, but it appeared word of the festivities had made its way to the wealthy citizens of Aadilor for them to seek entry.

Not that Arabessa would have postponed her errand if she had known of the crowds. What she held in her gloved hand could not wait.

As she slipped down a side alley, her feet swiftly crunching against the gravel path, the hairs on the back of her neck rose as she sensed two forms behind her peel away from the shadowed brick walls.

Not this too? she thought with further annoyance, gripping the glass vial in her palm more protectively against her cloaked chest.

While Arabessa wasn't wary of a fight, she couldn't afford anything else slowing her down. And foolish pickpockets were not worth her time. But thieves, unfortunately, were a tired detail in the Thief Kingdom. And these crooks appeared to believe they had found a mark. Especially when a third companion stepped from a dark cut in their alley to block her path. They danced a short blade between their fingers, their smile under their eye mask just as pointed. *Whatever you have is now ours,* their expression seemed to say.

Arabessa let out a tired sigh, coming to a stop. "I have no time for warnings," she said, angling her back to the brick, skirts rustling with her movement as she eyed her three opponents. "So let's get this over with."

"That suits us just fine," said a deep voice from the shortest of the trio, hood up and face covered in a stained leather mask. "Hand over what's in your pockets and whatever you're clutching so tight and we'll be on our way."

New flashes of metal winked in Arabessa's periphery: more knives pulled free.

Her magic thrummed in her veins, but it was not fear making her pulse skip; it was anticipation.

While she might resemble a lady of innocence, primed to be robbed in her gold disguise and plum silk gown peeking beneath her caramel cloak, Arabessa never went anywhere without her own choice of weapons close at hand. And though she was fitted with as many pointed accessories as these thieves, it was not her blades she hungered to use. Concealed within the sleeve of her dress was her ivory flute. No bigger than her forearm, it was a unique, compact design strapped securely in its holster and created for her exclusively.

While some hid knives, Arabessa hid music. For her notes sliced just as sharp.

And slice sharp she gladly would if any of these buffoons attempted to approach her.

"I apologize," she said, free hand twitching to set loose her flute. "I should have been clearer. Let's get *me* putting *you* three down over with so I can be on my way."

Gruff laughter floated forward from the group.

"You highborns are always so sure of yourselves," said the lankier man to her right.

"And always so fast to cry mercy," added the other, who continued to twirl their dagger.

"I fear you forget the kingdom which we are standing in," explained Arabessa, head tilting appraisingly. "Citizens here are never how they seem, highborn or low."

"You'll have to prove that, miss," said the man to her right as he sprang forward.

Arabessa spun away, dodging his slice. Her hood fell back as she tumbled into a roll, knocking a second attacker's feet from under him.

He fell with a grunt before a cry of pain as Arabessa landed a bone-cracking punch to his exposed jaw. She scurried back to her feet, one hand still clutching the vial protectively as the other stung from her hit.

Let us free, crooned her magic as it surged to her hands. *Let us play.*

Not tonight, she admonished silently, shaking out the pain along her knuckles. These rodents weren't worth her magic. She would take care of them as she sensed them to be: giftless.

With one down, the two left standing charged. As she twirled out of their way, she lifted an elbow, catching one in the nose. Blood sprayed, warmth landing on her cheek, before she ducked from a swinging arm to spring back up behind the last thief. She kicked him square between the shoulder blades, sending him tumbling to trip over his bleeding companion, who clutched their gushing nose. An unfortunate obstacle, for on the way down he fell upon his own blade. His pained roar shot through the alley.

"Proof enough?" asked Arabessa, breaths coming fast as she glared down at the cursing, grunting, and crying trio. She did not wait for a reply, however. Instead, she quickly turned and ran the rest of the alley's length to pop out onto a busy roadway. She had no more time to spare with this lot.

As she glided into the mass of pedestrians, she furtively glanced over her shoulder. Once assured she was not followed, Arabessa finally lowered her hand, which she had kept pressed to her chest the entire fight. "What an annoyance," she grumbled, muscles beginning to relax, but only just. What she held she could *not* lose, and if any other person tried to slow her down again, by the Fade, they would be worse off than those three thieves.

With renewed determination to reach her destination without another interference, Arabessa quickened her steps as she rounded a corner, entering the Gazing District. Here the buildings shifted from dark woods and brick to gray stone and white marble, a spotlight of bright in the shadowed cave kingdom.

As the domed glass ceiling of the Fountains of Forgotten Memories came into view, her pulse hummed excitedly in her ears. The building's towering columns stood like a centerpiece on a wedding cake at the end of the vast street. The surrounding temples were no less beautiful but lacked the reflecting glow from the pools.

Arabessa fought the desire to run the rest of the distance, her magic jumping in her chest with her eagerness. As she stepped into the large open rotunda, she glanced over the various basins of water, their illumination dancing across the disguised citizens who wove between them, all awaiting their turn to remember what was forgotten.

Arabessa searched out the shortest queue and added to the end.

Her grip on the vial in her hand tingled, anticipation spreading across her palm. Opening her fist, she peeked at the contents inside.

Strands of black hair tied together with thin blue yarn lay trapped in glass.

Her father had gifted it to her that very morning, on the eve of the Star Eclipse. Arabessa was near bursting with curiosity as to why.

Tipping her head back, she searched through the glass dome to catch the winking blue and green glowworms lining the cavern ceiling far above. The First Fade, the official beginning of the Star Eclipse, was not for a few days, so the stars still burned bright. Over the coming weeks they would dim as they reached the midphase, the Waning Sky, before continuing on to the Full Eclipse. While subtle, with their dimming, a shift of magic would transpire within the kingdom. The glowworms filling their cave's ceiling, the stars of this world, were preparing to die, shed from the sky to douse their city in utter darkness for a grain fall before birthing anew. And with that moment of rebirth, a shiver of ancient magic would race through the air. A shift of power from what once was to what now is.

Arabessa had been only five and ten during the last Star Eclipse, but she remembered the sensation well. Despite her heavy costume, a cold mist had fallen upon her skin as she stared up at the new bright stars, her sisters by her sides in the palace gardens. Her magic had purred in welcome delight as it soaked in the dusting. *Home,* it had whispered. *Our creators.* A bit of the lost gods turning over.

While her father had not said so, Arabessa was convinced that what she held in her hands was connected to this event.

Why else would he give it to me today over any other?

What memory does it hold?

Arabessa's question merely brought forward her own memory from earlier that morning, when she had sat playing her piano in her family's other home in Jabari.

Their sitting room was quiet, Niya still asleep as it was barely dawn, but Arabessa preferred to rise before her family, to swim in the silence before filling it with music.

Her hands stilled on her piano, however, as her father walked in, his form nearly taking up the entirety of the doorframe. His blue satin robe strained over his shoulders with his movements. Dolion Bassette spoke no greeting as he came to sit opposite her on the bench, no wishes of a happy day, his thoughts seeming elsewhere as he held up a small glass vial.

"She wanted me to give you this when it was time," he said, his blue gaze pinched with concern.

Arabessa's heartbeat tripped forward as she took the bottle, not needing clarity on who "she" was. "Time for what?" she asked.

"Time for you to know," he answered.

A rush of unease ran down Arabessa's spine as she peered at the hairs inside the glass. "Are they hers?"

Dolion shook his head. The sun had finally begun to creep into the tall windows, and the gentle rays caught on his copper beard and played through his combed-back hair. "They are yours, my melody."

"Mine?" Arabessa sat straighter.

"From when you were three."

She frowned, not understanding, which kept her a beat from asking more. Arabessa did not much enjoy not understanding.

Thankfully, her father saved her from her discomfort by clarifying. "You could have always used a strand of your own hair whenever you were inclined to, I suppose, but you would have needed to know what to look for, and this . . . memory your mother wanted unencumbered by four and twenty years of other memories. You won't have to search through so much to find what you saw as a child but could never explain."

Arabessa's gaze locked with her father's, a jolt of anxious expectancy to her heart.

What you saw as a child but could never explain.

At his words, the nagging visions that had wiggled uncomfortably through her mind every now and again pushed forward. A dark chamber, the metallic scent of magic accompanied by a sensation of fear and her mother's smile. But like always this was as much of the memory she could recall before the visions were sucked back into shadows.

And because her father never liked to speak much of her mother, the pain of her passing during the birthing of Larkyra still ever present in their home, Arabessa never felt inclined to burden him on the subject. He had enough to manage, and to forget specifics of her childhood, one that had been flooded with a plethora of vivid and lasting memories, seemed normal.

But Arabessa should have known nothing in her life was normal. Not even a gift.

"You must understand this, my child," her father continued, bringing Arabessa back to where they sat. "What you will learn from what's in there"—his eyes fell to the glass bottle she held—"I would have told you and your sisters if I could have."

Only the clicking of the metronome on the piano's top filled the room as Arabessa searched her father's blue gaze. But after years of slipping between his life as the noble Count of Raveet of the second house of Jabari to sitting on the Thief King's throne, of living two lives and many roles, Dolion Bassette had perfected the ability of shuttering his true feelings.

Her father was speaking with blatant opaqueness, however, which only meant he was unable to speak plainly. Or rather not allowed.

Magic, *her gifts crooned.*

Yes, *thought Arabessa, a flutter of hot excitement through her veins.*

A spell held her father's tongue in check. Secret Stealers or a silent oath, it did not matter.

We must go, *her magic urged.* We must learn what even our king cannot say.

"Thank you, Father." Arabessa stood, her urgency to learn this secret fluttering her pulse.

Dolion's large hand wrapping her wrist kept her from turning to leave.

"Also know this, my melody. What you may learn does not have to change your duties to this family. You can stay as you are with your sisters, do you understand? You have a choice." He released her. "You always have a choice."

Choice?

Arabessa blinked at the concept.

What choice did she have when born with her and her sisters' gifts, into such a family as theirs? When taught since a child that she was destined to lead her and her siblings, the terrifying trancing Mousai, in whatever their king demanded? What were choices when she had been so rigorously schooled in the importance of obeying a command, in the honor of duty? When her father mentioned the same familial duties in the same breath?

No, choice *was not a friend of hers. Duty was what Arabessa knew. What she believed to hold her virtue pure despite the acts they were meant to carry out in the Thief Kingdom.*

And still . . .

What was preserved in this vial sounded as though it might have the potential to change that.

And her father had given it to her. Her mother had wanted her to see it, when it was time.

An edge of unease twisted through her stomach as she looked back at the bottle, at the black hairs inside. Her *hairs. Trapped.*

"Would you want me to stay as I am?" she asked.

Tick, tick, tick of the metronome.

"I want what will fulfill you with a life beyond regret," her father replied.

"Next." A scratchy voice returned Arabessa to where she stood within the Fountains of Forgotten Memories in the Thief Kingdom. The soft murmuring of those around her dashed away her father's words.

She was now at the front of the line, where a Keeper of the Cup's charcoal-painted eyes peered at her from beneath their drapes of white robes.

"Skin, bone, nail, or hair?" they asked from where they sat before a small glowing basin of water: blessed liquid taken from the pools.

"Hair," said Arabessa, stepping forward. She handed over the strands from the container before depositing two silver into the jar by the Keeper's side. The coins clanked against past payments.

In fluid movements, the Keeper dipped their cup into the basin while feeding the hairs to a nearby candle's flame. They caught the ash in the glowing goblet and swirled.

"Drink," they instructed.

Arabessa took the cup, her magic swimming nervously through her limbs, a reaction to her apprehension.

I want what will fulfill you with a life beyond regret. Her father's words circled her once more.

"To a life beyond regret," whispered Arabessa before tipping back the liquid. She fought past the acute sour taste, ensuring she drank every drop.

Wiping her mouth on the back of her sleeve, she returned the cup to the Keeper.

"Sit over there." They pointed their bony finger to a bench along the far wall where other patrons were slumped, eyes rolled back, each twitching in the trance of a memory.

Arabessa's skin felt chilled as she took a seat, her head growing foggy. Her gifts swam quick in her gut, wanting to erupt and protect her. But for her magic to be set free, she would need to create music with her hands. Currently her limbs lay numb at her sides. It was impossible to activate the flute tucked away, leaving her magic to flip uselessly inside her.

Arabessa's greatest fear.

But her flash of terror dimmed fast as her lucidness slipped.

What you saw as a child but could never explain.

She forced her mind to hold on to this last instruction before her vision flooded with black and she toppled into the past.

The memory Arabessa saw next would rewrite every one that had followed.

CHAPTER TWO

*A*rabessa was late.

She was also flustered.

Two states of being she abhorred.

Still she was here, handing her cloak to an awaiting attendant before pushing into a crowded Macabris. As she breathed in the heady floral fragrance of the most exclusive club in the Thief Kingdom, she gazed through her eye mask across the low-lit sea of opulence. Ornate disguises, slices of painted flesh, gliding-by spirit trays, and multicolored threads of those wielding their gifts spun through the air. Yet none of it inspired much in Arabessa, for her stomach continued to churn with her recent shock from what she had relived at the Fountains, her mind reeling with overwhelm.

Arabessa was resisting her desire to turn around and find her father, demand he explain everything she had just learned and properly put to the test how much could be shared despite him being bound silent by magic.

But when Arabessa made a commitment, she stuck to it. She had promised her sisters she would meet them here, had promised a night of fun after they had been apart for so long, Larkyra in Lachlan with her duke and Niya sailing across Aadilor with her pirate. They needed Arabessa to start their time of revelry.

With a deep inhale Arabessa refocused on the room, and with shoulders pulled back, she pushed forward. As she maneuvered past masked patrons, she instilled an air of calm. Even with everything inside her screaming to be somewhere else, do something else, say something else, she would remain where and how she needed to be in that moment. After all, emotions were often wasted on the emotional. Later Arabessa could dissect and study her current innate feelings and come to a logical and reasonable conclusion and path forward. Just as she was the conductor to the madness of the Mousai, Arabessa would steady the madness currently coursing through her thoughts.

But our mother! pleaded her gifts through her blood. *She—*

Later, Arabessa silently commanded, curling her gloved hands into fists to keep them from shaking. *We will think on it later.*

A delighted shout brought her attention to the large steaming pool in the center of the room by which she walked. A handful of guests wriggled in its glistening waters. Most were still fully disguised, masks and beastly headdresses in place. While others, under the coercion of inebriation, carelessness, or a fit of boldness, floated nude, leaving any scars, tattoos, or other identifying markings clearly on display. Which, Arabessa knew, was the cunning ruse of the Macabris pool. An invitation of luxury hiding its true purpose: gaining leverage from guests.

Come relax in these warm waters, and do not worry if a bit of your disguise floats away.

It was a recently added design. One of many upgrades to the club since the Collector had come aboard, the infamous co-owner of Macabris who had brought it back to its former glory. If not better.

At the thought of him, Arabessa's pulse quickened, and she glanced up. High above the crowd, in the center of the second-floor balcony, stretched a long mirror. It reflected the debasing scene below, and behind the glass would be the man this kingdom called the Collector. Within these walls he collected identities and secrets in exchange for members' debts or, in other cases, to ensure payments were made.

Outside of Macabris he had become invaluable to the throne by pulling forth confessions from those charged with tyranny and other sins of this kingdom.

Though he rarely graced his guests with his presence, the Collector would be gazing down on them all, skimming his clever eyes over his costumed patrons reveling and gambling and swimming in the glowing steamed pool. Noting all who entered his domain, just as their king did of his kingdom.

You may not see me, but I always see you.

While not many knew the Collector, Arabessa did.

And he knew her.

At the thought of just how well, Arabessa's skin grew flushed, and she quickly turned her gaze from the mirror.

"There you are!" A blur of red hair and blue eyes beneath a half mask flooded her vision. Her sister Niya grabbed hold of her wrist and tugged the two of them forward. "Quick," said Niya. "I have placed too many silver on my next roll. You must bring me good luck."

"I thought you gave up gambling," said Arabessa, attempting to catch up with her sister's abrupt appearance while dodging drink trays and protruding disguises.

"I have given up gambling with the *pirate*," Niya clarified as she let go of her wrist to approach a crowded table of match-a-roll.

Second born, Niya was the dancer of the Mousai, her magic able to hypnotize and control others with her movements. As she seemed to be doing now as her boisterous presence caused guests to part, making way for her to grab hold of the awaiting dice and with a flourish send them scattering across the black felt. Those around her watched in rapture before they let out a wave of groans. Evidently a losing roll.

"Bad luck, then." Niya frowned over her shoulder to Arabessa. "Go stand over there so your dour energy isn't more catching."

Arabessa glowered as Niya became reengaged with the table, thoroughly preoccupied by her next roll. *Fine by me,* thought Arabessa as she scanned the crowd, searching for her youngest sister. She found the ivory hair and slight frame of Larkyra, who was in a nearby conversation with a group dressed like tropical birds.

From this distance Larkyra was a picture of innocence in her pearl disguise and soft blue gown, but her sticky fingers were playing their own game. If Arabessa wasn't trained in similar tricks, she would have missed Larkyra's hand dancing in and out of the folds of a man's suit pocket, a small bag of coin procured.

Criminals were a trying inevitability in this kingdom, and Arabessa and her sisters counted among them.

She was about to approach her sister when she stilled, watching the man whom Larkyra had stolen from spin to capture her wrist. Yet instead of growing angry at the sight of his bag of riches now dangling from her clutches, he smiled, a teasing grin that lit up his green gaze beneath his leather eye mask. Darius was here, Larkyra's duke husband, and appeared to have grown familiar with his wife's pilfering ways. Larkyra, the siren of the Mousai, tipped her head back on a laugh, and as she did, a small trace of her gold magic puffed out before Darius quieted her with a kiss. He pulled her close as he slipped the bag of coin back into his pocket, as if the incident had never happened.

A knot of discomfort twisted within Arabessa's gut.

It seemed her sisters did not need her to start their fun after all.

In fact, they appeared well enough on their own.

Her knot grew to an annoyed pang.

She had rushed here. Despite what she had learned at the Fountains, what she was desperate to gain more answers on, she had hurried here to be with them instead.

It seemed foolish now. And more foolish still to interrupt their merriment with this information. Arabessa was desperate to confide in her sisters what she had learned tonight, for it certainly affected them too. Her father might have been spelled silent on this secret, but she was yet not. Together they could figure out why they were learning of this history only now.

But Arabessa took in Larkyra's smile within her husband's embrace and the excitement gleaming in Niya's eyes from where she gambled. She could not disrupt that.

Even as her throat burned to share what she now knew.

Your mother wanted me to give you this when it was time, her father had said.

Why is this now time? she thought.

Why, why, why?

Arabessa shook the incessant question from her mind. *Later,* she told herself once again. She would find these answers later, when she had more time to digest everything, when this information would not change the course of their night. For now Arabessa would bottle it up. *What's another few grain falls?* she thought morosely.

For now, she needed a drink.

Snagging a glass from a passing waiter, she took the fizzy liquid down in one swig, the bubbles prickling slightly, before grabbing another.

This one she sipped, feeling the effects immediately, the welcome weightlessness to her limbs and mind. Arabessa needed all the help she could get unloading the burdens piling on her shoulders. The responsibilities and secrets and errands and tasks on top of the perception that she could carry them all gracefully. The flute hidden inside her sleeve tugged at her consciousness, her magic in her veins urging her to go somewhere private and let out how truly unbalanced her emotions were. Her music always helped her to settle.

Perhaps I should go, she thought; it was evident no one here would miss her if she did. With her decision made, Arabessa had turned to head for the door when a nearby conversation caught her attention.

"They say she's been like this since last night," said a guest to her right as they leaned closer to their companion. "A few have a bet going to see if she'll last until tomorrow's celebration."

Their friend huffed, incredulous. "Any who think otherwise are obviously not well acquainted with her endurance for revelry."

The pair was fixated on a rowdy scene at another gambling table. Arabessa followed their eyeline.

A woman sat surrounded by a hoard of admirers, all laughing riotously at something she'd said. Though she wore a gold mask and had a wig that twisted up into a beehive, the rest of her was on display. Or practically, with her dangerously low-cut dress spilling out ample white bosoms and no gloves covering the intricate tattoo of a snarling wolf on the top of each of her hands. Taking up a bottle of spirits, she flung herself atop her pile of winnings, showering herself in drink and inviting her entourage to lick her clean.

She might be in costume, but everyone who was anyone within the Thief Kingdom knew Kattiva Volkov. She was the only child of the Volkovs of the eighteenth noble thief house, and her parents were the other half of Macabris's owners. Kattiva was insatiable, sensational, and unpredictable. A living embodiment of what the kingdom represented of the wicked, the gluttonous, and the greedy. *A spoiled girl,* many would whisper. Though all cozied up to her if she ever shone attention on them. She was a gateway to the most debasing gatherings. A catalyst for the most chaotic. Whenever she was present, a party promised to grow wild. A good thing for Macabris, for no one entered here looking for a tame evening.

As Arabessa watched Kattiva slide from lap to lap, eliciting devious smiles from all, something hot and uncomfortable unfurled in her belly. What would it be like to be so free, so unburdened by responsibilities, even for one evening? Like her sisters appeared to be tonight? Like most in this room? What would it feel like to act on every desire, not caring about the consequence because someone else would clean it up?

Arabessa surely would never know.

But seeing Kattiva's boldness stirred her own. She might have come here to be with her sisters, but she was now hungry for another's company. One who, despite the panic sparking in her heart from all she had learned today, could always turn her worries to liquid. A danger of its own kind, to be sure, but presently she did not care.

With her pulse churning to a gallop, Arabessa's gaze swiveled to the one-way mirror high above.

Though she could see nothing but her own small reflection in a sea of strangers, she felt the voyeur's pointed gaze behind the glass as if he stood right in front of her. A tingling of warmth along the back of her neck that whispered, *Yes, I see you.*

Then come find me, she silently returned before charging into the mass of bodies.

She maneuvered unseen past where Larkyra and Darius still embraced, through the labyrinth of gambling tables away from Niya, along the steaming pool to turn into a corridor leading to the privies. It was not as crowded here, and her footsteps were muffled against the plush gold-and-black woven carpet. Every few paces she'd catch her masked reflection in one of the floor-to-ceiling mirrors that were patterned down the hall. Her black hair was piled into a complicated braid atop her head, and the bits of her cheeks peeking from beneath her eye mask were flushed. From the drink or from whom she was about to see, it did not matter. Arabessa needed an escape; she needed a moment to feel something other than worry or burden. Arabessa needed—

Her heart lurched as she was tugged quickly through where a panel opened beside her. The noise of Macabris was cut off with a whoosh as the wall fell back into place, dousing the tight corridor where she now found herself in utter black.

Strong hands held her waist, pushing her against a wall. The familiar scent of caramel and fire filled her lungs. Her magic roared awake along with her racing heart.

"I had hoped to catch you this evening," purred a deep voice in the dark. "I've wanted to do this since I saw you walk in."

Her next breath was stolen as soft lips pressed against hers.

Heat surged through her veins as Arabessa stood, fingers gripping strong arms, kissing the Collector.

CHAPTER THREE

*H*e tasted like his last sip of whiskey, warmth and comfort and *home.*

On that last thought Arabessa was tipped back to an altogether different time when this man, then a boy, had surprised her with a kiss.

Arabessa sat beneath the shade of a tree, annoyed. Her family's Jabari home stretched like a beached white whale on the far side of the lawn, and despite the summer day, one meant for far more relaxing activities, she found herself studying a pile of music sheets. Arabessa was meant to memorize them before her next lesson with Achak.

She was not fond of reading music. Preferred to play what she felt rather than follow what had been previously determined on a stave by a stranger. Her magic already felt so contained, limited to being set free only by her hands. To further restrict where and how it soared by obeying another's music sheet felt stifling.

To know where your gifts can go, you must first understand where your music can, *Achak had explained.* You may be musically inclined, child, but that does not mean you know all there is on the subject. All the melodies that can be created and with them the spells.

Achak was right, of course, but that only put Arabessa in a fouler disposition. Given the fine weather, her sisters were lounging in Niya's rooms with the windows thrown open. Enjoying their lemonades and layered cake as the soft breeze of jasmine filtered in from the front of their home. Yet here sat Arabessa doing homework.

A prickle of annoyance swirled through her.

She was not jealous of her sisters for much, but the ease with which their gifts could come alive, no instrument or study of music needed, was certainly one of the things she envied. Arabessa had often wished to trade with even Larkyra, despite her struggle to control the intentions of her voice. At least Lark could merely open her mouth to protect herself, to push out her gifts. Niya barely needed to flick her pinkie for a flame to be produced.

Arabessa stared down at her hands, felt the surge of her gifts fill her fingertips. But there it would remain unless she could create music, a sound, a beat: the door her magic waited to escape through.

"Are they dirty?" asked a familiar deep voice that had Arabessa glance up to find Zimri striding toward her. Despite the fact that she was sitting in shade, her skin grew hot at the sight of him. An ailment from which she had long suffered—ever since her thirteenth birthday, in fact.

Too long, she thought, given they were both now sixteen.

"Dirty?" she questioned, frowning up at him.

His dark skin shone smooth in the sunlight, his white shirt and casual trousers crisp for the hot weather.

"Your hands," he clarified, stopping at the edge of her blanket. "You were looking at them as though they were smeared with some atrocity."

"Dirt is hardly an atrocity."

"Blood, then."

She huffed a laugh, tucking her hands into her lap. "You're entirely too disturbed for so early in the morning."

"And you're working too hard." He slunk down beside her, lying on his side and propping himself up with an elbow.

He looked like a content cat, and she wished very much to pet him.

Arabessa blinked away the thought as she reexamined her music sheets sprawled in front of her. "Work hard now, play hard later," she said.

"I would agree, but we all know you will not do the latter anytime later."

Her annoyance flared. "I play."

"Not as often as you should."

She straightened. "Well, not all of us have the luxury to be idle. Some of us have responsibilities to manage."

Zimri raised a brow at that. "Certainly, but even Dolion takes time for himself."

Yes, *she muttered internally, teeth clamping,* time to visit his wife in the Fade. Time he should be spending with his family members who are still on this side of it.

Shame and guilt rushed through Arabessa at her thoughts.

She did not know where they had come from. Her father carried many burdens, and how he wished to unload them was not for her to judge.

"I'm sorry," said Zimri, appearing to take her silence and the emotions she was giving off as anger toward him. "I did not mean to offend."

"You didn't," she assured.

"You lie," he pressed, gaze assessing.

"Not every emotion you read is correct," she pointed out. "At least not with to whom it's toward."

"But I am usually correct," he countered. "Especially when I am with you." He slid her a disarming smile, full of flirtation and teasing. It set her heartbeat to tumble.

"I do wish you wouldn't pick apart my feelings."

"An impossible request." Zimri shook his head. "That is like asking you to not pick apart the notes played by a symphony."

"I hardly think my emotions are as interesting as a symphony, surely?"

"You, Arabessa, are the most interesting creature I have yet met as well as the most contrary. It's thoroughly enjoyable to watch you smile but know that you're actually quite outraged. Or see you paste on an expression of indifference when nothing but the sweetest scent of joy lifts from you.

You see"—*he leaned forward conspiratorially*—*"you may not share your thoughts, but feel them you certainly do, and loudly."*

Well, Arabessa didn't like that at all.

She certainly did not enjoy being described as loud.

Loud was Niya.

Loud was not nuanced, not graceful, not controlled as she was meant to be.

"Like now," said Zimri. "You have remained silent, yet I know I have hit a nerve."

"I'm sure my expression gives that away." She cut him a sharp look.

"Yes, but it does not give away that you also feel disappointment. It's subtle, but I can sense it coming from here." He lifted a hand to touch right above her chest, over her heart. His fingers were warm against her exposed skin, and she held her breath. "It is a heavy scent, sadness," Zimri continued absently, brows drawn in. "Like burning coals or charred meat."

She stared at him, his lips, his jaw, his warm hazel eyes. She could look at him forever.

"Why are you sad from what I said?" he asked softly.

She swallowed, forcing herself to speak true, for Zimri would certainly know if she did not. "I do not like being so easily read," she admitted. "It makes me feel as though I am not conducting my behavior properly."

Zimri slowly nodded, his hand falling from her, though the memory of it there stayed. "I understand why that would burden you."

"You do?"

"Certainly. You are the eldest child, meant to conduct yourself accordingly for your sisters to follow and for your father to be prideful of. You have duties others in your family do not. But I hope you know if ever there was a soul who needed to be described as one who behaved, it would most assuredly be you, Arabessa Bassette."

"But you said my true feelings were loud."

"To me." He smiled. "Most of the time, anyway. But I have the opportunity to look at you closer than others."

Arabessa felt her cheeks flush. "Certainly not too closely, I hope."

"On the contrary, not close enough."

"What does that mean?"

"It means"—his gaze grew serious, filling with something that had her stomach twist with nervous flutters—"if given the opportunity, I would love to see how much more I could pull out your fragrance of excitement that you are giving off now."

Arabessa laid a hand to her chest, where his had just been, as though she could stifle whatever escaped for him to sense.

She knew Zimri's gifts, of course, but they had never talked like this in regard to them: how they worked with her, could work on her. She felt raw, open, exposed, and not in a good way.

Arabessa had not thought to bring an instrument out to the gardens, seeing as she was still within the grounds of her home, but she was regretting it now. Her magic sat trapped inside her. No way to protect herself. She would never forget again.

"I do not wish for you to spell me," she said.

Zimri's brows dropped, features hardening, and he quickly sat up. "I would never do that," he assured.

"But you just said—"

"I do not need to use my magic to do what I described."

She didn't understand.

"Arabessa, you must know, I would never force my magic on you." Zimri appeared distraught at the very thought.

After a moment she nodded. "And I would never force mine on you."

"A promise, then." He held out his hand for her to shake.

She eyed it before taking it in her own. "A promise."

They kept their fingers entwined even after their agreement, and her skin grew flushed once more. With their gazes locked, a glint of something dark, something heated, filled his.

"Arabessa," said Zimri, his voice low. "I would very much like to show you what I meant about looking at you closer. No magic needed."

41

They were already close. So very close. And alone, hidden behind a low branch from the tree at her back. She could not breathe. Could not move. Arabessa sat in a moment she had never thought would come. She had fantasized about such a grain fall for too many nights to count, too many idle afternoons when he sat with her in her music room watching her play. When she could feel his eyes on her, caught his expression of want when she was done. But he was Zimri D'Enieu, the boy who had come to live with the Bassettes and be raised as one of their own.

And yet he was always more than that for Arabessa. Which terrified her.

But presently she was not scared; she—like Zimri had identified—was excited.

Here sat someone who knew what she wanted without her needing to say it. And she wanted him. She wanted him very much.

"Can I show you how much more I can make you feel?" he asked again.

Her breathing sounded loud in her ears. "As long as I can show you in return," she answered.

Zimri's smile was radiant. "Deal," he said before removing the last gap between them, pressing his soft lips to hers for the very first time. All Arabessa could feel from then on was Zimri D'Enieu filling every gap in her heart.

CHAPTER FOUR

A deep rumble of laughter filled the shadowed space, sending a cascade of goose bumps down Arabessa's skin. With a splash of clarity, she twisted out of the Collector's grip, pinning him against the wall instead.

"It's always so hard to best you," said his husky voice in the dark.

"You know you will always lose when we tussle," she pointed out.

"To tussle with you is to win." A gentle graze of knuckles fell along her cheek.

This, more than their kiss, had her disarmed, and she loosened her hold on him, stepping away.

There was a catch of a match striking before a flutter of orange light illuminated black skin, a strong jaw covered in scruff, and hazel eyes peering through a maroon eye mask. He moved closer, causing Arabessa to retreat, but because of how narrow the hallway was, she found herself once more against the wall at her back. Her breath hitched in anticipation, but he merely leaned forward to light a sconce beside her head.

He shook out the match and stepped away, but only just.

"I was headed to your office," began Arabessa, forcing composure. "There was no need to pull me in here."

A hint of an amused grin. "What is the point of hidden passageways if not to use them?"

"What is the point of running the most notorious club if not to enjoy your guests?" she countered. "Do you plan to show yourself tonight? I know everyone would certainly be pleased to gaze upon the elusive Collector."

"As I see it, I'm enjoying one of my guests now."

Arabessa's body burned as she drank in the heat in his gaze, the way it momentarily fell to her lips. Already her worries from earlier were fading, replaced by the tingling memory of their recent kiss. Her magic crooned its own desire through her blood. *Touuuuch. Feeeeel. Kiss again.*

Quiet, she commanded silently as fire pooled low between her legs.

Arabessa was glad then for the wall at her back, for her strength slipped ever so slightly. Which was the danger of him. Always the danger. She might have sought him out, but here stood the man who held the power to loosen her muscles as well as her corset. The man who softened her mind but blazed her body. Who made her feel. *Everything.* Right at the surface of her armor, threatening to break through. But if that was to happen, there would be cracks left in its wake, cracks where weaknesses could wriggle in. Where adversaries could poke and prod and hurt. It was always a delicate balance to be with him, for Arabessa could not afford any more cracks. Or distractions. Her family was already diverting enough, and this man counted among them. Plus, their work and loyalty to the throne were too wound up together: both trusted tools to the Thief King.

To jeopardize that relationship, that duty, was careless. And Arabessa was anything but careless.

So like always, she found herself reaching for him while simultaneously pushing him away, the secret she kept from her family—the secret of her heart.

"You appear tired," she said, concern prickling through her as she noted the heaviness in his magic in the tight corridor.

"And you're bleeding." His features pinched with equal worry as he stared at her chin.

"I am?" Arabessa rubbed at the spot. "Oh, that's not my blood."

He let out a huff. "Hardly reassuring."

"Yes, but certainly more encouraging. I had an unfortunate . . . delay on my way here tonight."

"Should I be worried?"

"Only if you care for the well-being of foolish thieves."

"I care for you and your sisters, don't I?"

Arabessa pursed her lips. "You're distracting from my earlier comment."

He looked away from her, his posture growing more rigid. "There is not much to add to it."

"You had a difficult interrogation tonight." Not a question, a Knowing. Arabessa saw how the harder ones, the ones where he needed to use pain, affected him. The problem with being an empath was that you couldn't ignore what you caused others to feel.

"Earlier today," he admitted.

"I'm sorry." Arabessa resisted the urge to go to him, ease whatever memory darkened his gaze.

"It comes with the territory." He shrugged.

"The Collector collects."

"You know I hate when you call me that." His tone held an edge as he moved to lean against the other wall. With his retreat, the space between their bodies felt cold.

"But that is your role here," she challenged. "Who owns Macabris."

"*Partly* owns," he corrected, eyes sharpening beneath his mask.

Arabessa didn't respond right away, knowing well enough how much this truth pained him.

"Nevertheless, Collector is your name."

"It is not my name to you. Here or anywhere else in Aadilor."

"No?" She lifted her brows.

"No," he repeated.

"And why not?"

"Because," he said, attention traveling to her lips once more, "we know each other better than that."

As he consumed her, she couldn't help but roam over his broad shoulders, shoulders she knew were smooth and strong beneath his flawlessly tailored suit. Clothes that hid a slash of a scar on his left side, one she had traced many times. "I would say we know each other as well as anyone else," she lied.

He watched her for a long moment. "You are attempting to incite me."

She snorted a laugh. "Seeing as you have dragged *me* into this cramped passageway, I would say you've already been properly incited, Collector."

"Then it appears you are looking to incite me further."

"And why would I want to do that?" She crossed her arms over her chest.

"Perhaps so I am forced to remind you just how well we know one another."

At his warning Arabessa's magic swirled hot in her belly. A tempting promise.

"Is that a threat, Collector?"

His eyes darkened as he pushed from the wall, gliding toward her, threat enough. He paused only a hair's breadth away, placing a hand against the wall by her head. She was cocooned in his solid form, his familiar heady scent, felt the pulse of his gifts at the surface of his skin. Hot and inviting.

Ours. Her magic reached out.

"It is only a threat," he rumbled softly, "if you're fearful of such a reminder."

Arabessa's chin tilted up, irritation sparking. "I am not afraid."

His gaze held hers. "Aren't you?"

Yes.

"No."

He dipped his head closer, lips hovering right above hers. Warm breath caressed her as he said, "Prove it, then."

Arabessa clenched and unclenched her fists, her gaze narrowing as her sensibilities tumbled through her: indignation, desire, frustration. But in the end—

Damn him!

Grabbing his lapels, she dragged him down, forcing his mouth to cover hers, his delicious weight pressing.

She was not scared of kissing him or touching him. No, it was everything that surrounded those kisses and touches. The years of *knowing* one another. Deeply. Secretly. Intimately.

Weakness, hissed that dreadful voice within her mind again. *Irresponsible.*

But to always be so responsible, reasonable, and logical was exhausting, and in this moment Arabessa was tired enough. Tired from what she had learned at the Fountains. Tired of always doing what was right and proper and needed for her sisters and father rather than what *she* needed, what *she* desired. Boiling pots required a place to let out steam, and he allowed her to boil over, if only for a grain fall while she leaned into his strength.

So instead of pulling away, she pushed farther in. Tipping forward, Arabessa wove her arms around his neck, greedy for everything he had to give, which usually was everything she would take. He rumbled his approval, strong hands traveling down to grip her waist, steadying her against him.

"Zimri," she breathed. *Zimri,* echoed her magic.

"Yes," he encouraged, cupping her cheeks and tilting back so he could look at her. "*That* is who I am to you."

"And who am I to you?" she challenged.

Zimri's gaze was liquid gold. "Arabessa," he whispered, said her name as if it were one of Aadilor's great wonders. "Music of my heart."

A deep ache pulled in her chest as he bent to take her mouth in another kiss. One that lingered, stroked, hot and needy, leaving her fingers to grasp in madness at his shirt beneath his jacket. She wanted to tear off every layer between them. She wanted to feel his warm skin against hers. She wanted to ignore everything from today and forget about tomorrow. She wanted . . .

"I should get back." She slid abruptly from his embrace, taking unsteady steps toward the exit of the corridor.

Zimri remained perfectly still, staring at the space she had just occupied against the wall, chest rising and falling.

Her own pulse was stampeding, her mind a hazy fog of conflicting desires. To stay with him, to be with her sisters as had been planned, to be alone with her thoughts. At the very least, she needed to pull herself together! She was *not* this manic. "Larkyra and Niya will be wondering where I am," she lied, knowing they no doubt didn't even notice her absence. But she needed some excuse to leave before she fell too far, unwound to the point where she couldn't pull herself back together. "And I'm sure you have—"

"Something is wrong," said Zimri, slowly facing her. "I can sense—"

"Please," she said quickly. "I am not one of your interrogations."

He grew rigid, eyes flashing. "You never could be," he assured, as if offended. "We promised never to use our magic on one another."

He was right, of course, but Arabessa was not thinking clearly. She had needed a moment of freedom, but it was always followed by a panic that she had been idle, ignoring one of her many responsibilities. At the very least she needed a moment alone to let everything from today settle.

"You are buzzing with worry," Zimri pressed, clearly wanting to go to her, but stayed rooted, no doubt aware of how close she was to fleeing. "Ara, what has happened?"

Tell him, whispered her magic. *He will carry our burdens with us.*

Yes, but should he? she countered silently.

"I learned of something today," Arabessa started slowly, knowing he deserved some form of the truth, "regarding my mother . . ."

His gaze narrowed, waiting.

"But I need to share it with my sisters first."

There was a flash of hurt in his eyes before he blinked it away.

Arabessa felt wrenched. She hated how that might have been interpreted. "Not that you are not like family." She took a step toward him. "It's just that this—"

He held up a hand, stopping her. "I understand."

She pressed her lips together. Tonight really was not her night.

She *would* tell him about what she'd learned at the Fountains, but her sisters deserved to know first. It was the responsible thing to do.

"Can you at least assure me that you are not in danger regarding this information?" asked Zimri.

Arabessa couldn't hold back her smile. "I am in danger every day. Blood on my chin, remember?" She pointed to the spot.

"You know what I mean." His expression remained serious.

Yes, she did. Being a part of the Mousai, the Thief King's preferred pets, meant a long list of creatures were left hungry for revenge. It was not uncommon that, when they were disguised in their black cloaks and gold masks or dressed for a performance, a foolish someone would attempt to get the better of her or her sisters. Pointy things did many costumes make, creative weapons creeping in disguises. But the Mousai were the Mousai for a reason, and very few had lived who had taken threatening steps their way.

Still, she felt the need to reassure Zimri.

"What I learned doesn't add any more danger to my life," she said. At least none that she currently knew of. "It's just . . ." She glanced away, mulling over her next words. "I need to talk to my sisters and father. There is much more to understand."

Zimri nodded, his shoulders easing ever so slightly. "Meet me later?" he asked. "Once the party is over? You know how to enter my apartments unseen."

"What of your meeting tomorrow morning?"

On top of conducting his interrogations, running his club, and carrying out orders from their king, Zimri had been preparing and saving and scheming for years for a way to finally remove the Volkov family from Macabris. So far he had been unable to make them budge even the slightest in the past half decade. Arabessa hoped that tomorrow, when he presented them with a gross abundance of overflowing bags of silver, their minds would finally be changed.

"I have prepared as much as I am able," said Zimri, jaw muscle working. "Nothing about tonight will affect that."

"Still," pushed Arabessa. "Surely there are papers you'll need to go over again or contracts. I do not want to distract you from—"

Zimri cut her off. "You are precisely the distraction needed," he said, his words echoing her very need from earlier. He pressed a button to his right, causing the panel beside Arabessa to slide open. The raucous sound of a celebrating Macabris flowed in. "Now, do try to enjoy the rest of the party," said Zimri. "But I ask that you save any dancing for me later tonight." Though his words were playful, his eyes remained hardened beneath his mask as he hung in the shadows of the passageway. If he could help it, he would not risk being seen by his patrons. His notoriety remained better notorious through rumor. Plus, it wasn't only the Mousai who danced with danger. The Collector collected vengeful creatures just as often as he did their secrets. More reasons for each of them to remain careful here and with one another.

Arabessa held his gaze, noting a flash of concern in it before it was gone and so was he, Zimri slinking back into the darkness.

As Arabessa returned to rejoin her sisters, she pushed down the squirm of guilt wriggling in her gut. Though she stuck to every commitment she made, Arabessa had never actually agreed to Zimri's invitation. It appeared both had thoughts of consequence to consider this evening, and in her experience it was best to do that alone.

So later, when Arabessa did not go to him, no promises would be broken.

CHAPTER FIVE

*I*n the center of a darkened ballroom, a bouquet of amaryllis stood rotting. Petals turned from vibrant red to crumbling black within the span of a breath, growing the pile of ash collecting around the vase. Arabessa was poised a few paces away, orchestrating the decay. Her magic prickled along her skin, a cascade of heat traveling to her hands. Her gifts exhaled through her fingertips as she dragged her bow in a slow tempo across her violin's strings.

Time, slip away, her spell demanded as it circled the flowers. *Die before the end of the day.*

The remaining blossoms crumbled in unison as if kissed by the Fade.

Arabessa's chest swelled in satisfaction, smile pressing her cheek farther into her chin rest as she danced her fingers up the neck of her violin, intent on continuing her spell's precision by lifting the water from the vase. But on a wavering vibrato, the glass burst, shards and liquid sent flying.

"Sticks," growled Arabessa as she dropped her violin to her side, abruptly ending the song she had been spinning into the expansive room. Her purple cloud of magic sizzled away. "What was *that?*" she chastised herself, whipping her bow against her skirts. "You *have* to do better."

Her gifts hissed at her reprimand, You *have to do better.*

"Yes." Arabessa huffed her frustration. "*I* am who I meant."

She had been practicing for a better part of a sand fall, waiting on her father's return to their second home in Jabari, the city outside the Thief Kingdom where the Bassettes lived unmasked. Though they hid other aspects of their lives here, like their roles and connection to the Thief Kingdom, along with their magic.

Magic that was currently not cooperating for Arabessa.

With a sigh, she stretched her fingers, working out the stiffness in her joints. Her corset had also begun to pinch, but there was nothing presently she could do about that. She always asked Charlotte, her and her sisters' lady's maid, to pull her stays as tight as possible when she planned to practice. *A straighter posture, a more perfect pitch,* Achak had always said.

And if Arabessa was not perfect in her playing, neither were her gifts. Or in extension, when they performed as the Mousai, her sisters. For in those moments they were also her instruments, her symphony reacting to her rhythm and tempo.

One slipup from her could do more damage than a broken vase. It could loosen a deadly note from Larkyra, a surging sway of fire from Niya. Which was why Arabessa still trained long after her childhood lessons had ended with Achak. She might have been musically proficient since birth, but even the most accomplished of musicians could not risk growing rusty.

Today her violin had called to her. *I am what you need,* it had whispered when she entered her music room. *My notes will calm your mind.*

And they had, for a moment. Until thoughts of her mother and what she had learned raced back in, upsetting her concentration.

Arabessa held a barrage of questions that had her chest tightening with confusion and frustration. *Why now?* she wanted to yell into the empty room. Why share this secret after keeping it hidden for all these years? What was Arabessa meant to do with it?

Dolion had not been at the palace, nor at their estate in Jabari, when she had come looking for him. Which meant there was only one other place he'd be hiding away, a place Arabessa would not go despite her burning questions or the fact that her father visited more often than he should: to see her mother in the Fade.

As Arabessa continued to massage her hands, she wondered how many years Dolion had allowed to be taken from him for a sand fall with his wife. For that was the trade the Fade required for the living to visit the dead.

Pushing down her growing unease at the thought of her father growing old too quickly, Arabessa turned, her slippers crunching and slapping over the glass and puddles of water along the tiled floor to focus on a new table. *Concentrate,* she instructed silently as she picked back up her violin. She eyed the fourth flower arrangement she had requested be placed into the ballroom. *And for the Obasi Sea's sake, maintain a simple vibrato!*

As she readied her violin, she prepared to awaken her new song, but a presence at the entrance of the ballroom stayed her bow.

Arabessa glanced over, her magic jumping beneath her skin, her pulse a matching quick beat as she watched Zimri approach. He carried the scent of the Thief Kingdom on him, cool night and perfumed smoke, as his graceful strides brought him just beyond her table. He was dressed in a crisp navy coat, matching waistcoat fitted impeccably across his broad chest. Noting the layer of irritation in his expression, Arabessa prepared herself.

"You never came," he said in greeting. He did not show the least bit of surprise at the state of the room or how it was arrayed with decaying flowers and shattered vases. The Bassettes always had their reasons, after all.

"No," said Arabessa. "I did not."

His brows drew together. "Why?"

"I had tasks I needed to complete."

"Tasks?" he asked dubiously.

"Yes." She placed her violin into the case set on a side table, clicking it closed.

"In the middle of the night?"

"The middle of the night is just as advantageous as the middle of the day."

He watched her evenly. "Did one of these tasks involve talking with your sisters about what you learned of Johanna?"

At the mention of her mother, of what she had been desperate to get off her chest for the better part of a day, Arabessa's muscles tensed. But thankfully she was no longer the distraught creature from last night. She was the composed Arabessa of today, which allowed her to hide her inner discomfort to calmly reply, "By the time I returned to my sisters, Niya was well into her cups, and Larkyra and Darius were primed to return to the palace for the remainder of the evening. So unfortunately no, I haven't yet had the chance."

And yes, I am annoyed by that, she finished silently.

"I see." His gaze was unyielding. "So you then left to do these *other* tasks you speak of rather than spend the night with me?"

"By the lost gods, Zimri," she huffed as she moved out of her ring of tables. "What is with the questioning?"

"It's quite simple, really," he said, crossing his arms. "I like knowing the reasons for why I have been jilted."

"You were *not* jilted."

"Oh?" He raised a dark brow. "So you did meet me in my apartments, and I have merely forgotten the entire experience?"

Arabessa flicked a piece of lint from her sleeve. "It's entirely possible."

"Ara," he breathed, his irritation showing.

"Zimri." She said his name with equal deference. "If anything, you should be thanking me for allowing you to concentrate on your meeting with the Volkovs today."

"I told you my meeting with Zhad did not change me wanting to be with you last night."

"But it should have."

His gaze narrowed. "What does that mean?"

"I cannot be a diversion from your goals, Zimri. I know how long you have prepared for—"

"Arabessa," he cut in. "As hard as it might be to believe, my cognitive abilities do not decline that easily. I am still able to put one word in front of the other after an evening with you."

She ignored how his sarcasm prickled her sensibilities.

"And besides," he went on, "despite your unwanted attempts to keep me focused, it did nothing to favor the outcome of this morning."

There was a beat of silence as Arabessa grasped his meaning.

Oh.

Oh no.

Her chest became weighted, knowing how much this must pain him.

"Zimri, I—"

"It's fine." He looked away from her.

"It's not fine." She took a step forward, feeling a flutter in her gut when he allowed her to place a hand on his arm. "What happened?"

"The usual. Zhad had his gifted bodyguard in tow, ensuring I didn't use any persuasive magic on him. Alyona was hardly allowed to speak, while Zhad gave nothing away. He had me bring in the money to inspect, read through the entirety of the purchase-of-shares agreement. I mean, by the Fade"—Zimri threw out a hand—"he allowed me to go on for two sand falls, all for him to merely smile at the end, pat me on the shoulder as though I were still the boy of nine and ten come to run Macabris, and say no."

Oh dear.

Arabessa wanted to bring her hands to cup his face, to kiss away his furrowed brow and silence the hurt in his eyes. But she kept still, instead assuring, "You'll think of something else. There has to be another way to get majority ownership."

"Or I can give up this hopeless dream," he bit out. "My parents are dead, after all. Who am I really doing this for?"

"You." She gripped his arm firmly. "You are doing it for you and for your family's legacy. What your parents worked for you to have. Macabris is your birthright. This is what you have wanted since I first met you, Zimri. The club was practically in shambles when you returned to reclaim your shares. You have brought it back to life."

"Yes, and because of that, the Volkovs are now more invested than ever," he added darkly.

"Then perhaps your way in is through something they invest in more. But whatever you do, do *not* let Zhad Volkov or any of their lot keep you from going after what is yours."

He merely shrugged, a tiredness creeping into his features, which pained her even more than his anger to witness. Zimri was not one to give up on anything.

"If it's any sort of consolation for the present moment," began Arabessa, attempting to cheer him up another way, "Cook made his chocolate biscuits this morning. I had him save you a few. Shall we call for tea and enjoy some?"

Zimri's gaze met hers, a small spark of warmth returning in their hazel depths. "You'll have to do better than that if you're trying to make up for breaking plans with me last night."

"I would if I had." She smiled coyly. "But I never technically agreed to meet you."

He blinked at her. "Pardon?"

"You asked if I knew how to enter your apartments unseen," she went on to explain. "Which of course I do, but never did I agree to your invitation to meet you there last night. No plans were technically broken."

A multitude of emotions washed over his countenance, but the one that settled was baffled annoyance.

"Arabessa." He ran a hand down his face. "It is fair to say I have been more than patient with all of your erratic—"

"Erratic?" She straightened, dropping her hand from his arm. "I am *never* erratic. In any sense of the word. I am the most dependable—"

Zimri cut her off. "In duty, yes, unquestionably. But with me . . ." He tore his gaze from her, staring at a spot at the far side of the room. His jaw worked along with his thoughts. It was clear he was attempting to speak his next words carefully, but as Arabessa regarded his pinched brows, his exhausted frustration, something sour twisted in her stomach. Something scared. Perhaps this would finally be the argument they had been dancing around for years. Arabessa knew it would come eventually. Knew it *had* to come. But knowing didn't keep one from hurting or running from it.

"Ara," he began more calmly, looking back at her, "I have always been honest with you, have I not?"

"Yes," she replied hesitantly. "Always."

"Then why can you not be honest with me? And I don't speak of whatever you learned of your mother yesterday," Zimri went on to clarify, saving her from an immediate reply. "Or other duties to your father or our king. I know with the amount of silent oaths and Secret Stealers between us, there is much neither of us can share in that regard. What I talk about is us."

Us.

"Why can you never be honest about your feelings regarding us?"

It was as if he had taken a slow dagger to her heart, spilling out a red pool of complicated, pent-up emotion.

Why can you never be honest about your feelings?

Because! she wanted to scream. *You are my greatest distraction and my greatest pleasure. Because I want to lie with you for sand falls instead of practicing. Because shared duties to our king complicate any relationship we may have. Because I do not know how to give more without having nothing left for myself!*

But Arabessa didn't say any of this, because how could she? What was the desired outcome here? What was the *right* thing to say? Arabessa opened her mouth before closing it. Lost. She was lost.

Zimri took a slow step closer. "I love you, Arabessa. So much so that I have been happy to hold only pieces of you for all these years even though I know there is much more of you that you hide away. That *we* hide from your family. But I can't keep this charade up forever. I cannot only care for you partially, love you in half measures. That is like asking the sea to not yearn toward the shore with its waves. I will forever be reaching for you, Arabessa, but the question I keep asking is whether you will ever reach back."

He was pulling her undone with every word. Her composure was slipping, her layers of discipline and duty and resolve. Which was precisely why she fought so fiercely to keep their love so neatly contained, controlled, a secret.

Because all that would be revealed if she opened the doors to her heart was a woman terrified.

Arabessa had seen what being in love did to others. All those who had knelt before her, treason committed against their king because of love. Love of their beliefs, love of another that caused them to murder, to steal. Love that still plagued her father despite the two decades since the death of their mother. The danger love had gotten her sisters into, the vulnerability they wore daily. Being in love was both a luxury and an ailment. And while her sisters might have married their duke or sailed the seas with their pirate, it was because of *her* that they could. Arabessa, the oldest, meant to remain, to be with their father and wrangle the Mousai when necessary. To look after their home, their assignments, their performances. What would happen to all that if she allowed herself to be ruled by her emotions, even for a moment? Or to allow Zimri to? He had plans and ambitions and dreams that needed his time and concentration to fulfill as well. And if ever there came a time when their duties to their king were in conflict with their relationship, if a personal quarrel kept them from cooperating, what then? For the gate to her heart to be thrown wide open . . . *no*, better to keep her love for him at arm's length. One always saw better in hindsight.

Plus, she was already beyond loyal to the man before her, to their history and what they slipped into behind closed doors. Just as she was loyal to her father, her sisters, their home, her expectations from her king. Danger enough. Leverage for others to claim. If she gave any more of herself to anyone else, would there be any pieces left for her? *Of* her?

"I do reach back," she eventually said. "As far as I am able."

Zimri's frown deepened, disappointment clear. "It's not enough," he said. "Not anymore."

She felt as if all the air had been knocked from her. *It has to be enough.*

"For the Obasi Sea's sake," Zimri went on. "We still hide *this*." He gestured between them. "Even when your family clearly knows something is going on."

"Perhaps something, but not everything."

He huffed his exasperation. "And what if they did? Aadilor would not come crashing down around us."

"Of course not," she replied, bits of her frustration showing.

"Then what is it? Are you no longer in love with me?"

"*Zimri*, that is nonsense, and you know it." She needed him to see reason, to remember what they had agreed to so long ago. "We have discussed this before. It is complicated enough that we live together in Jabari, work together for our king."

"I haven't lived here consistently in five years," explained Zimri. "And if it helps, I will move into my apartments above Macabris permanently."

Arabessa shook her head. "It's not only that. We can't risk this getting any more twisted up with my family. You have grown up with my sisters. We wouldn't hear the end of it. Every assignment together they'd drown us in their quips and jokes. It would be a mess of distractions. Plus, the expectations of my father—"

"Dolion would be ecstatic," said Zimri. "As for your sisters, their antagonizing has never stopped you from doing what you want."

"You're not being reasonable."

"I'm *only* being reasonable," he retorted. "You're the one making excuses. Ones that no longer have merit."

"Then what of our roles in the kingdom? We can't risk anyone learning of our feelings for each other there. I can imagine it now. The elusive Collector's lover gracing his floors for any to try to snatch in trade for a bit of their identities back or debts dropped. And the lost gods forbid if you were ever tied to loving one of the Mousai. Both of us already have enough danger to shake off with our current roles."

"Since when were you scared of anyone in the kingdom?" he countered. "The Mousai are hardly in the company of others in public. Why would that change now? Plus, it is quite easy to switch a disguise when needed. It's not as if I'll be waltzing through my club with you tied to my waist. Though that does sound like a pleasant evening."

"Zimri, please . . ." She rubbed at her temples. How was today already growing worse than yesterday and it was barely noon?

"Until you enlighten me to a better reason than these weak justifications—"

"Because I'm scared!" she burst out, hating how the ballroom echoed her words. Words she despised saying, was desperate not to feel lest he sense it.

She was Arabessa Bassette. The eldest. The leader of the Mousai. She had orchestrated the torture of dozens, felt the pain of broken bones and scarring magic, seen the most debasing to the most horrifying Aadilor had to offer. She was meant not to be afraid of anything.

Zimri appeared just as taken aback by her confession, but he remained quiet, waiting.

Arabessa's mind dizzied with how to even begin expanding on such a complicated admission. She didn't want to, of course, but Zimri deserved some portion of her truth. So she plucked forward the one that weighed heaviest. "I do not know how to be more without losing everything," she explained, unable to meet his eyes.

She felt him draw closer. "What do you mean?"

"I already wear so many masks." She looked up, finding his hazel gaze. "So many roles and responsibilities. To do this, to be with you fully, openly . . . you already feel I'm not giving you enough now, but what if I can't give you any more then, as well?"

His concerned expression shifted to warmth. "To be beside you is all I am asking."

"But you *are* beside me, Zimri, right now."

He shook his head. "No, I am living in a compartment. Taken out when convenient. Hidden and untouched when not. Being in love is not something to be organized."

Her chest felt tight. "But that's exactly my point. I don't know if I can love the way you need me to love. What I feel for you . . . how I know it could consume . . ." She shook her head. "To be distracted is deadly in our world, Zimri. For me to lose focus of what my family needs, what our king desires . . ."

"What about what *you* need, Arabessa? What do you desire?"

Her father's words from the other day grew up and around her. *I want what will fulfill you with a life beyond regret. You have a choice.*

But for what?

What did she desire?

Arabessa wasn't sure; she only knew she was tired of the role she had been forced into playing within her family. The conductor, caretaker, surrogate mother. Her father's words felt like a farce. But oh, how she wished they were true! To be given a choice rather than an order.

"Duty is important," Zimri went on. "But what is the point in living if you cannot feel, cannot enjoy? Your sisters are able—"

"My sisters are able to enjoy their love stories because *I* am still around to manage everything else," Arabessa said pointedly. "Do you think Larkyra comes to the kingdom unless beckoned from her castle in Lachlan? And Niya: don't get me started on the portal tokens we have needed to snatch her from all corners of Aadilor when she sails with her pirate lord. I am all that is holding the Mousai together. The one who eats with our father so he doesn't eat alone. Who has managed this household since I have come of age to do so. Do you think I do not wish to have ambitions and dreams of my own beyond these walls or demands from our king? Do you think I do not desire to be as free as my sisters? As autonomous in my duties? To only carry a single role rather than a handful? Though you might not believe me, I *yearn* to love you with everything that burns inside my heart instead of only what I can manage to hold in one hand. My other is always too busy carrying every other burden. I have been born into my place and responsibilities, Zimri, as we all have. If anyone, you must be able to understand that." Her breaths were coming out ragged, and there was something wet running down her face.

She didn't recognize it as tears until Zimri brushed his thumbs over her cheeks, wiping them away. "My music," he said softly. "I had no idea these were the thoughts burdening you."

"Only a few." She attempted a weak smile.

"This is exactly why I am here, you know. What I mean about being honest with each other about what's in our minds." He drew his arms around her, guiding her head to his chest. She inhaled his calming scent, listening to his steady heartbeat through his clothes. "We can figure this out together."

Together.

Could they?

It was a nice thought. Just as nice as to be given a choice in her duties.

"I'm sorry I did not go to you last night," she said after a moment, still nestled against him. It felt so good to lean on another. To lean on him.

"It's clear you have much on your shoulders, but you could have merely told me you needed to be alone last night," he explained, rubbing her back.

"I needed to be alone last night."

A warm laugh rumbled through him, and she soaked up the feel of it. "See." Zimri shifted so she could look up at him. "Was that so hard?"

"Utterly painful," she said, unable to stop herself from sharing in his grin.

His attention drifted toward her mouth, his arms around her tightening, and she knew he was going to kiss her.

She wanted him to kiss her.

"I do apologize," pricked a voice into their bubble. "Have I interrupted something?"

Arabessa sprang out of Zimri's embrace to find Niya leaning, arms crossed, with a hip against the doorframe to the ballroom. Her brows rose as she glanced between the two.

"No," replied Arabessa in the same moment Zimri said, "Yes."

Niya's eyes sparkled with amused mischief. "I see."

"What do you want?" questioned Arabessa, trying to calm her nerves from being found in such a state.

"Well," began Niya as she pushed into the room. "Now I definitely agree with Zimri."

Arabessa narrowed her gaze. "About what?"

"About having interrupted something," she explained. "Especially finding you so flustered and annoyed by my presence."

"I am always annoyed by your presence."

"And flustered?"

"I was practicing." Arabessa gestured toward her violin's case.

"Is that what we are calling it these days?" queried Niya. "Then I must be an expert for all the practicing Alōs and I—"

"*Niya.*" Arabessa tried again. "To what do we owe the pleasure of your presence?"

Her sister held up a letter. "This came for you. It appears His Grace requests you to run an errand for him."

As Arabessa glanced at the envelope marked by the black skull seal of the Thief King, that familiar tired weight returned to her shoulders. She had been looking and waiting for her father since last night, and this was what she would receive instead: orders to be his errand girl? "You have the letter," began Arabessa, annoyed. "Why can't you do it?"

"It's not addressed to me." Niya waved it toward her again.

"It's not addressed to anyone," Arabessa pointed out, indicating the blank front.

"By the stars and sea," Niya huffed. "Charlotte gave me the note to give to you. That is all that I was told. It showed up in the bin from the kingdom earlier this morning along with a messenger moth with your name on it. Now are you going to take it, or shall I write back that you said, *Thanks, but no thanks?*"

Arabessa snatched up the envelope. "Per usual, you are absolutely no help."

"On the contrary," Niya countered as she smoothed out a small wrinkle on her gown's skirt. "I graciously walked across the entire house to make sure you received this. I would say that's more than helpful."

"To Charlotte, perhaps."

"Then my actions are also charitable, for Charlotte's clearly over a thousand years of age. No one in her condition should be walking so far for a simple delivery of mail."

Arabessa kept herself from replying a multitude of ways, too tired to spare any more this afternoon. Instead, her mind filled with the list of actions she would need to take before returning to the Thief Kingdom and how this would most certainly rearrange the day she had planned for herself.

Letting out a weary sigh, she grabbed her violin case before momentarily meeting Zimri's gaze.

Later, his expression seemed to say. *We can figure this out together later.*

Though she knew better, a blossom of hope filled Arabessa's chest at the thought.

Later, she silently agreed, before catching Niya's watchful eyes studying them.

"You know," said Arabessa to her sister, "given you are being so magnanimous today, could you be a dear and gather Larkyra here for when I return? There's something important I need to discuss with you both."

A light of curiosity flashed through Niya's features. "Sounds ominous."

"It very well could be," said Arabessa as she made her way to the door.

For when it came to their family, let alone their family's past, nothing could be ruled out.

CHAPTER SIX

*A*rabessa was well accustomed to errands from her father. Nameless notes. Addressed letters. Messenger moths. Visits from one of her sisters or Achak or Zimri or Charlotte or any other confidant within their family, all sent to rush her here or there. Today the letter had only one line of instruction: *Parcel waiting at Amos's Apothecary.*

A *message glaringly void of any please* or *thank you* or *would you kindly, my most dependable offspring.* Just *do.*

And of course Arabessa would.

Because that was what had become expected of her.

As she hastened to her rooms to acquire the items necessary when traveling to the Thief Kingdom—masked disguise; sturdier boots; cloak; portal token; and her traveling weapons of choice, her short blade and flute, each inserted into a spring-loaded leather holder strapped to either forearm—Arabessa couldn't help but be reminded of doing this very action yesterday.

Except then she had held a different sort of errand, one that would reveal a secret her father had been spelled silent regarding. A past that still caused Arabessa's pulse to quicken in confused shock.

At the sense of repetitiveness, the burdensome memory she had relived at the Fountains of Forgotten Memories came rushing forward, overtaking her vision as though she had drunk from the Keeper's cup once again.

Arabessa was spinning, falling, before puncturing through light and color and sound. As if slamming into a wall, she collapsed into another mind and body. She stood very low to the ground: three years old. Her movements felt clumsy as she maneuvered in her childhood form, her surroundings a shiny new mystery.

She was in a dark chamber, a fire blazing behind her as she scooted along the ornate rug to hide under the legs of a large armchair. Her pulse fluttered in excitement as she peered around. Arabessa remembered how she had always been good at sneaking, slipping into places undetected as only a small creature could. A trait that would be cultivated into a skill later in life.

While her child self did not understand the significance of where she roamed, the Arabessa of four and twenty knew it well. They were in the Thief King's private rooms buried deep in the palace.

Her own rooms were not far, but as a child she had only ever been allowed entry to this domain with either her nursery maid or a parent present. Currently the chamber was void of both. Her baby sister, Niya, was a handful at one, leaving their nurse preoccupied with controlling a soul set on being uncontrollable. A perfect time, of course, for Arabessa to slip away to where she should not.

With excitement singing in her veins, she was about to scurry out from under the chair when the opening creak of a heavy door in the distance had her freeze.

The space flooded with a sharp fragrance.

Magic.

Though very young, Arabessa knew of magic. Not yet of her own but of its existence in this world. As she curled herself into the smallest of objects, cheek to carpet, she watched a figure wrapped in blinding white glide forward from the shadows.

Arabessa's eyes grew wide as they came to a stop beside a mirror hanging on a wall a mere few paces from where she hid. She could feel her younger self craning her neck in awe so she might take in as much as she could of the opulent alabaster disguise. Her heart flipped and flittered in excitement as her gaze traveled over the person's mask. It was woven of shells and pearls and other white scaling, which climbed up the headdress to two curling, sharp horns.

Here stood the Thief King.

The creature spun of myth and legend, the beast children were told would snatch them in the night, dragging them kicking and screaming underground, where the sun was snuffed out, unless they behaved.

Of course, Arabessa as a child did not yet know of these stories.

Who and what the Thief King was would not be understood until many years later. All that Arabessa of three could grasp was that this being was beautiful. Terrifying but beautiful.

As the Thief King went to unclasp their headdress, their white-gloved fingers paused, their chin tilting ever so slightly in Arabessa's direction—as though listening.

Neither Arabessa nor her child self dared make a sound, holding breath in anticipation.

The Thief King seemed to churn over a silent thought before they resumed their task. With the tiniest click at a clasp at the base of their neck, their mask was undone. They shook out of the headdress, placing the ostentatious crown on a nearby small table. Their gaze lifted to stare at their own reflection in the mirror. Pale skin, lips painted black, a strong nose, a pointed chin, and world-weary green eyes filled the glass. Green eyes that, despite the soot rimming them, Arabessa would remember until her final heartbeat.

This cannot be! *her magic hissed through her blood, knocking against her chest.* This cannot be!

But it is! *Arabessa silently cried.* It is!

Beneath her chair, Arabessa's surroundings shattered into pieces, all while her younger self looked on with confused curiosity.

As the Thief King's gaze moved from the mirror to lock eyes with hers beneath the chair, it was as if an arrow had been let loose to lodge into Arabessa's heart before being yanked free. With her blood spilled came every story she had ever been told, memory she had ever thought true. Why? she wanted to scream into the room. Why would you have hidden this from us? From me?

As though her quiet anguish were amusing, a hint of a smile played across the Thief King's lips, a glimmer of mischievousness in their eyes, of reasons and purposes unknown, before it was all wiped away as they turned.

They left the child just as they had found them: crouched and hidden under the chair, alone.

While Arabessa's younger self remained motionless, staring at the far corridor where the figure had disappeared, Arabessa's grown self, in contrast, fought against the suffocation that was her memory. Her nails desperately clawed against an elusive wall so she might rip herself free and flee.

Because while her father currently sat on the Thief King's throne, Arabessa now knew so had her mother.

CHAPTER SEVEN

*A*n empty, sunlit alley lay at Arabessa's back as she slipped through the portal door. A welcoming touch of cool night fell along her cheeks and filtered into her lungs as she entered the Thief Kingdom. As she retrieved her portal token from the ground, the image of a sunny midafternoon in Jabari closed behind her with a snap.

Her cloak rustled at her sides as she approached the rocky ledge. A twinkling midnight city pooled out below. There were many ways to enter this hidden caved world, but assuredly the easiest was with a portal token. The trick, of course, was finding one. Rarer than any jewel and harder to create than any deadly weapon, they were won by spilling blood or knowing a creature gifted enough to create one. Thankfully, the Bassettes had advantageous connections, and portal tokens they could obtain aplenty.

As Arabessa pocketed hers, she gazed across the colorful chimney smoke rising from tight clusters of rooftops, buildings that wove between reaching monolith stalagmites and stalactites. Within the dripping rock, thousands of other dwellings climbed up their base, warm pricks of yellow light from windows matching the winking blue and green glowworms peppering the ceiling far above. And in the center of it all rose the onyx palace with knife-sharp turrets of the Thief King. The watchful eye to the wicked.

Though Arabessa had stood in this very spot many times, never did the sight dull the flutter of excitement in her belly or the purr of her magic's contentment in her veins.

Home, her heart and gifts whispered.

Home, agreed Arabessa as her attention hooked onto the palace once more.

She was trying her best to set aside the emotional tidal wave that accompanied the knowledge of her mother as Thief King. Her growing pile of questions on the subject was becoming more and more paralyzing, and presently she needed to be able to move. She was desperate to complete this errand to Amos's Apothecary swiftly and without issue.

And yet her queries only bubbled up anytime she held the beastly ebony palace in her sights.

How had Johanna come to sit on the throne? How long had she ruled? How had her father come to rule after her? Was it directly following her death? Had they shared it?

Arabessa only ever remembered Dolion beneath the smoke and white disguise. Always her father whom they had come to kneel before. Their father who had created the Mousai and given them their orders. Dolion, who had always carried the burden of a kingdom of chaos on his shoulders. Never any history of her mother and the throne.

In fact, the only reliable narrative she and her sisters had ever been told regarding the Thief King's lineage came from Achak.

Like the sun and moon and stars, they'd said, *the Thief King has always been and always will be. They are as eternal as Aadilor.*

Well, thought Arabessa morosely as she turned down the tight path to her right, leaving behind the view of the palace, *evidently not eternal enough, given my mother is dead.*

Determined to shake off her tumbling emotions, Arabessa pulled forward the same strength she reserved for washing herself numb when torturing a guilty soul. She became stone. Became the cold, hard rock that made up this kingdom. She buried her internal chaos. After all, she soon would confide this secret to her sisters and come up with a plan together to confront their father.

Arabessa could certainly hold herself together a little longer until then.

Descending onto a wider footpath, she made her way through tight clusters of rocks to cross over a crudely constructed bridge. The quick rushing of the river below muffled her footsteps before she found her way into the southern bowels of the Mystic District.

The roads here were damp, as if the neighborhood had just suffered a great rain, though no such weather ever graced this kingdom. Her boots sloshed with each step, the bottom of her skirts growing muddy, and Arabessa held in a weary sigh. This district seemed to pride itself on its dilapidation. Shutters hung askew from cracked windows; lamps fluttered weakly, barely lighting her way as a warning fog crept along the ground. A rather dramatic ghoulish ambience to either keep those unwelcome out or persuade a curious someone in. The latter was in effect this evening, for despite the dreary environment, the streets were offensively more clogged with pedestrians than yesterday. And by the looks of the tittering laughter and swaying steps of the crowd, many were already in their cups.

"Haffy beginnin' of de eclipse!" slurred a disguised citizen as they bumped against Arabessa. "Care ta celebrate by buyin' me an' yous a bit o' grog?"

Arabessa checked to ensure she hadn't been pickpocketed before shoving the accoster out of her way. Her sigh turned into a groan. She had completely forgotten that tonight marked the official beginning of the Star Eclipse. A full swing of celebration would be vibrating in every part of the kingdom.

The Mousai were even meant to perform within the palace tomorrow night. A detail that it was very unlike Arabessa to momentarily lose sight of.

A rush of chastising annoyance flooded her.

73

These bloody unwanted distractions! she thought as she stomped forward. The past few days had been filled with them.

Her mood merely soured further as every sidewalk she maneuvered, road she crossed, and alley or tunnel she turned down was pressed with rambunctious visitors and those desperate to sell their wares. Arabessa twisted through the clusters in Vagabond Row, ignoring calls from proprietors leaning out from shop windows as they dangled weak spelled charms in masked potential patrons' faces. Business owners offering the services of their gifts to the giftless. All for a price not worth the bargain.

At this rate, she'd be lucky if there wasn't a line out of the door at Amos's, for nothing excited those born without magic more than acquiring magic potions.

Whatever parcel is waiting for Father better be of utmost importance, she internally grumbled.

Arabessa's only reprieve was in the shortcut she was racing toward. Hurrying to a hanging advertisement for Ida's Ingenious Incantations along a brick wall, she lifted the poster to reveal a dark alley. The air grew sour as she entered, but she still breathed a sigh of relief as her path cleared, no more crowds to fight.

Of course, there was good reason for why.

As she took careful steps forward, Arabessa's magic buzzed with awareness in her veins as she cataloged the sunken eyes attached to reedy forms who watched her pass.

Arabessa had entered Skin Stealer territory.

Along the walls leaned creatures so thin they looked skeletal in their suits and top hats. Starving schemes and shifty intentions oozed from each one she walked by, but what always gave Arabessa the shivers was what their bony fingers clutched to their chests. A true Skin Stealer's harm lay in the briefcase they held, each full of spelled mirrors. Disguised or not, they could snatch a person's likeness if they dared to look inside, stretching it onto themselves like slipping into a different suit. Havoc soon to follow.

"Hello, pretty thing," one cooed, voice deceptively warm and inviting as they slunk in front of Arabessa's path. "Care to see how you may add to your disguise? I've got just the detail to have your—"

"You would be wise to keep that closed in my presence," Arabessa declared, hand jutting out to knock away what they were about to unclasp.

The Skin Stealer hissed, clinging to their suitcase more tightly. *"Rude,"* they accused. "Very rude! Siblings, it appears we have a disrespectful patron in our midst."

Like piranhas floating to the surface of water, a sea of hollowed gazes and toothy smiles stepped forward from the shadows. In a blink Arabessa stood surrounded.

"We do not like those who are rude," began one in a voice eerily similar to the first.

"No, indeed," added another.

"Especially not in *our* place of business."

"But do not worry," said a different creature at her back.

"We will teach you better manners," finished the original Skin Stealer.

Arabessa's gifts raced to gather at her fingertips. *Let us free.* They churned, begging for her to take out her flute. *Let us steal more than their skin.*

Steady, she instructed, curling her hands into fists.

If possible, it was best to limit using one's gifts within the kingdom. Especially when Arabessa wasn't presently dressed as one of the Mousai. For just as a disguise could become an identity, one's gifts could be their own kind of marker. And Arabessa and her sisters' unique brand of magic was certainly well known here.

"I would suggest instead that you all step aside so I may pass," said Arabessa. "I merely wish to take this shortcut with no issue." She turned slowly, counting the surrounding numbers.

Seven.

Seven shouldn't be a problem.

"If we are offering up suggestions," replied one, "then show us more than what covers your face." Bold bony fingers whipped up to grab her mask.

Nearly in the same breath Arabessa caught their wrist while activating her blade. With a whoosh she severed the creature's hand.

A sharp-pitched howl erupted into the air, the Skin Stealer falling back into the arms of their brethren.

"Anyone else want to offer up alternate suggestions?" asked Arabessa as she tossed aside the detached limb while brandishing her blade.

A collective hiss filled the alley before it was replaced with the distinct scurrying of rodents.

Arabessa glanced up; her stomach dropped as dozens of Skin Stealers crawled down the brick like ravenous spiders toward a caught fly.

"Sticks," she muttered.

Throwing herself forward, she barreled into the smaller mass. Given how insignificant they were in weight, she was able to push most aside with her shoulder, but a few snagged at her braid, sharp nails tearing at her cloak and slashing her cheek beneath her eye mask.

Her skirts twisted around her hips as she spun to swipe her blade at any bony face, arm, or chest.

Let us plaaaaay, whined her gifts, pounding inside her hands. *Let us help clean up this mess.*

But Arabessa ignored her magic's protest, punching and slicing through another trio of Skin Stealers. She could see the end of the alley in the distance. The prick of light around the edges of another poster.

Running toward it, she used the momentum to jump and push off the brick wall, stepping onto the shoulder of a Stealer to then grasp a hanging lantern. She swung over the last cluster of creatures to land in front of the dangling flap. Arabessa dusted off her skirts while glancing behind her at the oncoming mass. "It's been a pleasure, my friends." She saluted before flinging back the cover and pushing through.

Arabessa's triumphant smile was quickly wiped clean as she found the road she was meant to be on replaced instead by a massive black stretching hall. No longer was she in the Mystic District but in a tall corridor where large burning fireplaces and half-carved stone guardians pressed against the length. The space was boiling hot and appeared to go on endlessly. She could just barely make out the gold door at the far end.

"What in all of Aadilor?" Arabessa spun around. The flap she had just exited was gone, now a solid stone wall.

She placed a hand on it. Cold. Unmoving. Very much real.

Her skin raced with goose bumps.

Not right, her gifts warned as they swirled through her blood. *Not right.*

No, agreed Arabessa. *This certainly is not.*

The Thief Kingdom had many mysteries, but for a path to suddenly shift and change was something she had experienced only within her home in Jabari. A house twisted up with magic. Never had Arabessa turned down a lane here to find herself instead in a place such as this.

There was an echoing of rock breaking, and Arabessa glanced behind her.

One of the large stone guardians came alive beside a fireplace. With each of its heavy footfalls, the ground shook, and Arabessa turned fully, steadying her feet. It dragged a chain mace, ripping up the floor in its wake until it came to a stop in front of her. Arabessa's head tipped up and up and up to gaze into the beast's lava-filled eyes. Steam shot from its nostrils with each breath.

She knew these guardians well, for they stood sentry at every important entry within the palace as well as lined the king's throne room.

But what were they doing here?

Or more importantly, where was here? And why was she now in it?

"Hello," she said. "Perhaps you can enlighten me on where exactly we are and why?"

By way of response, the stone guardian spit fire with its roar as it swung around its flail, holding every intention of sending Arabessa to the Fade.

CHAPTER EIGHT

Zimri had a problem. Despite the whiskey in his hand and the muffled clamor of inebriation filtering into his office from below, he was utterly sober. His thoughts were preoccupied as he slouched in his wingback chair behind his desk, absently swirling the amber liquid. The view beyond his one-way mirror was of an undulating Macabris. He had been informed the line outside curled through half the Betting District—citizens hopeful of entry into the madness—while the guests who were granted access celebrated the official first day of the Star Eclipse with untamed enthusiasm. The gambling tables were set at a higher price this evening, the spirits stronger and richer, the private dipping pools fully booked until tomorrow, and the opponents for the basement brawls primed to produce heavy bets. All advantageous for Zimri's pockets.

Yet still, he could revel in none of it.

Half of the proceeds would still fill the Volkovs' pockets, despite them hardly being of assistance in the grand affair. In fact, they had seemed intent on disagreeing with decisions almost finalized, slowing everything down.

A pattern of behavior not reserved merely for today's event.

Zimri bristled, finally taking a sip of his drink.

The smoky burn down his throat only slightly settled his maudlin mood.

He was not one to dawdle in melancholy, but he felt he deserved a few grain falls of sulk after getting rebuked by Zhad this morning. Which returned him to the problem that had begun the very day the Volkovs purchased half of his parents' club when he was still too young to do much about it. The Thief King had been right: ten years was a long time for Macabris to sit without a master.

Zimri had not been exaggerating when stating it was a hopeless dream to reclaim majority ownership. After years of acting on multiple contingency plans, his arsenal was nearly wiped clean. Despite his best efforts to sue, blackmail, coerce, and now bribe the Volkovs away from their shares, they continued to remain an immovable thorn in his side. He wasn't sure what he should or could do next.

A knock at his door stirred Zimri's thoughts back to his office. With a frown he swiveled around as the knock was followed by three more, a teasing beat. There were very few who knew how to find the private upper floors, and only one from whom Zimri ever desired a visit.

But Arabessa preferred her arrivals to be silent, a whisper of a breeze through a window. A thief who knew how to slip through doors despite them being locked.

Which left the Volkovs or a trusted employee.

Please let it be someone from the kitchen bringing me a bite to eat, thought Zimri as he picked up the maroon mask that he had discarded on his desk. Once it was settled into place, he pulled a latch by his desk, unlocking his office. "Enter," he announced.

Her perfume slunk in before she did, sweet and spicy, a perfect replica of her temperament.

"Kattiva," said Zimri, standing out of decorum as she walked in and shut the door behind her. She was covered head to toe in black, her headdress a braiding of leather over her dark hair, revealing only red-painted lips and piercing brown eyes. Her tight silk sleeves ended at her wrists, where her signature inked wolves sat displayed atop her hands.

Though she was the daughter of his nemesis, he and Kattiva had always been cordial. Mostly because she seemed to agree with Zimri regarding many of the changes he proposed be implemented in the club, helping on occasion to sway Zhad in his favor.

"What a pleasant surprise," he said. "Is your dipping pool not to your liking?"

Kattiva rarely visited him in his office unless it had to do with giving notes on a lacking element of one of Macabris's soirees. Or to complain about her father, probing Zimri to follow suit. Though he never would. While they were amicable, trust was not exactly a trait developed between them.

"The pool is perfectly filled with beautiful, slick bodies," she said in her husky voice as she sauntered forward. "Bodies who will no doubt become wetter once I rejoin them. Our turnout for our First Fade event must be historic. It's marvelous madness down there."

Zimri noted the heightened excitement wafting from her, honey-suckles in bloom.

"Then what keeps you from returning to your friends presently?" he asked.

"Isn't it customary to offer your guests a drink?" She slid into one of the two armchairs in front of his desk.

"Yes, of course." He strode to his bar, which was nestled in the center of a bookcase that spanned one wall of his office. "The usual fizzer? Or do you wish for something stronger this evening?"

"You make me sound so dull to have a 'usual,'" she huffed. "I'll have whatever you're having."

"Whiskey, then." He turned to pour her a glass.

"So long as it's rare and expensive, sounds marvelous."

"My dear, we only do rare and expensive at Macabris." He came to her side and handed her the drink.

Her smile was playful as she watched him settle into the opposite armchair. "You look very fine this evening, Collector," she mused, red nails clinking against her glass as her eyes perused his three-piece velvet suit. "Why do you deny our guests the pleasure of seeing you?"

"Our guests have much prettier items to keep them occupied than being burdened with my form."

"I'd happily be burdened with your form any grain fall of the day." Her gaze remained locked to his as she ran her tongue over the side of her drink.

He let out a low chuckle, unmoved by her blatant suggestiveness. "Unfortunately a sentiment the rest of your family does not share."

"Nor one you feel toward them," she countered. "Which brings me to one of the reasons I'm here."

"Only one of the reasons?" He raised his brows.

"Like I explained earlier, Collector"—her smile was serpentine— "someone as delicious as you should not go a day without being admired. How else could I picture you watching me in the dipping pools without seeing how you were dressed this evening?"

"That's right," he said. "Voyeurism has always been a favorite of yours."

"There you go again." She pouted, bending down to set her drink on the low table before them, allowing a generous view of her cleavage. "Making me sound predictable."

Kattiva was undeniably beautiful. A temptress at her best. Some would even say a reincarnation of Libida, the lost goddess of lust. But their flirtatious sparring had only ever remained as such. Zimri had no doubt she would allow him to bed her if he pursued, but something told him that she admired that he did not. Perhaps in her versatile tastes for pleasure loomed a desire for a relationship to be platonic. If she lived to be unpredictable, such a trait surely would suffice. Plus, despite the complicated relationship he and Arabessa had, he was not able to be in love with someone while also in bed with someone else. All parts of his body were reserved for one person and one person only.

"Given I have no guesses as to what your other reason for being here may be," began Zimri with a grin, "I can assure you, *predictable* is not a word I would use to describe you."

"Always a charmer," Kattiva tutted, settling back into her chair. "And for that I will speak my next point plainly."

He waited.

"I have a proposition for you."

Zimri raised his brows.

"Not *that* sort of proposition, though if you—"

"What are you proposing, Kattiva?" he urged.

She took a moment to reply, and only because Zimri held the gift of being sensitive to others' temperaments could he pick up her flash of nervousness. A sharp, tangy scent that wafted toward him. *How curious,* he thought. What could make such a creature as she nervous? Every other physical indication Kattiva exuded was utter calm.

"As you know," she began, "Mama and Papa have been less than . . . enthusiastic about how I have chosen to live my life since coming of age."

He nodded. Though the Volkovs had been born in the Thief Kingdom and were more than well versed in the idiosyncrasies of this world, Zhad and Alyona had never particularly enjoyed the reputation their daughter had acquired. Theirs was a first-generation thief house, new to noble life and thus desperate to continually raise their status. Nothing made a soul hungrier for riches than the taste of starvation still lingering on its tongue.

"Their opinions regarding my affairs have hardly caused much concern from me over the years," Kattiva continued. "My life is mine and mine alone. It's not as though I am hurting anyone. Well, unless they ask to be," she finished with a distracted grin.

"And the point of sharing this with me?" inquired Zimri.

"They want me to *marry*." She said the last word as though it were a grotesque disease.

"Ah." Zimri set down his drink. He'd be lying if he said he hadn't seen something like this coming. Zhad no doubt wanted to marry her off to another noble family, truly secure his family's lineage.

"And if I don't," she went on, tone turning sharp, "they said I will be disinherited! What utter nonsense."

"Surely your parents are testing you," Zimri assured. "A toothless threat. You are their only child. Zhad could never do such a thing, let alone Alyona."

"I thought the same at first, but they have already frozen half my accounts at Stockpiled Treasure to show their seriousness. They even gave me a deadline." She picked up her drink, taking a hearty sip. "I must be wed by the Sky's Return, the day after the Star Eclipse."

"The end of the month?" His eyes went wide.

She nodded, finishing the rest of her drink in one go. A wave of her annoyance floated forward.

Zimri stood, retrieving the whole bottle of whiskey. "This will no doubt be the weakest poultice to your troubles, Kattiva," he began as he refilled her glass and topped off his own. "But while such a date may be ambitious for some, you will have no issue catching a betrothed in that time frame."

"While I do not disagree, the issue here, Collector, is I don't *want* to catch anything of the sort. Marriage was not a line item on my list of dreams to come true and never will be."

He nodded, having assumed as much. Kattiva was not one to desire being tied to anyone, unless it was a different kind of bondage. "I'm sorry you have been placed into this predicament. No one should be forced into marriage."

"My sentiments exactly, but Papa says it's time to 'make a respectable lady out of me.' As though he doesn't gallivant around with his paramours, leaving my mother to her dens. Precisely the activities he judges *me* for. It's hypocritical!"

"Indeed."

She eyed him from beneath her braided mask. "I knew you'd understand. You and I have always seemed to live by similar philosophies."

"Similar, perhaps, but not exactly the same."

Kattiva waved a hand. "To be the same is trite. I merely point out how agreeably we seem to get on."

Zimri's magic prickled at her words, jumping from his skin to taste the warning in the air, the scheming. While Kattiva did not hold the lost gods' gifts, she was still cunning. Her emotions had turned insidious. Something was afoot. "What exactly is this proposition you came here for, again?" he inquired once more.

Her brown gaze held his. "I know how badly you want to gain majority ownership over this club."

Zimri's grip tightened around his glass. "And?"

"And I have the ten percent shares that can give you that."

His pulse doubled as the true intent for her visit began to crystallize.

"Marry me, Collector, and my ten percent becomes your sixty percent."

The room hung quiet before it was filled with Zimri's laughter. "You cannot be serious, Kattiva," he said after collecting himself, though he couldn't keep the grin from his face.

"I do not make a habit of joking about my shares in the club. Another similar trait between us, I believe."

That sobered him quickly. "But you admitted you have no intention of marrying."

"I don't, but if I had to, which it appears I do, you are the perfect candidate."

"And how's that?"

"We've proved to get along. Neither of us are occupied with sleeping with the other, and I don't care two silver for how you live your life, so long as you don't care how I live mine. I'd be tied to one of the oldest thief houses in the kingdom, so considered *more* than a respectable married lady in the eyes of my parents and whatever other society they care about, while still able to live my life as I do now, and you yours."

"A marriage of convenience."

"Precisely." She grinned. "And the cherry on top of the perky nipple is that you would gain majority shares with our union and I can maintain living the life I've grown accustomed to. Think of it, Collector"— she leaned forward—"you wouldn't need my parents to sign off on anything. You could finally be free to do with Macabris what you want."

Finally be free.

Perhaps your way in is through something they invest in more.

Arabessa's earlier words flooded his mind.

Kattiva was *certainly* something the Volkovs invested in . . .

Despite himself, Zimri couldn't help but taste the sweet victory, a heady imagining. No doubt because he had imagined it many times prior. His shoulders felt momentarily weightless. While this wasn't full ownership, it would be much closer to it than he was now. His dream of working the club with more autonomy lay with this path. Honoring his parents' memory, the name they had created for themselves, the legacy they had created for him.

We shall be so proud the day you rule Macabris in our stead. The whispers of his mother's hope danced around him, a suffocating tug of responsibility.

But what utter nonsense! *Marry Kattiva Volkov?* There were many reasons why that couldn't come to pass. His momentary daydream dissipated as if a strong wind had blown through.

"Even if disinherited," he pointed out, "you could still live well from your ten percent profits from the club."

Kattiva snorted. "I think you underestimate the sort of provocation and gluttony I enjoy, Collector. I need more expense than that sum."

"Then what would stop your parents from disowning you when telling them your intentions to marry me? It is no secret your father lives to irritate my every waking sand fall. Despite my family's nobility, he would not agree to such a union."

The grin that stretched across her lips, along with the devious spark in her eyes, almost had him shiver. "That's the most beautiful part of all. If you had majority ownership with me by your side, they'd never want to anger either of us. They'd want to keep us very happy indeed so we wouldn't shut them out of every decision. Plus, my family's financial trust will be all they have as leverage against me. They will want to keep me tied to them however possible." Her rumbling laugh had a diabolical tinge. "Oh, how delicious this will be! We both will be getting everything we want and more."

Not everything, thought Zimri.

Not Arabessa.

His heart felt like it was being torn in two.

Though this would be a marriage of convenience, Arabessa would *never* allow herself to be a mistress.

Even if it was her he wanted to spend the rest of his days with.

His head felt twisted up in every direction. His dream of reclaiming Macabris was so close at hand with the woman before him, yet his heart's happiness lay with another.

Another who still fought her feelings for him.

Who still wanted them to remain a secret.

Yes, Arabessa had admitted she was scared. That she feared loving him any more would have her losing herself, that they would become distracted, putting each of them at risk.

An anger boiled up inside him with surprising speed. *Excuses,* he thought. He appreciated that she had shared her doubts, but she had to give their relationship a chance before making such assumptions. Otherwise what was the point in doing anything, if always frightened of failure?

"So, Collector?" Kattiva asked, reclaiming his attention. "Shall we toast to our future union?" She lifted her glass.

His mind continued to spin as Kattiva waited for his reply. Her pulse of nervousness filled the air again despite her composure.

He studied her, this creature disguised for Macabris who knew the bones of this club perhaps as well as he. She was handing him a deal that would fulfill his promise to his parents, to his king, while ending a promise to another. A deal of impossibility. For how could he choose between the two things he loved most in this world, Arabessa and Macabris?

"I need time," he finally replied.

Kattiva's smile was like that of a cat who had caught a mouse. "An answer that is not no."

No, Zimri thought silently, taking a swig of his drink. Though it would be if Arabessa answered yes to a question of his.

CHAPTER NINE

*A*rabessa decided cloaks were hazardous accessories. She might have escaped the heavy blow of the guardian's flail by a hair, but her cape was not as fortunate. With the material's edge pinned to the floor, Arabessa's heartbeat exploded in her chest as she tugged frantically at it to no avail.

The stone beast let out another fiery roar, swinging around its other heavy fist.

Forget the cloak! thought Arabessa in a panic as she twisted out of the material. Slabs of rock erupted at her back, the guardian's hand punching the ground where she had recently stood.

"By the stars and sea," she breathed, covering her head. "We hardly know one another for you to despise me so thoroughly. But"—she pushed up, standing to face the guardian—"if you're looking for a real reason to kill me, I'm more than happy to oblige."

Tucking away her blade, Arabessa triggered her flute to jump into her hand. This situation warranted stronger stuff than a knife.

Magic, be free! she thought as she spun her flute to her lips. Her entire body sizzled with her gifts rushing out of her hands as she released a single sharp note. A blast of purple magic was channeled down her instrument to barrel into the chest of the stone guardian.

As it howled in pain, it took unsteady steps back. A burning hole now glowed from its chest.

Arabessa didn't pause in her playing. She twisted a spelled song into the air, which sent her fingers fluttering along her keys. *Lash out and seize,* she could imagine Larkyra singing along. *Bring this beast to its knees.* She pushed a steady beat down her flute's barrel, a rhythm of low to high registers, sending whips of strong magic to lash around the guardian.

Dozens of purple strings squeezed its rocky form, all connected back to Arabessa's flute.

The guardian roared as it tried to break free, attempting to tear Arabessa's instrument from her hands. But her spell was laced strong, rooting her feet, and she gripped her flute more securely. When the beast was completely wrapped up in her violet chords, she pulled the flute from her lips and yanked the beast to its knees.

"Heel," she instructed. "I don't want to fight any longer, for I truly have no quarrel with you."

A vibrating, fiery roar erupted from the guardian, who clearly didn't care about her desires. Errant licks of flames singed her already muddy skirts.

"Great," she grumbled, annoyance racing the length of her. "There's no saving this dress now."

Bringing the flute back to her lips, she pulled out notes that had her leash around the beast grow brighter and brighter, digging tighter and tighter into its stone flesh. A howl of agony filled the hall right before the stone guardian burst apart.

Arabessa curled into a ball, covering herself from the explosion.

All grew quiet save for the sound of the multiple burning fireplaces.

Standing, Arabessa held her flute and waited. She could feel the sting of a few cuts along her cheeks and, looking down, cataloged the state of her gown. She let out a tired sigh. At least her mask was still intact.

This errand is truly turning out to be a real pain in my arse.

As she tucked her flute back into her holder, she made her way toward the gold door in the distance. She didn't make it very far before she was rocked unsteady by the bursting of the rest of the stone guardians as they came alive from the walls.

"Sticks." Her eyes went wide as the fire-breathing giants angled her way. Each carried a deadlier weapon than the previous: sword, fanged hammer, spiked club.

Arabessa didn't have to contemplate long what to do next.

She picked up her skirts and ran.

The floor shook with the heavy footfalls of the pursuing guardians, but Arabessa kept her concentration on the gold door in the distance.

Please don't be locked. Please don't be locked.

She could use her magic to unlock it if it was, of course, but with how quickly the beasts were gaining on her, she had the bone-chilling realization that she wouldn't have the time. Such a spell still needed the proper song, and she couldn't huff that out while sprinting.

BANG.

A stone club fell at her heels, causing her to nearly topple over, but with a scramble, she righted herself.

The door lay ten paces away.

THUD.

A studded mace ripped at her skirts.

Four paces.

SWOOSH. Arabessa ducked from a swinging fist at her back.

She launched herself forward. The doorknob was cold in her palm, and a rush of relief filled her chest when she twisted it open, falling through.

Her breaths were loud in her ears as she pressed up against the back of the door.

She waited to feel the protesting boom of the guardians on the other side.

But none came.

And the longer it remained silent, the more in focus her new surroundings grew. Until she could make out very clearly where she now stood: in the throne room of the Thief King.

Arabessa's pulse continued to race as her mind buzzed in confusion. Never had she entered this chamber in such a way.

Five other masked individuals stood to her right, each in varying states of similar chaos. It was as though they, too, had fought their own beasts to make it to this hall. Ripped trousers, scrapes, blood, half-cracked masks, and even a broken arm with protruding bone marred her companions.

What in all of Aadi—

"Welcome." A thunderous voice filled with hundreds of others brought Arabessa's attention to the center of the room. Black smoke shrouded where the King of Thieves sat on his dais, rivers of lava churning on either side of the walkway leading to him. "I wondered whether our last candidate would make it," he began. "In truth I had hoped for fewer of you to have survived, but now that you are all here, I wish you luck during the beginning of this Star Eclipse, for your true tests have merely begun."

CHAPTER TEN

*A*s the eldest daughter to the Thief King, Arabessa had experienced her fair share of oddities and hard lessons over the years. The most important being that though her father sat on the throne, he was assuredly *not* Dolion in these moments. Any favors or leniencies or advantages he might bestow upon her and her sisters as the Count of Raveet of the second house in Jabari were void when he wore the disguise of the King of Thieves. So while another child might be shocked to hear a parent declare such a statement as *I had hoped for fewer of you to have survived*, when counted among the lot, Arabessa was not at all stunned.

In fact, she felt rather relieved to realize all the peculiarities of today were because of her king.

What Arabessa did not enjoy was not knowing why she was here.

"This throne has found each of you worthy," said a new voice, stepping from behind the curling smoke. Achak revealed themselves, their bald head and black skin made glossy from the nearby flaming torches. The sister's violet eyes found Arabessa's from across the room, sending a burst of unease through her. If Achak was here, this was serious business indeed. "Your ability to arrive alive proves that your invitation is deserving," they continued.

The word *invitation* snagged in Arabessa's mind.

"And because of that you will soon see what hardly any have and learn what no one but a few know. After which you may make your decision to stay or to go. But be warned: if you go, so will remembering the secrets you are about to learn." Achak gestured to the smoke beside her, silver threads grazing her hand. "Here sits a creature who has ruled this kingdom from before any can remember. From before even *we* entered this realm." Achak shivered and shifted from sister to brother. A wider, bearded face now looked out at them. "Tonight marks the beginning of the reason why," he continued smoothly, as though he, not his sister, had been speaking the previous sentences. "The Star Eclipse is more than just the rebirth of our skies every nine years. It is when there is a great shifting of magic in our kingdom, from old to new. It is when tired creatures and fountains and pools and blooms become rejuvenated. When a throne that holds the most ancient gifts may claim another to make a name immortal, our Thief King." Achak bowed low to His Grace as wind spun through the room, dissipating the king's cloaking cloud.

Gasps resonated from those around Arabessa as the resplendent-in-white form of the Thief King was shown to some for the first time. He beamed like a new star against his obsidian throne, curling headdress monstrously tall. Shrouded eyes slipped along each figure lined up in front of him: dissecting, calculating, curious. And then the King of Thieves stood, sending a powerful burst of silver magic to fan out, washing over Arabessa and her companions. A cold prickle of warning.

Listen up, the magic seemed to whisper. *Listen closely.*

"I have claimed this throne for as long as I am able," rumbled their king. "As done before me, it is now time to make way for the next generation of master. By the end of this Star Eclipse, a new Thief King shall rule, and one of you"—he paused as his masked gaze roamed over them—"will be my successor."

The room dropped from beneath Arabessa as her father's words punched through her. A loud whooshing filled her ears.

No. The denial came swift with the insanity of what she had just heard.

By the end of this Star Eclipse, a new Thief King shall rule, and one of you will be my successor.

This was a trick.

This was a farce.

This was impossible.

"Yes," assured Achak beside their king, apparently sensing the shock of the room. "You have heard our king correctly. Every nine years this title can be claimed by another so long as the current ruler is willing to give it up. The magic of this throne will be transferred to one of you during the final night of the Star Eclipse, and with it every history and lesson from those who have ruled before. It is a tradition eternal, done by one Thief King to the next, and the obstacle to claim such a prize the same. If you accept this invitation, you will find yourself thrown into three tests over the next month. Each correlated to a phase of the eclipse and designed particularly for you to prove if you are worthy. When they will begin is not exact, only that the first shall occur during the First Fade, the second around the Waning Sky, and the final by the Full Eclipse. On the Sky's Return, the day after the Star Eclipse, there shall be a new Thief King on this throne. There will be one of *you* on it."

The brother's words settled in the room like a rock in a pond, heavy and rippling. No one spoke. Arabessa felt unsteady and in the same moment paralyzed. The details Achak had just laid out barely registered as her mind was seized with overwhelm.

Her father was handing over his reign? Her father *could* hand it over? Was this how he had claimed it after her mother? A burst of frustrated rage flooded her senses. How could he not have mentioned his intentions of stepping down from the throne to her, his own daughter! The one he relied on for every favor and duty and obedience. Instead she was to find out like this, standing beside strangers after almost being pummeled by a stone guardian.

A pain awoke in her chest, a feeling of heartache and betrayal.

As if her father knew her thoughts, his deep voice filled the silent hall. "The secrets to this crown are vast and buried for a reason," he stated. "Only because of the beginning of the Star Eclipse have I and my closest confidant"—he gestured to Achak—"been given a small allowance of time to talk freely with you this evening. Soon we will be tied again by our silent oaths, just as none of you will leave this throne room tonight able to share what you have learned. As for when a new ruler stands in my place, our kingdom will know no difference. Our people will see what they are always meant to: their Thief King." On his last words the magic of the throne that swirled by his feet flooded down the dais. It washed over Arabessa in a demand of prostration, pushing her and those beside her to kneel as their king stood towering in his horned headdress.

Here is your leader, your ruler, your salvation, whispered the ancient gifts pressing her knee into the hard stone floor. *You are honored by their presence, humbled by their attention, and long for their love.*

Arabessa's heartbeat pounded against her ribs as these feelings bloomed true in her heart, a chilling reminder of the throne's power. What her father was giving up. Giving away.

"So, my children," said the king, indicating they could finally stand, "now that you understand your reasons for being before me, the uniqueness of it, I officially invite you to play."

Black envelopes appeared before each contestant. Arabessa stared at the shiny floating parchment, at the skull eyes in the pressed seal of the Thief King. The symbol, the creature, and the myth she had grown up serving. Now with the potential to be the one served.

Her mind was trapped in the fog of this moment. Nothing seemed real, but if this was a dream or a nightmare, she could yet not tell.

"I urge you to think carefully on your decision." The king's warning voice protruded into her thoughts as some took hold of their invitations.

"Just as the gifts of this throne invited you here tonight, they will also be the deciders of who may sit upon it, not I. Only one will be crowned. It is either to win or to lose, and to lose is to enter the Fade. So before you choose to open and sign, understand that once you do, there is no going back, no out, no mercy. The next Thief King *is* among you," he reminded. "But the question is, what are you willing to sacrifice to learn if it should be you? Now is your choice. Later is your fate."

The word *choice* rang in Arabessa's ears, sent shivers to race down her spine.

What you may learn does not have to change your duties to this family, her father had told her. *You can stay as you are with your sisters. You have a choice.*

Choice.

This was it.

This was what he had spoken of that morning. What he had warned of when he gave her the memory of her mother.

She wanted me to give you this when it was time.

When it was time for Arabessa to understand how deep her connection to the crown went, for the moment she would be invited to vie for it.

Her mother had been Thief King. Her father still was Thief King. And he was stepping down.

Now is your choice. Later is your fate.

Later could be her death.

Would be for most in this room.

Arabessa furtively glanced at her competition. A ragtag of individuals. Some broad and large, others slim or stocky. No disguises she recognized, but each gifted, each a potential Thief King. A stranger she and her sisters would have to obey as the Mousai if she were to turn away from this invitation. The idea had her magic racing forward in a surprising surge of protectiveness. This throne was her father's, her mother's, her family's.

Hers.

That last thought startled her. Arabessa had been raised to serve the throne, as well as the kingdom's best interests, but never had she known how possessive she was of it. Loyal, of course, but also protective of her family's connection to it.

But did that mean she wanted to claim it? That she should?

Yes, answered her gifts, sure and demanding. *Yessss. It is ours. It is what we have been raised to become. To lead. To command. To control. Our throne, our legacy. Our own.*

Arabessa's breathing grew quick. She knew in her heart she agreed. This was something of her own she could claim, she could work toward, she could do for herself.

I want what will fulfill you with a life beyond regret, Dolion had told her.

To remain as she always was, she would regret. She would grow bitter and resentful. She knew this because she could sense herself already slipping there.

But what would her father regret?

There is no going back. It is either to win or to lose, and to lose is to enter the Fade.

Arabessa turned her gaze to her king, met the shrouded stare she could feel boring into her from across the room. Her chest tightened. Her father was somewhere buried beneath that disguise and was no doubt terrified of losing a daughter. But was this not the world he had brought them into? A kingdom where they could die every day. He knew the risks; he had even known she would show up here today.

Choice.

It was her choice.

A commotion to her right had Arabessa turning to watch a candidate choose to leave. It was the one with the broken arm. They turned from their still-floating invitation, cradling their injury to their chest as they headed toward the exit at their back. The stone guardians on either side pushed the large doors open. A rippling of magic danced at the threshold, a spell to forget. As the masked individual stepped through, Arabessa could just make out their relieved sigh before the way out closed with a heavy huff.

The rest in the room stayed.

"It appears your competition has thinned," said the king. "A good omen, I would think. Now, unless there are others who wish to leave, please sign your invitation, and the secrets of today will be bound silent by blood."

Arabessa eyed the hovering envelope, indecision swirling, anticipation building.

Choice. Duty. A life beyond regret. Responsibility. Expectations. Roles. Family.

What do you desire? Zimri had asked her.

She now knew.

She desired autonomy.

A chance to be something other than the eldest Mousai, meant to conduct and control her sisters. A chance to be more than an executioner, more than a performer or an obedient daughter, a responsible sister. To have a choice about her future. A choice that *she* made for herself, one that still honored her family, continued her parents' legacy and her sisters' work, gave purpose to all she had been trained and taught and expected to be.

This was *it*. Possibly the only opportunity Arabessa might have to claim that desire. Death waited at one end and at the other a throne, but both began with a choice. Her choice. Not an order from a king or a father or an obligation to a sibling.

Arabessa snatched the letter, pulse stampeding through her veins as she broke the seal.

Inside lay an elegantly scrolled note:

Welcome, our child, our loyal Arabessa Bassette
A new Thief King is coming
A historic change that will remain untold
The end of the Star Eclipse, the final deciding

We invite you to test if you are worthy
To claim this throne, and this kingdom's vowed
Our magic will be yours to conduct
If you survive, you will be crowned

Sign in blood your silent oath to play
But remember, to lose is to enter the Fade
So think carefully, our darling, if this is worth dying
You cannot return from this decision once made

When Arabessa was finished reading, a silver pen winked into existence beside the invitation.

Siggggn, her gifts purred inside her. *Siggggn.*

Arabessa swallowed past the tight ball of nerves forming in her throat. Her skin buzzed with excitement, with fear, with a slowly solidifying certainty.

She looked to the Thief King once again, to where he remained on his distant throne at the end of the thinning walkway. Shrouded and masked, but in that slip of grain fall, she could feel her father there. A rippling of connection that sent cool wariness down her spine. What did he want her to do? What did he want her to choose?

In the end the answer would not matter. She had followed the path he had set her whole life. This was about what she needed. What she wanted.

Taking one last glance at the other contenders, at whom else the throne thought worthy, Arabessa teetered on a precipice of action.

We are worthy, reminded her magic. *Worthy like our mother. Worthy like our father.*

Yes, she silently agreed, chin tilting up with a surge of determination. *I* am *worthy.*

Worthy of my desires.

Arabessa had been invited here today, which meant she was worthy of this choice.

She didn't know what this meant for the future of the Mousai or Zimri or her father when he stepped down, but for once she knew what *she* desired. What *she* wanted.

And it was to be king.

To continue what her family had built.

Now was her choice. Later was her fate.

Arabessa grabbed the pen and, gritting her teeth from the slicing pain of the silent oath being carved into her arm, signed her name in her blood.

Chapter Eleven

*A*rabessa pushed into the private chambers of the Thief King, ripping off her mask as soon as the heavy doors behind her were bolted shut. Her magic was frenetic, thrashing through her limbs as her heartbeat pounded. Her raw blood oath burned along her forearm as she headed for his dressing room.

Her father might have eluded her for days, but tonight she *would* catch him. It was not a quick or easy task to remove the disguise of the King of Thieves.

As she drew closer to her destination, a metallic scent accosted her nose, a lingering of the throne's magic pushing against her. *Careful where you walk,* it seemed to say. Arabessa merely walked faster, pulse jumping with the confirmation that her father was here.

A sightless attendant stood outside Dolion's dressing room's door and, sensing her approach, raised a hand for her to stop. "He is not allowing visitors at this time," they said.

"He *is* seeing me." Arabessa pushed past, striding in to find Dolion with his headdress removed, surrounded by more sightless assistants.

"How could you not tell me?" she demanded, her intrusion stopping the busy fingers and hands unclasping and uncinching his costume. Achak glanced up at her from where they had been leaning in the corner, cleaning their nails.

Her father remained facing away as he said, "Leave us."

Beside Achak, the room quickly emptied.

Only then did Dolion turn on his platform to meet her gaze.

For a beat they each stared at one another, Arabessa noting a mixture of emotions in his blue eyes: pain, pride, worry, exhaustion.

Her ire slipped.

"How could you not tell me?" she repeated, softer this time.

Her father let out a long sigh. "How would I have been able to, my melody?"

"There is always a way," she said, coming to stand in front of him.

She hated how hurt she was, how angry, how stunned. Not from what she had agreed to do but because she'd had no warning of his intentions of stepping down.

"I am your daughter," she reasoned.

"A fact that has never mattered to the throne," he admonished as he loomed over her.

She kept herself from flinching.

He might no longer have worn his headdress, but his presence remained overwhelming, especially in the small room. She had always found his dressing room a calming space—circular, with a wall of closets and candelabras and soft rugs—but this evening none of the plush or familiar surroundings helped soothe her churning emotions.

Her father was leaving his role as Thief King. He was giving his reign to another. Possibly to her. Possibly to a stranger. And she had not known.

"If I had not been invited tonight," she said, trying a different angle, "when would I have been told about you . . . retiring?" She worked hard to find the word her silent oath allowed. "When would the Mousai have known? It's quite an important detail for those who serve you, don't you think?"

"The Mousai serve the Thief King," said Dolion. "Not me."

"But *you* created the Mousai."

"And you have now ended them."

Arabessa took a step back as though slapped. She was robbed of a response. Only feelings slid oily and unwelcome through her. Sadness and guilt because she knew he was right. Fury and frustration because of course when she was finally to go after what she wanted, there would be consequences.

But she was Arabessa Bassette, and she did not react emotionally even if her current state threatened tears as well as a scream.

"Are you . . . angry with me?" The question bubbled up quiet, fearful.

Dolion's expression softened. "My melody, how could I be angry with a path I myself have chosen? I am proud you are working toward a life you will not regret."

"But you just said—"

"I merely pointed out that nothing is lasting. Not my role here, nor yours or your sisters'. I am sorry I could not tell you what you've learned this evening, what I have been preparing to do or what you needed to prepare because of it, but this is the way of our kingdom, my child. Secret oaths and stealers and spells keep much inside. And the throne carries the most. I know you can understand this. You would not have been invited otherwise."

Arabessa wasn't sure if it was because of the dim candlelight or what had recently transpired in the throne room, but she noted the true tiredness in her father's eyes. The new lines along his forehead and gray folded into his beard. A collection of fatigue made from endless years of roles and responsibilities.

I have claimed this throne for as long as I am able.

A weight of remorse fell along Arabessa's shoulders. How had she not seen this exhaustion in her father earlier? Though even if she had, she would never have thought it could lead to such an outcome as this: him no longer being Thief King.

"Yes"—she nodded—"of course I understand, but surely if Achak was to know, so could I? So could Niya and Larkyra?"

"Achak has been beside this throne before me," Dolion explained. "They have known of what the Star Eclipse represented before I even knew of the Thief Kingdom."

This information settled hard in Arabessa's stomach. How old *were* the twins? She looked to the brother, who nodded, bearded expression neutral.

"It is true," said Achak. "We have seen *many* Star Eclipses come and go."

Meaning they had seen many Thief Kings. They were no doubt there for her mother, confidants as they were to her father and, as they stated, many kings before that.

Too many questions continued to flood Arabessa with every answer she collected regarding this throne's past.

Would she ever know them all?

Yes, whispered her magic, *when we sit upon it.*

A cascade of nerves danced over her skin at the reminder of the competition she had just entered. But it was not from the fear of her failing, of possibly entering the Fade. No, death did not scare Arabessa, for she faced it every day. It was the chaos this would cause in her family. Already had caused.

You created the Mousai.

And you have now ended them.

More guilt clawed at her chest. Deep down she had known before she had signed that she could not be king and remain a mercenary for herself. And if she did not survive to be king . . . well, the Mousai were three, not two. This consequence of her decision snagged at her heart the most. Not because she wanted to remain the leader of their group but because to decide the fate of the Mousai without consulting her sisters felt the most irresponsible, the most selfish. They deserved a choice too.

How was she meant to maneuver through this?

As if in response, the wound of her silent oath burned along her forearm. A warning of what she could never say: the truth.

She was now captive to these secrets, like her father was, like Achak. At least some of them.

"Is this why you gave me that memory of Mother being Thief King?" she asked.

Dolion might not be able to speak about Johanna's history, but Arabessa was not yet bound silent.

"Yes," he said, a pain creasing the edge of his eyes, as it always did when his wife was mentioned. "It was the best way we could think to ready you if a day like this ever came."

"So you knew this could happen?" Arabessa blinked, stunned. "That I could be invited?"

"Not exactly," replied her father. "But your mother . . . let's just say she prepared for all outcomes, especially ones that could involve you girls and our family."

"She really thought way too much about way too much," added Achak, a wistful grin edging the brother's lips from where he remained leaning against the far wall. "My sister and I used to tease Johanna that she wished she was born a future teller."

"Yes," mused Dolion, brows pinching. "I certainly would have appreciated knowing what was to be my future."

Arabessa sensed there was much more to this subject, a thousand layers to dig through, but she wasn't sure this was the moment to grab a spade.

"But you see, my melody"—her father looked back at her, expression carrying more than the worries of today—"it has been my time for a while now. I cannot serve this role as well as I once was able."

"I'm sorry," she found herself saying, more heaviness pressing.

Dolion regarded her quizzically. "What could you possibly be sorry for?"

"That I did not know you had been feeling this way. I should have known."

A soft laugh escaped him. "Not everyone is your responsibility, my child."

"Still, I should have been able to tell."

Dolion gave her a gentle smile. "You know, you might look like your mother, but you and I are alike in other ways," he admitted. "There is much inside us we hide."

For the first time Arabessa didn't know if such poise was a virtue or a fault.

"Your Grace?" interrupted a sightless attendant who bowed at the dressing room's threshold. "The Collector is here to see you. I wouldn't have disturbed, but he said it was quite urgent."

A flurry of panic erupted in Arabessa's stomach. Zimri, here? No, no, no. This wasn't good. She looked more than a mess; she appeared destroyed in her singed dress and bloodstains and scrapes. He would surely have questions. Questions she herself hardly had answers to, let alone ones she was allowed to give.

Unless . . .

"Does he know?" asked Arabessa.

"No," said Dolion. "Only those in this room and who were invited tonight. No one else in the kingdom."

"He can't see me like this." She gestured to her state.

"He won't," he assured before addressing the waiting assistant. "Have him seen into the smaller sitting room. I will be with him in a moment."

Arabessa frowned. "But I have much more to discuss with you."

"I do not doubt it," Dolion replied as he descended from his changing platform. "But perhaps a bath and some tea before we continue? That always settles my thoughts."

"Is that what you'll be doing before meeting the Collector?" she challenged.

Another grin lifted his tired features. "As much as I would like it to be, I have not had time for such comforts in a very long while."

As her father exited the room, the white robe of the Thief King still weighing on his shoulders, Arabessa had a flash to wonder how she might avoid such fatigue when she sat upon the throne.

That was, of course, if she didn't die in her attempts to claim it.

CHAPTER TWELVE

*T*he ring in Zimri's pocket was on fire. At least, it felt as though it were, with how it burned against his skin through the fabric of his trousers.

Take me out, it seemed to demand. *Hold me. Caress me. Give me to the one you love.*

Zimri certainly had every intention to, but first he needed to talk with Arabessa's father. Ever since his conversation with Kattiva, he had held a rush of urgency to settle what was in his heart.

As he stood waiting within a small room of the Thief King's private chambers, his nerves fluttered, erratic, like the nearby flames in the hearth. He had not felt this on edge in quite some time. Of course he knew why. He had come here to seek Dolion Bassette's approval. A prize everyone in his household had grasped at desperately over the years.

At the thought, Zimri was thrown back to when he was still a boy, learning the new ways of his new life with the man who slipped in and out of one of the most powerful roles in Aadilor, then, too, wanting nothing more than his blessing.

As the prisoner sobbed in the center of the room, Zimri fought against his wave of guilt. The air was filled with the acute stench of misery, an emotion he had purposefully amplified.

"And now happy," instructed *Achak from where they stood behind Zimri.*

Zimri refocused on the man. It had been easy to pluck out and expand on his sadness. To reverse it, however, and twist such heavy emotions to weightless ones was like turning over a boulder: rather laborious.

"I can sense you have experienced much pain," said Zimri softly as he bent close to the shackled man. "But surely you have a memory, a name, a place, that brings you serenity?"

Share with me what it is, *he urged his magic to caress gently over the prisoner's bent form.* I will help you feel better. *A graze to his cheek.* Trust me. *A press to his heart.* Share with me.

It was weak, but Zimri clung to a thin thread of floral as it began to waft from the prisoner. Love was always a potent emotion. It smelled like wildflowers: hopeful.

"Yes," he encouraged, daring to draw closer, his concentration an arrow in a quiver. "That is what can bring you peace. Hold on to it." The scent got stronger; the man stopped crying, his blindfolded head tipping up toward Zimri's voice. Zimri expanded his gifts then, a gold dusting to link onto the prisoner's small threads of calm. He breathed in deep, pulling out whatever thought this man held tight in his heart, cooing, Trust me, trust us, *with his magic until the prisoner smiled.*

"What makes you happy?" asked Zimri.

"Mary," the man sighed. "My Mary."

Like a window had been thrown open, any scent of melancholy was swept away upon the name being said. Despite his scrapes and cuts and soiled clothes, the chained-down man, who had been sobbing only moments ago, now grinned in utter bliss.

And as a result, so did Zimri, for it was very hard to manipulate the emotions of others without taking them on oneself.

"How long has he been practicing this?" asked Dolion to Achak from where he had been watching in a shadowed corner. With the intrusion of

his deep voice, the room Zimri stood in snapped back into focus. He, Niya, Larkyra, and Arabessa were all huddling in a prison cell beneath the palace.

An odd place, to be sure, for children to have magic lessons, but not the oddest they would ever experience.

"About a fortnight," replied Achak. "He's quite natural with his gifts. He can pick up quickly on the emotions of others."

Dolion stared down at Zimri, only twelve at the time, but three years older than he had been when first coming to live with the Thief King and his family. Still, he had not grown any bolder around his guardian. Especially not when he had surprised them with a visit this afternoon to watch one of their lessons.

"And he can always alter them?" inquired Dolion, not removing his gaze from Zimri.

He resisted squirming under his scrutiny, and knowing the sisters watched on wasn't much added help.

"He can for those not gifted," said Achak. "There are still some techniques to be smoothed out, but we believe he'll be a master of his gifts in no time."

Dolion finally addressed Zimri. "And do you feel this way? That you'll be a master in no time?"

A cold sweat broke out on his neck. He had learned early that his answers here would always be challenged, remembered.

"I—will not stop practicing until I am, sire."

His guardian's blue gaze sparked pleased, a subtle honeysuckle scent filling the air. The vise grip on Zimri's chest loosened, but only slightly.

"Carry on." Dolion nodded to Achak, not even addressing his daughters before leaving the room.

Achak quickly urged Zimri to the side, instructing Niya to prepare for her turn, the poor prisoner in the center the continued target.

"You did well," said Arabessa in a whisper as he came to stand next to her. "With my father," she added. "He might feel like a lot at times, but

he only tests those he believes are worthy. And you, Zimri, are certainly worthy."

With the mix of Dolion's contentment and Arabessa's words, a new sensation began to fill his chest. One Zimri hadn't felt in a very long time: a sense of belonging.

"I'm sorry to have kept you waiting," intruded a deep voice into Zimri's memory, snapping him back to the sitting room within the Thief King's private chambers.

"My king." Zimri bowed low as Dolion's broad figure strode in. "I do apologize for visiting when I know you are very busy."

"You are never one to waste my time," said Dolion. "Please, do sit." He waved a hand to a nearby chair, his countenance appearing as heavy as the weight he placed in the seat across from him. "Now, what is this urgency you spoke to my attendant of?"

"Well," began Zimri, gathering his resolve. "It's a matter involving your daughter, Arabessa."

A beat passed in the room in which Dolion hooked Zimri with his gaze, something he could not read flashing, though he could very clearly sense it in the air: unease flowed off his mentor, a sour scent. Zimri frowned, unsure what to make of this. Dolion was not one to be uneasy about anything.

"I see," said Dolion slowly. "Is she in some sort of trouble?"

"No." Zimri shook his head. "Nothing like that. I—well . . ."

No longer trusting his words, Zimri decided to rely on actions instead. Reaching into his pocket, he pulled out his mother's sapphire ring. Its sharp cut edges caught the fire's light as Zimri held it between his fingers.

Dolion's gaze fell to it, silence stretching. Zimri grew desperate to glean what his guardian might be thinking now that his intentions for coming here had been revealed. But as if a great wall shuttered his emotions, Dolion now gave nothing away, gave nothing off. He was a stoic father, a patient king, and an assessing adviser in this moment.

He only tests those he believes are worthy, Arabessa had once told him. *You, Zimri, are certainly worthy.*

This was his chance to prove how much.

"There's something of great importance I'd like to ask you, sir," Zimri began again. "Regarding a woman of great importance to us both."

CHAPTER THIRTEEN

*A*rabessa found herself stunned for the third time in less than a week. Her sisters had taken the news of their mother being Thief King in surprising stride.

In fact, they appeared not in the least bit put out as they sat opposite her, sipping their tea in their family's sunroom in Jabari. Was it possible that she had been more emotional than Niya?

Arabessa frowned, not at all enjoying that thought.

"I had prepared myself for you both to riddle me with more questions," she admitted.

"Are there some we have missed from the ones we have already asked?" inquired Larkyra, placing her cup back in its saucer. She was without her gloves this morning, and her half-missing ring finger was prominently on display. It was an injury she had acquired from a thievery gone wrong.

"I'm sure there are," said Arabessa with a frown. "But I shall not go through the trouble of figuring out which ones if neither of you seem to care."

"I care," mumbled Niya through a bite of her strawberry tart. "But you've been quite thorough with what you know and what you don't. Which we certainly appreciate."

This was true, of course. Arabessa had ensured she shared every-thing she could regarding her mother before she and her sisters were to give it away to a Secret Stealer.

Now that she had an even bigger secret looming over her head, Arabessa had been more than desperate to unload this one. Though she didn't feel as unburdened as she had hoped.

Perhaps having a potential end date to her life expectancy and knowing she would break up the Mousai come the conclusion of the Star Eclipse caused some added stress.

At the reminder, her stomach turned over with a mix of guilt and disquiet.

"Honestly," began Niya as she leaned forward to snatch up another pastry from the small banquet in front of them, "I would have put good money on such odds. From the stories Achak has told us about Mother, it makes complete sense that she was Thief King."

"One of the most powerful sorceresses in Aadilor, smart, beautiful," Larkyra listed. "Not to mention Father did tell us she was the one who showed him the Thief Kingdom."

"True," agreed Arabessa, a bit disappointed that she had not put this together as quickly as her sisters had. "But I still would like to have known about Johanna sooner."

"Of course," said Larkyra as she smoothed a wrinkle in her blue skirts. "But when have we ever gotten information from Father when we would have liked to?"

Niya snorted her agreement. "He does love to leave important details unsaid until the last possible moment."

Yes, like informing me that I've been invited to vie for a throne that he's stepping down from. Arabessa pressed her lips together as her silent oath burned awake along her arm. A warning.

I wasn't going to say it out loud! She tried to reason with the blasted spell, though her sisters had every right to know about their father and their fates as the Mousai.

Arabessa, of course, had the ability to tell them their trio was breaking up, but she wouldn't be able to explain why. That was what had her twisted up inside. The cause and reaction to everything.

"What I'd like to know," continued Niya, her red hair catching the light streaming through the windows, "is, how many Thief Kings have there been?"

"Does it matter?" replied Larkyra. "If there's been two, there have obviously been many others."

"True," Niya mused. "I wonder when they switch . . ."

"Will you be staying in the kingdom after our performance tonight, Lark?" Arabessa blurted the question, not liking where the conversation was headed, and neither did her silent oath, for the lingering signature carved into her arm began to sting in awareness. *Careful,* it seemed to whisper.

"No." Her youngest sister blinked over to her, blonde hair shifting from where it spilled over her shoulders. "I hadn't planned to. One of our maids recently bore a child, and Darius and I planned to call on the family."

"Didn't this maid just have a girl last year?" inquired Niya, flicking some crumbs from her sleeve.

"That was Rebeka," said Larkyra with a smile. "Her little girl is absolutely adorable. Hair redder than yours, Niya."

"No one's hair is redder than mine."

"Well, hers *is*," assured Larkyra.

Arabessa watched as her youngest sister's eyes lit up when talking of these children. Larkyra might have never mentioned it, but Arabessa knew she wanted a family. It was a topic that seemed rather strained between her and Darius. He had admitted his excitement about one day becoming a father, but such plans seemed on hold because of whom Larkyra was still bound to serve.

Pregnancy was not a friendly companion when ordered to torture or perform.

With that thought, Arabessa's heartbeat sped up with a realization. Could the Mousai ending actually be a *good* thing for her sisters?

Without her role tying her to the throne, Larkyra would be able to choose her future more freely for her family.

And Niya's expeditions *were* growing longer and longer with the *Crying Queen*. Her melancholy becoming rather insufferable when she wasn't with her pirate.

Could Arabessa's decision to follow her own path be able to help her sisters lean more into theirs?

For the first time in what felt like an eternity, a warm sense of hope filled her chest.

No matter her outcome at the end of the Star Eclipse, by dissolving the Mousai, Arabessa might have helped her sisters become free.

"I have missed seeing you three all together like this," said a familiar deep voice by the door.

Arabessa's moment of relief was dashed away with the skip of her pulse as Zimri strode into the sunroom. He was dashing in his burgundy coat and trousers, his brown skin warm in the morning light.

Hazel eyes found hers, a radiant smile spreading over his angular features, sending a pool of heat to her stomach.

She would never get used to how her body reacted to his presence.

"Zimri!" exclaimed Larkyra, popping up to give him a hug. "I had hoped to see you before our performance. We missed you at Macabris the other night."

"You know the Collector rarely walks his floors," pointed out Niya from where she remained sitting, though she blew Zimri a kiss in greeting, one that he playfully swatted away. She stuck her tongue out at him.

"What has you leaving your hovel in the kingdom to find us here?" asked Larkyra.

Zimri's gaze fell to Arabessa again. "I came to speak with your sister, actually."

The room grew quiet for a beat, no one seeming to misunderstand to which sister he was referring.

"Of course," said Larkyra with a too-bright grin, nudging Niya below her with her hand.

"But I'm not done with my tea," Niya whined.

"We'll get more tea in the kitchens," replied Larkyra through gritted teeth. "Now, come." She all but lifted Niya to stand.

A panic seized Arabessa then, as she watched her sisters shuffle toward the door. If Zimri was here to continue their discussion from yesterday, she wasn't ready. In fact, she might be in a *worse* position today. She was still working through how this competition for the throne would affect everything in her life, let alone the people in it. The First Fade had officially begun within the kingdom, which meant at any moment she would be given her first test. She needed her wits about her. Couldn't afford distractions more than ever.

Zimri would be able to sense these twisted-up emotions and seek answers for why she was feeling this way. Answers Arabessa couldn't give.

"I'm sure you both don't need to leave," implored Arabessa to her sisters as they moved toward the door.

"I'm sure we both need to leave *very much*," said Larkyra, linking arms with Niya. "But we'll see each other tonight for the performance at the palace. You'll be there, right, Zimri?"

"I had planned on it, yes."

"Good! The crowds during the Star Eclipse are always the most rambunctious."

And with that, her sisters slipped through the sunroom's door, closing it with a soft click.

"Oh dear," exclaimed Arabessa, coming to her feet. "I just realized I have so much to do before our performance. Costumes to check, my instrument to tune—"

"Ara," Zimri began softly, striding closer. "You can do all that is swirling in your mind *after* I ask you something."

His familiar scent filled her on an inhale, and a bit of her anxiousness slipped away.

"But—"

"Please, come sit with me a moment."

"Zimri—"

"For the love of the lost gods, Ara," he huffed. "You are truly taking the romance out of this."

That had her pause. "Romance out of what?"

He shook his head, though unable to keep an amused grin at bay. "I had this planned to go very differently. There was to be a lot of beautiful prose and heartfelt confessions, but I should have known that with you, time is of the essence."

Arabessa frowned. "I don't understand."

Zimri ran his hand down her arm to thread their fingers together. Arabessa's entire body suddenly felt like the sun: blazingly alive.

"I need to know something," he began. "Are you in love with me?"

She blinked, taken aback. "This is your question?"

"One of them."

"Zimri, how could you not—"

"Are you in love with me?"

Arabessa's heart squeezed with the thought it wasn't painfully clear. "Of course I am in love with you, you lunatic. You . . ." She needed to look away to find her next words. "You consume every part of my heart that my family doesn't."

His responding smile was resplendent. "And I am in love with you."

"Good." She nodded. "Now that we have that crystallized . . ."

"I need you to remember those two *very* important facts," he continued as he reached for something in his breast pocket. "For it is all that matters for what I will ask you next."

Arabessa stopped breathing, her heart stilling, as Zimri revealed a dazzling green sapphire ring tucked into a leather box. "Arabessa Bassette," he began, slowly lowering to one knee. "My music, my only love, I ask you to grant me the greatest honor of becoming my wife."

CHAPTER FOURTEEN

Arabessa remained speechless, and this time it had nothing to do with her silent oath.

"Your lack of an answer is not reassuring," said Zimri, still poised below her with the open ring box, his brows beginning to furrow.

"I . . . ," she began and then stopped. *I what? I what, Arabessa?* she demanded of herself, panic beginning to swirl. "I don't understand," she eventually tumbled out.

"Don't understand?" Zimri repeated, coming to his feet. "I would think it quite simple. I've asked for your hand in marriage. Now it is your turn to give answer to that request. People have been performing such an exchange long before the lost gods left."

"No, yes, of course, I understand that." She hated how flustered she sounded, but sticks, she *was* flustered! "I don't understand why you've asked me this right now."

He snapped the ring box shut. "Would you like me to ask again at a later date that better suits?" His hurt was clear in his dripping sarcasm.

Arabessa flinched. Though yes, that was exactly what she'd prefer. After the Star Eclipse would be much more convenient. "Zimri, you misunderstand me." She reached out to place a hand on his arm, but he shifted away. An uncomfortable grip to her chest. "Zimri, look at me. Please, will you look at me."

He begrudgingly obliged, and she hated the anger and pain she had placed in his gaze.

But marriage? Now? What is going on?

"I love you, I truly, desperately do, but I am merely having a hard time following how marrying you is the logical next step from our unresolved conversation from the other day."

"Why must it be logical?" he argued. "We love each other. We should spend every moment we still have on this side of the Fade celebrating that."

"And we do," she said. "Every free moment either of us gets, we are with one another."

"In *secret*," he practically hissed.

And here they were again.

She understood how it looked, how it must feel for Zimri. He was right regarding her family. They obviously knew *something* was going on. Even the potential danger and weakness this would set upon them in the Thief Kingdom could be managed, if carefully. As for the distraction of it, well, that was the snag that still held firm—if it wasn't, in fact, amplified.

Today was no longer the same as yesterday.

Arabessa didn't know if she'd be alive at the end of the month. Her tests were assuredly to be dangerous and taxing. She could not be caught unprepared, unaware, when thrown into them. Her life literally was on the line. To be openly with Zimri, engaged to be *his* wife . . . to be swept up in all that entailed: it wasn't possible. It would be the very definition of irresponsible.

The seriousness of her task ahead pressed down on her once more. But it was what she wanted: this chance, this choice. To continue the legacy of her parents, give purpose to all she had done as part of the Mousai. The most honorable duty she could imagine and her path alone to follow.

But she also wanted Zimri.

What she needed was time. She needed a way to stall without breaking both their hearts.

"You're right," she began. "There is no reason to continue to hide our relationship from my family."

This had surprise filling his gaze.

"And I am *extremely* honored that you have asked me to marry you, Zimri. But can we . . . I'd love if we could take this all a bit slower."

"We have known each other since we were nine," he said dryly. "Have been in love with each other since we were fourteen."

"Thirteen," she clarified. At least, that was how old she had been when she knew she loved him.

Zimri's gaze softened. "Thirteen," he repeated. "Going any slower would have us growing gray by the time we wed."

Arabessa hoped she would live that long.

"I'm not asking for years," she said. "Only for us to be together openly with my family for a while. For us to work out the logistics of how this will work with our shared duties to our king. Learn how we can be as safe as possible within the kingdom."

And time for me to deal with my trials for the throne and how to prepare for every outcome with my sisters and you and Father.

"This is not me saying no, Zimri." She stepped closer to him, her nerves settling when he let her grasp his hand. "It's me asking for a bit more time."

"And if I don't have more time to give?" he asked, gaze pained.

"What does that mean?"

"Please, Ara." He gripped her hand tighter. "Let us marry now. Let us elope and deal with any consequences later."

He was being erratic. She could hardly keep up. "Consequences? Zimri, what is going on? What has happened?"

He looked away as a small knot formed between his brows. "An . . . opportunity has arisen for me to be able to acquire more shares in Macabris."

"That's wonderful!" she exclaimed. "I knew you'd find a way."

He didn't even crack a smile, which sent a wave of unease through her.

"But this doesn't make you happy?" she questioned.

He glanced back at her. "It comes with a catch."

She nodded. "Like most things do."

"I will have to marry Kattiva Volkov."

Five. It was now five times Arabessa had been shocked silent. She stepped out of his embrace, and his expression crumbled.

"She came to me last night." He hurried to explain as he followed her retreating form. Arabessa butted into a nearby planter, forcing her to stop. "Her parents gave her an ultimatum. She must choose a suitor in the next week and marry by the Sky's Return or her inheritance will be taken from her. Kattiva proposed a union between the two of us. I would get her ten percent shares in exchange for her inheritance and marrying into my family's historic title."

His words were starting to come out muffled, a ringing growing louder in her ears. Zimri and Kattiva . . . Kattiva and Zimri . . . married by the Sky's Return . . . exactly when she would be either dead or on the throne.

"It would be a marriage in name alone," Zimri went on, his expression strained but his eyes earnest. "She and I . . . there would be no consummation. I do not desire her that way. I do not desire her *at all*," he clarified when Arabessa's brows shot up. "Ara"—he gripped her shoulders, forcing her focus on him—"I want you. I love you. I want to marry *you*."

"But then you wouldn't get majority ownership."

"Yes . . ." He took in a steadying breath. "But in time I will find another way. The Volkovs can't live forever."

"But this is your opportunity *now*. How can you turn it down?"

She noted how he regarded her carefully, was no doubt trying to decipher the emotions wafting from her. But Arabessa couldn't understand them herself. She felt torn, hurt, frustrated, heartbroken, confused. As for Zimri, it was clear his heart was desperate for two paths.

Like hers was.

"Would you have me if I was married to another?" he cautiously asked.

Bile rose in her throat. "A mistress?"

"You would be the woman I love," he corrected. "The *only* one."

Arabessa couldn't talk. A sudden sweeping of jealousy choked the words from her. A fiery burn consuming her insides. Share him? With *Kattiva Volkov*, the very embodiment of lust and pleasure? He might not want her that way now, but certainly after time . . . after they'd spent late nights together at the club, lived side by side under one roof, there was no denying a bond would surely grow between them. One Arabessa could never compete with. And though she hated to even think it, their pairing made sense. Both cared for Macabris, were involved in the business, were desired by their patrons. They would certainly be a force. A couple to rival.

Could she survive it? Arabessa knew how to wear many masks, but this one had tragedy written all over it. Had resentment promised. And if she did win the throne, such emotions surely would get in the way of her ruling. Being his mistress: it was an absolute nightmare to imagine.

"If it helps," said Zimri after a moment, "a different way to look at it is me being married to Kattiva would turn away any attention on the two of us. To your earlier point, Kattiva would have a target on her back, not you."

By the Fade. "You want this," she heard herself whisper.

His features fell, his gaze swimming with every kind of hurt: pain, irritation, exhaustion.

"I want *you*," he said. "But I needed you to know why I must have your answer now, not in time. Your father has already given his blessing. He—"

"You spoke to my father? About us?" Her magic jumped in her gut along with her alarm.

"Of course. His approval means a great deal to both of us."

"What did he say?"

"Only that he wished I would have asked for your hand much earlier."

Because he knows what tests I now face, she thought, a wave of heavy remorse hitting her. Did her father believe she would have walked away from her invitation for the throne if Zimri had asked her earlier? Perhaps more importantly, did Arabessa believe this?

"And I don't disagree with him," Zimri continued. "But I can't change the past. We only ever have the present. So I will ask again, Arabessa: Will you marry me?"

As she looked into his eyes, saw the loyalty in them, the love, she wanted to scream.

Despite the timing, how could she be the reason for him failing to obtain a lifelong dream? What he had been tirelessly fighting for all these years? How could she delay his reclaiming Macabris? If she said yes to marrying him, she would remove the one chance Zimri had ever had of regaining majority ownership; she would be keeping him from a promise he had made to his parents, a dream he had yearned for since a child.

If she said no, she would lose him, for she could never be his mistress, but he would get his club, his home closer to being entirely his.

Amid all of this there were her trials and all the complications that came with vying for the throne.

There was too much on the line for each of them. Too many sacrifices any way she turned.

Arabessa had already made a decision to go after what *she* desired for her future.

Zimri deserved that chance too.

"I can't have you give up this opportunity with Macabris," she said. "You would finally have majority ownership, finally be able to rule your club as your parents did."

Zimri shook his head. "I will find another way."

"How? You've been searching for a way for nine years."

A hardness crossed over his features, a stubborn fire. "That is my choice to make," he argued. "Now stop stalling, Arabessa. What is your answer?"

Her answer.

It felt more like a sentencing.

"I can't," she heard herself say. "I would never forgive myself if this was the only chance you were given and you didn't take it. I'm so sorry. I . . . can't marry you."

Zimri's gaze filled with an emotion that had her shiver. "And if I am wed to another?" he asked. "What becomes of us then?"

"You will have a wife," she stated, the words acidic on her tongue. "There will be nothing of us then."

A coldness slid through the room as Zimri's gaze hardened. The first wall ever falling into place between them. "I see," he said, voice hard stone. "And this is your final decision? You will give us up."

A burning of tears threatened to spill down her cheeks. "I'm letting us go."

Zimri became a rock before her eyes; he became a stranger with the blazing fury that overtook his energy. "Then I guess there is nothing left for us to discuss." His words were razor cuts.

"No," Arabessa said softly, forcing away the sob working up her throat. "I suppose not."

He did not grace her with a goodbye. Zimri stalked from the room, not a backward glance given.

Gone.

He was gone.

And Arabessa was left standing in the sunroom, hand clutching her chest as though that could stay the fracturing and falling pieces of her heart.

CHAPTER FIFTEEN

*Z*imri wanted to hurt something. He wanted to slam his fists into flesh and bone until there was another soul who felt even a sliver as broken and bleeding as he did.

He would arrange such a fight beneath Macabris. A lineup in one of the basement brawls where he could let out his magic, which twisted, hurt and damaged, through his veins. He would pull the agony from his heart to burden another. It was too much for him to take, too much to force himself to function through. Though Zimri did prefer wrath over sadness. Anger fueled; grief paralyzed. And he would not be rendered still. Not when he had lived in a limbo of his heart for so many years with Arabessa, only for it to end like this.

As if he had been sliced by a blade, pain oozed in his chest. Grief coming for him.

No! He gripped the sensation and punched it away.

He would not give in to it. Not now. He had something more pressing to attend to. Something that would give purpose to his pain.

Zimri pushed through the black curtain. The pungent scent of sweat and incense mixed with euphoria—a too-sweet wine—attacked his nose through his disguise. Naked bodies lay in low-lit alcoves that lined the circular space, groups of lovers occupying larger cushions in the center. Faces were buried in groins, limbs wrapping waists. A tangle of anatomy and motion and moans.

A man wearing only a thin gold loincloth came to his side, face hidden behind a black mask. "Collector, what a pleasure," he said. "Madam is with a customer at the moment, but we'd be happy to provide you with a service while you wait. On the house, of course."

"I'm looking for a friend." Zimri scanned the room.

"Certainly. A brunet friend? Blond? Old? Young?"

"A guest of yours who is here already."

"You wish to join their party? Of course. Please, have a look around and let us know if you need help in your search. Also, in case you are interested, anterooms two, eight, and twenty-six are requesting cuckolding, if you care to engage."

Zimri made his rounds through each adjoining room, attention sliding over breasts and chests and slick genitals. Though nearly everyone was nude, they still wore eye masks or headdresses, none of their disguises seeming to get in the way of what they desired.

Lussuri was one of the more high-end pleasure-houses in the Thief Kingdom, offering the widest variety of services with the best amenities. He never came here as a patron, only to discuss business with the madam, the owner. Lussuri and Macabris had a long-running history of working with one another.

Though now that he had been *let go* by Arabessa, he supposed he could do whatever he bloody well pleased here.

That carving pain caught him again, threatening to buckle his knees. Zimri desperately shook it off, grasping instead at his internal roar of frustration.

She had said no! Refused him even when he made it perfectly clear Macabris could wait, that she was more important than that dream— *they* were more important.

He should never have told her about Kattiva's offer. He should have known Arabessa would take the selfless road, the responsible path. Give him up so he could fulfill a promise he had made to his dead parents. Even though it broke them. Broke her. But Zimri couldn't force Arabessa into marrying him or being with him. He was not as desperate as that. Arabessa had made her decision. Even though he had nearly drowned in her devastation, clearly sensing how much her answer destroyed her.

But if it had killed her so much, then why say no? Why ask him in the beginning for more time? Zimri snorted his incredulity as he continued to pace the pleasure-house. They had been together for years now. In secret or not, they were forever devoted. But Arabessa always needed a plan, needed to prepare, and it appeared their relationship was no different. She wanted to work out all the possible issues they might hit up against before they walked down the aisle. But didn't she know life didn't care about plans? You could still wake up tomorrow an orphan.

Zimri's heart filled with more ghosts of anguish.

What had her so scared? He had caught the scent of her fear when he proposed. Sensed her energy churn like soil covering up roots one didn't want exposed. She wasn't telling him everything.

But when does she ever? he thought in another spark of fury. They had promised to never use their magic on one another, yet Zimri had never been so tempted to break that agreement. He had wanted to pry out all her secrets in that moment. Demand the truth of why she wanted to wait before he had confessed his opportunity with Kattiva.

Zimri huffed out an annoyed breath as he entered a new room. *None of it matters anymore,* he reminded himself. It was over. They were over. After everything. All the years of being patient, of sneaking around, of not wanting to scare her off, of pushing her too soon. None of it mattered. None of it had changed anything.

If she wanted him to follow his dream of reclaiming Macabris, then so be it. He was going full force forward.

A flash of a wolf on a pale hand caught Zimri's attention. He watched as it slid over the back of a head, tangling in white hair. Zimri quickened his strides.

He found Kattiva Volkov nude with her legs spread on one of the large round cushions in a corner room. Her head was thrown back, moans emanating from her pearl headdress as her spine arched, full breasts prominently displayed. A dark-skinned masked man and white woman bit and licked around each of her nipples, while a third party was attending to her between her legs.

At the height of her orgasm, her green gaze caught his.

Zimri's skin flashed warm at the unexpected connection, blood pooling low. Not even a cleric devoted to the lost gods would be unaffected in such a moment.

He cleared his throat.

"Collector, is that you?" she asked, breathless, as she came out of her height of pleasure. Dews of sweat glistened on her white skin as she lay limply against one of her lovers. At the mention of his name, nearby patrons glanced their way. Zimri was never more thankful for his full mask and heavy coat.

He managed a nod.

"What an utterly delightful surprise." Kattiva smiled. "Thank you, that was . . . well, it stunned me to find you standing there. And I am very rarely stunned."

"While not my intent in coming here to find you," he began, "I do aim to please."

Kattiva's gaze sparked, charmed, fingers idly stroking the abs of the man beside her as his hand fondled one of her breasts. "And what was your intent in finding me?" she asked.

"To accept your proposition."

Kattiva stilled the man's hand, shifting forward. "Truly?"

Zimri's pulse quickened, the sharp nails of grief threatening to rip open his heart once more, but he refused its presence yet again. Instead, he held tighter to his ire, burning away grief's clutches and fueling his resolve as he answered, "Yes, let us marry."

CHAPTER SIXTEEN

*A*rabessa was surrounded by the murmurs of excitement, but she barely registered a single guest. She stood unmoving, a numb statue, as she waited beside Niya and Larkyra on a small podium in the corner of a private anteroom.

Tonight they were the gilded beasts of the Thief King, the notorious Mousai soon meant to play and dance and sing in celebration of the Star Eclipse. While every sliver of them was covered from fingers to toes, hair tucked into complicated headdresses, any exposed skin painted to hide their natural hue, all here knew their purpose. This evening they were to entertain rather than torture. Though both actions could be considered synonymous by their awaiting crowd.

Arabessa's gaze traveled with indifference over the preperformance guests invited to clink glasses and ogle the Mousai. Those the king wanted to please. Court members he desired to shower in exclusive access to later pluck forth favors. The O'Crés were here, in their yellow thief-house colors, along with the Mendocis in their turquoise. Each eyed the Mousai with obvious intrigue, some even brave enough to approach and pay compliments to their costumes. Their real intent, of course, to collect a bragging token for later.

Yes, we talked with the Mousai and survived.

Arabessa hated this part of their duties. To be objects. But she understood the necessity. The Mousai were not merely a rarity in Aadilor; together they were some of the most powerful sorceresses. Any ruler who claimed them was, by proxy, also powerful. To show them off as they were being displayed tonight was both to inspire awe and collect fear. *Dare defy me and see what I can punish you with.*

Arabessa swallowed past the knot in her throat. Despite her earlier belief she might be freeing her sisters by ending the Mousai, her emotions were constantly shifting. Guilt to determination. Resolve to doubt. Her heart feeling as though it was forever being shredded from her and Zimri breaking up didn't help matters. She found herself currently questioning everything.

Especially as a voice whispered *selfish* in the back of her mind. *So selfish.*

Her stomach twisted with unease. Was she? To have chosen this path forward without being able to consult with her sisters?

Arabessa's resolve was cracking. Perhaps she had made a horrible mistake. Perhaps she should have turned away from the invitation to vie for the throne and remained as she was, kept the steady, predictable, responsible course.

A new voice rang in her head, a kinder one. *Yes, but it wouldn't have changed what happened with Zimri.*

Yes, she thought. That outcome would have still transpired. She could not be so selfish as to keep him from grasping this one chance to reclaim Macabris, to stop him from finally attaining closure on his parents' death. No matter how that erased a potential future together.

They were over. It was over.

Over.

Pain sliced like razors across Arabessa's heart once more, her lungs becoming crushed by an invisible weight.

She was suffocating, anxiously drawing in breath. Despite the thin silk of her costume, she wanted to rip the oppressive material off, wipe the thick paint from her skin. She needed to be alone. She needed out of this suffocating room! She needed to be free!

"We can postpone the performance," said Niya quietly beside Arabessa.

With a blink, she was brought back to where she stood between her sisters, a room of strangers tangling around them.

"Yes," agreed Larkyra at her other side, each of them seeming to pick up on her silent anguish. "We can push it to tomorrow or later in the month."

Niya and Larkyra had cornered Arabessa earlier in her private dressing rooms, immediately inquiring of Zimri and what he had wanted to discuss with her in their sunroom.

Arabessa had clamped her lips together, knowing that if she had spoken, only a sob would have escaped. But Larkyra and Niya evidently hadn't needed her to speak to know she was suffering. That her heart was broken. They had pulled her into a tight hug and whispered that whatever it was, it would all be okay.

That was when Arabessa had done something she had never done in front of her sisters. Hadn't let herself do even as she had watched Zimri walk away. She had cried.

Niya and Larkyra had merely held her closer, no more probing questions.

But Arabessa knew they would come, eventually.

"We cannot postpone the performance," she said, forcing at bay the overwhelm she could sense ready to crush her. "Everyone is here. We have a duty to our king to entertain. So we shall."

Larkyra and Niya remained quiet, but Arabessa could feel their shared glance behind her.

"How resplendent you three are this evening," said Achak, floating toward them as the sister. "But when are the Mousai ever not dressed to impress?"

"The same could be said regarding you, dear Achak," replied Larkyra.

"Yes," agreed Niya. "One might even feel you were trying to steal the show from us."

Achak's grin was coy. "My brother would no doubt agree with you. And—*ugh*—he's attempting to force his way—"

In a shiver, Achak's form shifted, height growing, face widening to sprout a beard and twisting their gold gown to accommodate a larger form. The brother now stood before them. "For once my sister is right," said Achak, the white jewels pasted along his eyebrows lifting. "But to properly turn heads, we all know it is *I* that must be in the room, not she."

The brother's expression strained for a moment, obviously containing his sister from shifting back so she might disagree.

"And you all say I am the one who stirs up drama," quipped Niya to the group, "when the real culprit stands before us."

"Speaking of drama"—Achak's attention fell to Arabessa, wary concern present in his swirling purple gaze—"how surprised we were to hear of Kattiva Volkov becoming engaged today."

Every muscle in Arabessa's body became stone.

"No!" gasped Niya, leaning forward. "To whom?"

Achak regarded the fire dancer, rather surprised, no doubt having assumed Arabessa would have already filled her sisters in.

"If our sources speak true," said Achak slowly, glancing quizzically at Arabessa, "we hear she's engaged to the Collector."

The room fell from Arabessa's sight as she became trapped within a tsunami of agony.

She's engaged to the Collector.

The words collided with her over and over.

She had known this would happen. She'd *known*. And yet it did nothing to keep her from being lashed by the truth, the reality. They were over. Done.

Zimri must have gone straight to Kattiva after leaving her this morning.

She was going to be sick.

135

As nausea swirled, Arabessa was barely able to sense her sisters' frozen shock beside her.

"Are we talking of the Macabris match?" A nearby masked guest slid closer, excitement clear in their voice to join in on the gossip. "It was certainly a delightful surprise to the kingdom, given Kattiva's proclivities," they went on. "But a rather sensible union, if you think about it. Both skilled at producing an entertaining evening. The Collector, no doubt, will gain some sort of advantage in the club with whatever slice Miss Volkov owns."

No one spoke for an awkwardly long time. Arabessa could feel the weighted attention of both of her sisters. This news and her crying earlier in her dressing room most assuredly had clicked everything into place.

"When"—Niya's voice tripped slightly—"are they to wed?"

Arabessa hung suspended as the guest answered, "I believe on the morning of the Sky's Return, after the end of the Star Eclipse."

The irony of holding oneself rigid, of attempting to freeze over all feeling, was that it merely took the right blow to the right place to break one.

Arabessa was being shattered into pieces. The sharp shards of herself falling into a nightmare of her own making.

The end of the Star Eclipse.

The end of her tests.

Possibly her life.

When a new Thief King would sit on the throne.

When she *needed* to sit upon it.

The morning of the Sky's Return.

The first day Zimri would be a husband.

To another.

The end of them.

The end of something she had not even given herself a chance to properly hold.

Arabessa didn't register Achak or their guest leaving. Didn't notice the crowd slowly pushing out of the room.

Arabessa was lost.

She was tumbling through the No More.

"Ara." A steadying hand along her shoulder; Larkyra's voice whispering close to her ear. "Are you able to go on?"

Go on.

"They are waiting for us to perform," said Niya at her other side.

At some point she and Larkyra had pressed themselves against her, holding on to her forearms. Holding her up.

"But we don't have to," added Larkyra. "We never have to."

But we do. A frustrated scream silently tore through Arabessa. *We must always perform, deceive, pretend. It is our purpose here.*

"We go on," Arabessa said, pushing out of her sisters' grasps, not knowing how she did it, just that she did; she held herself up.

She could not show how broken she was, how her magic was ripping through her veins, demanding to hurt another as she hurt.

Arabessa was their leader.

Arabessa was their guide.

She could not be weak.

She could not crack.

Larkyra and Niya would not agree to perform unless they believed she was able.

She.

Was.

Fine.

She.

Was.

Strong.

She was Arabessa bloody Bassette, eldest of the Mousai and invited to vie for the Thief King's throne.

Tilting her chin up, Arabessa funneled their years of training, of slipping on masks to become the picture of poise, of a creature unaffected even as a chaos of fire swarmed through her soul.

"We go on," she repeated as she glided toward the awaiting portable stage that would be pushed into the open arena. Her hands shook slightly as she bent to pick up her violin, but the instant her fingers grasped the familiar smooth wood, a sense of relief rushed through her. *Friend,* her magic cooed. *Ally.*

Her instruments could hold the emotions she could not. They could always lift the burden from her blood and send it spinning away. When everyone leaned on her, she leaned on her music.

"Play what you need," said Niya, she and Larkyra coming to stand close to her on the platform. "We follow you, *always.*"

"Always," repeated Larkyra.

Arabessa's chest tightened further.

Her sisters *would* follow her. Even if it was toward a day when the Mousai no longer existed.

Arabessa realized then how painful it was to grow. To move forward into something new. How hard it could be to carve one's own path and who might have to be left behind in the process.

I want what will fulfill you with a life beyond regret, her father had said. But could you live without regret if you also lived in heartache?

As their stage began to move, Arabessa turned her gaze forward, their masked attendants guiding their trio toward the open tunnel where the roar of the awaiting tiered crowd loomed.

When the spotlight swallowed her, Arabessa wondered if Zimri was watching. As he always watched.

Her grip tightened on her violin's neck, her gifts pulsing with each beat of her heavy heart.

Play what you need, Niya had said.

And she would.

Arabessa readied to play her devastation.

CHAPTER SEVENTEEN

imri was relieved to be in his private balcony two floors up as he gazed at the hungry crowd below. The mass was in rare form tonight. Double its usual size and thrice as heightened with impatience, waiting for the Mousai. The Star Eclipse always pushed the chaos within the kingdom, but mix in the promise of an exclusive performance by the most elusive and deadly beasts of the Thief King, and a tumultuous assembly one would indeed create.

Zimri noted the costumes that graced the circular cave. Spun of the rarest of rare: fur, silks, precious gems, carved bones, and soft leathers disguised guests. Headdresses seemed at war with one another. A battle of who could hold up the tallest, the most twisted, the most horned. It was a night to see and to be seen. Spirits flowed unceasing, rich food steamed, and the colorful smoke of those gifted pulsed as guests flittered from fighting to becoming needy tangling limbs, the overpowering scent of hundreds of emotions pressed together.

While he was in the business of entertaining, there was a reason Zimri preferred to watch his guests in Macabris from behind his one-way mirror within his office, and it had nothing to do with maintaining his anonymity. To be in the mix of crowds with such heightened emotions overwhelmed his gifts. The fragrance of lust mixed with fear, and every other nuance of feeling from those swarming around him became putrid. A nose-wrinkling experience that left him desperate for fresh air. But he had never missed a Mousai performance, so despite every logical instinct telling him tonight should become the first of many exceptions, he had still come.

Kattiva certainly would not have allowed her betrothed to be missing from her side during the kingdom's most exclusive event of the Star Eclipse.

"We should be down there among the people." Kattiva's husky voice brought him back to where she stood beside him on their balcony. "Instead of up here, separated from all the fun."

"The view from above is much less obstructed," he explained as he glanced to Kattiva. She sipped her drink, gaze beneath her red eye mask pinned to the chaos below. Despite the Volkovs belonging to a thief house, they had not been honored with many Mousai invitations. "Plus," Zimri added, "your restraints are more comfortable than what you'd be chained to down there."

"Not to mention," said another from behind them, "up here you are much better on display for the gossip you two have created."

"Achak." Kattiva smiled as the sister glided toward them, the curtain she had entered through falling closed behind her. "I didn't realize we'd have the honor of your magnificent presence this evening."

"I had to come and congratulate the happy couple," said Achak. "You two are all the kingdom has been buzzing about." The sister's violet gaze was unyielding as it met Zimri's. *What have you done?* it seemed to question.

Zimri clenched his teeth together, anguish swirling. *What has* Arabessa *done?* he wanted to counter but forced himself to keep silent. No good would come from him snapping at the twins in public.

Besides, he was under no delusions about what message he would be sending to those attending tonight when they saw the Collector accompanied by Kattiva Volkov. Which was rather the point. News traveled fast in this kingdom, but gossip, well, it was like a spark in dry brush: quick to ignite. He and Kattiva had only agreed to their union this afternoon, and already the entire kingdom appeared aware. Which meant, no doubt, so was Arabessa.

His stomach rolled with disquiet.

She pushed me here, he reminded himself, attempting to steel his nerves. Pretend his soul hadn't been charred to dust. By her.

"I will never be upset to be the topic of conversation," said Kattiva, wicked smile stretching. "I especially love knowing we were right to tell my parents no official announcement would be necessary." She looked toward Zimri. "They thought our news would get lost in all the eclipse celebrations. Turns out there *are* advantages for their daughter to have created such a name for herself."

"Indeed," replied Zimri.

"How are Zhad and Alyona?" inquired Achak. "Over the stars, I imagine?"

"They see the advantage of the match." Kattiva waved an unconcerned hand.

They certainly had, though they also saw Zimri's advantage. Still, their reactions were well aligned with what Kattiva had ensured they would be. Acquiring more status within court and the old thief houses, it seemed, was something mere money could not buy. To marry in— well, that opened particularly hard-to-unlock doors.

While none of it was shocking, it still left Zimri feeling rather, well, annoyed. What he had been working tirelessly toward acquiring for years had been handed over quickly through their daughter.

Perhaps your way in is through something they invest in more.

Arabessa's words from the other day circled through his mind, settling an ache in his chest. Never before had he hated for her advice to have been right. Zimri had gotten what he had wanted, but only by letting go of something else he wanted more.

"And you, Collector?" Achak asked. "I'm sure this union makes you very happy, considering the extra shares in Macabris this must provide you."

"Achak!" Kattiva laughed. "How admirably crude you are to discuss such a topic in public."

"My brother and I have existed too long to stand on the time-wasting formalities of decorum."

"Which is why you are the very best company."

"Yes, we are in high demand," agreed Achak. "But I do not want to tire you on the subject of us when we still have not heard from our dear Collector."

If Zimri hadn't been trained in the art of remaining poised when otherwise disturbed, he would have scowled under the ancient one's scrutinizing gaze.

But what could Zimri even say to the creature who had quite plainly been aware of his and Arabessa's love since it first blossomed? The twins who had practically raised him along with the Bassettes? Nothing would satisfy Achak as an excuse, because none of it satisfied Zimri. He was still angry, heartbroken, confused. Though he had yet to sign the contract of his and Kattiva's marriage, her shares were as good as his. And yet it gave him no satisfaction to know he finally had majority ownership in his parents' club. For it was not the way he had imagined such a day to be. A day without Arabessa.

"Tell me what you wish to hear," began Zimri, "and I shall see if I can please you by repeating it."

One of Achak's delicate brows rose. "Such amicability," the sister mused. "But also rather tiresome. I shall not push you further on the subject, Collector. My brother and I merely hope you both get what you are looking for with this union."

Zimri's hands clenched into fists at his sides as his gaze held Achak's. He was in no mood for their judgment this evening. They might play at being omniscient, but that did not mean they knew everything regarding the heart.

Though they did seem to pick up on his plummeting temperament, for Achak turned back to Kattiva to ask, "Before we leave, we wondered if we could announce the Mousai's entrance from your box?"

Kattiva all but clapped in her excitement. "It would be our absolute honor," she said, stepping to the side to allow Achak to approach the balcony's ledge. "This is so marvelous," she leaned in to whisper to Zimri. "Becoming engaged, and now this!"

For a flash Zimri heard the young woman hiding behind her disguise, and he had a moment to wonder who else made up Kattiva Volkov. But then his attention turned to Achak as the lights in the arena were extinguished. A spotlight winked on, illuminating their box.

The cavernous hall hushed, the sound of bodies shifting to glance toward Achak, who stood like a lost god. Especially when their form rippled from the sister to the brother.

"Esteemed guests," the brother's booming voice rang out, "deplorable patrons, in celebration of the First Fade, the start of the Star Eclipse, our king has bestowed upon us the most generous of gifts. He has called his magnificent Mousai here tonight to spin us into euphoria." The crowd roared its approval before growing silent again as Achak raised a hand. "Per usual, those who do not carry the lost gods' gifts may take leave now or, if daring to stay, must secure themselves. Get ready, my darlings, for the terrifying temptresses are here!"

There was a rustling as the giftless hurried to their chains, the crowd moving to secure better views.

As Achak turned to leave, the brother momentarily gripped Zimri's shoulder. As he leaned in close, he rumbled, "We hope you both know what you are doing." And then the twins were gone.

Zimri's stomach clenched, knowing they spoke of not him and Kattiva but him and Arabessa.

Grief rose once more with every intention to suffocate him.

"Time to strap me in, my love." Kattiva's voice broke through his haze of pain.

Zimri found she had settled herself into her plush chair by the railing, her wrists lying in the padded leather cuffs on either armrest. She gazed up at him expectantly, and despite himself, he felt a flash of protectiveness.

"You have watched them perform before, correct?" he asked as he came to her side.

"Of course," she answered. "Two other times."

Zimri drew his brows in beneath his mask, finishing tying her down. "Only two?"

She snorted. "What a snob you are, Collector. Not all of us are as well connected to the king as you."

"I only meant—" His words were cut off as a new spotlight flashed on to illuminate the very center of the concert hall.

Zimri turned, heart in his throat, as three forms were pushed into the light.

They were disguised in dripping greens and blues, a complicated wrapping of costumes that represented the Thief Kingdom's glowworm sky, but all Zimri could see, feel, yearn for, was the creature who stood tallest in the middle. The one who stood in perfect repose, shoulders back, clutching a violin close to her heart. His Arabessa.

Had been his.

Acid pain crept up his throat, his gifts tugging sharp behind his ribs.

Our music, it mewled.

No, Zimri demanded, leaning forward to grip the balcony's railing. *Ours no longer.*

Even in thought, it pierced him.

Zimri had come tonight knowing full well he'd see Arabessa, listen to her play, watch her magnificence from afar. No longer able to find her after the performance and conduct her body as she conducted the room. But he had thought his anger was greater than his heartache, able to burn away any longing he might experience.

He was a fool.

Zimri was being buried alive, not by his fury but by his desperate yearning. His air was slowly being stolen from him with each deep inhale as he stood in her presence. Unable to touch her. Hold her. They were no longer each other's.

Arabessa readied her violin at her shoulder, ornate headdress tilting as she tucked her chin. Zimri did not dare blink. He was wrapped in stasis, like the rest of the hall.

The Mousai were about to play.

With a graceful lift of her bow, Arabessa pulled forth her first chord.

By the Fade. Zimri's grip tightened as the notes speared him through the chest.

It was a deep, moaning sound. A yawning dark lake of grief, heartache, and loss.

Arabessa's music split open, layered and braided into the air. A raking purple claw of mourning magic.

And then Larkyra opened her mouth, her black-painted lips parting to send bone-shattering sorrow straight up into the skylight of the circular arena. She spoke no words, only created a melody that wove intrinsically with Arabessa's playing. Niya moved next, the light silk of her disguise unraveling to be caught in the red gusts of magic that were produced by her motion. She fell to the floor, an act of lamenting, before reaching out her hand to the crowd, a yearning of unrequited lust.

Tragedddddyyy, his magic cried. *Sadness.*

Control! he demanded, pushing his gifts to harden along his skin. He could not let this spell touch him, for nothing about this performance was euphoric. Nothing spoke of celebrations or rebirths.

Only death. Ends. Hurt.

But why?

Zimri gritted his teeth to keep his gifts from giving even a sliver to the lashing magic of the Mousai. His gaze was chained to Arabessa as she played. As were her sisters'. Arabessa was whom they watched, reacted to. Their conductor.

She was the one spinning this spell, creating the suffering.

Which only meant . . .

Arabessa was suffering.

Just as he was.

You fool! he wanted to cry. *It did not have to be this way.*

But it was.

She had refused him, broken him, and still he wanted to rush to her, pull her from the stage and stay her pain. Zimri wanted to wrap her in his arms and demand she forget reason and duty and his promises made to dead parents. They needed to be together.

But only her king and father could demand anything of Arabessa Bassette.

Duty.

Arabessa's guiding compass.

One that was apparently failing her now.

Zimri had watched the Mousai perform many times, watched them torture, watched them trance, and watched Arabessa play when she believed no one present. But always had she been in control.

Tonight was chaos, and not the purposeful kind.

Arabessa's emotions were frayed, pooling unchecked into the arena.

The way she dragged her bow over string, shoulders slumped almost in defeat. She was prisoner to whatever emotions swirled through her heart.

By the lost gods, thought Zimri in a panic, *Arabessa is distracted.*

She was not in control, which meant neither were her sisters.

The Mousai were unchained.

In time with his realization, sobs and cries rang out around him, mournful howls as the Mousai's spell grabbed hold of guests.

Their symphony was now lethal in its potency.

In his pulse of fear Zimri lost his hold on the magic that he had forced like armor along his skin. A quickly realized mistake, for a wave of the Mousai's spell lashed into the broken barrier, hot and unforgiving.

Paaaain, howled his gifts through his veins as they were attacked. *Too much suffering.*

And with it Zimri was slammed into the past, brought back to the last time he had felt so overwhelmed with hopelessness: the night he learned of his parents' death.

He stood alone in his rooms as his father's valet packed his items. Disbelief gripped him. Devastation.

They were dead.

His parents were dead.

He was alone.

Forever.

The visions blurred, and he was now in the sunroom in Jabari, listening to Arabessa tell him she could not marry him. His world cracking open, threatening to swallow him as he walked away from her.

Forever.

STOP! he silently yelled into the void of his mind.

Pulling forward a wave of his gifts, Zimri pushed out a gold crest of magic, driving off the trio's spelled emotions that burned like acid to his heart.

Resist, he demanded, gripping tighter to his lucidity, to the railing. *Be strong.*

It was a test of endurance to outlast the Mousai's performance. Their destructive harmony was unceasing.

But finally, exhaustingly, their tempo calmed. Larkyra and Niya quieted their magic as Arabessa's final chord from her violin soared through the tiered hall. The rainbow cloud of their symphony swirled up and out of the small hole in the ceiling, escaping into the glowworm sky.

The space descended into stillness.

A hush of destruction.

And then it was filled with screams.

Zimri's fingers ached as he loosened his grip, heart racing as he focused on the pockets of chaos below.

He couldn't yet make out what was happening; there were too many bodies moving and twisting together. He only tasted fear. Sour and everywhere.

"Oh dear," said Kattiva beside him, causing him to glance down at her. It took him a grain fall to remember they had come together. "Do you mind removing my binds?" she asked. "I think . . . my nose is bleeding."

"Are you all right?" Zimri scrambled to unhook her wrists, noting that Kattiva was right. Crimson flowed down beneath her eye mask from her nose. "Here." He pulled a handkerchief from his inside pocket.

"Thank you." She dabbed at her skin. "I fear this will not come out of your handkerchief easily."

"I do not care for a scrap of cloth," he assured. "Are you feeling all right? Let me take you from here."

As Zimri helped Kattiva to stand, frowning to find she was none too steady on her feet, new howls of anguish filled the arena.

With her weight securely against him, he leaned over to find a very different scene than what had greeted them earlier this evening.

The crowd had thinned and parted, leaving circles around a few masked guests who lay limp on the ground or who hung over a balcony's ledge, others in the arms of companions who shook them desperately to wake.

Unease climbed up Zimri's spine, his magic soaking in the heightened panic in the room. He searched for the Mousai, for Arabessa, but they were gone.

Leaving behind the innocent bodies of those they had sent to the Fade.

CHAPTER EIGHTEEN

Arabessa had only truly been afraid three times in her life. The first, when she'd learned of her mother's death. She had watched as part of her father was taken along with her mother that night, witnessing the power the Fade had over the living. The second was when she and her sisters had been playing in the dungeons below the palace as children and found themselves quite literally backed against a wall by a very hungry and very angry dungeon guardian. And the third, well, the third was right now.

With her hands tightly gripped in her lap, Arabessa's nerves buzzed along with her magic as she waited with her sisters in the private receiving room of the Thief King. It was unnervingly still. No fire in the hearth beside them. No hissing of a sandglass, the time measure fully run out on top of the mantel. The only sounds Arabessa could hear were her own chastising, swirling thoughts.

Irresponsible.

Selfish.

I have disobeyed my king.

I have disappointed my father.

I have led my sisters astray.

I have failed in my duty.

Her stomach twisted into a knot of guilt and shame with each lament.

Furtively, she glanced at the far passageway that sat in shadows. Its length led to the Thief King's hidden entrance to his throne room. He was in there now, taking an audience with those connected to the deceased. No doubt assuaging their grief with promises of punishment.

And she *should* be punished.

She had been foolish, stupid, impulsive.

All for what?

A moment of release for unknown consequences?

Pitiful!

Arabessa's magic hissed at her reprimand. *We needed to breathe!* it rebuked. *We needed to feel!*

At the time it had certainly seemed the only solution. The pressure that had been growing over the past week had become poison in Arabessa's lungs. The bruising weight of her responsibilities was too great for her to take on the added strain of her heartache along with the recent shock of Zimri and Kattiva's engagement. The only solution was to scream with her magic. That was how she had always dealt with the pressure, freed herself.

The difference being she usually did it in private.

Arabessa had certainly not been in the privacy of her music room this night.

She had gone too far.

She had lost control.

She had taken innocent souls.

She had conducted her sisters to murder.

All because she had been too distracted in her sorrows to rein herself in.

Her remorse felt as though it could strangle her.

"Ara." Niya's voice had Arabessa glance over to where she sat opposite her. They each had removed their headdresses when entering the

Thief King's sitting room, but Niya had unraveled her red locks to lie in her lap. She twisted the ends anxiously as she asked, "What happened?"

Arabessa blinked, unable to help the bitter laugh that followed. "I would think it quite obvious, dear. I have behaved abysmally, causing us to kill innocents. So we are awaiting our king's proclamation of our punishment. But I will take the blame, for it is I—"

"I do not care about what happened at the performance." Niya waved an unconcerned hand. "What I meant was—"

"You *should* care," Arabessa cut in, drawing her brows together. "We killed innocent people."

"Yes, you've said that already," Niya pointed out.

"And it apparently bears repeating, given, as you put it, you do not care." Arabessa's frustration was toward herself, of course, but she couldn't help how it was becoming directed at Niya.

"No one denies it is a tragic turn of events," said Larkyra, who joined in from where she sat beside Niya, "but everyone who attends our performances knows the risks."

"Yes, and guests grow ill all the time," continued Niya. "In fact, if none do, we have agreed on many occasions that we have not performed at our best."

"Vomiting and fainting is *not* the same as being sent to the Fade," Arabessa said pointedly. "As being *killed* as though they were a guilty party sentenced by the Thief King."

"Perhaps some of them were and we were being serendipitously proactive," argued Niya.

Arabessa's fury rose. "I don't know what leniency you have grown accustomed to, sailing on the *Crying Queen*, but in the Thief Kingdom, that is *not* how—"

"I have scars to prove how unwavering the *Crying Queen*'s captain can be," snapped Niya, hands curling into fists in her lap.

Arabessa was undeterred. "Then they will be welcome companions to the new ones we no doubt will receive."

"Sisters, please," interjected Larkyra, her soft voice sending a gifted pulse of calm through the room. "What has been done has been done. If I have learned anything from mistakenly hurting others with my magic, it is not how one feels after that matters but what one does next."

They slipped into silence for a breath, Arabessa's thoughts, no doubt, the same as Niya's. If any of them carried the guilt of dealing with the repercussions of their gifts, it was Larkyra. With her magic tied to her voice, her childhood had not been an easy one. Not when a simple howl from a skinned knee or a startled yip could slash skin to bone. Larkyra had come a long way in controlling the intentions of her powers.

"Father will not be happy, but he also can be reasoned with," Larkyra went on. "Either way, we told you to play what you needed to play. We *all* will deal with the consequences together."

"No." Arabessa shook her head. "You—"

"It's not up for discussion."

Arabessa's brows shot up at Larkyra's stern command, her gaze unwavering. Lark suddenly appeared much older. No longer was she her baby sister. She was a duchess now. Ran her own household.

When did she grow up?

"Agreed," said Niya. "We perform together, so we are punished together. The Mousai remain one."

Another hot twist of guilt jabbed into Arabessa, the words scratching up her throat to confess that soon the Mousai would be no more. But her silent oath gripped its warning beneath her skin. Arabessa swallowed away her confession. For how could she admit such a thing without being able to give reason?

"And now might not be the time to push this," continued Niya, "but what I had *meant* with my earlier question was in regard to Zimri." She leaned toward Arabessa, brows furrowed. "How can he be *engaged* to Kattiva?"

Arabessa held in a wince. Her heartache was too close to the surface, sharp broken edges wedged between her ribs. "You are right," she somehow managed to reply evenly. "Now is *not* the time."

"But—" Niya's response was cut off as a blast of warmth rushed into the room.

Arabessa and her sisters turned toward the far passageway. Arabessa's magic buzzed with anxiousness in her veins.

He's here, it warned.

Yes, she agreed. *He is.*

A figure in blinding white strode from the shadows toward them, and all three girls jumped to their feet. The lingering power of the Thief King's ancient gifts from his time on the throne pulsed forward, a metallic sting to Arabessa's nose. Though this private sitting room was large, his presence felt larger, and she had to fight from taking a step back.

Within his horned alabaster headdress, his shrouded gaze found hers, and a lash of dread shot through her. It was a consuming black void that threatened to pull Arabessa in if she looked too long. And though she could not see his expression beneath his complicated dressings, she knew with certainty he was none too pleased. The walls and floor and air seemed to radiate his displeasure.

You have failed me. Silent, weightless words that gripped into her flesh like hooks.

Arabessa steeled herself, stomach a spooling of fear.

The King of Thieves did not greet a one of them as he turned to unsnap his headdress and place it on a stand by a long mirror. The same stand Arabessa had watched her mother place her own disguise on all those years ago. There he waited in the silence, letting them fester, letting them worry.

It was working.

A movement from behind him turned Arabessa's attention, and it was as though a stone guardian landed a blow to her chest.

Zimri strode into the dim candlelight of their sitting room, accompanied by Achak.

Hardened hazel eyes beneath his mask immediately caught on Arabessa, and for the first time in her entire life, she wanted to flee.

Coward, a voice inside her sneered. *Weak.*

Her fingers clenched into fists at her sides, attempting to still her nerves, stop the chaotic beating of her heart. But it seemed futile as she drank in Zimri's chilled expression and stern lips. Arabessa realized it was far worse to find cold indifference in the man you loved than hurt.

"This has been a very long night," said the king, his tone a cliff's edge: precariously dangerous. As he turned back to them, he revealed the familiar features and thick beard of their father. An ancient creature he was no more, yet still a man commanding the room. "I have just met with the last of those connected to one of the fallen. From the thief house O'Cré. They lost their daughter."

Arabessa swallowed past the piercing ache in her throat.

"I will not mince words," Dolion went on, furrow to his brow as his attention returned to Arabessa. "I am extremely disappointed."

Daggers, claws, sharp talons all scraped across her heart.

Disappointed.

Her nightmare realized: to hear such a word delivered from her father's tongue.

Disappointed.

"You performed without thought to those around you," he said as though bewildered. "Without thought to why they were there. Why the Mousai were meant to be there. Where was your intention, Arabessa? What is your reason for acting as you have?"

Her face grew hot. Her shame burning as all in the room watched. As Zimri watched. It took an incredible amount of willpower not to glance back at him, see the reason she had acted as she had.

Your actions are your own, a voice chastened in her mind.

"It was all of us who performed, Father," interjected Larkyra. "It is *all* of us to blame."

"You all are culpable, yes, and will be dealt with accordingly," Dolion said darkly. "But your sister knows her role within your group. Yours and Niya's gifts are tied too closely to your natural behavior. You need someone to guide your powers when in that state." His blue gaze snapped back to Arabessa. "If you are to command, you must be in control."

She knew he spoke not merely of her role with the Mousai but of commanding a kingdom.

Still, it was the last word that splintered her resolve, fraying it like crackling, white-hot lightning.

Control.

Shoulder every burden of her family without room to break, without letting them see her trip or fall. It was an impossible expectation. She might be Arabessa Bassette, oldest of the Mousai, born to lead, invited to vie for the throne, but she was still *human.*

Just as her father was.

As her gaze bounced from Dolion's chastising expression to Zimri's emotionless mask to Achak's pitying frown, something inside her kicked free, teeth gnashing.

"You mean, be in the same control that has you slipping away to the Fade entirely too often?" she asked, voice as hard as the palace's stone walls. She ignored the collective gasp of Niya and Larkyra beside her. Ignored how the room grew very, very still.

No one *dared* confront her father on his visits to see her mother, how too frequent the meetings had become. His quickly graying hair and aging lines. But how could he speak of commanding and control when he couldn't even restrain his own behavior toward a woman who had been dead now for nearly twenty years?

"Leave us." Dolion's voice was a chilled wind. He looked at no one but Arabessa, yet they all knew it was her that was the only one meant to stay.

She clenched her teeth to steady her nerves, her magic slipping supportively through her veins. *We are here. We are with you.*

"Perhaps we should take a moment to collect ourselves before revisiting this conversation," suggested Achak from where they and Zimri stood on either side of Dolion, his confidants, his aides. "As you said, sire, it has been a long night. Some rest would do everyone good."

"Yes," agreed Niya, "and really, Father, it is the three of us you should be angry with. Ara—"

"I said, *leave us.*" The command was impenetrable, a steel door slamming shut.

No one else spoke as they made their way from the room. Niya squeezed Arabessa's shoulder along with Larkyra's touch to her hand. Achak sent her a *be strong* nod. While Zimri . . .

It could have been her imagination's desperate attempt to find a hopeful glimmer in this moment, but behind his frozen wall she caught a flash of concern in his gaze. A spark of what once was. Her chest ached to hear his voice. A whisper of advice. A passing of reassurance.

But he merely turned away without a word, leaving Arabessa, along with everyone else.

CHAPTER NINETEEN

*A*rabessa stood before a furious king.

His expression was dark, a hardened gaze that pinned her like an insect to a board.

Arabessa held tight to her gifts, which swirled through her fingers. A reminder of her tucked-away flute hidden within the spine of her costume's gown. *Play, and we will strike.*

She would never do such a thing, of course, but it settled her to know she had options. It was always good to have options.

As she drank in Dolion's calm fury, Arabessa was thankful he was not on his throne; his ancient magic was tucked safely away in the room beyond. Grateful that he was unmasked so she might look upon someone familiar, someone of this plane, rather than the being he became when crowned.

He might be her king, but it was a current relieving reminder that he was also her father.

"Sit," he ordered.

Arabessa sat, watching as Dolion strode to the unlit hearth. His white robes hung over his wide shoulders like rain dripping down a window: a gentle clinging. He removed his gloves to pinch ash from a small tin box on the ledge. As he threw the ash into the fireplace, flames burst alive on the stacked wood in the grate. The room warmed, their sitting area becoming drenched with light.

Arabessa grew more uneasy. In this kingdom, to make someone comfortable usually meant further discomfort was imminent.

Dolion stared into the fire, letting the sound of its sizzle and pop fill the sands' falling. Forcing Arabessa to wait.

But if there was one trait this father and daughter shared, it was patience.

Even though Arabessa had recently not displayed the best proof of that.

"You will never survive what you need to, acting as you have." Dolion's words hit like an icy wind against her skin. Cold and uninviting. "And you need to survive, Arabessa." His tone was almost a plea as he turned to face her, his shoulder-length hair shifting to one side. His thick beard tinted redder in the firelight. The lion, they called him in Jabari. "You *must* survive," he repeated.

Arabessa had never heard such desperation from her father, and it lit trepidation in her heart. The fight that had been swirling at the ready within her vanished in a whoosh.

"I will," she said. Though the words felt meant to calm a child, a baseless statement.

Her father did not reply, merely turned his gaze back to the flames. "I know I have been hardest on you compared to your sisters," he said. "And I know it must seem unfair, the responsibility you have taken on in our family since your mother . . ." Dolion paused, brows pinching in. "But you must understand, my melody, I would never have placed this role on you if I didn't think you could shoulder it. If I didn't think there was another way."

"I understand," said Arabessa.

Her father shook his head, eyes finding hers once more. "No, I don't quite think you do."

Arabessa frowned up at him, confusion prickling.

Dolion let out a tired sigh and settled into the large seat opposite her, the fire behind him illuminating his edges. "The Mousai were not written in the stars of this kingdom," he began. "Your fates were not a foregone conclusion; to come together as the trio who help retain order and law, who bewitch and entertain. But sometimes events set other events in motion, and when your mother . . . left us"—her father forced out the last two words like a gasp for air—"the direction of our family changed with it. The intentions of our lives were redirected down a path that I had not wanted for you three."

His meaning took shape slowly, an approaching ship on a horizon. When it came into focus, Arabessa held in a shocked breath. "You did not want us part of this world, did you?"

"I did not want you to have to be thrust into such danger so young," he explained. "Into experiencing such cruelty and hurt and chaos before knowing what those actions and ideas even were. When I met your mother, she was already sewn into the fabric of this kingdom. I knew what life I would be choosing to be with her, but I still wanted our children to have a choice."

There was that elusive word again. *Choice.*

"Johanna, however, seemed to have known better," said her father, a hint of a smile growing. "She always knows better."

Knows. Not *knew.* As though she were still alive.

With a squeeze to her heart, Arabessa realized that for her father, she still was. There was merely a door to another realm separating him from her.

"She knew to be a part of this kingdom, even a small part, there are risks," he went on. "But to be a great part . . . well, there will be sacrifices."

"And we were your sacrifice?" asked Arabessa.

"You three are my everything." The words fell from Dolion like a vow, his blue gaze a fire of conviction. "You three are what have kept me on this side of the Fade."

The statement slammed into Arabessa. A belief she and her sisters always wondered about, feared, proved true. If not for them . . ..

Arabessa shook the dark thought away, not enjoying how much heartache her father still harbored from being separated from his wife.

To be in love: a dangerous gift, a destructive magic.

"So I need you to see," said Dolion, "for me to be here"—he gestured to their surroundings—"I had to bring you and your sisters here as well. Not for visits or small stays as once planned with your mother, but to call this kingdom home. And to do that, I had to make sure you were safe."

"And to be safe here is to be feared." Arabessa finished what she knew would be his next words. She and her sisters had heard them enough from Achak growing up.

Dolion nodded. "I made you girls monsters in a monstrous world. The Mousai needed to be created. And you, my melody, were born to lead them."

Which is why I am the toughest on you.

Which is why you shoulder what you do.

Which is why which is why which is why.

The excuse for all of it, everything she had experienced growing up. Why Arabessa had always believed she could never afford a distraction, never be as wild as Niya or as fanciful as Larkyra. Arabessa had been forced to become the rock, the constant in their family, so they would be safe, so her sisters could play and their father could ease his conscience for dragging them into this world, for needing them close. For needing.

Something hot and laced with frustration unfurled in her gut. Had her choice, then, to go after the throne even been a choice? Or was it already predestined? An order disguised as an option.

Your mother wanted me to give you this when it was time.

Her father's words when handing her the lock of hair, the key to reveal her parents' legacy. Arabessa's known sense of duty to follow it.

Her chest burned. She was confused. She was angry.

Because despite how she now felt like a mouse running through a preconstructed maze, Arabessa still *wanted* to be king. She still wanted to claim the role her mother had occupied, her father currently held. She wanted to stand on her own and prove to herself she was worthy. Prove that all she had been taught, all her actions and inactions, was for a reason. A greater, bigger purpose than merely conducting the Mousai. She wanted to carry on the lineage and law and kingdom her family had protected for decades.

Her father might have felt he had forced them into this world, but to Arabessa this role felt like her birthright.

"And I will never forgive myself if the role you've chosen to take on . . ." Dolion's deep voice pulled her back to the room. She noted the blaze of fear in his eyes. "You *must* survive, my melody."

And here it was, the reason for his earlier words. *You must survive.* For if she did not, he would blame himself. It would be his fault for bringing his children into this hidden world of debauchery and mayhem. For raising them as he had. For raising her. All to keep them safe, only to end up killing his eldest daughter.

Her father had not shown any of this when they had spoken earlier in his dressing room after she had accepted the invitation to vie for the throne. He had shown only concern, exhaustion. Not worry. Not fear. Not guilt.

Here sat a true master at masking emotions.

A deep pool of sorrow filled Arabessa's chest, for she now understood him, more than she had ever known.

They were one and the same.

Both were people who shouldered others' burdens without complaint, who took on the added layers of responsibility because they felt they had to. Her father had carried more than she realized; not just from being king, father, single parent, but a guilt for making them the Mousai.

Pieces began to fit together in Arabessa's mind. This must have been the reason he had given them missions of altruism beyond the Thief Kingdom. Tasks that would take them out of harm's way in addition to giving back to Aadilor. Their penance for their behavior as the Mousai was his atonement for creating them to begin with. All so he could be closer to her and her sisters, to fold them into his role as king.

"I am not upset you raised us as you have," Arabessa said, tone earnest. "And I know Larkyra and Niya would say the same. Yes, there have been moments we each have hated our roles or assigned tasks, but none of us regret having a father who raised daughters to know what they are capable of. You have given us a greater gift than you may realize, and we love you for it."

A gentle exhale escaped from Dolion, and his eyes softened. "Thank you for saying that. But still, I know your childhood has not been an easy one—"

"Interesting people do not come from easy living," she pointed out.

Dolion's grin was still strained. "True," he agreed. "But my melody, please tell me you understand the severity of tonight. Why it goes beyond those killed. Tonight can *never* be repeated. In any measure, in *any* role."

Not if you are to live to be king.

"I understand," she said, her guilt swirling with a spark of frustration. "But Father, in all my years of leading our performances, I have remained steady throughout. Shouldn't that count for *something?*"

"No." His answer was a door slamming shut. "History books are not filled with peaceful tales but wars and plagues and curses. People hold firmer to tragedy than victory, and a ruler's reign is marked more by their failings than their triumphs. You say you were unsteady only once, and that once is all that mattered for innocent people to die. For *court members* to die. For you to be—" Dolion was abruptly cut off, his face pinching in discomfort, as though his next words were choking him. Arabessa realized it was his silent oath, tangling up his thoughts.

"To be a leader of great consequence . . . ," he went on, a bit breathless, "you *have* to be in control, Arabessa. It is not you in those moments. Not your feelings, not your wants. It is your people's wants. Your kingdom's feelings. You must make personal sacrifices every day. Every grain fall you wear a crown."

"Yes," she said, nodding, muscles growing tense with her resolve. "Yes, you are right. I truly am sorry for what I have done, Father. I acted childishly. Impulsively. I wasn't thinking clearly before performing. I had just learned of—" She looked away from him. "But it doesn't matter. It is not an excuse, like you said. My feelings will be set aside in those moments, even if I'm angry, even if I'm . . ."

Heartbroken.

Though the words were not spoken, her father still seemed to understand, for he leaned forward, features softening. "I heard of the Collector and Kattiva."

The Collector and Kattiva.

Letters strung together to create a nightmare.

"I am sorry, my melody. I know it was not an easy decision for you to refuse Zimri."

"It is what's best for him." Her jaw felt tight as she worked to get the words out. "He'll understand that once the majority of Macabris is in his hands."

It was the script that she had on repeat, hoping it would soon bring her peace to believe.

"And what of you?" her father asked after a beat.

"What of me?" She met his gaze, a coldness entering her spine. "I certainly could not guarantee I would be alive to meet him at the altar. And he needed my answer this week. Our timing . . ." She looked away. "Was never well met."

"Perhaps one day it shall be."

Arabessa regarded her father, brows furrowed. "What do you mean?"

"No story is ever truly over, my child, so we'll just have to wait and see. But for now, it certainly was the responsible decision on your part. This next month will not be easy for you. You must remain focused."

She took in a steadying breath, Dolion's approval of her decision bringing a small but necessary solace. His words mirroring her thoughts.

"I will," she assured.

Her father nodded. "There is one last topic I'd like to discuss. Your . . . obstacles that are to come." Dolion picked his words carefully, his blood oath at work again. "I do not control them. I do not know what they will be. It is the—" His jaw clamps shut, features twisting in pain.

"Father, it is fine," Arabessa hurried to say. "Please, do not test what we both know will not bend."

Her father cleared his throat, seeming to shake off whatever sensation had gripped him. "No." He raised a staying hand. "I must say this. Given the nature of events with your mother, my . . . challenges were different. I did not have to go through what you and the others will. So it's important to remember this about our kingdom: just as it knows everyone who enters, it also knows their secrets and strengths. This kingdom knows your greatest fears, so be sure you know them as well."

For they could be used against you.

The unspoken finish to his thought.

"Thank you, Father," said Arabessa. "I will remember that."

His features remained even. "A small gesture, I would think, given your punishment for tonight's performance will still come."

Arabessa stiffened, her magic swirling with a spike of trepidation. She should have known a king's generous deed always came with a catch.

CHAPTER TWENTY

Zimri barely listened as his lawyer read through the details of the marriage agreement. He had already read it thrice himself. Though his only real concern was the shares that were to go to him on his and Kattiva's wedding day. That line item he had made sure was rigorously ironclad.

It appeared, however, that Alyona Volkov, normally happily mute in all business affairs, was being rather particular regarding what items her daughter might receive—and, in proxy, herself.

"But what of the house they will live in?" she asked after Zimri's man of business was finished.

"Mother," chided Kattiva, who sat poised on a small armchair beside Alyona in her parents' office. The family wore matching green satin eye masks, the color of their thief house. A clear show of solidarity for this meeting. "What makes you think either of us have agreed to live in the same dwelling?" asked Kattiva. "My apartments on the east side of the Betting District have only recently been completed. I have no desire to give them up."

"And you shan't, darling," said Alyona. "But every married couple needs a communal home so they may entertain together on occasion. It's only proper."

"I'm sure the Collector would be glad to open his parents' wing for such occasions," said Zhad from where he sat behind his oak desk. "After all, it will also become Kattiva's by end of month."

Zimri's ire prickled along with his magic at the suggestion. No doubt the intended reaction Zhad was probing for. Zimri had no intention of doing any such thing. The Volkovs had already claimed his childhood quarters as their office. He had no desire to extend their greedy fingers any further into his past.

After having relocated to the west wing, Zimri had purposely avoided the Volkovs' private section above Macabris. Even redecorated with a glass wall similar to the one in his office, the space still held whispers of his old life, his old hurt. If he looked close enough, he knew he would find carved notches along the doorframe: markings of a child growing up in this room.

"I can commission a home to be built in the Gazing District," Zimri interjected, stopping this conversation before it got any more out of hand.

"The Gazing District?" Alyona's eyes widened from beneath her mask. "How dreadfully pious of a neighborhood."

"And where most of the older thief houses have second homes," explained Zimri.

This had the woman rocking back slightly. "Oh, well, yes, how sensible a suggestion, Collector. That sounds like a perfect prospect."

"You do not need to build anything," said Kattiva. "No one is under any delusions this is a love match. That building would sit empty and become a tomb for dust and vagabonds."

"How fortunate for you, then, dear," said Zhad, "seeing as the latter is your preferred company to keep."

Zimri frowned as he watched Kattiva shrink. Her usual daringness diminished like a flame snuffed by her father's words.

"This home *will* be constructed," said Zimri firmly, forcing Kattiva to meet his gaze. "And when it's completed, I will expect monthly gatherings of all the vagabonds and miscreants you may have the privilege to know. By the end of the year, with you commanding the soirees, Katt, it will no doubt be *the* invite the kingdom will hope to receive."

A small smile spread across Kattiva's red-painted lips, a smell of relief flowing from her as she tipped her head.

Thank you, her expression seemed to say.

Anything to annoy your father, he wanted to reply.

Instead Zimri nodded curtly before turning back to Zhad. "Now," he began, looking to where the thin reed of a man sat, their two lawyers columns on either side, "if we are quite done with the line items, I would like to sign and get back to running our club."

Our club, *soon to be* my club, thought Zimri.

Zhad made a show of conferring with his lawyer one last time, but in the end accepted the contract. Their men of business pointed to where both were to sign, along with Kattiva and Alyona.

Zimri's magic curled like a cold wind through his blood as he scrawled his name, a frost consuming his lingering doubts. Though he had dreamed of this day since he was nine, he now felt no rush of triumph. Only a sick pang of confusion.

This is what I want, he reminded himself. What he needed. This had been his ambition since the death of his parents. This was the necessary sacrifice to greatness.

Once finished, he didn't shake Zhad's hand since it wasn't offered in the first place. He merely nodded to the collective room and stalked out.

Zimri walked his lawyer to a side stairwell where a guard waited to escort him the rest of the way down to the exit. As the man took his leave, Zimri turned toward his office. His mind matched his sure strides, focused on what now lay ahead. He thought of all the plans he would begin as soon as his fifty percent became sixty. The upgrades and additions he could start without the required unanimous vote of both families. He did not think about the woman he had now officially lost.

The woman he had witnessed unleashing her pain to an entire audience. The woman who still held his heart in her perfect, powerful fingers.

No, those thoughts held nothing productive. And Zimri was now determined to follow his ambition, not hopeless yesterdays.

As he turned a corner, he traveled down another dark hall, a single sconce lighting his way every few paces. But Zimri did not need light to know the bends to take on this floor, to discern the small passageways that hid like soft folds in clothes along the walls. He did not need a lantern to sense when he approached a seam of new carpet that met old. A relic of a past life that set his pulse to jump with unease.

His mother and father had been in the middle of renovating this wing when they died, and for one reason or another Zimri could never bring himself to finish it. In fact, he had made quite a scene when Alyona had suggested replacing the carpets altogether.

It was a piece of his mother. An action of Briella's caught and kept for him to hold anytime he gazed from the maroon-and-black designs to where they met gold.

On occasion he was brought to rest one foot on either side, like he was doing now. Staring down at the thin line made from the two carpets meeting, desperately attempting to bring forward a thin piece of his mother. A sliver of her laugh, a fragment of her smile, a pinch of her perfume.

But in the end all he ever sensed was the soft reverberation of guests downstairs and the scent of oil burning in nearby lamps.

"Collector," Kattiva called from the direction he had just come. "I was hoping to catch you before you escaped back into your cave."

Zimri looked up, watching as her tightly costumed form drew close. "I would hardly call my well-decorated and lit office a cave."

"You're right." She stopped in front of him, brown eyes meeting his through her mask. "I should have said *den*, for you certainly were a wolf in there with my parents."

"And you admire wolves." It was not a question; the fierce creatures who inked her hand could still be seen even in these shadows.

Kattiva quirked a grin, and Zimri caught her scent of relief, perhaps for finding him willing to engage her. "They are magnificent creatures, don't you think?" she asked.

"I have never seen one in person to draw such conclusions, but I will take your word for it."

Her head tilted, studying him. "Do you know the people of the Valley of Giants revere the wolf? They believe they represent loyalty and intelligence. But if you were to travel north for two days to Shanjaree, you would hear a very different tale. They believe the wolf to be a bad omen. A sign of evil approaching. I always have found it fascinating how two very different beliefs can live so close to one another. That something can both be revered and feared. Celebrated and shunned."

"Our world is made ripe with contradictions," Zimri agreed.

"Yes," Kattiva mused. "People, I find, are the biggest culprits of such variance."

He watched her a moment, her words seeping in with new understanding. Here stood a girl whose life was painted in such variance. To have parents who loved her, but only if she acted as they wanted. Who wished for her greatness, but only if it also benefited them. A girl who screamed to be her own person, yet still thirsted for the approval of her mother and father.

Zimri was not judging her. He understood what it was to be many ideas in one body. Many contrary emotions pulled in different directions. No doubt all in this kingdom understood this to some degree, given they sought this place to free their differences. To wear a mask so they might slip into their other selves, live out their other desires.

"But I digress," said Kattiva, shaking away their shared moment. "I came to see how you were. I hope you are not regretting agreeing to our proposal?"

"Why would you think that?"

"Well, for starters, you stormed out just now rather abruptly. And you haven't seemed in the best of spirits these past few days."

Zimri frowned, not enjoying that his mood had been that easily discerned. It was his job to read those of others. "I do not regret gaining more shares of my parents' club," he said. "I will go through with this union, Kattiva. You may be sure of that. Now, if you'll excuse me, I have much to do this evening." He gave her a slight bow before continuing down the hall.

To his chagrin, Kattiva fell into step beside him. "Like what?" she asked.

"I cannot say," he replied.

"Mm, I see. I shall take that to mean our king has tasked you with something dreadful."

Zimri glanced over to her, eyes narrowed, but she merely waved away his expression.

"We all know you are close with His Grace," she explained. "Or as close as any being can be. A confidant of sorts. Am I right?"

He knew better than to answer.

Which evidently was answer enough, for Kattiva smiled, satisfied.

"If all you were curious about was my disposition," he began, "you can rest assured I am fine. I merely have much on my mind with the Star Eclipse and all the parties we have this month." He walked around another corner to come to a stop before the door to his office. To their right, stairs led down to the second, first, and basement floors, along with hidden passageways fingering through each landing.

"That is serendipitous," she said. "Because I also wanted to discuss our engagement ball."

Zimri's brows rose from beneath his mask.

"Yes," Kattiva insisted, reading his surprise. "We *are* to have one."

"All right." Zimri was in no mood to extend this conversation.

Kattiva let out an amused huff. "I take your enthusiastic answer to mean you are content with me making all the arrangements?"

"More than content." He pulled his office key from his pocket.

"Good."

"Great." He unlocked his door.

"I only had one other query regarding the event."

He paused, waiting for her to go on.

"I would like the Mousai to perform at ours."

Shock rattled down Zimri's spine. Ice shards piercing. He must have heard her wrong.

"I beg your pardon?" He turned to face her fully.

"There is no arguing that they are the most gifted performers in all of Aadilor," explained Kattiva. "Not to mention the most sought after. Having the Mousai at our party would make it *the* event of the Star Eclipse. Perhaps more so than the eclipse itself."

By the Fade, this could not be happening. "They do not entertain for private events," he informed her, tone a chilled lake.

"They do all the time for the king," she argued. "And what a marvelous idea for a wedding gift to his *close* confidant, the Collector, and his betrothed. To lend the trio to us for an evening."

Great lost gods, she was serious! "They killed people at their last performance," Zimri reasoned. "They gave you a bloody nose. You almost fainted."

"I know!" Kattiva grinned. "It is a night the kingdom won't stop talking about. Those who attended have been boosted in society. Those who did not are positively green with envy not to have witnessed the madness for themselves. We *must* get them, Collector. For our engagement to be their next event after such . . . devastation"—she breathed out the word on a dreamy sigh—"it would be historic. Please, see what you can do? And if you can't, I will seek an audience with the king myself to ask. One way or another, we *will* get the Mousai at our ball."

Zimri stood robbed of words. He was spinning with disbelief, sick with dread.

How were the lost gods this cruel?

What other twisted games were to transpire to thoroughly destroy the last bits of his soul?

"Collector." A deep voice broke into their moment from the nearby stairwell. A member of his inner circle of guards waited on the landing, shadowed gaze hidden behind a full black mask. "I apologize for interrupting, sir," he went on. "But we caught some flies at the match-a-roll tables, and I know how you like to be informed of these matters."

"Who would be dumb enough to cheat here?" asked Kattiva.

"It happens more than you'd think," said Zimri, words momentarily returning to him. "Thank you." He faced the guard. "I'll deal with it."

"What of my favor?" Kattiva caught his sleeve, stopping his retreat. His magic stirred with his frustration.

What of it? he wanted to growl back. It was a preposterous idea! Impossible. Foolish.

But for him, not Kattiva. To her it was a lofty request, but not wrong or out of character.

For him it was a nightmare. To ask his king, his mentor, whose daughter he had only recently asked to marry, for her to perform *as a wedding present* at his engagement ball to another.

It couldn't get any worse than this.

But Zimri also couldn't have Kattiva seeking out their king. If this was to be entertained at all, he had to navigate it carefully.

Placing on the calm mask of the Collector, Zimri pushed down the emotions of a man drowning in heartache as he replied, "I'll see what I can do."

Leaving Kattiva on the landing, he followed his guard down the stairs, desperate for a distraction. "Tell me about these flies," he instructed.

"There are two, sir," his guard informed him.

Zimri nodded.

"And they asked for you. Wondered if the Collector was at home tonight. In fact, they seemed rather keen on being caught."

"Did they now?"

"Yes," confirmed his guard. "They said they had been cheating for two sand falls and were growing tired of winning so easily. They've been quite overbearing, if I'm to be honest, sir."

Zimri pressed his lips together, speculation now growing about who these two flies might be.

CHAPTER TWENTY-ONE

*T*he basement of Macabris was constructed for two purposes: fights for entertainment and rooms to pry out confessions. Both housed pain, and both were scrubbed clean of sweat and blood nightly.

Zimri clung to the shadowed wall as he followed his guard past the tightly packed throng of guests yelling and waving their recorded bets at the two fighters in the center arena. Unlike the rambunctious onlookers, the opponents were maskless, but their swollen eyes, cut lips, and smearing of blood across features were disguises enough. The pungent aroma of sweat and body odor assaulted him through his mask, but it was nothing to the dizzying scent of adrenaline and heightened excitement wafting from those nearest. Their emotions pushed into Zimri in the same moment his gifts reached out like greedy gold fingers to pluck at the sensations.

Food, his gifts purred. *Feelings.*

Behave, he demanded silently, tugging his magic inward. He had no desire to examine those in this room nor become overwhelmed with their emotions.

Putting his back to the crowd, Zimri turned down a darker hall, stalking behind his guard as they passed through where smaller brawling dens rested on either side. These were private rooms that could be reserved for those desperate to hurt or be hurt. A warden stood sentry in each, ready to break up a fight before it became deadly. When Zimri was nineteen and had first returned to Macabris, he had been naively shocked that this floor was filled quicker than the pleasure floors above. As he got older, however, he began to understand that anger grew faster in hearts than love. The desire to let out souring emotions lest they fester and grow into something different, something that could not be controlled, was ripe in this kingdom. Zhad had pushed Zimri on more than one occasion to reserve a room. And Arabessa, well, his almost consuming ache to be with her every grain fall, touch her whenever near, go to her each night they slept under the same roof, found himself seeking this floor so he wouldn't seek her.

"We put them in your interrogation room, sir." His guard stopped before a nondescript metal door that hung at the very back of the hall. "Would you like me to accompany you?"

"No," said Zimri. "You may return to your duties. I can take it from here."

The man nodded but did not budge until Zimri safely stepped through.

As the door closed behind him, the hum from the distant fights disappeared with its click. He was swallowed in stillness save for the flickering lanterns peppered down the hall. It was a gray stretching of space. No decoration or finery. Just bare, raw, like the end state of those who were brought here. Zimri now stood in the Interrogation Wing. Or as his mother liked to call it, the Debt Collection Corridor.

Briella, with her *senseer* gifts, had been the mistress of this domain. Zimri had been invited here once to witness her interrogating.

Briella had hardly spoken as she had stared at the woman sitting in front of her, a guest who had either owed or stolen or broken some loyalty. There had been a thick quiet in the room, but Zimri knew his mother heard plenty. With her mind reading abilities, she was a spider creeping into ears, up nostrils, and through mouths so she might have a look around. She listened to thoughts and gathered them into her web. Food to feast on when ready.

Zimri had often wondered which had been more unnerving for the detained: his mother or the silent boy in the corner who had watched.

Coming to a wall at the back, Zimri looked at the only hint to it being a door. A small keyhole rested in the center, which in fact was shaped less like a space for a key and more like a pad for a thumb. Pressing his finger to it, he pushed out his desire for the door to open, the emotion of need. With a rush to his hands, his magic listened and lit up the lock with gold. It opened with a soft escape of air.

Two sets of eyes glanced up from where they sat on a velvet couch. The only other furniture in the colorless room was a red armchair that directly faced the culprits.

Despite their flashy disguises, Zimri knew them instantly.

"You truly keep your guests waiting an unfashionably long time," said Niya, who was hidden beneath a bushy red beard and leather eye mask. Her hair was swept up inside a top hat that matched her yellow pin-striped suit.

"But we do appreciate such comfortable seating in the interim," reassured Larkyra, stroking the soft fabric on which she sat. She, too, was dressed as a peacocked gentleperson but was adorned with a curling white mustache and matching mask. Where Niya was painted loudly, Larkyra's suit was a muted mix of greens and blues.

"I would remind you both that this is a holding cell and not a receiving room, but I know such reasoning would pass through one ear and out the other." Zimri shut the door behind him before approaching where they sat. He stopped behind the armchair rather than taking a seat. "What are you doing here?"

"We always come to Macabris midweek," explained Niya.

"Yes." Zimri shot her an unamused glare. "But why did you cheat—no, let me rephrase that." He held up a hand, stilling the sisters' readying replies. "Why did you want to get *caught* cheating tonight?"

"How else could we collect the Collector?" asked Niya by way of an explanation. "You only ever showed Arabessa the way up to your private floor. Not that we couldn't find it ourselves eventually, but this felt a much faster approach. Oh, Zimri, do not frown so." Niya waved a hand at his scowl. "Ara never *told* us she had been up there, but we are no fools. No one needs to be in the lavatories that long *or* that often."

"Unless they suffer chronic irritable bowels," pointed out Larkyra.

"True," mused Niya. "Arabessa does suffer irritability, but I would say it plagues her overall demeanor rather than specifically her—"

"Why did you need to collect me *here?*" Zimri interrupted what surely would be a never-ending volleying conversation between the girls. "You could have sought me out in Jabari."

Both sisters eyed him dubiously from beneath their masks.

"Like we stated," said Niya, "swiftness was imperative. When would you have come home to Jabari?"

Home. The word spoken so plainly, so matter of fact. When it was never so easily defined to him. An orphan who had lost his claim to the home of his past; the boy who was raised within a family but knew he was not of blood; the man who was treated like a brother but was in love with a woman he would never call a sister.

"You haven't stayed in your quarters there in a turn," Larkyra pointed out.

Because I cannot sleep there, knowing Arabessa sleeps there too. I cannot pretend that nothing has changed when everything has.

But of course Zimri said none of that. Instead, he evenly replied, "Perhaps not, but if you needed me to return, you could have simply sent me a summons."

"What about us stating we needed to see you *now* is not being understood?" asked Niya, eyes narrowing with confusion.

"You might have also said no to our summons," added Larkyra. "Or left it unanswered."

"When have I ever done either of those?" he challenged.

"There are always firsts for everyone," said Niya.

"A sentiment I wish I'd have exercised tonight," Zimri muttered.

"That only proves our point further, you know," explained Niya.

"Nevertheless," said Larkyra, flicking a small piece of lint from her trousers, "*I* recommended this way of meeting because, honestly, I no longer have endless sand falls to wait around. I'm a duchess now, you know?"

"Yes," quipped Niya, cutting her sister a glare. "You remind us far too often for any of us to forget."

"All right," said Zimri, raising his hands in defeat. "You have explained your essence of hurry quite thoroughly. You now have my undivided attention. What is it that you want?"

Larkyra settled her blue eyes on him, a pulse of her determined resolve filling his lungs on an inhale. "We don't want you to marry Kattiva Volkov."

Zimri physically flinched, a wash of cold hitting him. "And why not?"

"Because you're in love with Arabessa."

He stood very, very still.

You're in love with Arabessa.

Skin burning, razors piercing, a thousand knives scraping; Zimri only felt pain. "So?" he asked.

"*So.*" Niya waved her hands emphatically, her scent of exasperation potent. "She's in love with you!"

She's in love with you.

The chains Zimri had wrapped tightly around his heart shivered.

"Evidently not enough, given she did not want to marry me."

Neither of the girls looked surprised by his statement, which meant Arabessa must have confided in them that he had proposed. Which also meant she had told them what her answer had been. Embarrassment and ire pushed heat into his cheeks. Here stood Zimri, the ever-lovestruck pup, pining after their sister. But blast if it wasn't true. Or had been true. He was over pining, however. He was now a man who got what he wanted and entertained only those who truly wanted him and weren't afraid to show it. He wanted Macabris, and he would entertain Kattiva for the same reasons she entertained him: personal advantages. This was the way of the Thief Kingdom, after all. To be ruthless was to succeed. And he had been born to this kingdom; he needed to start acting like it.

"She only refused your proposal because she didn't want you to lose your chance at majority ownership," said Larkyra.

Excuses, he spat silently. *Defenses.*

"Perhaps," Zimri ground out. "But did she share that I had told her I would find another way to get it? I want her more than the shares, more than the potential of the shares. My feelings apparently don't matter, though, for she refused me anyway. And you both know there is no way of reasoning with your sister when a decision of hers is set. I am not going to beg. And I am not going to force her into something she clearly does not want as much as I do. I have done that already for far too long."

His heartbeat raced with his quick breaths. The girls let his words settle in the room, sink into their understanding. He had known long ago that Larkyra and Niya most likely had inklings of what was going on between him and Arabessa. They were her sisters, his friends. If they didn't know the full picture, they at least saw admiration, the longing, the want. Zimri had never desired to hide their relationship. So he had never been the one to rein in his expressions around Arabessa or his compliments toward her.

"Why did you tell her?" asked Niya.

"Excuse me?" Zimri frowned.

"Why tell Arabessa about Kattiva's offer? You know our sister, perhaps better than we do, as we've come to learn. She is sickeningly honorable. Painfully selfless. *Of course* she would refuse you once she learned of this opportunity to fulfill one of your childhood dreams. Of course she would remove herself from being an obstacle in your way."

"I never saw her as that," he argued. "She has never been an obstacle."

"Then we have found our problem." Niya leaned back, folding her arms over her chest.

Zimri's annoyance flared. "What does that mean?"

"It means you're as thickheaded as she is sometimes."

"Well, that certainly must be a new record, Niya." Zimri glanced to his pocket sandglass. "I've been here less than a quarter sand fall, and already you have found reason to be insulting."

Niya's lips twisted into a sharp grin. "I certainly can find more reason—"

"*I think,*" interrupted Larkyra as she placed a steadying hand on Niya's leg, "what Niya is trying to say is, perhaps in your love for our sister you forget the role she carries for our family?"

"Never," said Zimri, gripping the top of the chair he stood behind. "Her role has been the very excuse for why she never wanted anyone to know about us. The distraction of it, she would say. That was me, her distraction. When she was my—" *Guiding light.* He cut himself off, not wanting to bare himself publicly any more than he already had. He still had his dignity to cling to, for the lost gods knew there was no hope for his shredded heart.

"It was not *you* that was her distraction, Zimri; it was her fear of her feelings for you. And I think we all saw proof of what happens when she does not have control over her feelings."

No one spoke for a moment. Memories of their performance the other day and the bodies left in their wake no doubt floated forward into all their minds.

"Arabessa has shouldered responsibility from a very young age," Larkyra continued.

"And so have we all," Zimri pointed out.

"Yes, but this is different. Her responsibility is unbending. What she has been expected to do for us, for our father. You say you did not see her as an obstacle, but that is the very definition in which she has placed herself in our family. She is the obstacle who blocks Niya and I from performing wildly. She is the reproachful wall that keeps our father from visiting the Fade whenever he pleases. She is the one who takes on the sacrifices of a mother, of a wife, of a conductor for us, her symphony. She takes the blame with all falls, and it appears she may have hit her own wall with you. When she learned you could hold more of Macabris in your hands, she obviously could not stand in the way of that. Not even if that meant losing you."

"But that is not her sacrifice to make," said Zimri, frustration pouring through his veins. "My goals and dreams are my own. They are *my* choices. She was my choice."

"Perhaps she fears you'd regret that choice," said Larkyra.

"How could I regret loving her?"

"Do you regret it now?"

Now that you can't have her. Now that your heart is bleeding. Now that you feel like half a soul. Do you regret it now?

Did he?

"No," said Zimri, fingers digging farther into the chair's back. "Never."

"Then there is hope yet," said Larkyra.

Hope.

The word took the wind from him. *Hope.* A naive, childish emotion. An airy, subtle fragrance. One that could easily be blown away by any other feeling. Anxiousness, fear, anger.

No, there was no hope here.

"She will not be with me." Zimri shook his head. "And even if so, it is too late. I have just come from formalizing the marriage agreement with the Volkovs."

"You are not yet married," said Larkyra. "It is never too late. Not even death is the final say in Aadilor."

"Nevertheless," began Zimri, looking away, not enjoying how desperately he wanted to believe that thought, "I need to make the most of what I have left on *this side* of the Fade, and what I have left is this club."

"And us," said Niya. "You still have us."

He glanced to both women, drank in their strong wills, tasted their determination wafting, their love warming. These girls who had grown up beside him, never questioned it when he had shown up in their lives. Who had shared their homes and the attention of their father.

Perhaps this was the hope Larkyra had spoken of. Hope for him and them. Hope to retain a piece of the family he had puzzled around himself. Even if that no longer included the piece he wanted to place into the center of his heart.

"Even after I marry Kattiva?" he challenged, needing to press the realities. "Even if your sister and I will never be able to be mended?"

There was a beat of quiet, a spike of sadness through the air.

"Yes," said Larkyra. "Even then. You must have learned by now that it takes a great deal to get rid of a Bassette."

"Worse than weeds, we are." Niya nodded.

A warm, floral embrace surrounded him: their love. And because Zimri needed it more than he had known, he allowed himself to lean into it, just this once.

"Thank you," he said. "That means more than you know."

"You are still our brother, Zimri," replied Larkyra, gaze steady. "We love you as we love Ara, no matter the divide between you."

"Our loyalty is with our family," added Niya. "And you are family."

You are family.

A blossoming of guilt filled Zimri as he recalled Kattiva's earlier request. It would not be a sign of loyalty to ask it, but he felt this was as good a place as any to test what he would soon be forced to say to his king.

"I will likely challenge these sentiments of loyalty with a situation that has arisen," he admitted, feeling more than sick to his stomach.

"What is it?" asked Niya, brows furrowed.

"First, I preemptively ask for your forgiveness for what I'm about to share."

"Oh dear," said Larkyra.

"Oh goody," replied Niya.

"I understand the inappropriateness of it," Zimri continued. "But to speak to you both before your father is probably best."

"Well, spit it out, Z," urged Niya. "You can't intrigue us so and continue to drag out the matter."

He took a steadying inhale. "Kattiva and her family are inclined to have an engagement ball."

Niya nodded. "That seems appropriate."

"Yes, but my betrothed is quite set on asking the king for the Mousai to perform at the event as a wedding present."

Larkyra's brows rows above her eye mask.

Niya's mouth popped open.

No one spoke for a painfully long time.

"The Mousai are not for hire," Niya finally said, her tone a frozen tundra.

"I explained this to her," said Zimri. "But she is rather set on asking the king anyway. Having *me* ask him as a favor to one of his confidants, the Collector."

"That is absurdity!" Niya threw up her hands, standing.

"I know," assured Zimri, stomach rolling in nausea at the thought. "And I hate to even entertain this request, but if there is one thing you should know about Kattiva Volkov, she is very similar to a Bassette. She fights for what she wants until she gets it. I'll have to ask the king; otherwise she will, and I do not trust what else she may push for when given an audience. I need to take care of this myself. I know that Dolion would be disappointed if I didn't."

And that outcome pained Zimri almost as much as the request itself. Disappointing Dolion was not something he could take on in addition to everything else.

"Arabessa will never agree," said Niya.

"No," replied Larkyra, who still sat contained on the couch. "But it might not be her decision to decline," she explained.

Niya whipped her gaze toward her sister, expression horrified with her realization. "He would *never.*"

Larkyra sighed, a sad exhale. "When it comes to the Thief King, nothing is off the table. And besides, he has yet to set the Mousai's punishment for their performance the other night."

"By the Fade," breathed Niya, her trepidation pungent. "This will be a disaster. It won't only be a handful dead at the end."

Zimri stood out of body. Even in his fear of bringing this request to his king, he had been certain a quick *no* would follow. A definitive dismissal. But after Larkyra mentioned the Mousai's punishment, on knowing how twisted and brutal the Thief King's forms of lessons could be . . . he realized with bone-freezing dread that this performance was not out of the realm of possibility.

The room swayed, bile rising up his throat.

"Zimri." Larkyra's voice remained a muffled echo until he blinked, his surroundings slamming back into focus. "We will do what we can to manage the Mousai," she said, gaze earnest. "But please, this performance . . . *if* it comes to pass, it will not be easy for Arabessa. No matter what you believe she may or may not feel for you, this could very easily be the final breaking weight on her shoulders. We ask that you be gentle whenever you again cross paths."

Gentle? The very idea that he could ever be purposefully callous to Arabessa awoke fury in his veins. "I would never be cruel," Zimri stated, tone chilled.

The sisters appeared mollified, if only just.

Zimri's agitation grew, for while Larkyra spoke of how hard this would be for Arabessa, the very thought of watching the woman he loved celebrate his marriage to another—well, it might be her punishment, but it would undoubtedly be Zimri's torture.

CHAPTER TWENTY-TWO

*A*rabessa sat staring at her reflection in the glass, wondering how she was not marked with wrinkles and grays for how tired and ancient she felt. On her vanity lay her invitation to vie for the throne. It was an open black splotch on the pristine marble top. Arabessa stared down at the words she had read over a dozen times, to the lines that hooked into her psyche.

> *We invite you to test if you are worthy*
> *To claim this throne, and this kingdom's vowed*

And then farther down, the last section:

> *But remember, to lose is to enter the Fade*
> *So think carefully, our darling, if this is worth dying*
> *You cannot return from this decision once made*

It felt impossible, all that had transpired this past week. That she had agreed to this competition, signed her potential death certificate, ended the Mousai, and lost Zimri, and she now waited with impatience for her first test so she could possibly, hopefully survive to rebuild her confidence in her decision.

It was maddening, not knowing exactly when it would come.

The Waning Sky was nearing, the middle of the month, which meant her first test was imminent, if not close to past due. Arabessa certainly had believed it would have happened by now. Whatever *it* was, of course.

She still did not understand how she was meant to enter her challenges. Another leveraging token for the throne, she supposed. Another small test: survival favored the prepared.

Taking in a calming breath, Arabessa knew it wouldn't come from sitting here. Refolding the invitation, she put on her leather eye mask and stood. Walking to a painting depicting the starry glowworm ceiling of the Thief Kingdom, she pushed aside the frame to reveal her wall safe. When she rapped a beat onto its surface, her magic pulsed out a purple mist from her knuckles to slide into the lock. With a quiet click, it opened.

She placed the invitation atop a stack of small valuables—a few portal tokens, bags of silver, old letters from Zimri she dared not glance at—before locking the safe once more.

Arabessa had stayed in the palace last night, wanting the solitude of her chambers. There was no noise of household staff here, no formal luncheons or dinners requested. Only quiet, darkness, a place to hide unless you rang to be found.

Arabessa had been so full of unease in her heart after her performance that she needed this stillness so she might recalibrate her mind. Plus, such silence allowed her to imagine how she might fill it with music, a calming sound.

At the thought of playing, her fingers absently grazed the flute tucked into her gown's sleeve. Her gifts jumped awake in her veins, sensing her intent, but it was her piano that called for her today. Thankfully, such an instrument was only a few paces down the hall from here.

With some urgency, Arabessa opened her door and, stepping through,

fell
fell
fell
into the dark until—
With a grunt, she landed along her side on a hard surface.
What the—?
As she blinked to pure black, her heartbeat tumbled on top of itself, a panic scrambling.

Arabessa pushed to her feet to find she now stood in nothing.

It was not merely a darkness brought from covered windows. This was devoid of anything.

It was not cold or hot or scented or shadowed.

The *only* tangibility was whatever surface lay beneath her feet.

Solid. Real. There.

Her quick, panicked breaths punched like thunder in her head as she turned in a circle, not knowing if she had turned fully or half or thrice around. Arabessa was utterly disoriented.

Like a glowing reprieve, a thin, scrawling light began to grow in front of her, a knife dragging through a veil to create glowing words in the air.

Arabessa squinted as parts flickered brighter where the tracing moved.

A message . . .

> *Welcome to your first start*
> *Though it might be your finale*
> *We ask that you face your greatest fear*
> *If you're worthy will be yours to tally*

Not a message, a test.

Her first test.

With a jolt, Arabessa's gifts gathered at her fingertips right as she released her flute from its holster to jump into her hand.

She readied the cool metal at her lips, not taking any chances to fight with anything but her magic. She needed to win this test. She needed to survive.

Like a fog lifting, the space around her grew into existence. Edges of rocks, a dirt floor, a falling waterfall feeding into three glowing pools. Arabessa stood in a small cave, one of the grottoes that she knew were tucked away in abandoned parts of the kingdom.

But something felt missing, felt off.

Her eyes snagged on the waterfall again, watched as the waters hit the illuminated pools below.

She drew in her brows, but before she could connect the reason for her unease, a vibration beneath her feet caused her to turn as the wall to her right exploded.

Arabessa tumbled out of the way of the spraying rocks, coming to crouch behind a heavy boulder. She peeked over the edge to find a giant wriggling beast that looked like a rabid canine, but whose four legs had been replaced by thick slime-covered tentacles.

Sticks, Arabessa silently cursed, her pulse racing along with her churning gifts. She dipped back behind her rock.

A *skylos lak*, another guardian of the palace, was not a creature to be trifled with. If their black, beady spider eyes didn't catch you, their heightened senses would, followed by their razor-sharp teeth. They were not easily slain, hence their role as guardians.

Arabessa's breaths came out quick as she searched the cave, hope spiking as she noted a small doorway beyond where the *skylos lak* hovered.

She didn't know if it was *the* way out, but it was *a* way out, and that was better than no way out.

Lifting her flute, she blew out a sharp chord, one she knew would send any creature back on its heels.

But no note was produced.

Confusion swirled.

Arabessa blew again.

And again.

She fluttered her fingers over the keys until they ached, her chest burning, but the only music was the rhythmic sound of her labored breaths inside her head.

With a sharp slice of dread, she realized what was missing from this scene: sound.

There was not one whisper or echo or splash from the waterfall or ringing of sound from the beast.

No no no no no no no, thought Arabessa as she gripped her flute firmer, the illuminating script from earlier filling her mind.

We ask that you face your greatest fear.

And then the words of her father.

This kingdom knows your greatest fears, so be sure you know them as well.

The reality of what was happening slammed into her like a blow from one of the *skylos lak's* tentacles.

She could not make music here. She could not make noise. Not a small beat. Not a hiccup of a tempo.

Which meant her magic was trapped.

Contained inside her as if her hands were bound, no way to escape.

Her biggest fear realized.

Her powers lay useless within her. Reduced to a pleading buzz.

Let us out! her gifts screamed. *Let us protect.*

But Arabessa couldn't.

With a rush of panic, she stood before the approaching beast completely and utterly giftless.

CHAPTER TWENTY-THREE

*W*hen Arabessa was not yet nineteen, she had been sent away from her home and family to experience her *Lierenfast*. It was a time when she had to live for a month in the lower quarters of Jabari without using her magic. An initiation of sorts during which Arabessa had been meant to learn how those not blessed with the lost gods' gifts existed without the benefits she and her sisters were born into. *A time without,* as her father liked to put it. Niya and Larkyra had followed in her footsteps before they came of age. And though she had grown up in the Thief Kingdom, Arabessa had never learned lessons so fast and so brutally as she did in that month. Larkyra had even lost her finger during her bout.

But the benefit of hardships was learning your potential when overcoming them.

It was this teaching that Arabessa pulled forward now as she stared down the beast, who had caught sight of her and charged.

She might be without her gifts, but she knew she was more than her magic.

As a thick, furry tentacle swung her way, Arabessa dove from behind her boulder just as the rock burst apart.

She rolled into a squat as the guardian rounded on her, fanged teeth baring with another silent scream.

There might not be sound, but from the putrid aroma that filled the cave upon the guardian's exhale, there was certainly smell. And she still had her sight, along with feeling, given the vibrations the *skylos lak* made with its heavy movements. Three senses she knew were just as much a gift as her magic.

The trouble, of course, lay with what to do with them. For now she settled on running. As she pumped her arms and legs as fast as she could while wearing heavy skirts and tight sleeves, she focused on the door that now sat unobstructed on the opposite side of the cave.

Unfortunately the beast was fast, if not faster, and it was upon her within a few grain falls. Arabessa's exit was quickly blocked by one of its furry legs flopping in front of her, sweeping quickly her way. She jumped over it, a child playing a deadly game of crisscross, before rolling to hide behind a new boulder. Her dress was an annoying tangle around her legs, her corset a cursed iron grip. She had trained in such ensembles, but it was a crazed person indeed who preferred to fight in them.

Switching her flute for the blade that was strapped to her other wrist, Arabessa began to tear through the material. One benefit of the silence: she did not make a sound as she stabbed and ripped and pulled. Soon she was in nothing but her drawers and corset, the stays of which she enthusiastically sliced open. Now able to take in a larger lungful of air, she attempted to calm her panicked breaths, her magic a similar tumbling craze through her veins.

Free us! it demanded, pushing relentlessly against her fingertips. *We will destroy. We will kill!*

I wish I could! Arabessa silently cried back. *I wish I could let you out to let me out!*

But she couldn't.

Her gifts were caged, just as she remained caged within this cave. Giftless. Useless. Weak.

No! she screamed internally. *I am more than my magic. I am Arabessa bloody Bassette.*

Her resolve was fortified as her gaze locked to the gleam of metal in her hand. Her blade. It caught the glowing reflection of the blue pools not too far to her left. She turned toward it, eyes drifting up, up, up to a small lip where a gathering of large rocks was piled around the waterfall's edge.

An idea wiggled alive in her mind, sending Arabessa's pulse to flutter with renewed hope.

Her magic might be trapped, but she had other tools in her arsenal. She had cleverness.

The ground around her began to vibrate with more urgency, a sign of the *skylos lak* nearing.

Sending a feeble prayer to the lost gods, Arabessa jumped to her feet.

The beast was in the middle of the cave, searching between other rocks, but Arabessa's movement quickly snagged its attention, and with a frantic, hungry burst, its legs twisted and gripped the ground, sending it barreling toward her.

Arabessa didn't spare it a second glance; she ran straight toward the glowing pools. Her legs pumped with more freedom with her shredded skirts left behind.

Skidding to the edge, she stopped in front of the wall beside where the waterfall fell, the spray a welcoming cool along her exposed skin. She turned fully to watch the approaching crazed guardian.

MOVE! RUN! GO! her magic hissed in her head. But she couldn't. Not yet.

Not until—

She jumped into one of the pools by her feet just as the beast reached a few paces away. The ice water was a shock to her senses, and she let out a silent scream below the surface, air bubbles rising as she blinked her eyes open through her mask. Dozens of glowworms wriggled along the bottom of the pool, creating the illumination. Though the sight of a moving floor was unnerving, she pushed herself down toward it just as a shaking vibration rippled her surroundings.

As Arabessa had hoped, the *skylos lak*, unable to stop its hurried movements in time, had slammed into the wall of the cave above. Two of its thick tentacles flopped into the water where she floated, half of its body becoming submerged. She kicked away as it swept its legs along the bottom, thousands of worms clinging to its matted fur.

As she swam, Arabessa's lungs burned: time running out.

Quickly she twisted toward where another pool's surface hovered above like a circular glass door. Arabessa pumped her way toward it.

With a greedy, silent gasp of air, she pulled herself up and over the lip.

She lay on the hard floor of the cave for less than a grain fall, wiping at the water dripping into her eye mask before scrambling to her feet. She would rip the bloody disguise from her face, but she needed her magic to release the spell that kept it in place. And as she already knew, her magic was trapped.

She turned, and her heart leaped into her throat as she found the wiggling *skylos lak* closer than she had realized. If she had lifted her hand, she could have touched it. As she took staggering steps back, she was thankful that it was facing the other way.

The waterfall fell unceasing atop where it lay, and the beast shook its head, sending water spitting and smacking against her. Arabessa wasted no time as she scrambled up the nearby wall. She wedged her booted toe into small grooves, grunting as she pulled herself up, using her knife at times to help scale the cave. Her fingers slipped on a wet rock, and with a shot of panic she found herself dangling for a moment with just her hand desperately grasping the handle of her jammed blade. She swung back to the wall, nails digging into dirt to cling to the side, her muscles burning. With another few scrambles, she was pulling herself up onto the opening of the waterfall.

Arabessa slumped along the ledge, collecting her breath before she braced her weight against the wall at her back. With feet raised, she heaved against a large boulder by the fall's edge. The rushing waters smacked like icy blows along her side, her body beginning to grow numb, but this was her chance. Perhaps her *only* chance. As she grasped a renewed surge of will, Arabessa let out a quiet scream as she pushed with all her living might. The rocky wall dug into her spine as her muscles strained, her fingers gripping in desperation the slick stone on either side of her. She ignored the cold, ignored the pain, ignored her magic, which thumped its frustration through her body. All she concentrated on was the boulder beneath her feet. She pushed and stomped and whacked past the agony radiating like a thousand needles up her legs.

And then, like a gasp of relief, the heavy rock shifted, moved forward.

Hope blossomed warm in her chest as she gave another blow. She slipped as she knocked the boulder free, the cold rushing of water drenching her entirely.

Arabessa gasped and pushed herself up, scrambling to the ledge just as the massive stone fell the great length to land on the *skylos lak*.

If there could be sound, she imagined a high-pitched wail filling the cave as the beast was shoved farther into the pool. With its head fully submerged, its legs, which remained topside, flopped wildly, hitting every part of its surroundings, desperate for purchase. But with the force of its blows, it merely set loose more rock to fall from the caved ceiling.

Arabessa slid back, tucking herself as far into a pocketed crevice in the wall as she could, clinging against the onslaught of the waterfall rushing out and down. Her teeth chattered from the chill mixing with the vibrations shaking the room. And despite the chaos, there was an odd beauty in watching destruction when it was silenced. The quiet falling of stone kicking up dust storms when crashing into the ground. Arabessa had a moment to imagine the music she would spin into this scene, the companion piece to the madness.

But then it all stilled, save for the waterfall, which still pushed around her legs to spill over the ledge. The rest of the large grotto was at rest.

Carefully, Arabessa loosened her grip, edging her way to the lip. A deep breath of relief exhaled as she found the *skylos lak* smashed inside one of the pools below.

Drowned.

Picking her way down the wall, Arabessa landed back on the cave's floor.

Though the grotto stayed unmoving, Arabessa kept her knife at the ready, not trusting that this might be the last of her test. But she wasn't about to stick around to find out either. With quick strides she hurried toward and through the small exit the beast had first guarded.

The air instantly changed from cold and damp to warm and dry. From a glowing blue cave to an empty candlelit hallway. Arabessa now stood within the passage she had first attempted to enter back in the palace. Twisting around, she found the open door to her private dressing rooms. No longer the way to return to the hidden grotto. No longer a scene of tangled legs of a half-submerged carcass of a *skylos lak*.

But what might be the ultimate gift of relief was that she could *hear*.

The soft hiss and flicker of flames in the sconces along the walls, the rushing of a nearby sandglass. Such mundane quiet sounds were now made loud by their recent absence.

Arabessa strode back into her rooms, sheathing her blade and shutting the door.

Then and only then did she let out the bubbling laugh she had felt fighting up her throat.

She had survived!

She had passed!

She had made it through!

She was alive!

Her elation was only compounded when her laughing vibrations were met with sound. *Her* sound. Her happiness. Her triumph.

Releasing her flute, Arabessa flipped it to her lips and sent soaring notes into the room. She played a marching melody of celebration that had her gifts bursting from her hands in purple euphoria.

Freedom! they crooned through her blood. *We are set free!*

A hard knock at her door sliced through her joyous moment.

Arabessa furrowed her brows beneath her eye mask, lowering her instrument. She was in no mood for company.

"We know you are in there," said a familiar voice from beyond her door. "Your music rather gave it away."

"Sticks," Arabessa muttered.

She unlocked her chambers to find Achak standing in the hallway.

They were in the sister's form, and her brows rose as she took in Arabessa.

"By the Fade, child, you look near death."

Arabessa glanced down to find, to her dismay, the sister was right. She appeared like a drowned beast. Her hair had come free of its braided updo, now a plastered dark mess around her shoulders. Her ivory corset and drawers were a muddy, soaked disaster. Her legs and chest were peppered with scratches and small cuts. The only pieces of her in good shape, she knew, were her mask, because of magic; her sheathed flute and blade; and her brown boots. They were soaked through, of course, but in one piece nonetheless. A testament to the gifted cobbler she and her sisters favored in the Thief Kingdom.

"Yes, I look it probably because I was, indeed, near it," said Arabessa. Despite her appearance she still felt elated. "For reasons I cannot say," she went on, "but you certainly know of."

The one relief in Arabessa's invitation was that Achak was in the know.

Understanding flashed in the sister's violet gaze. "Well done." She smiled. "Your state of aftermath is not nearly as bad as the others'."

Arabessa's ears pricked hot, a jolt to her heart.

The others? she thought.

The other contestants. The other players. The others who could claim the throne.

With everything else going on in Arabessa's life, she had forgotten "the others."

Her competitive curiosity burned.

"Interesting," she said in the most uninterested tone she could muster. "If my state is qualified as near death, I'm curious as to what you'd categorize as worse than that."

Achak quirked a knowing grin, not fooled. She knew what Arabessa was asking. *How many still live?*

"I'm certain you are curious," said Achak. "But we came to find you for another reason. The king has requested an audience."

Arabessa's joy from passing her first test sank below the surface. "Now?" she asked.

"I'm afraid so." Achak nodded. "He has asked for the Mousai."

Our punishment, she thought. *My punishment.* He must have finally settled on the sentence.

Exhaustion and apprehension tugged at her bones. "I must change," she said.

Achak placed a staying hand on her door to keep her from closing it. "Four," said the sister, eyeing her intently.

"Four?" queried Arabessa.

But Achak was already walking away, down the hall, to be swallowed up by the shadows.

As if a flame caught light in her mind, Arabessa's understanding grew. *Four!*

Four contestants.

Four left who could potentially sit on the throne.

Three guaranteed to enter the Fade.

One to remain. Hopefully it would be her.

Despite the looming audience with her king, Arabessa could not ignore the underlying buzz of excitement in her veins.

The odds of her victory were steadily growing in her favor.

CHAPTER TWENTY-FOUR

*A*rabessa's ears rang with disbelief as she stood in the Thief King's throne room.

This surely must be her second test, the next obstacle she was forced to overcome or die trying, for the words alone cut fatally.

You shall perform during the engagement ball of the thief houses D'Enieu and Volkov.

The slicing order of the Thief King whipped through her mind and dragged across her heart over and over.

The engagement of thief houses D'Enieu and Volkov.

Of Zimri and Kattiva.

A celebration of their union.

A declaration of Arabessa and Zimri's end.

Was this a sick, twisted joke?

Arabessa certainly was not laughing.

Beneath her Mousai disguise of gold mask and black robe, she glared at her king atop his throne, consumed with an emotion she had not yet felt for him: pure, thick, hot rage. Arabessa was the lava churning on either side of the walkway where she and her sisters were gathered. Her magic wanted to spill out of her and burn everything in her path. Destroy the decree that hung like a dagger above her head in the towering hall.

I dare you to disobey, the mounting tension whispered. *You shall see what happens if you do.*

But Arabessa had already been stabbed clean through, fists clenching at her sides to hold in her furious scream, her gifts already wailing through her blood.

This cannot happen!

This cannot be real!

We must stop it!

She knew her father's lessons to be brutal, but never were they so cruel.

To force his daughter to perform at the engagement ball of the man she loved, celebrate his union to another: it was disturbed, vicious.

It was a punishment for her and her alone.

Yes, she could feel the radiating anger from her sisters, but their pain would be for her, not for their own hearts and beliefs becoming eviscerated.

Arabessa would rather have been lashed for a week.

Flesh wounds could heal. But this . . . the trauma would haunt her the rest of her days.

Which, of course, she realized was the appalling point.

You will never survive what you need to, acting as you have. You must *survive.*

The austere words of her father.

To be a part of this kingdom, even a small part, there are risks. But to be a great part . . . there will be sacrifices.

Was this, then, to be her sacrifice? Her proving that she could control her emotions through any torture? That she could still think clearly, act properly, when drowning in her own grief, in her own mourning, as she toasted the marriage of Zimri to another?

But what of the test she had recently survived? Had passed? Did none of that matter? Did none of what she was to go up against this month count toward her proving her worth? Her abilities?

You must *survive.* Her father's plea.

This must be him ensuring that she would. His own test for her to learn what she was capable of.

A twisted action of his love, his guilt, for raising her on this path to make sure she did not die.

"The ball is at week's end." The booming layered voice of the Thief King stirred Arabessa from her swirling thoughts. Her eyes refocused on the extravagant white form sitting high on his black throne. "I trust you will think carefully on what piece you wish to perform," he went on, his ancient magic pulsing from him in oppressive silver waves. "Though I shouldn't have to state it, I will remind you there is no room for repeated misbehavior. Not unless this throne decrees it. Do you understand?" Though his horned headdress shrouded his gaze, Arabessa felt his attention burrowing solely into her.

You have to be in control, Arabessa, he had said. *It is not you in those moments. Not your feelings, not your wants. It is your people's wants. Your kingdom's feelings. You must make personal sacrifices every day. Every grain fall you wear a crown.*

Her father wanted to give her a lesson she could never forget. Never ignore. That such a time as this might come again and again and again if she lived to rule. For Zimri and Kattiva would be a permanent part of her life, whether she accepted it or not. And she needed to be confident that she could act not with her heart in mind but her kingdom's.

This sliver of understanding was the only reason she was able to push past the chaotic circling of fury in her soul to answer alongside her sisters, "Yes, my king."

He waited a beat, the clawed, gloved fingers of one hand thrumming pensively along his armrest. He must have grown satisfied, for his only response was a dismissal. "You may go."

Exiting the throne room, Arabessa remained mute as she and her sisters filtered down the onyx hall, past where others waited for an audience with their king. She ignored their hushed chattering as they took in the presence of the Mousai.

This was the one time since their performance Arabessa was glad for the fear they had reinstalled in hearts. None dared block their path or stop to talk, allowing Arabessa to silently stew and simmer in her growing anger.

Once they reached their private floor beneath the palace, gathering into their joined receiving room, door shutting with a click, Arabessa rounded on her sisters.

"Did you know this request was coming?"

Niya and Larkyra furtively glanced at one another behind their gold masks.

Arabessa's outrage spiked. "And you didn't think to warn me?"

"We didn't know if it would actually come to pass," explained Larkyra, hands raised placatingly. "When Zimri told us of Kattiva's request—"

"Zimri knows of this?" Arabessa took an unsteady step back, as though hit. She had been sure this was to be a surprise for him as well. "When did you speak with him? How could he have . . ." She swallowed up her next words. The pain in her voice too obvious to her own ears.

How could he have entertained such an idea?

Did he hate her as much as this?

Arabessa didn't believe her chest could ache any more, but it was seized with another unceasing clench of pain. Her breathing became desperate gasps. She had done this. She had caused Zimri to loathe her to the point of cruelty. All because she felt she had been placed into an impossible corner. But she could never have chosen herself over his family's legacy.

It was all too much. Too demanding. As soon as she felt she was moving forward, achieving something, she got knocked back behind the starting line. She couldn't see her way forward. Her way out. She couldn't breathe, couldn't—

"Ara, calm down." Niya's voice was gentle as she approached. "You're giving yourself a panic attack."

"I can't . . . I can't . . . I can't . . ." Arabessa shook her head, the room beginning to tilt, the walls closing in on her. *I can't do this. I can't perform at his engagement ball. I can't watch him with another. I can't remain in control. I can't. I can't. I can't.*

Arabessa was falling. Tumbling. Failing.

A gentle layering of a wordless song pushed into her mind. A heated blanket against a winter's cold.

Calm, it whispered to her gifts as it caressed through her veins. *Be at peace.* It stroked along her lungs.

The room dimmed; Arabessa's breathing slowed, the song continuing to twist around her like a warm summer wind.

Arabessa blinked up to where she now found herself slouched in an armchair, Larkyra ending her quick sung spell. "Better?" she asked. Her sister had removed her mask, and her delicate features were pinched in with concern.

"Yes," said Arabessa as she sat up, rubbing at her chest, which now felt expanded rather than tight, her pulse steady rather than erratic. "Thank you."

"Of course." Larkyra squeezed her hand reassuringly.

"Ara," said Niya where she stood in front of them, mask also gone, though their black robes still clung to each of them. "I want you to understand that Zimri did not ask for any of this. It was Kattiva who wanted it and was adamant to ask the king if Zimri did not. As horrible and messed up as it is, remember she does not know who we are. She doesn't know what she is asking besides a bragging right."

"Are you defending them?" Arabessa frowned. Though the residual effects of Larkyra's calming spell were still at play, she knew she'd assuredly be annoyed at Niya.

"I'm trying to help you see this performance for what it is. *A performance,*" explained Niya. "To this kingdom we are not people who feel or have thoughts of our own. We are the king's creation. We are a pet. We do what we are told. Kattiva does not understand there are humans with hearts beating beneath our disguises because that is exactly what we have wanted everyone to believe. We are pretty ornamentation with deadly abilities that anyone at court would kill to rent for an evening of entertainment or revenge. This order of our king's is certainly the lowest of the lowest blows for us personally, but we must remember not even he is who we know him to be beneath that disguise. He is as much an adornment for this kingdom as us, performing for his citizens, not himself."

You must make personal sacrifices every day. Every grain fall you wear a crown.

The room hung in silence, Arabessa's frown deep as she soaked in her sister's words. "By the stars and sea," she huffed, "since when did you become so bloody reasonable, Niya?"

Niya shot her a smug grin. "Sailing aboard the *Crying Queen* isn't merely filled with lessons of buffoonery and fun."

"No," mused Larkyra. "But it mostly is, certainly?"

"It has its perks," admitted Niya.

"Well, I am in no mood for what wise lessons you may have learned," said Arabessa, still distraught. "I do not see how I can survive this."

"As you once have said to me, sister," began Niya, "you will survive it as we must all things. One sunrise at a time."

"That's horrible advice," muttered Arabessa, not enjoying her own words used against her.

"I thought so, too, at the time." She smiled. "But do you want to know the worst of it?"

"Do I really have a choice not to?"

"You were right," she said. "You're always annoyingly right, Arabessa. Which means you'll get through this. We'll *all* get through this, together."

"And we hope you do believe that Zimri was just as upset," said Larkyra. "If not more than he even let on when we talked with him."

Her heart twisted.

"How is he?" she asked. "Other than seeming upset?"

This might be the longest they had gone without speaking, and it was like she was slowly being swallowed up by quicksand. Her air soon to be used up.

"He . . . ," began Niya, appearing to choose her next words carefully. Never a good sign. "Is concentrating a lot on his club these days."

Arabessa nodded, feeling a sliver of relief, of validation. "That's good."

He has his club, she reminded herself. He might not have her, but he was able to claim the other part of his heart: that of his parents, his home.

"Speaking of soirees of debauchery and decadence," continued Niya, "we are taking you out tonight."

"We are?" asked Larkyra, brows lifting.

"We are," repeated Niya. "The Waning Sky approaches, and there are many parties to attend."

"I am in no mood for a party," grumbled Arabessa.

"Which is exactly why you need one," reasoned Niya.

"I was expected back in Lachlan," said Larkyra, "but sister duty does presently seem more important than dinner with Darius. I'll send word to him not to expect me tonight."

"I appreciate you giving up your plans," began Arabessa, "but it's not necessary. I also do not take kindly to being qualified as one who needs 'sister duty.'" She folded her arms over her chest.

"Of course you don't," huffed Niya. "But you are in need of it, nonetheless. So I suggest you put on your most comfortable dancing shoes, old girl, because tonight we are going out."

CHAPTER TWENTY-FIVE

Zimri was regretting a lot of his decisions as of late. Assuredly among them was his most recent one to accompany Kattiva and her companions, better known as tonight's bed partners, to a Waning Sky party taking place in one of the towering stalagmites within the Thief Kingdom.

The drinks were top shelf but overpriced. The music was delightfully hedonistic, but the disguised guests' dancing felt lacking. Worst of all, the rooms were small, connecting one level to another by even tighter winding staircases. The intended effect was, no doubt, an intimate atmosphere, but for Zimri it only caused discomfort as the emotions of those surrounding him pressed close. A claustrophobic cloud.

Lust, envy, and excitement mixed sourly in the air along with the escaped bursts of magic from those gifted. It quickly became too much, and Zimri was forced to retreat to the nearest balcony. He took a relieving inhale of the cool caved world as he stepped from the party. The landing was blessedly near empty, and here was where he found the one complimenting piece of tonight: the view.

Gazing from beneath his maroon eye mask, he took in the magnificence of the Thief Kingdom. A twinkling expanse stretched out, other dwellings carved into the soaring and pouring rocks. The weaving of thatched roofs far below and the colorful puffs of smoke lifting from the Mystic District. Nearby loomed the shiny corridor of the Gazing District. The Betting District was a thick dark vein threading through it all, and far in the distance he could make out the cluster of masts and ships docked at port. Farther still would be the waterfall portal they could sail in and out from to an unmapped section of the Obasi Sea.

His gaze snagged on the intimidating onyx palace in the very center. Its turrets reached like talons up to the glowworm caved ceiling. Their world's sky was dimming, approaching the Waning Sky: hazy stars soon to flicker out before being reborn in a wave of bright blue-green light. The Sky's Return.

Zimri's muscles tensed at the reminder. The stars were his slow countdown to his new life, barely a fortnight away. To be married and finally fulfill a childhood promise to his parents. Their home reclaimed.

But at a price. Always at a price.

A future without Arabessa and a lifetime knowing she was near. Working with her father, always to wonder after his eldest daughter. Watching her perform as the Mousai, never to again seek her out after a performance and spin her as she spun him: into madness.

A sharp pain radiated through Zimri's chest, and he tore his gaze from the fading sky.

He had lost everything once and survived.

He'd do so again.

Was doing so again.

A slither of a voice filled his head. *Lies. You suffer. You hide.*

A bitter laugh rumbled out of him. *Who doesn't suffer and hide in this kingdom?* he challenged before pushing off the banister where he'd been leaning. Despite Kattiva's better intentions to help him find a distraction to "put some sweet into that sour mood," attending tonight had been a glaring mistake.

Zimri's retreat was brought to an abrupt halt, however, when a familiar voice hooked his attention. His pulse tumbled back as a slim figure in a cascading moss-colored dress and delicate sleeves stepped onto the balcony. Her black pearl eye mask caught the dim light of the room inside as she finished replying to two companions at the threshold. "Don't worry, I won't be able to escape from here," she said dryly. "Though I wish it, I have no wings so I may fly to a better gathering than this. I need some air, is all, so stop hovering and I shall return shortly."

As she turned forward, her gaze met his from where he stood in the center of the veranda, and she froze.

A warmth so consuming it burned.

A blast that sent Zimri flying back before snapping him forward.

Our music, his magic crooned in a sick ache.

She might be wrapped in a disguise, her half mask reaching up into a woven headdress that covered her hair, but Zimri would know that voice in the dark, would recognize those blue eyes in a sea of azure. Arabessa Bassette was imprinted on his soul, and nothing in Aadilor could hide that fact, not even the desperate lies he tried to bury himself in.

It appeared she had suffered a similar fate, for she held him in her sights as waves of her grief, anguish, panic, and—the sweetest but most poisonous to his resolve—scent of yearning filled his lungs on an inhale.

His gifts wanted to lift from his skin and go to her. Urged him to touch her. Pull her close. *Our music,* it pleaded once more. *We want our music.*

Stay! he ordered, fists clenching.

Arabessa broke their connection first, her emotions snapping inward as she glanced to the other couples on the balcony. Calculating risks, liabilities, her mind always working with a sense of duty, of correctness. It both enraged Zimri and had him envious.

Here stood the creature who could so easily separate emotion from responsibility.

Except when she plays her emotions for all to feel, said that voice inside him again. *Her emotions for you. Her devastation.*

Our devastation, Zimri wanted to yell.

A devastation she could have avoided by saying yes to him.

Of course she would refuse you once she learned of this opportunity to fulfill one of your childhood dreams. Niya's words to him at Macabris rushed fast and hot through his mind. *Of course she would remove herself from being an obstacle in your way.*

An obstacle. Her blasted noble actions. Selfless for those she loved.

He had hated that he knew the sisters were right.

Ever since that morning in the sunroom, Zimri had replayed his and Arabessa's conversation over and over, turned around their moment like an impossible puzzle. *Was* it a mistake to tell her? *Should* he have kept secret the proposal with Kattiva? But how else could he have given reason for why she needed to commit to marrying him that day? The purpose for the rush of it when she would have most assuredly found out later? Been furious at him later. But he would have gladly taken that fury over her absence.

She would have called it off. The taunting words prickled up inside him again. *She would never have gone through with it if she found out you lied. If she had found out what you were giving up. You'd be left with no love and no Macabris. You'd have nothing.*

Nothing.

Funny how a part of him felt like he had that now.

Arabessa walked past him to the farthest end of the balcony: a place for quiet conversations.

Zimri's magic skittered with unease and excitement, a mix of contradicting emotions. He glanced to the party taking place inside, to the way out, but of course in the end he followed her.

As he came to Arabessa's side, her familiar scent wrapped around his skin like delicate torture. He gripped the balcony's railing as they both gazed out to the kingdom.

Neither of them spoke for an achingly long time, their bodies so very close. Always so very close.

"I did not expect to find you here tonight," she said by way of greeting, or perhaps by way of an excuse. *I would not have come if I knew I'd find you here.*

"Nor I you," he countered.

"Yes." She huffed an amused laugh, a sound he clung to like a flower reaching toward a bit of sun from its spot in the shade. "This certainly is not a party I would have picked to attend. I was rather dragged here by my sisters."

"Then we share more in common, as I was all but threatened with death if I did not follow Kattiva to tonight's event."

The air around them shifted, silence descending like a dungeon door.

Zimri bit back a curse. He had not wanted to get here so quickly. He had not wanted to get here at all.

Arabessa glanced over to him, and he hated how soothing it was to meet her gaze.

Home. His magic spun in his veins. *We want to come home.*

"I apologize," began Arabessa. "I believe a congratulations is in order on your engagement."

Fire crackled awake in his blood.

"Don't." He shook his head. "Don't act right now."

"Act?"

"Like we are nothing but acquaintances owed surface-level pleasantries," said Zimri. "Despite what has happened between us, I still *know* you. And you me. To pretend like we don't, it makes a mockery of what we had."

Had.

No longer have.

The word fell from his tongue like a knife plunging into his heart. It merely twisted deeper when a wafting of sorrow, of fruit turning sour, emanated from Arabessa.

"You're right," she replied softly. "But I *am* happy you are able to reclaim what has always been yours."

For some reason this had him growing more frustrated. "Are you?" he challenged. "Happy?"

He did not need to breathe in her emotions this time to tell she was not in the least bit happy.

"If this shall be the tone for the rest of our conversation," she began tightly, "then I'll leave you to swim in it without me."

Zimri mumbled a curse, snagging her arm to stop her retreat. "Wait."

They both glanced to his grip on her, the first time they had touched in too long. He wondered if she also felt the heat radiating. Felt the desire for him to move his fingers up to her shoulder, along her back, as he desired.

Zimri dropped his hand. "I'm sorry," he said. "It's just . . . this"—he gestured to the space between—"does not come easy for me."

"Nor I," she admitted, which was the briefest of a poultice to his pain. "But if we cannot in the very least be civil, even if that means we must *act* every once in a while"—she eyed him meaningfully—"whatever our past may be, I can assure you, we will not have a future."

"And you want that?" he heard himself asking without thought. "A future with me?"

The falling grains of silence were tormenting.

"I want . . . ," she started, before biting her lip, obvious thoughts racing.

Risks. Calculations. Responsibilities.

Not right now, Arabessa, he wanted to say. *Not with me. Please, speak your mind.* But of course he understood why she might not, why she was holding back. Because so was he.

Still, he found himself urging her by asking, "What do you want?"

Arabessa looked away then, through her disguise, to the view of the kingdom. She took a deep breath in. "I want to be able to salvage *something* of our childhood. Of my . . . love for you." She rushed out the words that both stung and soothed. "I want to be able to keep the memories of us together unspoiled, for even if we can't ever again have this"—she looked between them—"I'll always know we once did and that it was beautiful." Zimri's chest was being torn open as he listened. "But perhaps most of all," Arabessa went on, "I want to be able to play at your engagement ball and not kill people."

Zimri saw the pool of desperation in her eyes and the anguish that threaded with her truth. Her admission. Her fear. He smelled it in the air around them.

It turned the shards of his heart into further dust. She had learned what he had asked their king. Her father. What had made him sick to ask but he had done nonetheless.

"Ara," he said quietly, her name only for her to hear. "You must know, that request came from Kattiva. I would never—"

"Yes," she cut in. "I know. My sisters told me they spoke with you. I was not . . . pleased to be handed this task, but I understand the purpose of this performance."

We must act once in a while.

They were living in a world of masks, layered identities, a play of characters, of responsibilities.

Zimri was not her past lover; he was the Collector. She was not his childhood sweetheart; Arabessa was an elusive fixture in the Mousai. He produced entertainment; she was created to entertain.

This was what Kattiva saw. What their guests would expect.

What they would continue to fabricate because they must.

Identities to keep hidden, roles to keep up.

All, no doubt, a case for why Dolion had agreed. It had been a tense meeting, private, unmasked in the count's study in Jabari. Zimri hated to admit he had been too fearful to ask him as the Thief King in his throne room.

The magic that gripped him there was unpredictable, and Zimri valued his life.

Dolion had been quiet a long while after Zimri had explained his predicament: Kattiva's request; her tenacity; how it looked for him, the Collector, a known close asset of the king, to be unable to produce such an engagement present for his future wife.

Dolion's age and exhaustion had shown in those moments, in the crease between his brows and the way his shoulders sagged. Zimri feared this new burden might be the one that finished him, but in the end his mentor had nodded. He had told Zimri he was sorry, too, that they found themselves here, but these sorts of predicaments tended to work themselves out. *Tests in Aadilor are given for a reason,* Dolion had said. *To learn from. Let us hope we all learn from this.*

Zimri had left feeling much worse than when he had come.

Arabessa was to play at his engagement ball, and he was meant to sit through it. Applaud. Smile.

His stomach twisted once again in nausea and dread. A true nightmare come to life. He could not even begin to fathom how Arabessa was taking such an order from their king, her father.

"So you are not mad with me for requesting this?" he asked.

She smiled up at him, a sad pull to her lips. "Are you with me?"

The question rocked him back. A quick panic to untangle the knot of emotions he felt for this woman. He was angry, for sure, but with her? Or their situation? Their fate? If she had asked him this a week ago, he would have said yes. But now . . .

When she learned you could finally hold more of Macabris, she could not stand in the way of that. Not even if that meant losing you.

By the stars and sea, he hated how he understood this now. Hated how he might have even done the same for Arabessa if roles were reversed.

"I am not angry with you," he eventually said, noting her scent of relief. "I still do not agree with it, but I now understand why you refused me."

She nodded, words seeming to remain trapped in the bob of her throat.

"But I will tell you this." Zimri stepped closer, their bodies a grain's distance from touching. "If there was a way to still convince you to say yes, I would hunt it down."

He should never have said it, never admitted he still yearned for her. But blast if her nearness didn't split apart his control. There was so much of *her* control he wanted to unravel, set free, expose. When they were alone like this, the teasing heat of her so close, it was more than temptation to touch her—it was a compulsion. Especially when a puff of excitement burst from her skin upon hearing his words. A flicker of desire in Arabessa's gaze caused hope to stir in his ripped-apart heart.

A childish emotion: hope.

One he now clung to despite his better judgment.

"If there was a way I could agree," she returned, her voice a determined hush, "I would hunt it down with you."

Agony tore further into him, hands twitching to embrace her. To kiss those stern-set lips. To find the answer with her in his arms. To prove they'd find it together, because why couldn't they have it all? Perhaps not all at once, but in pieces, as they had enjoyed each other before.

"Ara," he breathed, a quiet prayer. To the Fade with holding back. Zimri would take any piece she might give him. He hungered to settle her skin to his, have their bodies slick with sweat and reprieve. He needed her. He loved her. He—

"There you are," said a familiar husky voice from behind them.

A wash of cold reality intruded on their moment as Arabessa took a step away, both turning to find Kattiva Volkov eyeing them curiously from beneath her mask.

"I see you found a fish for this evening, Collector," she cooed, walking forward. "And a lovely one at that." Her gaze roamed over Arabessa with appreciation.

Zimri caught the spike of ire from Arabessa, noted her hands curling at her sides, no doubt stopping herself from going for one of her hidden blades or tucked-away flute.

This is not good, thought Zimri. Never had he ever intended a one-on-one meeting of his future wife to the woman whom he still loved.

"Is there something I can help you with?" he asked Kattiva, hoping to expedite whatever *this* was to be.

"Oh dear," Kattiva began, eyes widening. "I see my interruption was poorly timed."

"What else is an interruption if not poorly timed?" asked Arabessa, who, despite her tone, plastered on a smile.

Kattiva studied her with further intrigue. "How delightfully coarse you are," she began. "I do enjoy a good talking down. Collector, you must invite your friend to join our party. We have hardly been gifted your presence this evening, which is why I have come to fetch you. If this is what has distracted you, please, bring your companion. They will fit right in with tonight's pleasures."

Zimri caught the further pungent rage that escaped Arabessa, tensions mounting. But if Kattiva sensed it, she showed no sign. Merely grinned her lascivious grin.

By the Fade, thought Zimri. *Could this get any worse?*

He wanted Kattiva to leave. He wanted to spin Arabessa toward him and tell her there would be no pleasures to be had tonight, at least none from him with some stranger. Not that he owed her an explanation, given they were no longer together. He merely wanted to return to their moment moments ago, when she had looked up at him with desire, with need.

What could that have led to?

Zimri desperately needed to find out.

"While I appreciate the generosity," said Arabessa to Kattiva, voice deceptively even, "I have my own party waiting. As for pleasures, I fear what I desire is no longer available."

Zimri snapped his gaze toward her, magic buzzing, pulse rushing.

I fear what I desire is no longer available.

Arabessa desired him. Wanted him.

Her open admission filled him with something dangerous: determination.

"If your pleasure pertains to the gentleman you stand beside," returned Kattiva, quickly picking up on her meaning, "I can assure you, darling, he is very much available."

Arabessa tilted her head, obviously perplexed. "Aren't you marrying this gentleman?"

"I see you know who I am." Kattiva's gaze sparked pleased. "How delightful."

"Everyone knows the one who wears the wolves," Arabessa pointed out.

Kattiva grinned at the mention of her exposed tattoos. "And who are you?"

"No one of consequence."

"If you've caught the elusive Collector's eye, you are someone of great consequence, I would say."

"And when do I get a say in any of this?" asked Zimri, having enough of this back-and-forth. He needed Kattiva to leave.

"If you'd like one," began Kattiva, "I'd claim it now by requesting this beauty join us. More is *always* the merrier, but you already know that, don't you, Collector." She shot him a salacious grin, one that spoke of the night he had caught her in the midst of receiving the height of pleasure. To those standing by, however, it could be interpreted in all manner of ways.

A waft of pungent jealousy, a tangy spice, lifted from Arabessa, and it might have been wrong of Zimri, but he reveled in it.

It meant he was still something she wanted, something she did not enjoy another having.

I can still be yours, he wanted to tell her. As Kattiva had mentioned, his and her marriage was a contract and nothing more. Merely leverage for both of them. But to convince Arabessa of that was a different matter.

"Kattiva Volkov!" a voice boomed from the threshold of the balcony.

Zimri turned to find a figure in a dark cloak walking toward them, eyes beneath their disguise trained to Kattiva.

"Yes?" she questioned.

"This is for the masters of Macabris!" A glint of a jagged knife was pulled from their robe.

Zimri surged forward to stop the attack, but Arabessa was quicker, a whip snapped alive. She spun in front of Kattiva, brandishing her own blade, which had been tucked beneath her bodice. A rush of fluid grace as she bent and sliced and twisted back to standing.

A pained howl from the assailant as they fell to their knees, holding their now-bleeding hands, knife forgotten at their side. Arabessa kicked it away.

Kattiva tumbled into Zimri's arms. Her fingers gripping his suit's sleeves. Fear and shock rippled out of her and into him.

"No!" the masked assailant cried from where he scrambled along the ground, blood smearing. "They took everything from me! Everything! I *must* take something from them!" Despite their injury, they lunged at Kattiva, but Arabessa flipped her dagger around and whacked them on the back of the head with the hilt. The attacker slumped to the ground, unconscious.

"By the stars and sea," breathed Kattiva, leaning farther into Zimri.

"Are you all right?" he asked, holding her firmly.

She merely nodded.

Gasps and shouts of excitement filled the doorway, party guests spilling out to see the commotion.

Zimri caught Arabessa's gaze from where she was folding herself into the crowd.

His pulse rushed to follow her.

But he didn't, because he couldn't.

Arabessa disappeared quicker than she had first appeared.

Leaving Zimri standing on the balcony, holding his betrothed.

CHAPTER TWENTY-SIX

*S*urely you are not as shocked as all that," said Zhad gruffly to his
daughter, who was curled into a thick blanket beside her mother
on a settee. Though Zimri was quickly beginning to regret his decision, he had immediately sent word of the attack to the Volkovs. They
had quickly gathered in Kattiva's newly renovated apartments. "What
number is this even now?" asked Zhad.

"Five," said Alyona, her gaze reproachful from beneath her mask as
she glanced to Kattiva.

"So the fifth attack in less than two years," admonished Zhad, his
leather disguise picking up the orange glow of the nearby fire's light.
"And you sit there sniveling."

"I am not sniveling." Kattiva frowned. "I am just . . ."

"What?" challenged her father. "Wondering how this could have
happened?"

"It was because of us," said Zimri, guilt still heavy on his shoulders.
"Because of Macabris. They were trying to get revenge through Kattiva
on a debt I most likely called in for us. I have yet to learn the attacker's
identity but will make arrangements with the king to do so."

The assailant had been dragged to the palace dungeons by the kingdom's patrollers. Thievery was tolerated here, but murder and attempts
at murder were always reviewed.

"See that you do," huffed Zhad. "But the blame is not on Macabris. If Kattiva didn't flaunt who she was everywhere she went, she wouldn't put our club in such danger."

Club, not daughter.

Zimri's temper grew dangerously on edge.

"What do you have to say for yourself?" Zhad demanded of Kattiva, whose head was lowered, staring at her hands in her lap. "So reckless and bold, yet when the consequences of your actions catch up with you, you're conveniently lost for words."

"You yelling at her, I'm sure, is not helping matters," pointed out Zimri. He was leaning on the fireplace mantel but had a mind to become sentry beside Kattiva.

Zhad shot him a pointed glare. "You are not married yet, Collector. You have no say on how I reprimand my daughter. And even then, there are certain matters only fit for a father to deal with."

"Like reprimanding a daughter for almost being killed?" Zimri's tone held nothing but disgust.

"For the *fifth* time."

"It doesn't bloody matter the number," returned Zimri. "Almost being killed is sure to startle anyone, no matter the frequency."

"She doesn't even have a scratch." Zhad waved an unconcerned hand. "Besides, the assailant sits in the dungeons. More than sufficient for my peace of mind."

"Well, as long as you are satisfied . . ."

"Collector," Zhad huffed. "Even *you* must see the idiocy here? What does she expect from brandishing her tattoos as she does? Carrying on with who knows who nightly. Do you have to be reckless in every aspect of your life?" He stared down at his daughter. "This attack might have to do with Macabris, but what of the last one? You should know better than bedding a married woman. At least choose discretion when entering into a liaison with one already claimed."

"You're right," said Kattiva, voice a sharp blade. "Next time I'll be sure to apply how you deal with your many paramours, Father."

"*Kattiva!*" scolded her mother.

"Oh? Is there something you disapprove of in what I said, Mother?" She scowled at Alyona. "Tell me, is it that Father has just as many companions as I or that I stated it out loud?"

Alyona's exposed neck and décolletage flushed red. "What has gotten into you tonight?"

"Perhaps almost being stabbed and then yelled at has caused me to be bad company."

"We do not enjoy scolding you," reasoned her father.

Don't you? Zimri wanted to retort but held his tongue.

"We merely do not understand what you assume will happen when you so boldly flaunt who you are in this kingdom," continued Zhad. "*Especially* when you are connected with a thief house such as ours, who is partnered to the most exclusive club in the kingdom. There are places to stand out here but crowds where we all must blend in. For the Obasi Sea's sake, you were born here, Katt. You must recognize the risks you put yourself in and the consequences that can follow?"

"You know your father speaks true," pushed Alyona. "Why did you have to get those gruesome tattoos, anyway? When we clearly advised against it?"

"Perhaps *because* you advised against it," volleyed Kattiva.

"You are a *fool*," spat Zhad. "A fool that will one day feel the pain of their stupidity. There is only so much your mother and I can protect you from. This kingdom hides even itself from Aadilor. Should that not teach you exactly how *you* must hide parts of yourself?"

"*I do!*" Kattiva yelled, appearing to startle even herself with her outburst. No longer was she the creature who oozed contentment and disinterest. "I hide what you have always been ashamed of. What makes your perfect daughter not so perfect. At least be satisfied I do not share *that* with the kingdom!"

"*That* you did to yourself," her father shot back.

"Zhad!" gasped Alyona, eyes wide beneath her mask. It seemed her husband had finally gone too far.

The room was tangled with emotions, twisted up with the sharp tang of shock, the pungent aroma of fury, the too-sweet scent of sorrow. And Zimri had no idea who was feeling what or if they all were feeling these emotions together.

"I think it's time you both left," said Kattiva, voice a frozen lake.

Zhad puffed out his chest as though grasping the last of his resolve. "You know we are right in our frustration."

Kattiva merely looked away, silent.

"Very well," said Zhad, chin rising. "Alyona." He held out his hand for his wife.

She looked unsure for a grain's fall, glancing back to her daughter, but Kattiva acknowledged neither of them.

With a tired sigh, Alyona stood, but she did not take her husband's hand, though she left with him nonetheless.

In their absence, the room filled with the snap and crackle of the fireplace. Zimri regarded Kattiva staring at a nondescript part of the carpet, at the complicated weaving of the pattern spreading across it.

This was the first time Zimri had been in her apartments, and with no great surprise, he had found them impeccably decorated. High ceilings, handsome patterned wallpaper, gold- and silver-adorned accessories, and the art: it was everywhere. The den they occupied felt warm and inviting, the furniture comfortable as well as fashionable. It was an interesting glimpse into the mind of Kattiva, a woman whom he had been around for many years but never truly interacted with in a meaningful way until recently.

Zimri pushed off from the mantel to sit by her side.

While he did not approve of Zhad's and Alyona's methods for showing concern for their daughter, they had been right regarding the dangers of this kingdom. There were many reasons the majority of citizens here hid themselves behind masks, why he did. The threat of death was merely one of them, their lives beyond this cave world another. And the few who walked here without disguise did so because they usually were more lethal than the danger that endangered them.

But Kattiva . . . what Zimri had witnessed tonight, she was no fighter. She had no skills to keep herself safe. It was indeed foolish for her to so boldly share her identifying tattoos as often as she did. Part of a thief house, court member, and daughter of Macabris: she would be a leveraging coin to anyone.

"I did not know she was married." Kattiva's words had Zimri glance to her. "The other attack my father mentioned. I do not discuss such things with my companions."

"Perhaps you should?" offered Zimri.

She shook her head. "It is not for me to judge the actions of others. If they seek pleasure outside their homes, who's to say that is not how their arrangements have been settled? You and I certainly will share such behavior. And anyway, they could easily lie and say they were not."

"That is true."

Another stretching of silence.

"Why do you show your tattoos so often if they have brought you threats before?" Zimri asked.

"I am not ashamed of my markings to need to hide them."

"I mentioned nothing of shame in my question."

A spike of annoyance shot off Kattiva, but toward him or herself, he wasn't sure. "Why must I hide who I am?" she retorted.

"This is the Thief Kingdom," reminded Zimri, knowing he sounded like her father. "Everyone disguises who they are here, for precisely what could have happened to you tonight."

She took a deep breath in, her glossy black eye mask catching the reflective flames of the fire. "All my life I have been told how to be," said Kattiva. "How to act, how not to be, how not to act. That dangers lurk outside my door, yet never was I taught how to become a danger myself. I have been bred to marry and marry well, and that is all. If that was to be my lot in life, I decided early that I would do my very best to live despite it. I have never been a spirit to want to hide. To follow rules. I am a creature of this kingdom, and I want to taste every part of it and have every part taste me."

"Then why wear a mask at all?" countered Zimri.

Kattiva's brown gaze met his, a churning look of uncertainty and recklessness. She reached to take off her mask.

"What are you doing?" Zimri stilled her hands, his pulse tripping into a fast beat.

"I trust you," she said, her words heavy with her belief.

"You shouldn't," he advised, grip still on her wrists.

A stubborn fire flickered across her features. "So we shall be married and never see each other's full faces?"

He blinked, having not thought of that. To him their union was for the shares; he never wondered about their relationship, of their companionship, beyond that.

"I am not ready to show you mine tonight," he admitted.

"That is fine." Kattiva tugged out of his hold. "But I am done hiding what you will one day see. What makes up all of me. You should know what you are marrying." With a small click of a latch, her eye mask fell away.

Zimri looked at a face that was much younger than he would have thought, her eyes larger than they appeared in her disguises, though they matched her full lips. What his gaze caught on the longest, however, was the puckering, twisted flesh that ran along her cheekbone under her right eye, across the bridge of her nose. A severe burn scar.

"I was eleven," said Kattiva, knowing exactly what Zimri stared at, what he was wondering. *How did this happen?* "Perhaps the beginning of my rebellion with my parents." She smiled softly, as though it was all an amusing memory now. *"If you keep playing with fire, Kattiva, you'll get burned,"* she said in a mock voice of her father. "If I had a silver coin for every time I had heard that in my youth for some trivial misbehavior . . ." She shook her head. "Well, it appears no amount of warning worked on me. I decided to take my father at his word. I played with fire, a bit too much of it in the end, and, well"—Kattiva gestured to her face—"I now have a constant reminder of the consequences of my foolish actions. I think my parents hoped it would calm me, put me back in line, but it merely sparked more fire in my heart to prove I could handle the responsibility of my actions and the ramifications of them. I would rather suffer the fate of my own mind than from the decisions of another."

The words settled like antagonizing blows to Zimri's chest.

I would rather suffer the fate of my own mind than from the decisions of another.

So much of what he suffered, he realized, was from others' decisions. His parents' passion to create Macabris, to pass it down to him, which forced his responsibility to reclaim it. He loved the club, to be sure, the memories it held for him of a mother and father he had too short a time with. It was his family's legacy, what they had made for themselves by themselves, but too often Zimri's time at Macabris was tinged with the threat of overwhelm. The barrage of emotions lifting from his guests was suffocating. Zimri thought better in smaller settings, his gifts more easily able to catch feelings and pull out secrets when alone with another.

And then there was Arabessa and her choosing not to be with him. She had given him up—them up—for him to marry another, all because she felt she needed to, that she knew better than he what he might regret.

That hot prickle of rage mixed with exhaustion swam through Zimri's gut once more.

Despite how foolish Kattiva could be, he envied her resolve to live as much of her life the way she wished as possible.

"But I understand it is an ugly part of me I will always carry." Kattiva's words shook Zimri back to where he sat beside her in her den. She played with the corner of the blanket she was wrapped in, her scar catching the fire's light as she glanced his way. "And I suppose an ugly part you'll have to look upon every now and again after we marry."

"It is not ugly," assured Zimri.

"It ruined me being perfect." Kattiva frowned. "A sentiment my mother liked to remind me of when I was younger."

"Your mother is an idiot," said Zimri.

Kattiva choked on her startled laugh. "Collector, you delight me with your candor."

"It is less candor than fact, for perfection is not real."

"Says the man who is no doubt perfect under that disguise."

"Hardly." He shook his head. "And despite what scars mark my skin, you and I both know appearance is an illusion, especially in this kingdom. Those who most deem ugly often carry beautiful souls, and those beautiful, foul ones. Perfection is a made-up construct. It is much like time: it cannot be held, and only fools would waste sands falling in an attempt to try."

Kattiva regarded him for a long moment, her brown gaze assessing. "And here I thought your best asset was in your form," she admitted. "Who knew the Collector to be so wise?"

Zimri huffed his amusement. "I do not know about being wise, but I do know that Kattiva Volkov, the creature who thrives on being different, hides her most beautiful difference of all." He placed his hand atop hers and squeezed.

With his touch, a blush rose to her pale cheeks, a gentle wafting of pleasure. "Oh my," said Kattiva. "I would be careful with your words, Collector, or you might persuade me to want to bed you after all."

Zimri laughed, a real laugh, one that warmed him, eased the tension in his shoulders.

He had not laughed like that in a turn.

"That is a lovely sound," admitted Kattiva. "You should do it more often."

"With you near, I have no doubts I shall." He lifted his hand from hers.

They shared a grin, and Zimri realized how nice it was to sit like this, with a friend. Something else he had not done in some time. The Bassettes had always been his sanctuary, his place to laugh and relax and enjoy. But his surrogate family had not been such a reprieve as of late.

"Speaking of those near," said Kattiva, "I would like to thank your friend for her help tonight."

Zimri's breath of lightness fell quickly away. "She is not a friend."

"No?" Kattiva tilted her head curiously. "You certainly seemed friendly."

Zimri remained silent.

"Ah." She gave an understanding nod. "More than friends, then."

"Perhaps once." Zimri wasn't sure why he said it, admitted to it; maybe because he felt he owed her some honesty, given that she sat before him so exposed.

"Do you wish for more again?" queried Kattiva.

"What I wish for doesn't seem to matter." The bitterness in his tone was more than apparent.

"Collector," said Kattiva, brows pinched. "Does our union affect your happiness?"

He blinked, taken aback. "What do you mean?"

"Well, as I've mentioned, you've been awfully moody as of late, and while you've always carried austerity around my family, this, in comparison, feels rather . . . sulky."

"Sulky?" he repeated, fully offended.

"I may not have your gifts, but I can still read people rather well. So yes, sulky."

"How repugnant my company must be for you, then."

Kattiva grinned, the expression scrunching up the scar along her cheek. "Your company has become my preferred."

"Then I question your taste." Zimri cut her a look. "For maudlin is certainly tiresome."

"We may argue the subject later." She waved a hand. "I'd much prefer you answer my earlier question. Does marrying me no longer suit?"

It should have been a simple answer, but for some reason Zimri's pulse tumbled with uncertainty along with his magic. Here lay a moment where he could change the current course he walked, but to what outcome? What alternate end?

Arabessa was still firm in her corner. More shares in Macabris were still held with the woman beside him.

It was the obvious answer, the responsible one, the reply that would keep intact his parents' dreams, but it still felt wrong as it left his lips. "It still suits."

Kattiva seemed to mull over his response like a sip of wine: searching for whether it tasted right. "Are you sure?" she asked.

"Macabris needs to be reclaimed under the D'Enieu name for my parents."

She nodded slowly. "Yes, for your parents, certainly. But what about for you, Collector? What do you need?"

What do I need?

Zimri's hands fisted in his lap. This *was* for him. This *was* what he needed . . . wasn't it?

"It suits," he repeated, more firmly this time.

"Very well," she said, seeming to take him at his word.

"Does it still suit you?" he had to ask.

To this Kattiva laughed. "It strangely suits me better each day. Which is why, despite your friend not being your friend, I would like to thank her for stopping my attacker."

He had wondered about Arabessa's behavior tonight. How quickly she had stepped in front of Kattiva. Quicker even than he, when she had clearly been annoyed by Kattiva's presence, been jealous. Her noble heart had still risen, her instinct to be good, to protect, even when the action would not benefit her in the end. Arabessa would always put the importance of another's life before her own, and how frustrating it was that such deeds that had torn them apart were also the very ones that had him love her all the more.

"You might have trouble finding her to do so," said Zimri. "I never know when or where she might show up."

"Yes," Kattiva mused. "That is a predicament we often suffer in this kingdom. Well, perhaps if you run into her again, you can pass on my appreciation? She saved my life, after all. I must get word to her *somehow*. My parents are afflicted with many shortcomings, but one thing they got right was teaching me to be grateful."

"Indeed." Zimri raised a questioning brow, not seeing how that fit into how he knew Zhad and Alyona to be. "Well, I shall endeavor to make sure your gratitude reaches her."

"Thank you." Kattiva placed a hand on his forearm. "Despite your sulking, you are a good one, Collector."

The touch was a friend's affection, and it warmed him. Kattiva, Zimri was realizing more and more, was a good one as well.

"Now," stated Kattiva, sitting back. "One thing my parents certainly did *not* teach me was to be skilled with a blade, like your companion. That was very impressive."

Only a glimmer of her impressiveness, thought Zimri.

"I can teach you," he said.

"Truly?"

"Of course. There are quite a few simple techniques with blades that are very effective."

"Wonderful!" She beamed. "That way I can save my own life next time and with it your extra shares in the club."

It was meant as a jest, but it pinched something uncomfortable inside Zimri nonetheless.

Perhaps because it was those very shares that were becoming less and less appealing. Here grew a burden in the place of a goal, of a sense of duty. Macabris was becoming the ghost of his parents, shifting to haunt him.

What about for you, Collector? What do you need?

Zimri was fearful that it was not what he needed but whom.

CHAPTER TWENTY-SEVEN

*A*rabessa's eyes were closed, but she saw clearly the song she spun into her music room with her cello.

Peace. Release. Forgiveness.

Violet light pulsed beneath her lids with each undulating wave of her deep vibrato. The dusting of her gifts as the full and gentle chords she drew out washed over her skin. Her fingers pressed with a mother's care to the strings along her fingerboard, her cello cradled within her arms, its hips nestled between her knees. Her head swayed along with the melody she set free.

Time did not exist in these grain falls. Thoughts beyond the way the notes flowed into the air to thread back into her heart were of no consequence. Arabessa was alone: no audience, no sisters, no watchful king, no purpose for her playing besides her own need for solace. To empty the emotions compounded within her heart.

She never repeated the pieces she played for herself. They were created for this moment alone. Her confessions. Her diary of feeling she needed to sonorously spill into an empty room, a burden leaving her shoulders, yearning lifting from her chest.

The buildup over the past weeks, the worry of tests to pass, secrets kept from her sisters, the Mousai ending, seeing Zimri with Kattiva, the preparation to perform at their ball, along with proving herself worthy to her father, to the throne: it was too much to hold together, and Arabessa had been starved for the reprieve of her music room in Jabari. A safe place to play it all away.

With a final pull of her bow over string, fingers pressed down to release a silky end to her song, Arabessa opened her eyes.

Purple trails of her magic dissipated between the dust motes dancing in the sunlight that spilled through the windows in front of her. Her hands prickled with her magic settling back inside her blood.

Rest, it purred. *Happy,* it sighed.

Arabessa breathed in her own contentment. The view beyond her window was the cascading of terra-cotta roofs down the hill of her city of birth. Birds flittered past, and in the distance sounded the chime of bells: a prayer session to the lost gods ending. Arabessa had missed Jabari. Here it was easy to forget what lay waiting in a caved kingdom through a portal door. Here her mask did not press into her skin along with the pressure of what she hid beneath. Here she could look to the sky and not constantly see the countdown dimming glow of stars. Of her future, her fate, waiting to be written. It was no doubt why Dolion had kept their home here: to give them all a place of light to chase away the shadows.

"I've missed catching you playing like this." A familiar deep voice had Arabessa's heart jolt, and she twisted to find Zimri leaning against the doorframe to her music room. He appeared a languid tiger, gazing at her from where he stood, eyes assessing, muscles evident beneath his fitted clothes. Per usual, he was impeccably dressed in deep royal blue that complemented his black skin, his cravat pinned in the center with a ruby.

A heat unfurled in Arabessa's stomach as he approached.

"I distinctly remember shutting that door," she said.

"Your memory serves, but you remembering to lock it does not." He came to stand beside her piano, only paces away. He tinkled the keys idly. "And as our past has proved," he went on, looking over to her with a dangerous glint, "an unlocked door is as good as an invitation inside."

She tried to ignore the fluttering in her belly that accompanied his words, that awoke sentiments shared by him the other night.

If there was a way to still convince you to say yes, I would hunt it down.

The sight of his strong hands grazing the delicate piano keys helped little in her endeavors. It merely pushed forward memories of Zimri similarly playing his gentle touch along her body to arouse sound. This music room was her haven, decorated in rich, deep colors, but it was also a room filled with a history of the two people now in it.

Zimri always loved to watch her play, and she certainly enjoyed his audience.

It is how I can hear what you too often do not say, he had told her once. *Your music is your language, Arabessa, and I could listen for eternity to your words.*

"Have you come to speak with my father?" she asked, wanting to push the conversation away from closed doors, locked or not. "I fear he is not at home at the moment."

"I came to speak with you." He stepped away from the piano, approaching.

"Oh?" She feigned casualness, though a heated rush danced through her, watching him draw near. She placed her bow in its case, which rested on a nearby table, cello still between her legs as she looked up to where he stopped in front of her.

The sun streaming into the windows outlined his broad shoulders.

"I wanted to thank you," he said. "For what you did for Kattiva the other night."

A tight grip to her chest followed by a wash of disappointment. Arabessa wasn't sure what she had expected him to say, but it wasn't this. Wasn't for him to talk of Kattiva. The woman she had watched Zimri hold protectively in his arms, clear concern for her in his gaze.

A hot lick of jealousy had torn through her then as well as now at the memory.

"It was nothing," said Arabessa, rubbing at a smudge along the neck of her cello.

"It was *not* nothing. You saved her life."

"*Possibly* saved," she countered, glancing back at him. "We do not know whether the attack would have been fatal."

Zimri huffed a laugh. "Always fighting the point, even when it's one that compliments you."

"I merely do not want to be painted a hero when you no doubt would have done the same. Or anyone else capable, for that matter."

He regarded her, his hazel eyes searching. "All right," he said. "Either way, know appreciation is felt on my behalf and hers."

A knot too large to swallow formed in Arabessa's throat.

On my behalf and hers.

A sentence spoken by a future husband, indeed.

Arabessa merely nodded.

Silence stretched through the room, but Zimri did not move from standing in front of her or offer more conversation. He kept his attention pinned to her, as though he was studying every outline to later recall, or perhaps to never forget. It left Arabessa with a sick ache. She did not want to be forgotten.

"Was there something else you needed?" she eventually asked, unable to handle his examining any longer.

"Despite all the resplendent costumes you have worn when performing," said Zimri, as though he had not heard her question but spoke a private thought, "you are always the most stunning when you play like this." He stepped closer, and Arabessa stopped breathing as he bent to graze his fingers down her loose braid, which was draped to one side. "When you play for yourself."

Arabessa sensed the blush to her cheeks, the warmth to her chest beneath her casual gown, before it was followed by a chill of anguish.

"Zimri," she said, voice hushed, pained, her grip on her cello tightening. "You cannot say such things."

His expression dripped with danger, a challenge. "But I have."

Yes, she thought as warnings spun through her blood. *You have, and now my heart cannot unhear it.*

"And do you also speak as such to your betrothed?" It was a low blow, she knew, a reality she had pushed him toward, but she needed him to step away. She needed him not so close. His familiar scent only goaded her to pull him even closer. To pull him to her lips.

Her comment did the trick, for Zimri's features hardened, cooled, as he stood back to his full height, dropping her braid.

"You very well know my agreement with Kattiva is that and nothing more," he said, tone the sharp edge of a knife. "Why do you feel the need to talk as though it isn't?"

Arabessa looked away, to a spot in the corner where a bouquet of anthurium stood bright. She tried quickly to douse the rippling of desire that still swirled through her body. That *he* caused to swirl.

"I do it so I do not act in other ways," she admitted.

Zimri remained very still. "And do you want to act in other ways?"

"You very well know I do," she said with slight exasperation, moving her cello from between her legs so she could stand. She needed to get farther from him. "I'm sure I am a puff of all my emotions around you, despite how I wish not to be."

Zimri seized her arm, keeping her dangerously close. His attention dipped to her lips, eyes shadowing with hunger, his grip tightening, jaw muscle flexing. "Then do them." His words came out a soft rumble, the very definition of temptation. "Act on every desire you have for me, Arabessa. They are assuredly no match for the desires I have for you."

Her magic crackled through her, flames erupting where he held her. *Yesssss,* her gifts crooned. *Let us play him. Let him play us.*

By the lost gods, how she wanted that. Needed that. Zimri was always her safe place to unravel. Within his arms, under his caring, caressing hands. He settled her into the present, his magic a gentle lapping of waves to her internal churning worry, tangle of responsibility. She missed floating within his calm. Having him conduct her.

"But then what?" she forced herself to ask as she pulled free. Neither of them stepped away, however. "You will still marry another at the end of the Star Eclipse."

"Yes, but it is in name only," said Zimri with frustration. "You heard Kattiva. I am available. Available only for you." His tone was a rumble of need, desperate for her to understand. "We *can* have it all. We can be together and have the protection of my marriage to keep eyes away from you. To keep you and the Mousai safe. I can have majority ownership in Macabris. And besides your family, our union would be a secret to all others. The other night's attack clearly proved you were right regarding the dangers in the Thief Kingdom when it comes to who I am involved with publicly. The Collector and you shall never be connected."

The Collector and you shall never be connected.

It was a sentiment full of sense, but it still burned to hear.

Because though she would have him in private, he still would have another on his arm in public. Arabessa might hold his heart, but Kattiva would forever hold his name.

The twist of jealousy she had felt from seeing Kattiva clinging to him the other night roared once more.

"I would still be a mistress," she said.

"And many love their mistresses," he countered. "But do not get caught up in titles. What you are to me is more than a wife or a lover. You are my whole heart, Arabessa. Surely the past days have proved us being apart is not an option. At least not for me."

As she looked into his stunning face, felt the power of him, breathed in his familiarity, his words coiled into her resolve, threatening to snap it to smithereens.

Yes, thought Arabessa. It had been unbearable. Like she had been walking around half a person, half a heart.

Could Zimri be right? Could they do this? The lost gods knew she and her sisters had not lived a conventional life. Why start now?

Because of your next tests, hissed that voice of responsibility inside her. *The throne. The engagement ball. Distractions kill. Distractions lose. You could lose. You could die. Not now. Not now. Not now. Later. Decide later.*

"Or I could end my agreement with Kattiva today," said Zimri, snapping her out of her thoughts.

"Don't be ridiculous." She frowned.

"I'm being completely serious."

"But what of Macabris?"

Zimri's face twisted, annoyed, a strange look flickering through his eyes before he turned from her. He stared out the window. "I have already told you. In time, another opportunity will present itself. And if not"—he shrugged—"perhaps my future is not from what my parents built but from what I can build."

Shock rocked through her. "What are you talking about? You've wanted to reclaim Macabris for so long."

"Wants change," he said. "People change."

Arabessa stared at him, confused. Where was this coming from? How could a goal he had longed for since a young boy, a promise he had made to his parents, so quickly dissolve?

The same way your goals have changed, said a voice inside her. *Your duty.*

Arabessa shook away the thought, not wanting to see the similarities. "So what are you saying?"

Zimri let out a long sigh, scrubbing a hand down his face. "I don't know. I'm merely trying to make the point that my decisions are mine to make, and how I might acquire more of Macabris is not one for *you* to make."

She blinked, momentarily taken aback. That was not what Arabessa had intended to do. "No," she began. "No, it is not for me to make, but what *is* my decision is whether or not I support the opportunity you have now. And I truly believe you should take it. You have waited for six years for such a one to arise."

"But you will not have me if I do," he implored, brows drawn in with anger.

She was quiet for a turn; her maddening confusion over what she wanted versus what she needed versus what she should do mixed into a muddy mess. What was the correct way forward? The responsible one? They were now in the Waning Sky phase within the kingdom, her second test ready to pluck her into its chaos at any moment. She still could be sent to the Fade before the end of the Star Eclipse. Still had to play at Zimri's engagement ball. Still had to figure out a way to tell her sisters of the Mousai. And if she and Zimri were to reunite now, how would she share with him *her* new goal? Her new ambition that could cost her life: becoming the next Thief King.

Distractions.

Distractions kill.

Distractions lose.

Later.

Decide later.

"I do not know what I will or won't have at the end of the Star Eclipse," said Arabessa. The weight she had tried to rid herself of by playing her cello returned tenfold. "But what I do know is right now, with your engagement ball coming up and the Mousai performing at it, I think it best if we remain on our present course and learn to become friends."

Zimri's gaze snapped to hers. *"Friends?"*

She nodded. "We once were just that, Zimri. Surely we can be again."

"We were children at the time," he pointed out dryly, "who did not yet comprehend what it meant to be *more* than friends."

"Perhaps, but I . . . *we* need to get through this next part without casualties. And this"—she gestured between them—"feels ripe with casualties if we were to give in to what we want to do right now without thought of the consequences. I do not want you to regret breaking things off with Kattiva. And I do not want to lose focus during my next performance."

Or my next test for the throne.

Arabessa needed to stay on alert, and being with Zimri, captivated by him, was not smart. For his sake as well as her family's, and most certainly for herself. "Nothing good comes from rash decisions," she went on. "Look at Niya's history."

"I'd rather not." Zimri pursed his lips.

His response caused Arabessa to smile. "You know I am right, though."

"I know you make me more frustrated than any other soul in Aadilor."

"Oh dear," she said teasingly. "Not a good start to a friendship, I'd imagine."

Zimri cut her a pointed glance. "Not ideal, no."

"But it is better than not ever seeing one another again, wouldn't you say?"

His gaze narrowed, and Arabessa watched, skin heating, as his attention fell to her mouth, on what felt like his intended next meal, before he again met her gaze. "Fine," said Zimri, a bit of dark mockery in his voice. "We shall see how we do as friends."

CHAPTER TWENTY-EIGHT

The carriage bounced with vigor along the cobblestone streets, merely agitating further Arabessa's nerves. It was an uneven clomping rhythm disturbing settled sediment. She was not accustomed to suffering such a state before a performance, which only caused her to grow irritable for suffering it now. Not the most choice of moods to arrive at the engagement ball of an ex-lover with the intention of redeeming past behavior, but certainly understandable.

With their coach windows drawn shut, she and her sisters were given the privacy required to travel within the Thief Kingdom maskless. A reprieve met only with a disadvantage, as Arabessa could not see how near they might be to Macabris. The ride felt as though it was going on for eternity.

"We will be in and out," reassured Niya from where she sat beside Arabessa, Larkyra swaying on the bench across from them.

"Yes." Larkyra nodded. "We have arranged it so we are to arrive just when we are meant to entertain. Then we'll be directly back in this coach heading home."

"Thank you," said Arabessa, her mounting tension easing slightly. But only just. There had been no use in pretending she wasn't still distraught by the prospect of tonight, even with her and Zimri's new truce of friendship from the other day. And her sisters might be foolish, but they certainly were not stupid. They knew she could not stand to organize tonight's event. Quickly did they take the reins on planning this evening's proceedings. "I truly appreciate you both handling the details of tonight," said Arabessa. "I know I am usually the one to manage these affairs, but this . . ."

Was too much.

"Ara, we love you." Larkyra leaned forward, placing a gloved hand on her knee. "You do not have to thank us for doing a job that you have done for us our whole lives."

"Especially when we have never thanked you once for doing it," added Niya.

"You can remedy that, you know," Arabessa pointed out, appreciative for the distractive sparring.

"Yes, I suppose we could," mused Niya, "but why break old habits now?"

"So you can practice new habits?" suggested Arabessa, brows rising.

"I'm rather content in my ways," admitted Niya, stroking the gold mask in her lap. They each held their signature Mousai disguises, their full complicated costumes hidden under their black robes, headdresses for tonight in the cases tied atop the carriage. "But if Larkyra wants to change for the both of us, I give her my full support."

"That surely is a new habit you are practicing now," quipped Larkyra. "For you have never given me your support, let alone your *full* support."

"Well, never before have you made me look good by doing so," explained Niya.

Arabessa smiled as the two went shot for shot, a blessed lightness entering her chest for the first time in many days.

Thank the lost gods for fickle sisters, she thought.

While Arabessa was glad she and Zimri had been able to air out their issues, she had most certainly left their meeting from the other day frazzled and physically frustrated. They had agreed to a friendship, and while their relationship had always held that, what she needed, though, was to not be as attracted to or in love with her friend.

That would certainly make tonight a lot easier. And every night without him easier.

Arabessa breathed through the tight grip in her chest. *This was my suggestion,* she reminded herself, *my action to cause these ripples.* It was her responsibility to find a way to live with it.

And with her sisters by her side, their continuing prattling surrounding her now, perhaps she could get by tonight as intended: without casualties.

Arabessa merely needed to remember who she was. What she had already achieved. Her decades of practiced restraint carved into her spine. Her countless past performances where she had held it together, tortures she had orchestrated down to the final scream.

Arabessa would get through tonight the same way she had gotten through any other hardship: because she had to.

Just as she had survived her first test, she would survive this.

"We're here," announced Niya from where she had pulled back a sliver of curtain to peek outside. Soon the carriage slowed.

Arabessa took in a deep breath, steadying the quickly ignited buzz of her gifts through her veins.

Tonight we play, we play, we play, they sang excitedly through her. *Tonight we will be set free.*

Only so much, Arabessa warned before she and her sisters settled their gold masks into place.

She rapped for their driver to open their door. The noise of the Betting District cascaded in just as they stepped out.

The celebrations taking place in Macabris could be heard even through the thick walls of the room where Arabessa and her sisters waited. It was one of the lounges, created for members to smoke or drink and sit comfortably in front of a fire before returning to the gambling tables or dipping pools or basement brawls. A place of calm in the midst of swirling movement.

Presently, it had been cleared out, meant only for the Mousai and their sightless attendants.

Arabessa held still, doing her very best to channel a tranquil demeanor while her corset was tightened and her headdress was situated securely against her scalp. The pain was a nuisance, but it helped ground her to the present. She was not her emotions in her heart but the sensations taking place along her skin.

"Mistresses." One of their cloaked attendants bobbed a curtsy in front of them. "The ancient one, Achak, wishes to speak with you before you go on. Shall we invite them in?"

"Of course you shall," said Achak in sister form as she strode past the two large bodyguards stationed at the side entrance. They were meant to block any unapproved visitors, but a quick snap of Achak's fingers was all it took to prompt their escorts to bow. "And we take offense to the mention of our age," she said, coming to stand before Arabessa and her sisters. "We are wise, yes, experienced, certainly, but *ancient* makes it seem as though we are weak, and we can assure you"— Achak looked toward the attendant who had spoken earlier—"we are furthest from weak."

The servant bowed with their apology, a nervous flush blossoming along their exposed neck. "Forgive me, wise one."

"Pay them no mind, dear," advised Arabessa to her helper. "Achak suffers from warped realities due to their advanced age."

A bark of a laugh filtered out of Achak, who draped herself across a nearby settee, her gold gown rippling around her feet. "You should be thankful my brother is not here," she said. "He would never find such offensive sentiments amusing."

"Your brother hides, no doubt," began Niya from where she stood beside Arabessa, getting similarly adorned in her costume, "because he could never pull off such a delicious dress. Where did you get this garment?"

"I shall never tell you," assured Achak, "or it will go out of style instantly."

Larkyra snorted a laugh from behind Niya while Arabessa bit hers back.

Niya merely pursed her lips, unamused.

"We are done, mistresses." Their attendants stepped to the side. Though without sight, they held precious gifts others did not: heightened senses. Their ability to notice details and capture a vastness of understanding in a simple graze of their fingertips was unparalleled.

"Thank you," said Arabessa. "You may leave us." As their staff hurried out, she glanced from beneath her shrouded headdress to study her and her sisters' costumes. She wore an emerald-green gown and Niya a black, while Larkyra was wrapped in a deep cobalt. None of their white skin showed. Parts that were on display were colored to match their costumes, nails included. Each a weaving and threading and stitching of nuanced opulence, all capturing an embroidery of glowing stars. The Thief Kingdom's night sky.

Tonight would be their Star Eclipse performance that had been meant for the week prior.

This evening Arabessa *would* have them play a celebration.

A celebration of the Collector and Kattiva's union.

Arabessa's pulse flared in beats of doubt, of heartache and mourning bubbling to the surface.

No. She stomped it down. *Tonight I am part of the Mousai. I am not Arabessa Bassette. I am not an ex-lover. I am not a friend. I have no past. I have no emotion. I am a creature created to conduct this trio.*

"You look marvelous," said Achak as she stood, her shaved head gleaming in the candelabras' light as she took them in. She had dusted gold along her smooth black skin. The effect, along with her dress, had her appear like a dipped statue of a lost god. "Shall I introduce you now?"

Arabessa nodded, her words caught in her throat with the realization that this was it. She was about to perform for the guests of Zimri and his future wife.

Could she do it? Could she push away the grip of grief on her heart?

I think it best if we remain on our present course and learn to become friends.

Her own words floated forward as a reminder of why she stood where she did.

Friends.

He was her friend.

That was what she had wanted. What she had asked for. She needed to stay her course, needed to stay focused on the bigger game she was playing, the throne she was angling for, the danger she had invited into her life. *After the Star Eclipse,* she silently recounted. *After I prove I am worthy, like my mother, like my father. After I make a future for myself. After Zimri gets what he wants in Macabris.* Then and only then could she entertain what it would be like to be a mistress.

There was a touch to Arabessa's arm, and she blinked to the awaiting room, finding Achak had neared. Her violet eyes spun with worlds not found in Aadilor. "You will be magnificent," she said. "You *are* magnificent."

"Thank you," said Niya, stepping closer to Arabessa. "That is kind of you to say."

Achak arched a brow in her direction. "I wasn't talking to you."

"You mentioned being magnificent," said Niya. "So of course you were."

"You always know how to ruin a moment," huffed Larkyra as she mimicked Achak and placed a supportive hand on Arabessa's shoulder.

"I know how to make light of one," quipped Niya, adding a third touch to Arabessa. "Which could be argued to make many moments better."

"If they start out with you around," stated Larkyra, "your argument is already lost."

"How did I ever succeed in teaching you three anything?" Achak shook her head.

"I'm not sure," began Arabessa, "but could you all remove your hands from me now? I feel like I'm about to be hauled away to the dungeons."

"It was meant to be a reassuring gesture." Niya frowned as they dropped their arms.

"One, I repeat, that you ruined," countered Larkyra.

"Let us argue the point later." Arabessa stepped from their claustrophobic circle to pick up her cello. "We have a crowd waiting." The feel of the sturdy neck in her grasp and lightness of the bow between her fingers grounded her.

Time to play. Her magic jumped to her hands, a prickling of excitement. *Time to make the room ours.*

"I will leave to announce you," said Achak. "But before I do, I did have something to share." She looked pointedly at Arabessa. "Something I hope can help occupy minds in an advantageous way while performing."

"Yes?" asked Arabessa, her intrigue skipping.

"There are only two," said Achak.

For a beat Arabessa had no idea what to glean from such a random statement. And then—

Her breathing quickened, realization falling fast.

There were only two.

Only two contestants left.

Only two in my way to claim the throne.

Arabessa was a step closer, her chance materializing as a real possibility. She felt a burning validation that her decision with Zimri had been a sound one. For them to wait, for her to survive these tests so she could then think of their future.

"What in all of Aadilor does that mean?" asked Niya. "Only two what?"

"I shall see you girls out there," said Achak by way of an answer as she turned and left through the side door from which she had entered.

"I think Achak's age is starting to get the better of them," muttered Niya as she and Larkyra gathered around Arabessa where she waited by the closed double doors.

"It was a rather odd note to leave on," admitted Larkyra. "Do you know what it means?" she asked Arabessa.

"Achak is filled with riddles," she said, facing forward, heart still pounding in excitement. She did not want to lie to her sisters, but now certainly was not the time to attempt an explanation as to what the twins had been referring. "We can worry about untangling their words later. Presently, I suggest you prepare yourselves, for we are about to go on."

"Are you prepared to go on?" asked Niya softly as they each pressed closer.

Her question sent a ripple of tension through Arabessa, but it was now a feather's touch compared to the determination spinning through her heart.

"I am," she said. "I'm prepared for all of it."

As the doors swung open, spilling in the spotlight trained to where they stood, Arabessa did not search for where Zimri might be watching. Her attention remained straight ahead, on the empty platform that waited.

Tonight she would master this performance as she had her last test. As she had with her temptations to fall back into Zimri's arms.

Arabessa would prove to her father she could be more than her emotions and prove to herself she could, like both her parents, be king.

CHAPTER TWENTY-NINE

*T*he room hung in silence as Arabessa pulled the final chords from her cello. Its purple melody stretched into the room, a colorful cloud of celebration dissipating along with the last echo of Larkyra's song and vibration of Niya's movements. Their performance was finished.

And no one screamed.

In a wave, Macabris erupted in cheers. From the main floor to the two ringing balconies, guests shouted their praise and love and awe.

Arabessa let out what felt like her first real breath since entering this building. She had done it; she had conducted perfectly. The Mousai had spun the room with light and joy and new beginnings. They had played a performance of hope and happiness, and its effects sparkled through the club. With heartbeat racing, Arabessa's magic preened and bubbled in her veins at the crowd's surrounding reverence. With the spotlight still pinned to them, she gazed out to the silhouetted mass as she lowered her cello's bow.

Her sisters gathered behind her as she stood to give a collective bow.

Arabessa smiled from beneath her masked headdress. She had done it. She had remained in control. She had made it through this punishment, and she was bloody proud of that. Dare she even admit she felt happy?

The spotlight flickered out from above as the hanging candelabras were relit, bringing the soaring space into full sight. The gambling tables had been pushed aside to make way for a larger dance floor and an even larger buffet in the back. A queue had begun to form in front of them, guests daring to speak with the Mousai and offer their compliments.

But Arabessa saw these details only in her periphery, for her gaze had instantly snagged on the couple directly across the room, who sat on their own raised platform. Kattiva Volkov and the Collector were poised together on a velvet couch. Kattiva fanned herself as she leaned over to talk with a companion sitting by her feet. Her grin was radiant beneath her half mask, matching her salacious gown and husky laugh, which floated through the air. Arabessa hardly spared her a glance, however, for the man at her side was anything but smiling.

Zimri's eyes burned from beneath his maroon mask, his attention solely on her. His lips were pressed tight, scruff-filled jaw sharp as tension radiated from his entire form. His black-gloved hand gripped his armrest, his magic curling gold around him, a haze of warning. But Arabessa did not exactly know for what. She only felt heat pooling low in her belly, taking in the way he was consuming her from a distance, the way he was every bit the dark prince of this domain, the tempter of pleasure and gluttony and decadence. Here sat the Collector who had collected many secrets of those in the room, hers included. Zimri regarded her as though he knew one in particular he wished to leverage now. Nothing of friendship was in his shrouded expression.

A shiver ran the length of Arabessa.

Dark desires.

Ones that were plunged into ice water when Zimri abruptly stood, stepping from his dais and striding from the room.

Arabessa angled her head to see where he might be going, heartbeat racing with the desire to follow. She of course stood rooted still, watching the imposing figure of the Collector disappear from her view.

Arabessa swallowed past the discomfort tightening in her throat.

Was Zimri okay?

Had she done something wrong?

Whatever had him stalking away, she needed to find out.

She hated for him to suffer. Hated that she could be the cause, again.

Perhaps something had happened since their last encounter. Something he needed to unburden on another that he trusted.

A friend.

Arabessa settled on this thought.

She would go to him later tonight.

After all, this was a perfect first chance to prove their new relationship. And as she had already proved she could stay in control this evening, surely she could master her emotions once more.

For a friend.

The Betting District was no less packed despite the indecently late hour. Arabessa slunk through the masses unnoticed in her plain black trousers and brown hooded cloak. Her blades were strapped securely along her sides, flute holstered at the ready on her forearm. Her skin felt flushed beneath her leather mask from her quickness to return to this part of town, but her strides were even, her breathing calm.

Arabessa was a thief on a mission, and it set her emotions to glide smooth. Tonight she would reenter Macabris, but not through the door. She would break into the private apartments of the Collector. And not for the first time.

Arabessa traveled past carts that wafted the scent of fried rice cakes, through a tangle of onlookers watching a heated dice game, to find a boisterous line that had gathered outside Macabris. The engagement party seemed to have escalated since the Mousai's exit, and it appeared regular patrons were being invited to take a peek inside. A decision from

Kattiva, no doubt, but the havoc it created at the entrance was all the better for Arabessa.

The guards had their hands more than full, taking no interest in a shadow dancing up the side gate to land in the private alley along the exclusive club.

The sounds of the main street softened as Arabessa wove out of the lamplight peppering down the thin lane. Her magic skipped with excitement as she came to a storm drain running the height of the building. It did not rain in the Thief Kingdom, but glowworms did fall regularly, and the washing of roofs was a common maintenance among those who could afford it.

Hooking her hands around the sturdy metal, Arabessa began to climb. Her arm muscles burned along with her thighs as she reached the top, pulling herself up to balance on the thin landing. Large glass windows stretched where she stood, a view into the private apartments of the Collector. Here was his bedroom, dark, empty. Arabessa's pulse pitched faster as she moved toward the glow of firelight farther down, her cloak fluttering at her back.

Her gifts skipped through her veins as she peered into a study to find Zimri slumped on a couch before a large fire. He faced her, but his eyes studied the flames before him, expression distant as he sipped from a glass. He was still in his clothes from earlier, but his mask was a forgotten accessory on the carpet by his booted feet.

Arabessa stood there watching him for an indecently long time, the echo of busy streets forgotten far below. It was rare she got to be the voyeur, and a dark part of herself reveled in it. She felt like the hunter tonight, the silent gust of wind, studying the man who usually studied her.

Zimri was devastatingly handsome. His nose strong, his jaw angled to perfection, but it was his eyes that stopped many. Not because of their color but because of what they saw, how they looked at another: openly, empathetically. Whether it was because of his gifts or his true nature, it did not matter. All Arabessa knew was that he could put many a soul to find peace just by being in his presence.

But every coin had another side, and she had witnessed such calm turn to crippling sorrow under his emotional ministrations. If the Collector could not get what he wanted with pleasure, he squeezed it out with pain. Just like the Mousai.

Arabessa's heart stopped as his gaze suddenly hooked to her.

Zimri did not move or get up to let her in. He just watched her watching him, and a lick of flames cascaded down her skin. She was on a precipice, and not just because she stood on a ledge. Arabessa was in a moment that had a distinct before and after, and she had a quick panic of doubt that perhaps this was not the best idea after all.

But she was here, on the other side of his window, many floors up.

And she was not one to retreat.

Taking out her blade, she jammed it into one of the windowpanes on hinges and pried it open. Arabessa left her doubts outside as she climbed in.

CHAPTER THIRTY

imri watched Arabessa approach from the dark like a phantom. A specter added to the visions of his parents who roamed these private apartments above Macabris.

She stopped before him, the fire running a soft glow along her brown cloak, hood pulled down to reveal her raven hair braided to one side. Her eye mask was dark, but the blue eyes beneath were bright.

"Are you real?" he asked, his glass of whiskey poised at his lips.

"Are you drunk?" she countered, head tilting appraisingly.

"Not nearly as drunk as I'd like." He took a sip, relishing the burn, the way his thoughts of this very woman and her earlier performance softened to a blur.

He had left the ball as soon as they had given their final bow, and he was of a mind to not see anyone anytime soon. *Especially* not her.

"What's wrong?" She came to sit beside him, the couch shifting with her new weight. He did not like it. Her being so close. He wanted to fall into her lap, lay down his head, and have her stroke his cheek as she had once done many times before in this room.

But they weren't in the past. They were here. As *friends*.

Zimri scoffed at the ridiculous idea before asking, "What are you doing here?"

"I saw you leave after our performance," explained Arabessa. "You seemed . . . distraught, so I wanted to make sure everything was all right. That's what friends do, is it not?"

Friends.

He was growing to loathe the word.

"Well"—he gestured to his general disposition—"you can see that everything is in order. You may be on your way."

"Are you angry with me?" she asked, worry clear in her voice.

Zimri looked over at her, considering the question.

The Mousai's performance tonight was unrivaled, unraveling.

Arabessa had birthed pure euphoria from her cello, and his euphoria was to be with her. But it had not just been the effects of her and her sisters' spell that gripped him. It was knowing with utter clarity what it was like to be as her instrument: between her legs, held in her arms, inspiring her eyes to roll back, her body to sway and fingers to play along his back.

He had been drowning not in happiness but in pure white-hot lust. Like a pubescent boy he had grown stiff beneath his trousers. For the Obasi Sea's sake, Zimri had needed to dig his fingers into his armrests to near pain to keep from charging the stage and taking Arabessa right then and there. To stop himself from seducing her to open wide for him and all their guests to see.

Kattiva certainly wouldn't have minded.

But it was not at all the reaction of a *friend.*

"I am not angry with you, silly," he said, lifting an arm that felt entirely too heavy to boop her on her masked nose. "I'm angry with me."

Arabessa frowned. "You really are drunk."

"Would you like to be as well? I've got a bottle and a glass right over there." He waved a hand in the direction of his spirits cart. "But I don't need to tell you that, of course. You are more than well acquainted with these rooms."

Arabessa twisted her lips to the side, eyes narrowing, before she stood, going to the cart. When she returned, she plucked the glass from his hands to trade it with another.

"You know I do not care for clear spirits," he said.

"Then it is good that is water."

"Even worse." He scrunched his nose as he leaned forward to discard it on the table beside him.

"Drink it or I shall keep pouring you more until you do."

"And I shall merely keep placing them there," he said. "You'll run out of glasses eventually."

"Don't test my patience, Zimri."

"Or what?" He cocked a brow. "You'll spank me?"

She blinked at him, clearly startled by his words.

Good, he thought. *Be so startled you'll leave.*

But then a grin twisted onto her face, and he quickly grew uneasy. He knew such a look from a Bassette, and it was followed only by unwelcome mischief.

"Yes," declared Arabessa. "That's exactly what I'll do."

"I beg your pardon?"

"You need a good spanking, Collector." She pulled at his arm, attempting to spill him onto her lap.

"Absolutely not." Zimri jumped back, nearly knocking the nearby table and glass of water over. "The only spanking happening will be from me to you when you beg for it."

Quiet fell like the plunge of a knife, sharp and painful.

Arabessa's neck blushed red, her emotions radiating from her with a mix of fear and excitement. Her mouth opened, but no words came out, only a quick inhale.

Zimri's knee-jerk reaction was to apologize. He had not meant to say such a thing out loud, not that such an act had not been experienced between them before. But perhaps that was the problem. Many an indecent act had been experienced and enjoyed. Many he wanted to do right now.

But she had asked for friendship, a truce so they could remain in each other's lives while they worked out if and when they could be more.

Zimri wanted that too. He wanted more.

Which was why Arabessa being here was of no good. Not when he was a few drinks deep. Not when he was seeing her on the tails of a performance when he could still taste her power. Savory and fragrant and entirely too delicious. It had become a need for both of them after a performance to come together for an encore. To allow their release of tension to be devoured by the other, held and smoothed out.

It was too dangerous for her to be here with neither of them able to offer such a reprieve.

But if she wasn't going to leave, he would.

"I need to go to bed." He stood abruptly, finding himself slightly unsteady on his feet.

"Let me help you."

"No, thank you." He pushed her arm from where it was angled to wrap around his waist. By the Fade, the last thing he needed was Arabessa any closer. "I can get to my bed on my own."

Zimri strode from his study, brushing a hand along the wall as guidance through the following hall and into his bedchamber.

It was dark, the only glow from the waning stars outside, but he knew the way to his bed with his eyes closed, which, thank the lost gods, was where they were about to be.

Zimri collapsed onto his soft sheets, letting out a moan.

Behind him was the catch of a match lighting, a gentle warmth filling the room as candles were lit, before a clink of a glass being placed on his side table.

"If that is water, I will pour it over your head," he mumbled.

A soft laugh that felt better than it should to hear. "If you drink the entire thing," said Arabessa, "I promise to leave."

He turned his head so he could look at her. She stood hovering above, cloak draping her shoulders, her mask now off, features soft but holding a whisper of worry in her brow.

She worried about him.

Cared for him.

She had come here to see if he was all right after he had walked out from his own engagement ball. One in which she had performed. Had been forced to perform at. To please his betrothed and complete a punishment from her king. Arabessa had done all that and still was before him, kind, considerate, selfless.

Zimri's chest tightened with disappointment in himself but also in their situation.

"Give it here," he said, sitting up, kicking his feet to the floor.

She gave him the glass, a waft of relief floating forward.

He drank the whole thing, the liquid cool, an instant clearing of his mind.

Blast if she wasn't right to force me to drink this.

"Good boy," said Arabessa, taking the empty cup to place it back on the table.

Zimri glared at her. "I shall not be patronized in my own home."

"I apologize." There was a hint of a smile in her voice. "I'm just so very proud of you for drinking all of your water."

His gaze narrowed further right before he tugged her to the bed. She squeaked her surprise. "I fear that sarcasm is just as bad of an offense," he declared, attempting to position her across his knee. "And I also fear I must punish such insolence as you wished to punish me."

"You shall do no such thing!" Arabessa knocked his arms away before twisting on top of him. But they had both been trained in fighting by the same teacher, so Zimri soon found himself her better. Not for long, of course, before they flipped from top to bottom, tussling across his bed.

There was the sound of metal being pulled free before the prick of a knife was brought to his throat. "Truce! Truce!" exclaimed Zimri, one hand palm up, the other pinned beneath her arm. He lay under her. "No one said anything about knives being allowed," he protested.

"Knives are always allowed."

"Noted for next time."

Arabessa smiled down at him, her body draped across his as they held each other's stare. The hiss of a sandglass somewhere in the room filled the space, in which neither of them moved. Her blade's tip was still angled at his racing pulse, but he did not care.

In fact, he hardly wanted to breathe to bring her awareness to how they were situated.

All he wanted was to remove their clothes so he could better feel her curves and breasts and move his open hand to glide down to her bottom and pull her tighter to him.

Her braid draped forward against his arm; her chest pushed into his with each of her shallow breaths. She was a lost goddess come to torture him. Her eyes fell to his mouth.

Heat pooled low in his groin, followed by a flash of anguish when she blinked her gaze clear, angling to push away.

"Stay." His hand came to her hip, gripping to keep her from leaving.

"Zimri," she said, a hushed plea.

Her knife was still by his throat.

"I hate being your friend," he admitted.

Her gaze roamed over him, brows pinching in. "No, you don't."

"Yes, I do. You are by far the worst friend I have ever had."

A glint of amusement dashed away her frown. "I'm sorry to hear that."

"I am not."

"No?"

He shook his head. As much as he could, anyway, without getting stabbed. "You are much better being more than that."

"I don't know," she said thoughtfully. "I can recall quite a few complaints from you when I was more."

"You obviously are not remembering it right."

"On the contrary, I have a great memory," argued Arabessa.

"Not as good as mine," said Zimri. "And I can prove it."

"How?"

He glanced to her lips, full and open and perfect. Every drink he'd had tonight evaporated from his veins as his magic surged through them with his need. "Let me touch you and you'll see."

Everything became very still very fast. Arabessa's breath seemed to hold as her body poured desire straight into him, warm and fragrant and torturous.

"You are touching me," she whispered.

"Not in the way you and I both would like."

"We can't," she said, but the protest was barely that.

"We can," he reassured. "For tonight, at the very least."

She did not answer him, merely grew tense as an obvious swirl of thoughts and conflicts rushed through her mind.

Do not think, he wanted to tell her. *Do not worry with me.*

"My music." Zimri brought his hand from her hip to glide it along her jaw. "Let me remind you how much better we are when we can be more."

Arabessa's eyes fluttered closed for a beat as she leaned into his touch. "And come tomorrow, when I cannot forget?" she asked in pain.

"Know that I could never forget in the first place," answered Zimri. "The memories of us are forever a part of my soul. They are the only thoughts that have kept my heart beating these past weeks. I could never forget a single moment with you, Arabessa Bassette." He brushed along her cheek. "Be with me tonight, my music. Tomorrow is tomorrow, but tonight, let go. I am here to catch you. I will *always* catch you."

Arabessa stared at him, the scent of her fear mixed with her desire, worry tangling with need, but soon only hot determination filled her gaze. *Yes,* he coaxed, shifting slightly beneath her so she might feel what she did to him. *Let me show you what I, too, can do to you.*

She growled the sweetest sound of frustrated defeat before her blade fell away from his neck.

Arabessa let go. She kissed him, and Zimri caught her, exactly as promised.

CHAPTER THIRTY-ONE

*I*t was their first kiss all over again. Arabessa felt as though she was back beneath the tree in their garden, her pulse bursting along with her magic, her skin blazing too hot for her clothes. Clumsy excitement and eagerness and pleasure pumped each beat of her heart, but unlike that summer morning, she and Zimri were not so delicate now. Arabessa straddled him, hands twisted in his shirt, greedy for the strong muscles that lay beneath. Zimri's fingers gripped her rear, pulling her tightly to where he was hard for her, moaning against her mouth. He tasted like his last drink of whiskey, sweet and lasting.

Arabessa arched up, ripping off her cloak and holstered weapons as Zimri made quick work of the buttons on her shirt. He snapped the last one free, baring her breasts for him.

"By the stars and sea," he hissed, pushing himself up to kiss down her neck before lifting one of her breasts to suck a nipple into his mouth.

The sensation was liquid lightning through her body. Arabessa groaned, angling farther into him.

None of this should have been happening. She certainly knew she would pay for it later, but her need was too great, her desire drowning. Reason was an eviscerated carcass somewhere far away from where she burned in Zimri's bedroom. There had been too many close encounters between them. Too many almosts, barelys. She was sick of grazes, of whispers. She wanted to be grabbed, pulled, pressed against. She wanted to moan and scream her pleasure to echo through the kingdom for the man she straddled.

With a quick flip, Zimri had her pinned to his bed, held her hands above her head as he kissed down her neck, bit her skin. Arabessa's vision blurred with ecstasy as Zimri's mouth claimed hers once more. He was ravenous like she, a hungry beast let out of a cage. No longer were they he and she, but they. There was no end to his hand sliding along her body or her legs tangling with his.

Let me remind you how much better we are when we can be more.

More.

She needed so much more.

"Zimri," Arabessa groaned, pulling at his shirt.

"Yes, my love, I will give you what you need. I will give you what you want."

"I want you without all of this." Her fingers felt clumsy at his shirt's buttons.

He let out a rumble of a laugh as he pushed off her.

Arabessa almost whined at his weight leaving, but her mind was quickly distracted by the vision of him poised at the edge of his bed, slowly unbuttoning his shirt.

Zimri's eyes remained hooked to her, hooded, starved, but in control.

More in control than how she currently felt.

But wasn't that the point?

Zimri was the only one who could take the ropes of Arabessa's sails so she could be the wild wind.

She could soar free with him, and tonight she would revel in every grain fall of that freedom.

Tomorrow is tomorrow, but tonight, let go.

Let go.

As Zimri revealed his strong form, his trousers quickly falling to the ground along with his shirt, Arabessa more than let go: she was free-falling.

She sucked in her bottom lip as she took in his need for her, strong and powerful. Zimri gave himself a lazy stroke as he watched her watching him, and the ache between her legs intensified.

By the Fade, he was perfect.

He was hers.

Zimri grinned, lascivious, as he bent to tug off her boots, her pants following suit.

They were both bare, but neither touched.

She lay in his sheets, studying every ripple and smooth line on his body bathed in candlelight. Zimri did the same, a dangerous glint in his eyes.

The air between them snapped and sparked, his magic a gold dusting coating his skin, his own emotions overflowing.

"My bed has missed you," he said, a slow glide of his hands starting at her ankles and moving up her legs as he came to drape himself over her. "*I* have missed you."

His skin was warm against hers, a delicious bath of familiarity, settling her magic to purr content in her blood.

Home. Our home.

Bursts of desire overwhelmed her with the sensation of Zimri gripping her, kissing her.

More. More. More.

It had been entirely too long since they had done this. Had been with each other like this. Arabessa had almost forgotten how wrecking it could be, how consuming.

"Easy, my music," said Zimri, lifting off her slightly. "I have waited to be with you again for far too long. I will not have it rushed."

"Zimri," she protested, grabbing his rear to attempt to push him back down. Push him in.

He chuckled. The cheeky bastard chuckled!

Arabessa snaked her leg around one of his and flipped them. She straddled Zimri once more, glaring down into his smug face.

Zimri placed his hands behind his head, stomach muscles stretching, biceps flexing; a pleased dark prince.

Her gaze narrowed. "You wanted me on top, didn't you?"

"For now," he said. "I will be having you in every position tonight."

Tonight.

But tomorrow . . .

Her heart tumbled with a quick shot of fear, a sliver of her responsible self fighting for air.

Wrong. This is wrong.

Though it felt more than right.

This will not end well.

"Ara." Zimri spoke her name softly, calmly, bringing his hand up to run smoothly along her waist. "Look at me," he instructed.

Heated hazel eyes pooled into hers.

"We can stop if you want," he said. "If that is what you need, we can stop." The words must have been painful for him to say, to offer, for they certainly hurt to hear. But he had forced them out for her.

Her choice. With Zimri she always had a choice.

Her chest squeezed with her love for him. It was too much to contain. To stop.

I am here to catch you, he had said. *I will* always *catch you.*

"We can't stop now," she said. "Not when you still need to show me how much better more is."

His features remained unamused, Zimri no doubt able to sense her lingering wave of unease. "Are you sure?"

"No," she admitted. "I'm not sure, but for once in my life I don't care to be. I care to be allowed to feel, to have what I want in this moment."

Zimri's hands gripped her hips. "With me you can have it all."

Not quite, she answered silently. *I will never be your wife.* But she pushed away that ache in her chest as she leaned down to kiss him again.

He guided her mouth effortlessly, coaxing open her lips for tongues to brush. He grazed up her back to run fingers into her hair.

The touch was reverent, devoted.

But Arabessa wanted untamed, savage.

"I want to feel you in me," she whispered, setting loose Zimri's own groan.

"A request I will never deny." His voice was a silky rumble as he moved against her, slow, teasing. "So wet for me," he said through gritted teeth.

"Now, Zimri," she demanded. "Please."

"Look at me," he asked of her again.

Her eyes opened to hold with his. They burned with lust, with love, with a promise.

I've got you.

I will catch you.

Arabessa's chest was flaming, searing through every complicated tangle of emotion for this man: desire, trust, fear, reverie, obsession. Zimri was everything to her. Every one of her strengths and weaknesses. He was the blood pumping through her tumbling heart, part of her soul living outside her body. To be apart from him was torment, but to be with him without fully having him was excruciating. Zimri caused her control to be paper thin. And as he easily lifted her hips only to deliciously and slowly lower her onto him, Arabessa's last wall of defense shattered. Zimri filled her, consumed her, claimed her, proved to her just how much better they were as more.

Arabessa had not expected anything less.

CHAPTER THIRTY-TWO

Zimri was being split open, undone by the woman above him. And however he was meant to be put back together later, he certainly would not be the same.

But he was glad of it.

He did not want to be the Zimri from earlier or the Zimri from yesterday, from a month ago.

Tonight, what was transpiring in this room, was beyond anything he and Arabessa had ever shared.

Each of them had been broken, cracked straight through, when she showed up tonight and now were stitching together their new eternity.

They were crazed with lust, with weeks of pent-up desires and constrained thoughts. They were climaxing endlessly, emotionally and physically. There was not a grain fall when one of them was not commanding or taking or groaning or teasing. Arabessa was telling him everything she had felt, was feeling, without saying a word, and he caught every piece only to respond in kind.

She was forever his complex symphony to which he would listen longingly.

While much of their future was still unsure, Zimri knew the one element that was not was Arabessa being in his life. As *more* than a friend.

Whatever he needed to do to convince her of the same Knowing he would walk the ends of Aadilor to achieve. They were beautiful together. Perfect. Made for one another.

Her pleasure pulsed from her pale skin in the most delectable scent of iced sugar. Zimri wanted to lap up every drop.

Digging his fingers more firmly into her hips, he guided her to grind deeper into him. Arabessa moaned, throwing her head back to push her breasts forward. He felt his cock stiffen further, his mouth watering to suck in her nipples. He pushed himself to sit, keeping her straddling him. With one hand wrapping her waist, following her undulating movements, he used the other to cup her heavy bosom.

Arabessa's nails dug into his back as he gently bit her sensitive bud.

"Zimri," she pleaded.

A new wafting of bliss escaped her, and he took a deep breath in, head growing dizzy with the hit.

He could not get close enough.

Deep enough.

Zimri shifted them down the bed so he could stand, lifting her. He gripped Arabessa's thighs, keeping her connected to him as he pushed her against the far wall. Her hands wrapped around his neck, legs squeezing his waist as he pumped into her. The sensation was eviscerating. He needed so much more. The art along the wall rattled with his thrusts, the flames in the lit sconces fluttering a matching ravenous rhythm.

"My music," he growled. "You wreck me. We can never stop. I will never stop."

"Not even for water?" Arabessa teased.

Her playful tone had him tipping back to find her amused gaze.

That will not do.

Zimri pulled out to sink into her deeper.

He watched with dark satisfaction as Arabessa's eyes rolled back, a beautiful gasp escaping. "I will drink you instead," he said, his voice a rumble of an approaching storm. "And if I grow hungry, I know exactly what I'll eat."

He angled himself so he could rub along her most sensitive spot, did not let up until she screamed another release.

"Zimri," she whispered, limbs growing limp in his arms, weight settling. "Zimri," she said again.

"I have you, my music."

He carried Arabessa back to his bed and laid her on top of the sheets. It was a heady sensation to gaze upon the creature who contained such power and know he had so thoroughly undone her. To have Arabessa trust him enough to hand over her control: it was humbling.

Zimri knew he was the only soul in Aadilor whom she had ever given such authority to, such faith in her heart. The responsibility of it pressed into him, but in a yearning way, a desire to prove how worthy he was to claim it.

Spreading her legs, he dipped his head low.

"Wait." Arabessa stilled him with a hand to his shoulder, her eyes half-closed with her satisfied exhaustion. It brought him the most wicked pride. "What about you?" she asked.

"This is about me," he assured as he secured her hand back to the bed. "Lie back, my love. I told you I will have you every way. This is merely the first course."

"Oh dear," she said before it was replaced with, "Oh, lost gods!" as he licked her.

Like a good girl, she listened to him again and lay back, fingers gripping his sheets before his head, legs wrapping his neck as he devoured every fold of her.

When she danced the edge of her next climax, he pushed away, smiling as she cried her disappointment. "Easy," said Zimri, draping himself against her before slipping back inside. Arabessa sighed, content. "You will get what you want," he assured.

"You give me more than what I want," she said, gaze a blue pool of desire. "You give me what I didn't even know I needed."

"Which is what?" asked Zimri, stilling for a moment. An excruciatingly hard exercise, given she tightened around him. He held Arabessa's gaze, breathed in the vulnerability seeping from her.

"The security to let go," she answered.

Zimri's shredded heart reformed, her admission more seductive than any sexual act. He did not last long after that. As Zimri spilled himself onto the sheets between her legs, head buried in the crook of her neck, her scent all around him, in him, he found his euphoric end.

※

Zimri lay with Arabessa tucked into his arm as she trailed lazy fingers over his bare chest. The candles had long since burned down to extinguish the room into darkness, but the soft blue-green glow of the caved stars outside filtered in through his windows.

The sand fall was unknown, but Zimri did not care for the time. He had no intention of disturbing this moment.

He had never felt so satiated but also so on edge.

Zimri could sense it in Arabessa as well, the subtle scent of worry mixing with her calm. Each of them appeared to be grasping tightly to the present.

But whether he liked it or not, it would be morning soon, or perhaps it already was, and they would have to deal with what this new day would bring.

Zimri, of course, knew what he wanted, but it terrified him to his core to wait for Arabessa to say whether she would side with him this time.

He had set out to prove to her tonight how the best future, the *only* future, between them was one that allowed more. More than friends. More than acquaintances. They belonged as they were now, naked, satisfied, and fitting beside one another perfectly.

Arabessa let out a heavy sigh, and Zimri tightened his arm around her. "Don't," he said.

"What?" She tilted her head back to look at him.

Her hair was a tumbling raven river down her back, her pale skin smooth, and as if they hadn't just made love for the better part of three sand falls, Zimri felt himself growing hungry for her once more. Arabessa was a vision, especially when she lay like this, loose, free.

"Don't think yet," he said. "We can remain like this a little longer."

"I fear thinking is never far from my mind." Her brows drew in slightly. "Zimri—"

"Unless you are about to say you want me to ravish you again," he cut in, "or that you love me and will be in this bed every night henceforth, I do not want to hear it."

She smiled, but it was strained. "I do love you."

Despite the declaration, his stomach dropped, sensing a *but* was imminent. "Then let us leave it at that." He kissed her on the forehead.

Arabessa shifted out of his embrace to sit up. "Zimri, we must now be serious."

He stared at her exposed breasts, heat pooling low. "I don't see how that will be possible."

"Zimri," she admonished as she reached to cover herself with the sheets.

"Fine," he huffed, pushing to settle his back to his headboard. "You want serious, then here is mine: I want to be with you, and by what I experienced of you tonight, you want to be with me too. And"—he raised a hand to stop her from cutting in, as she was poised to do—"I do not want to hear anything about how you cannot be a mistress or this opportunity with Kattiva is the only one I shall ever get to regain majority ownership. As I stated before, that latter part is *my* decision to make, not yours. What will be constructive now is how we can come to a solution for us to be together."

Arabessa remained silent, an edge of fear wafting toward him. He had not expected that.

What are you afraid of? he thought.

"Well?" he pushed. "In what circumstance will you be with me? For I will be with you in any, *without* regrets."

"Without regrets?" she repeated, a bit dubious.

"Yes, but if we want specifics, I'd prefer *you* to be my wife rather than Kattiva."

The scent of Arabessa in pain lifted sharply from her skin.

"Why does that hurt you to hear?" he asked. "Would being my wife be so horrible?"

"No," she answered quickly, not showing surprise that he could tell how she felt. "I . . . merely wish we were having this conversation after the Star Eclipse."

"Why?"

"It would be easier."

"How? I could be married by then."

"Yes . . . there is that."

He watched her closely, studied the way she worried her bottom lip, breathed in her swirl of emotions. "Ara," he began, "what are you not telling me?"

Her gaze locked with his, her expression troubled.

Zimri shifted closer to her, taking both her hands in his. "I am here for you," he reassured. "I am always here. You can tell me what troubles you."

She glanced away from him, anguish clear in her frown. "I know," she said. "But I can't."

It was as if she had landed him a blow.

"What do you mean, *can't*?"

"There is something I must do, complete, before I can allow other distractions."

He physically flinched, her words spiking awake fire in his gut. He let go of her. "So I am merely a distraction, then?"

"No." She shook her head, touching his thigh to keep him from retreating. "That's not what I meant."

"It sounded like that's what you meant."

"No, what I mean is, I . . . need to be focused on other duties presently, and I fear . . . there are decisions coming that could . . ." Her words appeared to stick every few beats, as though what she wanted to say and what she could say were misaligned.

Zimri frowned, never having heard her so tongue tied before. Something indeed was troubling her. "My music," he said softly, cupping her cheek. Her blue eyes blazed with some silent torment. "You do not need to hide from me."

"Zimri," she whispered, agony pouring. "I *do* want you. I want this"—she gestured between them—"but . . . I need time."

"Time?" he repeated, blinking. *Time?*

An incredulous, harsh laugh barked out of him.

Here they were again.

Forget they had been in love for a decade. Forget that he had patiently stood beside her while she laid excuse after excuse at his feet for why they needed to hide from her family, keep their love secret from those important in their life.

No, it was not *time* that was needed here.

What was needed was the *why*. Why did Arabessa need time? Why wait until after the Star Eclipse when so many of *his* duties were riding on right now? What was Arabessa not telling him? What was she so scared of?

They had not come together like this, proved further what they both already knew—they were not souls meant to be long without each other—for her to be too scared to say what truly plagued her heart.

What was this last wall keeping them from being together? She *needed* to tell him. She *would* tell him.

Zimri's patience was dried to the bone, gone. He was beyond desperate for her truth; he was furious for it. He knew what he was about to do was wrong, *very* wrong, but his sense of reason was no more. Arabessa might have magic, but it could not help her unless she could let it out, and currently her flute was somewhere buried under her clothes on the floor.

"Zimri, please," Arabessa pleaded. "You must take me at my word."

"All right," he said, tone a gentle ripple of a lake as he forced an air of calm to settle over him, to push into her.

Arabessa blinked, obviously confused by his sudden quick acceptance. "All right?"

"Mmm." He nodded. "You will tell me your reasons when you are ready."

She appeared even more taken aback but said, "Thank you. I know it is unfair of me to not say more at present, but . . . thank you, Zimri."

A thrash of guilt befell him, but he shoved it aside.

You will *tell me more,* he thought, *and you'll tell me now.*

But for that he needed Arabessa relaxed. He needed her trusting as he allowed a sliver of his magic to seep from him, a serpent slithering unnoticed beneath the sheets to caress her legs.

He felt the gentle pull in his heart as it worked into her skin, heat absorbing.

"I am here for whenever you can say more," he replied, eyes never wavering from hers as his gifts crept unnoticed. "You will tell me then, yes?"

"Yes." She nodded slowly, her gaze growing slightly out of focus as more of his magic lifted unseen behind her in a gold cloud.

Now, he thought, pushing his spell to fall over Arabessa like a net catching a fish.

Arabessa stiffened before relaxing, jaw growing slack.

Trust, his magic crooned. *Truuuust us.*

She nodded softly. "Yes," she said. "Trust."

Zimri had hold of her, and his pulse wanted to rush, tumble, but he needed to keep himself steady to keep her calm.

"Why do you need more time?" he prodded. "What truly keeps us from being together now?"

You want to speak, stroked his gifts. *You want to share.*

Arabessa's mouth opened, but nothing came out.

"Say it," he encouraged. "If you say it, I can offer a solution, my music."

She took in an exhale, words once again primed, but only a strangled noise grunted out before another until Arabessa's features grew panicked, hand going to her throat as though she couldn't breathe.

"Ara!" Zimri tipped forward to grab her shoulders, snapping free the command on his gifts, his spell breaking. "Are you all right? I'm so sorry, my love. I'm so sorry. Breathe. Please, *breathe.*"

Arabessa took a blessed gasp of air, face regaining its natural pallor with each continuous heavy intake.

Zimri's confusion swirled as he watched whatever had grasped her lift, and then, like a douse of ice water, clarity raised his brows. There was only one reason Arabessa would have suffered such a reaction in telling the truth: she was held silent by magic.

She was bound by a silent oath.

A torrent of questions filled him.

A silent oath for what? For whom? What has she gotten herself into?

"You bastard!" Arabessa scrambled off the bed, diving to find her flute along with her knife. She held both tight in her grasp, ready, waiting as her anger at his betrayal burned white hot through the room. "You used your magic on me!"

Though he was beyond devastated at this truth, his frustration was still palpable, and his defenses bared their teeth. "You left me no choice!"

"Choice?" She reeled back, and by the lost gods, did she not look magnificent standing there, naked and fierce. "You certainly had a choice, and you *chose* to break your promise! *Our* promise to one another. How could you?" The question came out raw, shattering, and Zimri hated that he was shattering along with it.

"I am not proud of it," he admitted, "but I could tell you were in pain, hiding something that brought you fear. I was worried, and yes, I was angry, thinking you were purposely holding yourself back in some stubborn, selfless act. It would not have been the first time, Arabessa. I merely want to help you."

She did not respond, just stared at him, eyes wide and shocked and furious.

How had this night gotten so turned around?

"What is going on?" he tried, a bit gentler. "I now understand you are bound silent by an oath, but please, Ara, tell me in whatever way you can what's happening. What have you gotten yourself into?"

"Nothing I shall now ever trust to tell you!" she seethed.

In a flash of movement, Arabessa swiped up her clothes before heading for the door. She was still naked, exposed, devastating as she marched her way out.

"Ara." Zimri jumped from the bed to stop her. "We must settle this!"

Spinning toward him, she whipped her flute to her lips, sending out a sharp note. The power of her magic slammed into his chest, sending him soaring to thunk against the far wall.

"Do not follow me," she warned, teeth bared.

But presently Zimri could not go after her even though he wanted to, for the air had been knocked from his lungs. He bent over gasping, the burning a torment up his throat. When Zimri finally could stagger to his feet, he searched through his apartments only to discover the windowpane Arabessa had earlier entered through now stood open. Zimri stared through it to the skyline of his kingdom and the distant dimming stars, hardly feeling the cool air coming through to prick along his skin.

Arabessa was gone, leaving behind far more than broken promises.

CHAPTER THIRTY-THREE

*S*he was the thunderous roar of a storm as she charged through the streets of the Betting District. Citizens cursed at her as she barreled through, knocking them aside with her shoulders. Arabessa was in no mood for *excuse me*s or *please do step aside*s. These excess visitors who clogged the throughway for the Star Eclipse could eat dirt, for all she cared.

Zimri had used his magic on her!

He had attempted to pry free her secrets without her consent.

Yes, she had retaliated by then using her gifts on him, both of their promises to one another now blown apart, but *how dare he*!

Arabessa had wanted desperately to speak freely in those moments before Zimri attempted to collect her. But she had been challenged to spill all that was in her mind: her father stepping down as Thief King, her mother ruling before him, the throne available for the taking, herself vying for it and with it activating tests that had the potential to send her to the Fade, least of all the ending of the Mousai. She needed this chaos behind her. She needed to *survive*. Otherwise her commitment to him now could all be in vain. Zimri could give up his additional shares in Macabris for naught.

Arabessa *wanted* to tell Zimri these were the reasons why she needed bloody time. If only she could. If only her silent oath was not tying her thoughts and words down like an anchor. One omission was merely a catalyst for another wave of questions whose answers she could not surface. She had felt stuck and frustrated and had hoped he could trust her to tell him when some of these complications were behind her.

But then Zimri had used *his magic on her!*

When Arabessa was defenseless.

Naked.

Without a weapon of her own to fight back.

He had used her vulnerability with her gifts for his leverage, curled his magic behind her to where she could not even see its approach with her Sight.

Traitor, her gifts growled. *Betrayer.*

Arabessa wiped harshly at a tear that escaped down her cheek from beneath her eye mask.

Her chest felt torn through. Stomped to smithereens after having been forced open mere moments ago.

She knew she had asked much of Zimri, challenged his patience, but could that truly justify what he had done?

I was worried, and yes, I was angry, he had told her, *thinking you were purposely holding yourself back in some stubborn, selfless act. It would not have been the first time, Arabessa.*

No, it would not have been.

She had held herself back from being with him, pushed him to fulfill a promise to his parents instead.

My decisions are mine to make—Zimri's words from the other day awoke hot in her mind—*and how I might acquire more of Macabris is not one for* you *to make.*

Arabessa had accused him of forcing his magic on her, but had she also forced this direction for them?

Had she really taken away his choice regarding what *he* wanted as his path forward with Macabris?

Arabessa's resolve twisted uncomfortably at the thought as she charged down a new road, the smell of fires in canisters warming cold hands accosting her nose.

All Zimri had ever talked about growing up was reclaiming the club, placing majority ownership back in D'Enieu hands. For the past six years she had watched him try and fail to edge out the Volkovs from their shares. Had consoled him after each meeting, each fruitless fight.

Wants change, he had said. *People change.*

Could that really be true for him?

It is for you, said a voice deep inside her. *So why not him?*

Arabessa frowned.

Her entire life the Mousai had been all she cared for, her sisters' well-being and duty to her family. But now she saw a new responsibility she wanted to explore. A role without her sisters in tow, one she felt she had been raised to fulfill: alone.

Could Zimri feel the same with his club?

Perhaps my future is not from what my parents built but from what I can build.

As her thoughts continued to swirl, Arabessa drew up short, realizing she had taken a wrong turn somewhere in her hasty retreat.

The alley she had thought would lead her toward the Gazing District and then on to the palace was blocked. A moldy wooden door sat at the end.

Turning, Arabessa went to retrace her steps, only to find a solid brick wall now stood at her back.

"What in all of Aadilor?" She spun in a circle, finding the far door had moved closer, the wall behind her now pressing in to confine her in a small four-walled space. Her magic thrummed in panic through her blood. *Tricks, games, tests.*

A chill raced down her spine.

Nonononononono. "Please, lost gods, no," Arabessa growled out. *This* cannot *be the start of my second test!*

Glancing up, Arabessa took in the waning stars high above. The only visible way out was up. But when she attempted to scale the brick, an invisible force shoved her down. Arabessa landed on her backside with a grunt. She tried again, but again she was stopped. She screamed her annoyance, but her voice went unheard. She was a fish in a bowl, seeing her freedom through glass but unable to make the jump.

She eyed the door again, lips pursed in irritation.

It stood unassuming. Quiet. Waiting.

"Sticks," Arabessa muttered.

It *was* the start to her second test.

But of course it was.

This kingdom knows your greatest fears, so be sure you know them as well, her father had told her.

What Arabessa had been most fearful of as of late was being caught unaware and unprepared for her next challenge.

And here she was, suffering both.

"Fine!" she declared to whatever invisible entity was at play. "You've caught me. Good on you!"

Silence replied.

Arabessa huffed in frustration, attention returning to the unwelcome way forward.

She chanced a touch to the worn wood. Freeze kissed her fingertips, and she drew back.

Magic lay beyond.

With this finality of understanding, nerves began to replace Arabessa's swirl of rage, block out the residual hot fire from her and Zimri's fight.

She knew once she entered through this door, she might not make it out.

Her stomach twisted with unease.

So much would be left undone, unsaid, unexplained. But such was her agreement for the prize she desired.

As she straightened, focus settling, sharpening, Arabessa found herself letting go for the second time this day. With no other option than through, Arabessa opened the door and stepped in.

The blaze of lettering in the dark came and went much too quickly, and Arabessa hurried to take in its meaning.

> *Welcome to your second beginning*
> *An outcome up to you*
> *Pay heed to your next choice, dear one*
> *Lives depend on you ruling true*

Arabessa's pulse vibrated, her magic in her blood a matching rhythm of anticipation and fear. What monster would be placed in her path this time? What test would further prove her worth for the crown? Might end her fight for it?

Only another beat did Arabessa wait until light spilled over the dark like liquid illumination to reveal a cavernous throne room.

It was not her current king's throne room, but shifted and reshaped. A new space for a new Thief King. Around the circular dais on which she stood, lava churned, a moat in the middle of the soaring obsidian hall. Arabessa stood in front of a vicious sculpted throne, its back made of similar volcanic rock reaching in spikes all the way up to a domed skylight far above.

Everything waited quiet, waited ready.

Though there were no further instructions, Arabessa sensed that whatever was to happen next, she needed to somehow start it.

She stared at the throne, a pull tugging in her gut.

Yours, a dozen voices whispered at once in her mind, a layering of kings.

Mine, she thought, a skip to her heartbeat, a grip of desire.

Arabessa lowered herself into the chair, magic thrumming, anticipation vibrating.

The rock surface was warmer than anticipated, welcoming, and she leaned farther into the seat.

As she laid her hands atop the armrests, gripping the black carved skulls decorating either end, silver magic snaked around her wrists.

Arabessa gasped as the restraints dug into her sleeves, rubbing raw her skin as she tried to pull herself free.

The magic was unyielding while her own thrashed in her veins to help.

We will protect, it vowed in a cry. *We will avenge.*

But she was bound in place, unable to activate her flute, let alone bring it to her lips.

Arabessa's gifts were trapped. Once again her nightmare realized. A new panic erupted in her chest.

Was she to continually live this fear? To be tested by losing her greatest weapon?

I am more than my magic, she reminded herself, desperate to force calm into this moment.

I am more than my magic.

As she pulled in deep breaths in an attempt to soothe the stampeding of her heart, Arabessa glanced up as a portal door opened in front of her.

The sound of chaos flooded the room. Her pulse stopped, lungs suffocating as she stared into a scene of horror.

It was a view of the Gazing District on fire.

The ancient architecture crumbled; sacred magic unique to Aadilor was being burned from existence. The Fountains of Forgotten Memories' glass dome was being eaten by flames. The library of spells consumed by a blaze. The ancestral homes of thief houses were bursting with the heat that raced through the buildings. Citizens yelled and ran and screamed. Some were on fire themselves as they fell into the street, howling in pain.

"No!" cried Arabessa, panic filling her as she attempted to stand, to run through the portal, but her binds kept her from getting very far. She fell back into her seat.

"Let me free!" she demanded into the throne room, tugging desperately.

But then a new portal door opened beside the other, a new scene that further stopped dead her heart.

Niya and Larkyra were standing back to back, bloody and bruised and near their end as a dozen stone guardians attacked. They were in a caved arena, one no doubt created precisely for this fight, one this kingdom fabricated as quickly as it created the doors that Arabessa was made to walk through for her tests. Fire shot from Niya, a gold whip of song from Larkyra, but their magic was not enough to take on such a horde. They needed her; they needed the combined power of the Mousai. Arabessa's blood drained from her face as she watched one beast get the better of them and swipe both away with a heavy blow. Niya and Larkyra rolled like tangled rag dolls.

"Sisters!" A roar poured up and out of Arabessa's throat as she wrestled with her restraints. "Sisters, I am coming!" She thrashed and screamed as she attempted to break free from the glowing silver chains. But no amount of pull or leverage would loosen them. Blood only soaked farther into her sleeves and dripped down her hands. Arabessa's skin was being broken and sliced from her attempts. But she felt no pain along her arms, only the explosion taking place in her chest.

"Our king!" A civilian's cry brought Arabessa's attention back to the scene of the burning Gazing District. A figure in a half-shattered mask and charred flesh reached for her through the portal door. "Save us! *Please*, save us!"

"Arabessa." Niya's voice was a mere groan, but she could hear it from where she sat as though she was right beside her. Niya attempted to stand next to where Larkyra lay, but her knees gave out.

What madness is this? thought Arabessa, her body beginning to shake with her trapped hysteria to help, to stop, to protect. *Is this real? Is this happening?*

The cries of fear and pain certainly sounded real; the smoke smelled real; Arabessa's agony from watching it all unfold was more than real.

But what is the point? she cried silently. "Why show me this!" she yelled into the throne room.

Which? asked a layering of voices in her mind. *Which?*

"Which?" repeated Arabessa, brows drawn in as she hurriedly glanced from one portal door to the other.

Your choice, the throne's ancient magic continued. *Your choice to make. Your choice to save. Which?*

"Both!" she demanded.

Noooo, the throne hissed, reprimanding her with a sharp tug to her wrists. She cried out at the acute burn. *Which?* it asked again. *Which? Which? Which? Which? Which?*

The question echoed dreadfully in her mind, and Arabessa squeezed her eyes shut as though that could save her from this fate.

She was meant to decide whom to save, which to protect. Only one choice, one option. One right answer in a decision that would kill either way.

Save her sisters or save the historic district of her kingdom, the sacred magic that was housed there and the citizens who resided there. Arabessa sat paralyzed. Cold. Confused.

In her grain falls of indecision, words from her father rushed forward.

To be a leader of great consequence . . . it is not you in those moments. Not your feelings, not your wants. It is your people's wants. Your kingdom's feelings. You must make personal sacrifices every day. Every grain fall you wear a crown.

"No." Arabessa shook her head, tears spilling from beneath her mask to slip salty into her mouth. "There has to be another way," she ground out before yelling, "there *has to be*!"

The throne remained silent.

She heard only her sisters trying to push out their last bit of strength to survive, the crackling and toppling of buildings mixed with terrified and dying citizens.

Arabessa knew whom she *wanted* to save, but that was very different from whom she *needed* to save. And she hated, loathed, and detested that she understood this difference. She had been raised to carry out these very acts most of her life.

To kill to stop murder.

To steal to give back to those needing.

Do evil to bring good; fight in wars to bring peace.

Such was the burden of the Mousai, of being a Bassette.

And so, too, was it to wear a crown.

Knowing the needs of the many outweighed the needs of a few.

It is not you in those moments. Not your feelings, not your wants. It is your people's wants. Your kingdom's feelings, her father had said.

Her kingdom.

Her kingdom.

Her kingdom.

But these were Arabessa's sisters! Her family! Her heart! She needed to help them. *They* needed her to help. They were outnumbered. Larkyra's magic was coming out in weak spurts of gold, her jaw broken by a blow. Niya's foot was twisted at an unnatural angle, her movements hindered. Their injured gifts were no match for the continued onslaught. They screamed for Arabessa and her music. "Please, sister!" cried Niya once again. "Help us, Ara!"

Arabessa's barely threaded stitches of her heart were once again severed by the pool of her pain. She was amazed she was even still breathing as she watched the two nightmares unfold. But breathing she was, in big gulps and shaking nerves and toppling-over rage.

Yet the throne held her still, held her in place. The ancient magic of kings forced her to sit as though composed as she came to her decision.

She had a quick wondering if this same power was what always gripped her father as he sat on the throne, what held him appearing calm when delivering a severe sentencing or watching a soul be torn open. Did he sit tied down as Arabessa did now, screaming inside for it all to stop, hating knowing the choice that would end it?

You must make personal sacrifices every day. Every grain fall you wear a crown.

Could Arabessa live through such sacrifice?

Which? the voices asked once more. *Chooooose,* they insisted, impatient.

Arabessa's chest rose and fell like a storm at sea, each breath bringing more waves of misery, for she knew her decision. She knew which path would lead her to the Fade and which to be king.

With lips trembling, gifts crying through her blood, she gripped the skulled armrests tighter and gave her answer to the throne room and turned to watch her sisters die.

CHAPTER THIRTY-FOUR

The man wept before Zimri but elicited from him no pity. The prisoner's tears merely pushed him to further dig in his magic, a gold hand tugging the man's head back.

Tell us everything, his gifts demanded. *Tell us your story.*

"What debt did you owe?" Zimri asked, voice as cold as metal.

"I . . . bet my home," said the man on a gasp, eyes wide, snot dripping to mix with his tears.

Zimri's mind flipped through all the recent debts he had called in, which ones had included estates. Two names came to mind from his books: Tanner and Maxerly.

"M-my house," hiccuped the man. "My family . . . my *children,* they have nothing now. *Nothing!*"

Zimri's lip curled. This was Tanner, then, for Maxerly had no children he was aware of.

He looked down at the lamenting creature from beneath his full face mask. When Zimri did the more torturous collecting, he covered himself as much as he could.

Rodents, Zhad had called people such as this man, who came to play at Macabris without knowing, or caring for, the stakes. But Zimri thought of them as worse than that. Rodents were resilient; this soul was weak, selfish, to have placed his family's well-being on the line for a roll of chance.

And then blame *them* for his predicament, blame him.

"That is your doing, not Macabris's," said Zimri, glaring down at the man who knelt before him, chained to the ground. The attacker no longer wore a disguise. That protection was the first that had been stripped from him when brought to the dungeons beneath the palace. He had been younger than Zimri had expected, but his youth still lent him no mercy.

Zimri had been working on the man who had attacked Kattiva for the better part of half a sand fall. Slowly pressing him to be more malleable to his desires for answers. He could have gotten to this point of his investigation much quicker, but Zimri was filled with his own rage. Emotions that had little to do with Tanner seeking revenge for a forced payment and more to do with Zimri's own pain that pulsed through him like poison. He needed another to suffer as he suffered. Needed his mind on something other than the visions of a shattered Arabessa and her scent, which burned with his betrayal.

You used your magic on me!

He had, but blast—he still was not entirely regretful of it.

"What shall we do now? What will I tell my family?" sniveled Tanner at his feet.

"That is not our concern," said Zimri. "What is my concern is you never gracing Macabris's doorstep again or going near Kattiva Volkov."

The man shook his head violently. "No. Never. I shall never."

"Promise it," said Zimri, tightening his gifts on him.

Tanner let out a pained gasp, spine arching farther. "I promise. I promise. I promise."

Something twisted sour in Zimri's chest as he watched Tanner reduced so quickly. Here sobbed a man who had taken for granted his family, the love of his children, the trust of his wife, and thrown it away so easily. All because he believed he had luck on his side. Because he thought he had the right to gamble with his family's well-being.

Zimri was disgusted. He was outraged.

You are a coward. He fed more of his thoughts into his magic, which wrapped around Tanner. *You are useless.*

Weak, his gifts hissed in agreement. *Worthless.*

An agonized whine filtered from Tanner, but Zimri did not stop.

You are a fool, sang his spell, worming into the man's blood. *You will never be happy. You will never be free of this shame, of this betrayal to your family, to those who loved you, trusted you. You are weak, weak, weak. Selfish, selfish, selfish. You are worthless.*

"I am," sobbed Tanner. "I am worthless. I am weak."

Zimri released his magic, and the man collapsed to the ground, sobs filling the dark prison cell.

"Attempts at murder do not go unpunished or unnoticed by the Thief King," explained Zimri, his voice a frozen expanse. "Especially if the reason does not fit the action, and yours certainly does not. You should be lucky if you can walk free after our king decrees your punishment."

Zimri turned from the bent and broken figure, the sound of Tanner's tears and chastising mutterings fading as he exited the holding cell.

The heavy door closed behind him with a decided click, a warm rush of magic locking.

Violet eyes met his in the shadowed corridor.

"Well, that was . . . thorough," said Achak in the brother's form as he regarded Zimri.

"His surname is Tanner," said Zimri, not entertaining the twin's comment. "He bet his home on a losing hand of Cutthroat."

"I shall relay his situation and name to our king."

Zimri nodded. "Let me know what his punishment shall be."

Achak raised a brow. "Dear boy," he began, "I have a feeling Tanner's punishment might have already been carried out."

By you. The words unsaid but meant.

Zimri cared not for Achak's accusation. All he could focus on as he turned from the twins to travel through the dark halls of the dungeon was finding Arabessa. Finding her and praying to the lost gods he had not destroyed his last chance for them to be together.

CHAPTER THIRTY-FIVE

*A*rabessa surely was in the Fade, for she felt more than dead inside. Her limbs had somehow carried her from the Thief Kingdom's streets to her family's private quarters beneath the palace. She remembered very little about surviving her second test.

Surviving.

An odd word for her current state.

Though her decision to save the Gazing District had unchained her from the throne, dissolved where she stood in her nightmares to send her back to the empty alley of the Betting District, Arabessa felt she had failed her test.

She had allowed her sisters to die. She had *chosen* for them to die.

To save her people.

And she had been rewarded for it.

Nausea pushed up Arabessa's throat as her tears continued to stream down her cheeks from beneath her mask. The sharp, pointed claws of grief raked over her chest. She needed to get to her rooms so she could be the only witness to her breaking.

With a hurried shove, Arabessa pushed into her chamber and nearly tripped over her own feet at whom she found inside. Her skin rushed with a chill.

"Ara?" asked Larkyra, brows set in a worried furrow as she regarded her from where she stood beside Niya. The two of them had been huddled together without their masks in the center of her room but had glanced up as Arabessa entered. "You look horrid," exclaimed Larkyra.

"You smell it too." Niya waved a hand in front of her nose.

Arabessa let out a strangled cry, flying toward them. She drew them into a tight embrace.

"Oy, careful now," said Niya, trying to create space between her and Arabessa. "This dress is fresh from the modiste."

"What has happened?" asked Larkyra.

Arabessa didn't reply right away; she merely squeezed them tighter, breathing deep their familiar fragrances, reveling in their voices not filled with anguish and pain.

They are alive! They are alive! They are alive!

Her magic swelled within her blood, a tsunami of relief threatening to knock her to her knees.

"Are you unwell?" pushed Larkyra as Arabessa finally stepped back.

"No," said Arabessa. "Not any longer, at least."

"But you've been bleeding," pointed out Niya, gesturing to her ripped sleeves and crimson-crusted arms. "Are potentially still bleeding. Does Lark need to heal you?"

"You both being here has healed me."

Her sisters regarded her as though she had more than a few dull blades in her arsenal.

Arabessa's wide grin no doubt fueled such thoughts, until she caught sight of what Niya held in her other hand and her smile fell.

The room tilted, panic shooting back through her blood.

Seeming to notice where her attention had gone, Niya lifted the black envelope still sealed by the white skull stamp of the Thief King. "What is this?" she asked.

Arabessa did not answer, not only because she could not but because she was now busy taking stock of her room. Her gaze swung to her wall, finding the painting thrown open, along with the door to the safe it covered.

"What have you done?" Arabessa hissed, attempting to snag the envelope from Niya's fingers.

But Niya was a master of movement and must have sensed what was about to transpire, for she easily spun away from Arabessa. She placed herself on the other side of a nearby couch.

"Why are you rifling through my things?" Arabessa growled.

"You were very quiet after our performance at the engagement ball," reasoned Larkyra from where she stood between her and Niya, "and then disappeared. We wanted to check on you."

"And checking on me includes breaking into my safe?"

"We may be your sisters," explained Niya. "But do not forget, we are also thieves. Breaking into a hidden safe is too tempting to deny."

"How did you even open it?" she questioned with further agitation. "It has a magic lock."

Niya shrugged. "When sailing with Alōs Ezra, you pick up a few new skills along the way. But now it is your turn to answer questions. This is from the Thief King," she accused. "What note did you get from the king that we did not?" Her tone was laced with offense rather than concern.

"Something obviously only meant for me," said Arabessa through clenched teeth, sticking out her hand. "Now please, give it back."

"Is this why you are so . . . disheveled?" asked Larkyra. "What has the king asked you to do that could not be done by the Mousai?"

Arabessa shook her head, frustration prickling awake. By the Fade, was she to go through this again? First Zimri, now her sisters. Both people she *wanted* to tell, she needed to confide in. "It is nothing like that," she explained, annoyed, her eye mask beginning to press too tight.

Her head was pounding, and with a dramatic flourish, she unsnapped her disguise and threw it onto her nearby vanity. Arabessa rubbed at her temples in an attempt to ease the pressure. She was tired and dirty and cut up and was in no mood for this conversation.

"What is it like, then?" asked Niya, folding her arms over her chest, envelope still tight in her grasp. "It won't open for us, so you'll need to explain in your own words."

Her own words.

Words that she had pledged to keep silent.

"I cannot," she stated.

"What do you mean, cannot?" Niya frowned.

Further exhaustion gripped Arabessa. This moment was a song on repeat.

"Exactly as I stated: I *cannot.*" She threw out her hands. "Though I might want to, I am unable."

Larkyra's gaze was the first to fill with understanding. "You are bound silent by an oath."

Niya glanced from their younger sister back to Arabessa, brows shooting up. "What have you been tasked with that you cannot share?"

"She obviously can't tell us, now, can she?" said Larkyra with an eye roll.

"Oh yeah. Well, perhaps we can guess?"

Arabessa snorted a sardonic laugh as she slumped into a nearby armchair. "You may certainly try," she said. Every one of her muscles felt bruised. "But I fear we'd be here for a very long time."

Niya harrumphed while Larkyra came to Arabessa's side. She placed a gentle hand on her shoulder, looking down at her. "Can you at least let us know if you've been put in danger?" She eyed the blood staining Arabessa.

Tightness gripped her again. She hated for her sisters to worry. That was her job, but presently she was too tired to lie. "Yes, quite a bit of danger," she admitted because she could.

Larkyra nodded, lips pressing together pensively. "I see," she said. "And did you have a choice in whatever is written in that?" She pointed to the envelope Niya held. "Could you have said no to our king's request?"

An ease of relief lapped through Arabessa as she once again found herself able to reply. "I could have said no."

"Then I have no further questions," said Larkyra, moving to settle into the facing couch.

Arabessa blinked. "What?"

"Yeah, what?" asked Niya, eyeing Larkyra with confusion from where she stood behind her.

"Arabessa is more responsible than either of us," explained Larkyra with a shrug, "and has taken on many burdens from the throne and for the Mousai. Whatever you go through now, sister"—Larkyra met her gaze—"I trust you with. Just know we are here when and if you need."

Arabessa stared at her youngest sister in a mix of amazement and guilt.

What I go through will end the Mousai, she wanted to confess, but how could she share that without being able to answer why?

The fire of her frustration burned hot once again.

"When did you become so *reasonable*?" asked Niya, incredulous.

"Perhaps when I became a duchess with more than myself to think of?" Larkyra pointed out. "Am I to believe you do not trust Ara with the responsibilities she takes on?"

Niya scrunched up her face with the question, an obvious silent war waging. "Fine, yes." She waved her hands before coming to flop beside Larkyra. "I, *too*, then suffer this sickness of being reasonable. After traveling with a ship full of pirates and a demanding captain, I've accepted that we don't always get the luxury of an explanation. Here"— she leaned forward to hand the envelope back to Arabessa—"we have followed you faithfully for all our performances. We trust you'll handle well whatever this is too."

Arabessa was lost for words as she held the letter. Was this really happening? There would be no continuous badgering from her sisters?

No dramatic pouting and feeble threats if she did not share what was in this invitation? Niya and Larkyra were . . . trusting her.

"You will?" asked Arabessa, still dubious.

"Yes," answered Larkyra. "We trust you to your choices, Ara."

A sizzle of magic pushed a gust of wind through the room; the black envelope in Arabessa's hand jumped into the air.

Trussssst. A layering of voices slithered through Arabessa's mind. *Trust revealsss.*

She looked to her sisters, wondering if they, too, heard the voices, but they were too busy regarding the letter as it unfolded and floated down to settle onto the low table between them.

Trust reveals.

Arabessa's pulse thrummed along with her magic as Niya and Larkyra met her gaze. Their features held a flash of astonishment before they each leaned forward, reading the invitation that inked Arabessa's fate.

CHAPTER THIRTY-SIX

*T*he room had descended into chaos. Her sisters were pacing, throwing question after question her way. At the onslaught, Arabessa's head spun from where she had remained seated.

"All right." She raised her hands for them to stop. "All right, that is enough for the moment. By the Fade, I had thought this was how you'd be when I told you about Mother."

"Well, be lucky we saved it all for now instead." Niya plunked a fist onto her hip. A red cloud of her gifts swirled from her heightened emotional movements. "Now share what you can."

Arabessa took a deep breath in, attempting to recall the order of the questions and which ones she could answer. "No, Zimri does not know. Obviously Achak does, as well as Father. And no, I didn't know he wanted to retire. Yes, I am well aware the full eclipse is less than a week away. The rest you unfortunately must put together yourselves."

Her sisters were quiet for a few grain falls, evidently doing just that.

Their father's rule was ending; their eldest sister was hoping to claim it; she could die in the process; and all of this was to be settled in a handful of days.

Similar to her first test, her second had come during the end of the Waning Sky. Tomorrow would mark the third and final phase of the Star Eclipse. It was the shortest period, when the last of their stars would die, dousing their kingdom into the eclipse. The time when the throne would silently change over to another king. When Arabessa's fate would officially be sealed.

She breathed through the constant churning of disquiet and determination in her stomach at the thought. Arabessa wanted the throne desperately, wanted her choice to be the right one, wanted to have the opportunity to lead this kingdom as her parents had. She also wanted to live.

"Is this why you refused Zimri's proposal?" Larkyra's question brought Arabessa's attention back to her sisters.

"It . . . is one of the reasons, yes." She refused to acknowledge her heartache.

"What Zimri can gain by marrying Kattiva is the other," said Niya. Not a question; this they had known.

Arabessa could only nod, her and Zimri's fight from earlier today still raw. The memory of his touch along her skin still burning.

By the Fade, how could she have been in his arms, in his bed, only this morning? Arabessa had been floating in bliss and calm and happiness only to now be bruised and crushed and exhausted.

Swallowing past the anguish edging up her throat, she picked up the forgotten invitation on the table and refolded it. She stood, returning it to her safe.

As Arabessa swung the painting back into place, she remained there for a moment, her weight pressing into the frame through her hands.

Every part of her hurt.

"It has been a very long month," she admitted to the room.

There was a rustling behind her, Larkyra and Niya coming to her side. She felt out of place in her wrinkled trousers, cloak, and partially blood-soaked shirt compared to their pristine gowns.

"We are sorry you have been suffering this alone," said Larkyra, hand to her shoulder.

Arabessa turned, meeting their blue gazes. "So am I," she said before offering a small smile. "But now you know, and what a relief, for I have wanted to tell you since the very first day."

"We never knew you wanted something like this for yourself," admitted Niya.

"I didn't know I did, either, until I was offered the chance," Arabessa confessed. "I *really* do want it, though. Not only for what our parents have built but for what I could build for this kingdom."

"It makes sense for you," said Larkyra. "You are a great leader."

A warmth flooded Arabessa. "Thank you."

"Yes, despite being an annoying one on occasion," added Niya, "I would agree."

The emotions washing over Arabessa were too great.

Her sisters' blind faith in her, trust in her to make her own decisions— the right ones for her and possibly them—was the biggest honor to hold.

Trust reveals. The secret to learning another's truth.

"You will be a great Thief King," proclaimed Larkyra.

It was as if a fuse was lit inside Arabessa's heart, hearing those words spoken out loud.

"I have not made it to the end yet," she reminded them, reminded herself.

"You will," said Larkyra.

"You must," added Niya. "Though I don't relish the idea of you being able to command us about, I'd much prefer that outcome over you being sent to the Fade."

"*Niya,*" chastised Larkyra, brows furrowed.

"That's a compliment!" explained Niya. "I want our sister to live."

"You could have just stated that."

"I just did."

Larkyra let out a long-suffering sigh. "How you've been able to remain in line for our performances is a testament unto itself regarding Ara's leadership abilities."

At the mention of the Mousai, a pang of unease surfaced in Arabessa's chest.

"There is something else you both should know," Arabessa began slowly. "Something I have not known how to share without being able to talk of . . ."

"You vying to be Thief King," Larkyra finished for her.

"Yes." Arabessa shot her a grateful smile.

How much easier it was to talk now that her sisters knew, though they both would need to pledge their secrecy soon. For her safety and their own.

"Well?" pushed Niya, brows drawn in. "For the Obasi Sea's sake, now that you can say it, say it."

Arabessa readied herself. "No matter the outcome at the end of the Star Eclipse, the Mousai will be no more."

The room was swallowed in silence, Arabessa a ball of nerves as she watched her sisters' expressions change from shock to confusion.

"And why is that exactly?" asked Niya slowly.

"Because," began Arabessa, "I might be in the Fade or . . ."

On the throne.

"And you cannot be Thief King *and* part of the Mousai," stated Larkyra, rather matter of fact.

Clarity washed over Niya. "Oh, yes. Those are rather tricky pairings."

"And Father knows of this future for the Mousai?" asked Larkyra.

"He does." Arabessa nodded.

A flash of hurt now danced in Larkyra's gaze. Arabessa could tell she was working to settle her emotions before she went on to ask, "And if we had not been able to learn tonight, when exactly were *we* to be told of this rather drastic change in our lives?"

Guilt swam fast. "On the Sky's Return," answered Arabessa. "Father would figure out how to deliver the news if I was unable." *Because I'd be dead.* "Or I'd reveal myself like Father did to us as children for you to learn."

The following quiet sat heavy.

"I'm sorry," said Arabessa, chest aching. "I am sorry I could not have shared all of this earlier. That I could not have come to you both before I agreed to . . ." Her next words were taken from her, the blasted silent oath choking them down.

She coughed for her next breath.

"Ara," said Larkyra quickly, leaning forward in worry. "We understand why you could not. It is okay. Do not try to speak what you know you cannot."

Arabessa sucked in a gasp, the tightness of her lungs releasing. "Still," she wheezed before regaining her breaths. "I am sorry. It has not been easy, keeping this a secret from you both."

"Well," sighed Niya, bringing her hands to settle on her waist, "I'll share a secret that might be just as shocking. I'm in full support."

Arabessa drew her chin back, her surprise vibrating through her. "You are?"

"Of which part?" added Larkyra, brows furrowed.

"All parts. But mainly that the Mousai will be retiring," explained Niya. "I obviously love you both, dearly, and being a part of our trio has been one of the most spectacular experiences of my life, but I'd be lying if I said I haven't wanted other spectacular experiences as of late. Ones that could not come to pass if I were still bound by such responsibilities."

"You want to sail more with your pirate," said Arabessa, having grown her own suspicion of this.

"I hate to admit it," said Niya, cheeks blushing. "And please, do *not* tell Alōs, or I shall never hear the end of it. But I do. Our voyages are always on a time limit, and as you both know, I do not like to be constrained if I can help it."

"We do know that." Arabessa huffed a laugh.

It felt foreign and odd after such an intense day, but blast, did it also feel good.

"If this is confession time," said Larkyra, hands smoothing over her blue skirts, "then I, too, have one of my own."

Arabessa, along with Niya, turned to her expectantly.

"Darius and I have talked often of wanting a family. And before you jump to conclusions," she went on quickly to say, "no, I am not pregnant. I merely have wished to one day be, but I did not know if that ever could transpire with our particular responsibilities to our king. It has been a rather difficult conversation for Darius and me." Larkyra frowned as though recalling a recent fight. "So to hear this . . . well, is it wrong to say I am relieved?"

"That is not bad *at all,*" said Niya earnestly, pulling Larkyra into a hug. "I am so excited for you and Darius! We are going to be aunts!" She stepped back to look at Arabessa, eyes wide with excitement.

"Well, not quite yet," said Larkyra with a laugh. "*Much* still has to transpire."

Yes, thought Arabessa in a mix of happiness for her sisters and unease for herself. *I still must make it to the end, alive.*

Something felt lodged in her throat, the building of tears, but Arabessa shook it away as best she could. No matter her outcome, it appeared all would be well for Niya and Larkyra, and *that* was the best she could ever hope for.

Her father had admitted how it had pained him to bring his daughters into this world. In a way, Arabessa was undoing this regret of Dolion's, allowing her sisters to each choose their own path as he had always wished for them.

Arabessa was not killing the Mousai; she was freeing them.

At this realization, a wave of peace settled over her, exhausted relief.

"So neither of you are mad at me?" she asked, wanting to make sure.

"Mad?" Niya frowned. "Not at all!"

"We could not continue forever like this," said Larkyra. "Though I had feared we might. Plus, how could we be mad at you for wanting something different for your life, as we want for ours?"

That pressure to cry threatened Arabessa again, but not because she was sad; quite the opposite. Her sisters finally knew what she had been shouldering this past month. They knew and *understood*. Accepted. Supported.

Wants change. Zimri's words came fast in Arabessa's mind. *People change.*

It appeared he had been right.

As if Larkyra knew the subject of her thoughts, she said, "Not to sober this moment, but speaking of what you want for your life, I think Zimri deserves to know what's going on. He should know this is a reason you've denied him. Especially if, well . . ."

You do not survive were clearly the unsaid words.

Arabessa's shoulders refilled with tension, stomach with disquiet. Her and Zimri's argument from this morning resurfaced in her mind. *Of course* she wanted to tell him, just as she had wanted to tell her sisters.

"Yes, well," began Arabessa, her tone a prickle of agitation, "it's not as though I have much say in how any of this transpires, now, do I?"

"True," said Larkyra. "But don't you think, given what's at stake, being with him now is better than possibly never having moments with him ever again?"

Niya let out a whistle of shock. "You're really living dangerously with these questions, Lark."

"I merely want Arabessa to have no regrets," Larkyra argued.

I want what will fulfill you with a life beyond regret.

Their father's words echoed.

Despite her sister's good intentions, white-hot annoyance erupted within Arabessa, not because she disagreed with Larkyra's sentiments but because she was scared she was right.

"There is no point in being engaged if one of us ends up dead," Arabessa said, doubling down.

Both of her sisters physically flinched at the mention of her life.

"But if he could know what—"

"He can't!" Arabessa's outburst cut off Larkyra, surprising even her, but by the Fade! She was so very tired of having to defend herself on this subject. "I am incapable of telling him," she went on. "Do not think I haven't wanted to. Tried. But I cannot! No invitation has been there to magically open and explain. Now, do not press me any further on the subject."

"Yes, of course," said Larkyra, and Arabessa watched as her sisters shared a quick look of pity.

It merely pushed her ire further. She could not be sad for her current situation. She *could not.* She had already sacrificed too much to get to this point. She had the chance to be *Thief King*, and by the stars and sea, she was reaching for that chance with all her might.

"Now, if you don't mind," said Arabessa tensely, "I'd really love a bath right now. As you pointed out, Niya, I really do smell."

"We'll let you bathe," said Niya. "But we *will* be back with tea and food. If ever there needed to be sister duty, it is now."

Arabessa didn't fight them on the matter as they put on their masks to make their way to her door. Despite her being tired and frustrated, after her last test, her heart yearned for them to never part. Sister duty was more than desirable. For who knew how much longer they'd have together.

No, do not think like that, Arabessa admonished herself, shaking away the prickling of fear.

"Oh, hello, Achak," said Niya in surprise as she opened the door to find the sister on the other side of the threshold.

"Hello, ladies." She smiled sharply, tall figure silhouetted by the dark corridor behind. "I have been made aware that some secrets have been shared this afternoon. Advantageous, since I have come to steal them." She displayed an intricately carved silver cylinder.

"Oh dear," said Larkyra.

"Sticks," sighed Niya.

Arabessa's stomach fell.

Achak held up a Secret Stealer. Their time of talking freely of her future appeared to have come to a fast end.

Even so, Arabessa knew, despite what loomed to claim a throne, she would continue her fight to survive so she might one day see her sisters' futures as well as her own.

CHAPTER THIRTY-SEVEN

*A*rabessa was shadow as she slid silent along the dark carpeted corridor. Her breaths were even, despite her pounding heartbeat, her gifts a tumble of trepidation through her blood.

She should not be here, but she desperately wanted to be.

From two floors down, the muffled sounds of Macabris celebrating the third phase of the eclipse vibrated up through her booted feet.

Arabessa did not know if Zimri would be here, but it was as good as any place to start her search. Larkyra's words from the other night had come to haunt her over the following two days.

I merely want Arabessa to have no regrets.

A sentiment similar to her father's.

Perhaps a warning that Dolion and Larkyra had learned from experience.

With these incessant voices in her head, Arabessa had come to realize that she would regret entering her final test without seeing Zimri one last time. They had both been hurt, angry, frustrated, and heartbroken at their last parting. She needed to make peace between them now. Needed for them to hold happier memories so she could walk into her unknown future with no regrets if she never stepped out.

As Arabessa approached the next corner, careful not to step into the illumination of the low-lit sconces peppering the hall, she furtively glanced around the bend.

A masked guard hung near the only door in the following corridor, stairs directly in front of him leading to the lower levels. Arabessa's pulse tripped forward with elation. He would not be standing sentry if his master was not inside.

Unholstering her flute with a quiet click, Arabessa pressed it to her lips.

She breathed out a note to jump high across the darkness to echo somewhere down the stairs. The guard turned toward it, body stiffening.

Arabessa fed him another misdirected note. This time he shuffled to the landing, looking down. On the third, he descended to search out whatever might be within the stairwell, leaving his post abandoned.

Arabessa made fast work of her next actions, for this was not the first time she had broken into the Collector's office. Placing the end of her flute directly over the keyhole, she sent a flutter of low notes through, her magic sizzling down and out of her fingers. *I will open this for you,* it said.

In the next breath, there was a shifting of a lock, and Arabessa stood, twisting the handle before she slid inside.

Zimri stood maskless, looking out his large one-way glass to the party below, hands together behind his back, strong shoulders stretching his immaculate black coat. He turned as she entered, a multitude of emotions playing over his features at finding her standing there: shock, desire, frustration—but the one that rose highest to the surface was sorrow.

Arabessa had never found Zimri surprised when she broke into his office. Pleased, to be sure, but never taken aback. Tonight, however, he appeared as though he was looking at a walking heartache and he was not quite sure what to make of the visit.

Arabessa's pulse skipped as she pressed against his closed door. She rushed to work out what to do now that she was here. Especially since the space was instantly buzzing with tension, with yearning.

His deep rumble broke into the silence first. "I have been looking for you." Neither of them moved from their opposite sides of the room.

"I have been avoiding you," she admitted.

"And yet now here you are." Zimri raised a brow, as if to say, *Why?* But he didn't give her a chance to answer. "I need to apologize for the other night." He turned fully to face her, tone edging urgent. "My actions . . . they were unforgivable, Ara. But I will do whatever is needed to fix that mistake."

His features held his clear pain, and Arabessa's chest tightened.

Yes, he had broken a promise they had made to one another, and that betrayal still stung, still prickled in her heart, but she had come to understand how forced into a corner he had felt. How his actions came from a place of concern, of his need to protect her, help her. Sentiments she, too, felt in regard to him.

But Arabessa had not come here to discuss that night.

She had come to change how it had ended. How she had needed it to end.

"I know," she said, pushing off the door to make her way toward him. Zimri eyed her approach with wariness, and a dark part of herself reveled in it. In her power in this moment. "I am sorry that evening got so turned around," she went on. "That we both pushed each other to places we didn't want to go. But I did not come here to talk of what happened."

"You didn't?" His brows furrowed as she removed her cloak and unclasped her mask, absently depositing them on an armchair she passed.

Her newly exposed skin sighed, the air in the room a welcome warmth.

"No, I didn't." She stopped only a pace away from him. "I came here for something else."

Zimri's gaze grew dark with her nearness, attention falling to her mouth.

It was as if lava filled the gap between them. Arabessa's entire body was on fire with her desperation to press against him, feel his strength beneath her fingers, lean in to better breathe his familiar fragrance.

But she didn't touch him. And he didn't move to touch her.

"Whatever you need," said Zimri, his husky voice sliding over her like silk, "I will ensure you receive."

"Good." She nodded, her stomach fluttering with her resolve. "I want a better ending to that night. I want the ending we should have had."

A spark of fire lit in Zimri's hazel depths at her words, his lips slightly parting. He regarded her as though he was dying of thirst and she was a crisp, clear abundance of water.

Every nerve ending in Arabessa raced with greedy need, magic sparking in her veins.

He might be getting married to another. She might be walking into the Fade.

But responsibility and duty and future outcomes could hang tonight. This evening Arabessa would savor every grain fall she could get with this man. For later might not be a possibility for either of them.

"And what sort of ending do you believe we should have had?" Zimri questioned, clear fight in his tense shoulders. It was obvious he was restraining his desires, ensuring Arabessa truly got what she sought in this moment.

It had her love for him swell further. She knew without a doubt he was distraught in regard to his earlier betrayal, unforgiving of himself. But she forgave him. She understood all of him.

"The one we deserve," she whispered, closing the last gap between them.

A shuttering breath escaped Zimri, his expression pained as he looked down at her pressed against him, her hands flat on his quickly rising chest.

"I want a night with you that eviscerates all of our other nights," admitted Arabessa.

Liquid heat pooled into Zimri's features, a dangerous glint of the Collector becoming drunk from drinking in her lust-filled emotions.

"If that is what you need," he said, his tone a deep abyss of desire, "then I will ensure you receive it."

Sliding a hand into her hair, another around her waist, he ever so carefully brought her in for a kiss. But that gentleness was swept away as soon as their lips touched. Devour and devotion: that was how he now claimed her mouth, her soul. Every part of Arabessa erupted in white-hot euphoria with the change, with the hunger in which Zimri fed on her, gripped her body, groaned as she gripped his.

He tasted like whiskey and warmth and home.

Turning them as one, he had her pressed against his desk, her backside scooting onto the top as he spread her legs so he could fit between. Forgotten papers shifted and slid under her as Zimri pressed his weight to her length. Shirts were being torn open, cravats ripped off, vests and jackets quickly discarded. They were rapid animals fighting for who could touch bare the other quickest.

As Zimri pulled off her boots, then pants, gazing down to where she rested wet and ready, a low growl rumbled out of him.

"You are too perfect," he said. "Too beautiful."

Arabessa could say the same to him as his stomach rippled with abs, his length hard and intimidating. But it was not only his body that had Arabessa aflame; it was knowing what lay within, the beautiful soul filling him.

"You are the magnificent one," she breathed. "You are the one who makes me whole."

He moaned, as though in pain from her words, before he dropped to his knees, head coming between her legs. Arabessa arched up as he made contact, pure pleasure shooting into her every vein. She did not muffle her groans, her exclamations of ecstasy. Somewhere in the distance she could hear the faint celebrations taking place below, the Macabris party swirling behind the glass where Zimri was bent over, worshipping her.

Arabessa dug her fingers into his shoulders, a constant string of desire escaping her, as one of his hands pressed her thighs wider. Too soon she was soaring, shattering with her climax, but no part of her was satiated as Zimri stood. He regarded her like the prince he was in this domain. Smug, dangerous, not nearly finished. He could taste every part of her emotions, every yearn and want and knew exactly how to play with it.

"I think you are ready for me, my music," he said, moving himself to her entrance. He pushed against her gently, a tease.

"I am never ready for how you make me feel," she admitted from where she remained sprawled across his desk.

Something in Zimri's gaze softened, grew serious. "I am always here with you, Arabessa," he reassured. "You hold me up as much as I hold you. Do you trust me?"

It was a question to answer his earlier apology, his earlier devastation. A way for him to be confident in moving forward without regrets, as she had needed from him this night.

Her chest ached to console his fears as he consoled hers. "I trust you with all of me," she said, and it was every bit true.

Zimri's expression lit with pure love as he pushed into her. Their groans of bliss filled his office, consumed each of their breaths, before he was bending toward her, taking one of her nipples into his mouth. The sensation rocked through Arabessa, and she dug her fingers into his back, gripped his backside to feel each of his thrusts. She was spinning, falling, coming apart only to snap back together with each climax he pulled from her. Zimri was making good on his promise. He was eviscerating any past memory of them lying together. He was creating a new lost god for them to offer their devotion to: each other.

They showed their commitment in every corner of his office: against the glass, on his carpet, Zimri seated in one of his large armchairs as Arabessa rode him. It was a night of forevers, of gorgeous exhaustion and groaning praises.

When they finally came to lie in respite on his soft rug, Zimri asleep with her curled at his side, Arabessa brought herself to whisper what she could not when he was awake. "You are the eclipse who will forever consume my heart," she said. His even, sleeping breaths had her head rise and fall as she listened to his heartbeat. "I love you, Zimri D'Enieu, and I am so sorry I could not share what is about to happen."

Sliding from his embrace, Arabessa quickly and quietly re-dressed. After scrawling a note that she left on a nearby side table, she chanced a few grain falls to study him one last time: his angled jaw, beautiful features, and long, lean power relaxed as he slept. She was consumed with rivaling emotions: wanting to stay but needing to go.

In the end, as she found the hall beyond his office door momentarily clear, she slipped out. Arabessa walked away from Zimri and toward the final phase of the eclipse: to a future that was coming for both of them, whether they wanted that ending or not.

CHAPTER THIRTY-EIGHT

Zimri no longer recognized himself.

He had become a visceral being: pure emotion, all need and desperation, and short fused.

Arabessa had disappeared after they had shared a night that rewrote every fiber in his soul, and he was unsure what that meant or how he was to go forward.

It was driving him to madness.

Especially when he found her still missing among the palace's guests tonight.

Sure, she had left him a note, the smallest reprieve in her absence after he awoke, explaining she had a duty to the throne to attend to. But was that duty to have taken her all week?

He had attempted to seek her out in the coming days to no avail.

Arabessa remained not at home in Jabari. Empty did he find her private quarters beneath the palace. Zimri had sent letters and messenger moths and even asked her whereabouts of Dolion. What he had not yet done, however, was talk with her sisters. They, too, had been elusive in his search, no doubt each off with her pirate or duke. But he hoped to remedy his fruitless labor tonight, for he knew all three women were meant to be in attendance at the palace's soiree as regular guests.

Standing within a shadowed corner of the large courtyard, Zimri ignored the drink in his hand as he gazed through his eye mask at the lavish party. His gifts fizzled through his blood at the emotions swarming him: excitement, intrigue, jealousy, desire. It was a tittering of court members and esteemed visitors in layers upon layers of intricate beading and feathering and scaling. A contest for who could carry the most opulence the most boldly.

Come stand next to me, and see how I may eclipse you.

A fitting craving, given the event they were celebrating.

Per tradition, the palace was hosting a grand viewing party, as tonight was *the* eclipse: when the last of the sky's stars would wink out and with their deaths send an extinguishing wind through the kingdom. Every light would be snuffed out to push their cave world into pure black.

It was the breath when all would look up, waiting for the rush of magic to crackle through their sky and absorb into their skin as their new stars were born in a wave of color. Brighter, more brilliant, alive. The Sky's Return.

A time for new beginnings, said many.

Which was likely the reason for the Volkovs settling on such a day for Kattiva's wedding.

Our wedding, Zimri corrected himself silently, finally taking a sip of his drink. The burn did nothing to settle the fight twisting up in his gut.

The only new beginning he wanted for tomorrow was with Arabessa. The memories from the other night played like a punishment over and over through his mind. Their glorious sweat-soaked euphoria, broken hearts mending, trust reforming.

She had said she had come not to talk about their fight but to redo how it ended. To give them an ending they deserved. Zimri had not thought her words foreboding until she had left him as he slept. Now they spun with a finality that caused him to feel sick, panicked.

The silent oath she harbored rose wild and unanswered in his mind.

Was this the duty to the throne she had mentioned in her note?

The idea that it could be connected to a demand from the Thief King made Zimri's skin crawl with unease. Especially if a silent oath was tied to it.

Nothing pleasant was made from such a combination.

What task would have Arabessa talking in finalities, keep her in fear that they could not be together until after tonight?

These were the questions that Zimri had hoped to ask after they awoke, *together*. But he had been robbed of the chance, which kept them swirling through his mind and fueled his desperation to find her.

But as the days went on, he had begun to wonder a different question: Did the truth even matter? His truth was simple: He loved Arabessa. Desperately. And nothing would change that.

Zimri had been a fool to believe he could walk this path without her, that Macabris alone would be enough to fulfill him. Despite what his parents had built, what he had been determined to reclaim in their name, it was no longer a sense of duty but instead a self-placed burden, a curse. His parents had been proud of Macabris, to be sure, had wished for him to one day help in running it, but from what he remembered of their teachings, they had always stressed what was most important was making one's own name in this kingdom, not following in another's. Macabris might be part of his past, but was it to be his only future?

There are many paths you can walk to become one of my confidants, if it is not destined to be through Macabris. Words from his king so very long ago. Zimri knew he could find a new way forward that still held purpose, that he could make for himself and his gifts.

And then there was Arabessa . . .

I do want you. I want this. Her own proclamation from after his engagement ball.

Zimri wanted only to build a future with her in it. What they had between them was not for forgetting, for letting go and moving on.

If the past month proved anything, it was that they were born to be together. To *work* as one, side by side.

But to convince her of such a thing, have her committed to him despite whatever spelled secret stood in their way, he wasn't quite sure how to achieve. Especially if he couldn't find her tonight to attempt to do so. But it *had* to be tonight, for tomorrow would be too late.

Zimri's impatience roared as he scanned the crowd. *Come on, Arabessa, I know you are meant to be here.*

"I thought I'd catch you sulking in a corner somewhere," said Kattiva as she slid to his side. The black ink of her wolf tattoos seemed darker in the low-lit courtyard as she held a long-stemmed glass. "I promise not to force you to attend any such future soirees when we are wed, Collector, unless *you* promise you'll enjoy them."

At the mention of their wedding, Zimri's chest tightened with further unease and frustration.

"I'm enjoying myself," he lied.

Kattiva let out a boisterous laugh that grabbed the attention of more than a few guests. "You must do better than that if you wish to fool me," she said, her amused eyes meeting his from beneath her raven-feathered headdress.

"I'll take that under advisement."

"Please do."

"I'm assuming you are enjoying yourself?" he forced himself to ask. After all, Kattiva wasn't to blame for his foul mood.

"I always enjoy myself," she replied, attention flitting to a nearby couple who smiled coyly at her. Kattiva lifted the speared strawberry from her drink and slowly sucked on the tip, not breaking their gazes.

"Yes," mused Zimri. "That you certainly do."

Kattiva turned back to him. "I hope you find someone to play with tonight. It is tradition for those betrothed to snog wild hogs and all that before they wed, is it not?"

"I'm not quite certain that is how the saying goes," said Zimri as he returned to scanning the disguised mass, picking apart each of their costumes, looking for something, *anything*, that was recognizable as whom he sought.

"Really?" quipped Kattiva. "Well, however it's said, it's a fine tradition. Though I'll be sure to curb my vices as best I can, for I am the furthest from an early riser. No doubt the reason Mother insisted on the wedding being so indecently early. It certainly is one way to have me behave," she said in a dry tone. "My vanity keeps me from looking anything but well rested and breathtaking for the day."

Zimri did not respond, his pulse quickening as his attention snagged on two forms who were possibly Niya and Larkyra, but after finding brown gazes, his disappointment settled harsh in his chest.

"Are you looking for someone?" asked Kattiva, attempting to follow where his eyes roamed. "Perhaps that beauty who caught your attention the other week?"

"No," said Zimri much too quickly. "I am not looking for her."

"What a pity." Kattiva frowned. "I had hoped you had reconnected when passing along my gratitude for saving my life."

"Are your parents here?" asked Zimri, very much wanting to move the conversation away from Arabessa. His mind was already filled with her.

"They are," she said. "Somewhere over there, talking to the Suyis." She waved a hand in the general direction of the grand carved waterfall in the center of the courtyard. "I shudder to think what they are discussing. My mother will do anything to get into the good graces of the older thief houses. I'm sure they are regaling them with how they've saved prime seating for their family for tomorrow's event."

At every mention of their upcoming nuptials, it was as if a hand squeezed Zimri's lungs tighter and tighter. He was suffocating in guilt at doubting what they had agreed upon. For not knowing what tomorrow would bring for him, but knowing he was no longer committed to his and Kattiva's agreement. Zimri was not a man to go back on his word, nor was he one to revel in hurting a friend. The very thought of doing either made him sick. Kattiva had become a friend, a surprise after she had been so long merely the daughter of his biggest adversary.

And a friend certainly deserved better than being jilted at the altar.

Zimri had to tell her. He had to *at least* share with her his wavering, what was wrapped up in his heart. He certainly would want Kattiva to tell him if she felt as though she were walking to the Fade rather than to the altar. For that was how he felt: that his life was ending after the Star Eclipse.

"Kattiva," he began. "About tomorrow . . ."

"Yes?" She glanced back at him.

"I'm not sure . . . ," he began as his magic spun, along with his racing pulse. "I'm not sure if—"

Two forms drew his gaze as they parted the crowd behind Kattiva. They were horned beasts of paradise, dripping in blues and greens and silver. The Sky's Return.

Familiar Bassette-blue eyes met his from beneath their disguises. One short, one tall.

Zimri's body was seized to fly, to run to them. He hardly needed Niya nodding in a *follow us* gesture to do just that before they dipped back into the crowd.

"I'm so sorry," said Zimri quickly to Kattiva. "You must excuse me."

"Really?" Kattiva raised an incredulous brow. "You are going to leave me on such a precipice regarding tomorrow?"

"I'm sorry," he repeated, placing his glass on the tray of a passing waiter. "I will return shortly."

Zimri dove into the mass, keeping his attention hooked to the two figures whose headdresses were draped in horned beadwork. He ignored his gifts, which wanted to catalog every emotion of those he passed, every buzz of excitement, lapping of desire, shaking of fear. He forced himself to keep focused, keep steady, as he turned from the boisterous party in the courtyard to a shadowed and secluded hedge grove. Sharp-petaled blooms graced the edges, vines reaching for his feet as he passed.

Rounding a corner, he slowed as he caught sight of the two sisters in the dark garden. They huddled in front of the statue of Yuza, the lost god of strength, who was carved in black rock with a raised sword.

As his footsteps transferred from grass to gravel, the crunching announced his approach.

Larkyra and Niya glanced over to him.

"I have been looking for you both for entirely too long," said Zimri by way of greeting. "You must tell me where I can find your sister."

"Such serious demands for a celebratory night," came a calm voice from behind Niya and Larkyra.

"Achak," said Zimri with a frown as the twins stepped forward from the shadows. They were in the brother's form, his beard woven with glowing beads mimicking the stars. Zimri's unease heightened. It was never a good sign when Achak was mixed within a whispering group.

"It is serendipitous that you have been looking for the girls, for they have been waiting for you," Achak explained.

"Is this about Arabessa?" Zimri questioned, pulse growing quicker. "Where is she?"

"Are you sure this is a good idea?" Larkyra turned to Achak, ignoring Zimri's question. "I still think we are breaking important rules here."

"Bending," clarified Niya. "We'd never be able to break the magic of the throne, but bend we certainly are able."

"Call it what you'd like," returned Larkyra. "But I'd argue our king and Arabessa would not appreciate either. What if this hurts her chances?"

"It was with *your* insistence that he know," reminded Niya, "that this plan was formed."

"What are you talking about?" Zimri asked, confusion swirling. "Know what? Is Arabessa all right?"

"Yes, he deserves to know what's been going on," said Larkyra to Niya as though Zimri wasn't even there. "But perhaps there is another way."

"We've been through this already," huffed Niya. "We clearly no longer have the ability to tell him." She shot Achak a glare. "And we are out of time to think of alternatives. The twins offered this, and I think it a fine idea. The best one, in fact. He needs to know, and he needs to know before tomorrow."

He needs to know before tomorrow.

Zimri grabbed hold of Niya, impatience flaring. "Do you know what secret Ara has been spelled to keep silent?"

Niya's eyes went wide beneath her mask. "You know she harbors a silent oath?"

He had been right! Zimri's pulse tumbled in chaos along with his gifts. "What is it?" he demanded, tightening his hold. "You must tell me!"

"Not so loud," hissed Larkyra, glancing to the hedged path that led back to the party. "We do not want to draw a crowd."

"You also will not get my words out, squeezing me as you are," pointed out Niya. "But you *will* get my fury."

Zimri held Niya's gaze, knowing she was more than capable of keeping such a promise. With a shaking breath, he stepped back. "I apologize," said Zimri, attempting to calm his racing worry. "I merely agree that I *deserve* to know what's going on. It's imperative I know, in fact. Not merely because Arabessa's future depends on it. *Please*," implored Zimri, quieter this time, desperate.

"I . . ." Niya glanced questioningly to Larkyra, then Achak, uncertainty clear in her gaze. "I'm sorry, I can't."

I can't.

The same words Arabessa had spoken.

By the Fade, was there to be no end of this!

"You are bound to silence too?" asked Zimri, hope plummeting. He looked to the group. "*None* of you can tell me?"

"It is better if we show you," explained Achak.

"Show me?" questioned Zimri, brows coming together.

The brother nodded before turning to the girls. "Before we go on, I want to assure you that if trouble is to be had from tonight, it will be directed at us. For trouble has never stopped my sister or me from doing what we felt necessary."

"Are we sure?" probed Larkyra once more, worry still clear in her voice. "What if . . ."

"All will be fine," assured Niya, a hand to her sister's shoulder. "Achak has promised."

"Well, we didn't promise that," corrected Achak.

"Not helping," Niya singsonged through clenched teeth.

"Will one of you *please* explain what in all of Aadilor is happening?" interjected Zimri, not hiding the panic now edging up his throat. Arabessa was shouldering an important secret, one her sisters and Achak knew of and could not tell him. "Where is your sister?" he demanded. "You *must* tell me where to find her."

"We will do one better," said Achak. "We will bring you to her." Reaching up, the brother pricked his finger on the blade of Yuza. A dark drop of blood glistened on the tip before the sword glowed blinding white. The illumination rushed down the figure to disappear into the ground. There was a breath when nothing happened, merely the muffled revelry of the palace party in the distance. Then there was stone scraped over stone. Tiles at the base of the statue shifted away, revealing a dark and steep staircase. Achak's swirling violet eyes met Zimri's. "Come." Their only instruction before they disappeared into the abyss, expecting them all to follow.

Chapter Thirty-Nine

*T*hough she had grown up in the Thief Kingdom, Arabessa had never worn as many weapons as she had on her tonight. At least, not all at once. She had no fewer than eight knives strapped, tucked, and sheathed along various parts of her cloaked body. Her flute was in its usual holster, hidden beneath her shirt's sleeve along her forearm, while one of her violins was strapped in its carrying case across her back.

Yet still, none of it felt remotely enough.

Arabessa had been on edge for the past three days, waiting, searching, anticipating when creaking open a door or rounding a corner would throw her into her final test.

Even the simple act of stepping out of bed she had grown to fear would cause her to spin, fall, or blink into a new room. One that was designed to be her end.

She would never again be caught unprepared.

Arabessa couldn't afford to.

You must survive. The desperate words of her father, mixed with the determined gazes of her sisters and the devoted touch of Zimri, filled her mind.

Arabessa's magic stirred restless in response to her constant thrumming pulse echoing her final duty.

I must survive. I must survive. I must survive.

"Would you like another?" asked a masked server who stopped beside her.

Arabessa looked to the full drink between her hands. She hadn't taken one sip. "Thank you, but I still need to finish this one."

"Aye, that you do," they said in a way that meant *drink more or get out*, before they squeezed their way to another table.

Arabessa sat by an open window in a small, gritty pub on the outskirts of the Mystic District. It was not a choice establishment for those wishing to view the eclipse. It butted up against an alley, allowing only a sliver of the dim stars above to peek through. Despite its location, however, it was overflowing with patrons. Too many meager tables were crammed together, guests pinched even closer as the crashing wave of chatter and laughter and drunken revelry filled the stuffy air. The lighting was a glimmer of sagging, overused candles, and the smell of sweat mixed with boisterous belchings of ale continually forced Arabessa to lean out of the window to her right.

But she had chosen this establishment for a reason. It was not a place anyone she knew would think to find her, and it was as far from the palace as she could get while remaining within the city.

She knew she would otherwise be too tempted to accompany her sisters to the royal eclipse party tonight.

And she needed to avoid that gathering at all costs.

As Arabessa had suspected, after their night together Zimri had been on the hunt to talk with her. Her lady's maid in Jabari as well as her father had told her of his visits, and it might be the cowardly way out, but she could not afford to face him again. To disturb her last memories of them entwined together, his devoted gaze drinking her in between their kisses. It was what she needed to fuel her resolve for whatever was about to happen next. Arabessa had made sure to leave each of the people she loved without regret.

And with that settled, she had chosen to stay at an inn in this district, waiting like the guilty for the gallows, for the throne to come to collect her before the Collector could. She waited for her final test.

Final.

Test.

She had a moment to marvel at how far she had come. How much she had survived.

How has a month gone by? she wondered in disbelief.

Achak had said two contestants remained. Did they still? Would she ever face them?

What last twisted evaluation did the throne have in store to decide who would be crowned king tonight?

Arabessa stared into her drink as her nerves jumped in ripples similar to those of the ale in her mug. The patrons around her sang and slammed the rhythm of a popular kingdom ballad onto their tables.

Come over, come over,
To our kingdom of trouble;
Your sins shall not follow you home

You can fight, you can drink,
Live life like a gamble;
Only our king watches where you may roam

Come over, come over,
To our kingdom of no mercy;
Your silver ain't all that we'll steal

You may hide what is yours,
Lock it away in a safe,
But all vices are always revealed

Arabessa smiled softly as the song continued on. It was a favorite of hers and her sisters, and when together, they would always join in. Such moments felt distant now, simpler, but too often memories were reshaped to be bittersweet. Still, she resisted the urge to lean back and look out the window to the barely there stars. Take in the last balls of light that desperately held on to this side of history.

Though Arabessa was an impatient flutter inside, part of her was holding tight to this moment.

Tomorrow morning Zimri would be married to Kattiva. He would have his additional shares in Macabris.

Tomorrow, if she survived, she would be his king.

She would be holding her biggest achievement but have lost her greatest love.

Her grip flexed on her drink.

No, she thought, *not lost him. Reshaped our future.* For if she won the throne, she would be able to reveal to him herself upon it and with it every answer he had sought. And then one day, hopefully, if he could forgive her this secret, be with him again as they once had been.

Well, perhaps not quite like they had been.

I'd be his mistress.

Arabessa frowned at the beaten-up tabletop her drink rested on, a fissure of sorrow worming through her with the word: *mistress.*

I'd prefer you to be my wife, Zimri had once said.

She swallowed past the ache in her throat. She would have preferred that too. If only that was how their story could have been written.

You must make personal sacrifices every day. Every grain fall you wear a crown.

Perhaps this was another of her sacrifices. To settle for becoming a mistress over a wife.

Arabessa shook her head, clearing the heavy emotions that stirred there.

See, she silently reproached, *this is why I cannot be near him before my test.* Even at this distance, her mind became preoccupied.

Focus, she reprimanded. *Focus.*

"One sand fall, mates!" shouted the bartender from the back of the room, pointing to a large sandglass in the center of one of the shelves.

Patrons erupted in excited cheers; more drinks were ordered.

Arabessa sat still.

One sand fall.

One sand fall.

Her magic skipped in her veins. *Danger,* it whispered. *Danger approaches.*

Arabessa should get up now. She should move, walk the alleys, search for her tests.

Yet she remained seated.

Arabessa's entire life came down to tonight. This one sand fall.

Soon she would have to prove that everything she and her sisters had gone through, been taught by her father, was not in vain.

This was the thought that kept her paralyzed, for the question it stirred up in her mind held her deepest fear: Was she worthy?

Arabessa let out a shaking breath, finally sipping her drink. The ale was bitter and had turned warm. Disappointing.

Disappointing. Disappointing. Disappointing.

What she could not bear to become.

As Arabessa placed the mug back onto the table, it ended up clattering to the ground, liquid spilling onto black stone.

She blinked, glancing up to find she was no longer sitting but standing. The tight crowd and gritty bar gone. Replaced instead by the soaring throne room of the Thief King.

Her blood rushed through her in a panic, her magic whooshing to fill up her hands.

Protect! Protect!

The heat from the lava surrounding her was oppressive, the smell sulfuric and mixed with ancient magic.

Arabessa's stomach twisted with further anticipation as she caught the shrouded gaze of the Thief King sitting at a distance atop his throne. No protective smoke surrounded him. He sat revealed in his bright-white splendor, tall horned headdress holding his focus on her, silent, unmoving: a moon in the sky bearing down on his world.

Here sat the current king, soon to be the old king, waiting to crown the new king.

Her father was to be witness to whether his eldest daughter lived or died.

It should have terrified any child to stand before their parent as Arabessa now was, knowing what could follow. But she had not been raised to be like others. She had been raised as a Bassette, to be a monster in a monstrous world and to know the difference between the two.

Arabessa stood ready, prepared to write her own fate and claim a throne.

CHAPTER FORTY

*T*he glowing insects scampered away into cracks and corners as Zimri and his group passed through the damp tunnel. The bugs were the only illumination in the tight corridor, the crawling blue light coming from large clicker critters and the fluttering green wings of below beetles. Zimri held in a cringe as the sound of tiny legs skittering here and there filled his ears, the air stale and tasting of dirt along his tongue with each of his quick inhales.

"I did not know of this passageway," said Niya behind him, her tone clearly meaning, Why *haven't I known of this passageway?*

"I didn't know of it either," added Larkyra.

"You are young," replied Achak, who guided them in front of Zimri. "There is much you do not know."

"Always so charming," muttered Niya.

As they shuffled forward in a line, Zimri was thankful for the single path, or he might have needed to grab hold of Achak's gown. So dark it was down here. He could just barely make out edges of the brother every few paces as they came close to a slithering or flittering glowing creature.

"Oy!" yipped Niya. "One got into my headdress! Get it out! Get it out!"

"Stand still or I won't be able to," instructed Larkyra as they all stopped. Niya squirmed and squeaked while her younger sister unclasped her horned disguise. No fewer than three bugs fell to the dirt floor, scampering quickly away.

Niya shuddered, her red hair now spilling down her back, face exposed. "That's it," she said. "If another one of those vermin comes remotely close, I shall squash them." With a twist and flourish of her hand, she called up a small flame to flicker in her palm.

The spot they stood in awoke with orange light, the bugs hissing at the offending brightness and disappearing in a rush into the farther shadows.

"Why didn't you do that as soon as we came down here?" asked Zimri, not hiding his prick of annoyance. He didn't enjoy bugs any more than she did.

"I didn't realize we'd be walking so long in nightmare alley," Niya sulked.

"Are we ready to continue?" asked Achak. "Or would you prefer to stand around some more and miss what you are meant to see?"

Zimri's heart skipped with unease. "What do you mean, 'meant to see'? You said you were taking me to Arabessa?"

"If you'd let us go on," pointed out Achak, "you'd get all your answers."

"And there's that brotherly charm again," replied Niya.

"You know," began Achak, glaring over Zimri's shoulder at her, "these used to be people." He gestured in the general direction of the bugs.

"What happened to them?" asked Larkyra, voice edged in wonderment rather than horror.

"They got on our nerves," said Achak, before he turned and continued forward.

"He lies," whispered Niya, but still she kept from commenting further the remainder of their journey.

Soon—though not soon enough, in Zimri's opinion—they came to a crumbling staircase that led up to a small trapdoor in the tunnel's ceiling.

Achak ascended, tracing a finger along the outline of the hatch. White magic sizzled and sparked, and then, with a creak like old knees straightening, the door opened.

Zimri's gifts gathered at the ready for whatever he might face as he climbed up and out, but he merely found them standing in a new windowless space. A solitary torch lit the obsidian room from where it flickered in its holster along the far wall.

"We are inside the palace," he said, spinning around slowly.

"We are," confirmed Achak as they glided to the wall directly in front of them. It was so smooth and spotless Zimri could see his reflection. His maroon eye mask matched his three-piece high-collared suit. His black cravat pinned with one of his father's amber brooches. Though he looked put together, he felt anything but.

He was a swirl of impatience and frustration and fear. Fear that he would be too late in talking with Arabessa; frustration that perhaps he had followed Achak too readily, blindly, and it was all a trick. The ancient one loved the Bassettes, to be sure, but they were also fickle, as old creatures were. They followed the rules of this world only for as long as it suited. Then bend them they would, break them certainly and without care if it caused a stir worth watching, entertainment after an eternity of monotony. It was why, he knew, Achak preferred the Thief Kingdom to all other places in Aadilor: for the chaos.

But the sisters seemed in on whatever *this* was, even if Larkyra was a bit hesitant, and that served as scales tipped for him to follow.

We don't want you to marry Kattiva Volkov, they had practically ordered him. *Because you're in love with Arabessa.*

Despite being less than pleased when Niya and Larkyra had first shared their feelings with him in the basement of Macabris, he was glad of it now. Everything was out in the open, and what he was prepared to do next would startle none of them.

"Is your sister meeting us here?" Zimri asked, his need to hurry rising tenfold as Niya and Larkyra came to stand beside him. How much longer did they have until the full eclipse? Until today became his wedding day?

"Patience," instructed Achak.

"I've been *quite* patient," argued Zimri. "Lark, Niya"—he looked intently to each of them—"I don't blasted care about your silent oaths. Tell me whatever you can about what is happening. Why are we here? Where is Ara?"

He caught the shared glance between them, their waft of worry, which only fueled his panic further.

"If you do not tell me this instant—" His next words were cut off as Achak placed a hand on the mirrored wall, its black surface rippling away to reveal a wide view of the Thief King's throne room.

Zimri's pulse ran fast through his veins, his magic jumping in tandem as he took in the soaring hall. Lava snaked around the T-shaped pathway from where the large stone guardians stood by the entry doors. The Thief King sat at the far end of the narrowing lane. No cloud of smoke shrouded him as he rested in his throne, his splendid white costume and horned headdress on display. His attention seemed pinned to the closed doors, as though waiting.

"An observing room," said Niya. "I didn't know the throne room had these." She turned accusatory eyes on Achak. "Why didn't we know it had these?"

"You don't have to know everything, child," the brother said, before he shifted and twitched into the sister. "But now you know this," she finished more gently.

"Yes," began Niya, fists plunking on her hips. "But I would think the Mousai and the king's closest confidant would be among the 'need to know everything.'"

"I know about these," said Zimri, twisting back to the group. "But what I want to know is why we are in one."

"Hold on." Niya drew back. "You *knew* about these observing rooms?"

"Did I not just say I did?"

"Oy!" She raised offended brows. "That attitude won't help you here."

"And neither will pointless conversation," he snapped. "But if answering your questions will answer mine, then *yes*, I know of these rooms. How else would I be able to observe those I was meant to interrogate for the king? There are many peppered around the throne room. Now, if you're quite satisfied, one of you better explain—"

His fire died on his tongue as he saw her appear out of thin air. Arabessa stood at the entrance to the throne room. She was masked, but her cloak's hood was thrown back, and her raven hair was tamed into a braid down her back.

Zimri took quick steps to the glass, heart in his throat. "Ara," he said, though he knew she could not hear him from where he stood. She was dressed as a thief. Trousers fitted for easy running and climbing; boots with soles for gripping ledges. He caught the glint of metal along her thigh, ankle, and wrist. But what prickled his awareness, his warning, was her violin strapped into its case at her back.

She was not dressed as a thief. She was dressed for a fight.

But why?

A new figure appeared on the exact opposite part of Arabessa's path. Zimri frowned, regarding the tall, muscular man who was similarly armed to the teeth with blades and daggers and spiked metal shoulder pads. His gray hair was pulled back, matching his silver mask.

Zimri watched as the man's gaze caught on their king on his throne before he found Arabessa far down his path.

There was the familiar singing of metal being pulled, his sword unsheathing.

Zimri cried out in warning at the same instant the man let out a bloodthirsty roar and ran straight for Arabessa, blade raised in a painful promise.

And all Arabessa did in return was unstrap her violin and begin to play.

CHAPTER FORTY-ONE

*S*he was going to have to kill him.

Arabessa knew this even before the words of her last test flashed quickly in the air.

Your final test is not one but two
Of ambition and of sacrifice
Be prepared to go until death
For one crowned is all that will suffice

She was fighting for the Thief King's throne. Having the last two contenders battle it out was the most logical next step. Arabessa had a spike of annoyance for not assuming this sooner. Claim a life to claim the crown: indeed, proof of one's ambition to be this kingdom's ruler.

Luckily for Arabessa, she had taken her fair share of lives, and though each of those souls nicked away small pieces of her own, she had learned to compartmentalize.

Her killing innocents during her performance had been negligent, wrong. Her attempting to take this man's life tonight was necessary.

As her magic poured hot into her fingertips, Arabessa had her violin tucked to her neck, bow raised in the sand fall it took the man to pull out his sword. She set loose a full-bodied set of chords, her instrument lighting like a struck match, shooting out a purple wave at the oncoming threat.

But her opponent was gifted as well, for with his Sight he apparently saw the impending blow and swung his sword in a quick circle, sending blue wind to gust her spell away.

Sticks, thought Arabessa in a rush as she pumped out harsher and more complicated music.

Waves upon waves of her sharp gifts forced the man to stop and protect himself. He batted and swung and swiped his blade, which glowed with his own magic. A shield of blue power punching away everything she threw at him.

He must have an affinity with metal, thought Arabessa, brows furrowed in concentration beneath her mask as her fingers began to ache with the speed at which she forced them to work along her violin's neck. While they both held the lost gods' gifts, her advantage lay in the fact that he could release only a single point of attack from his blade. Arabessa was commanding notes that could be threaded, split, splayed, and wound together. She conducted her gifts to untether, her song to grow into dozens of individual chords as it reached for her opponent. They were the hot tentacles of a jellyfish stinging and striking, eventually knocking his sword to the ground.

He screamed his torment as her gifts sliced against his chest, face, hands. Rakes of crimson awoke across his skin.

Cut, her magic sang. *Shred.*

With a heavy grunt, the masked man held an arm as sacrifice to shield the rest of his body from the onslaught of her spell. He dug the other into his leather holster along his ribs.

There was a winking of sharp silver turned ice blue as he flung razor-edged circles forward. Arabessa was forced to duck, pausing her playing as the deadly razors whooshed past her. Her heart skipped a beat, a relieved breath escaping her before she howled in agony. The blades had spun back around, two lodging into her shoulders.

The pain was overwhelming, a blaze of fire with each of her quick inhales.

The man twisted his hand, working his blue magic, which was still connected to the weapons, to dig farther in.

Arabessa's vision swam with the torture, and she dropped her violin as she fell to her knees.

Her magic cried its agony as her song was cut off. Her gifts lay trapped inside her hands.

Let us out! they pleaded. *Let us fight! Let us protect!*

But Arabessa was preoccupied, trying to remove the circular cutters from her back. The man's hold on them was unceasing, and her fingers slipped, catching on sharp edges to suffer cuts.

"Arrgh!" yelled Arabessa in determined anguish as she finally was able to grip the centers of each. She ignored the nauseating feel of more of her flesh being torn as she fought to rip the razors free with another strangled cry.

She threw them with a grunt, and there was a puff of steam as they disappeared into the lava that churned on either side of their walkway.

Arabessa's chest rose and fell in great huffs, a pool of warmth running down her back and soaking her shirt and cloak. Blood. She glanced at her hands. They were covered in crimson, slices along her fingers that sent an acute sting to radiate down her arms.

She hissed as she attempted to flex them, the strength and precision feeling drained from the injuries.

Nononononono.

Panic erupted cold and uninviting through her veins as she forced herself to her feet.

She would not be able to play her violin with fighting purpose. Her fingers would slip on the strings. The music would come out messy and unfocused, and with it so would her gifts, her spells.

Her opponent grunted as he pushed himself to stand as well, his front shredded in a fashion similar to what she assumed was the state of her back. But his hands were protected by thick gloves, and he easily unsheathed two more hooked knives from his hips. He gripped their handles with determined strength as blue sparks of his gifts lit them up.

Arabessa's concentration wavered at the fear that grabbed her.

I'm going to die. The poisonous words slithered fast through her mind.

You must *survive.* A whisper of response.

Arabessa's heartbeat galloped as she glanced to the alabaster figure far down the walkway. The Thief King loomed large as he remained unmoving in his sharp obsidian-backed throne.

Was Dolion sitting prisoner as she had been in her last test? Handcuffed to watch the fate of his ruling, what he had set into motion when creating his daughters to be the Mousai, when deciding to step down from the throne. She was filled with anguish for her father, sorrow for herself.

But then a glint of metal soaring fast pushed Arabessa to drop her current thoughts and regain her focus. She twisted and ducked away from one of the blades her opponent flung her way. But they, too, were tethered to his blue gifts and quickly were whipping back around in the same instant he ran forward, second glowing knife raised.

You must survive. You must survive. You must survive.

A surge of white-hot determination filled Arabessa's veins.

I must survive.

Retracting her flute from her holster, she brought it to her lips. Despite the pain in her hands and the taste of blood smeared on the lip plate, she blew out a single piercing note.

Her gifts were a sizzle through her fingers before they sent a gust of wind down the body of her instrument, barreling from the end into her attacker.

He lifted his blade to take most of the hit, but her spell managed to push him back a few paces. It gave Arabessa time to spin away from the other knife whirling close. The benefit of her simplified flute was that she could move easier with it while playing.

Her spells were not as nuanced as what she could do with a violin or cello or piano, but her work with a flute most certainly could do damage, and damage Arabessa was set on achieving.

She ignored the throb of her stab wounds along her shoulders and reclaimed her attack.

Fluttering out a marching song of battle, her magic erupted in a storm through her hands. It filled her flute with a purple blaze of light as it struck like a venomous snake. Her violet gifts clashed with her opponent's blue as he pushed a spell from his dagger. Puffs of magic tangled and smacked through the air, clawing to get past each other.

It was a dance that Arabessa had practiced on many occasions with her sisters, but the end would be wholly different from in their sparring room. To kill was her intention as sweat dripped from beneath her mask, her breathing labored with the fight.

In her periphery she could see the white glow of their king still remaining in his sea of black. The last star of this realm waiting to light another.

I will survive.

Arabessa was filled with the truth of this thought, how it *must* come to pass, for her father, mother, sisters, Zimri, and most of all herself.

The throne was testing her ambition, but what would push her to win was *her* dedication. No one else's.

With a great roar of breath, she pushed out a barrage of her gifts from her flute, finally knocking unsteady her opponent. She rushed forward, taking advantage of his missteps to engage him in hand-to-hand combat. Or rather foot to hand, as she kicked free his last blade.

"No!" the man screamed as it soared toward the lava and sank away.

Arabessa did not hesitate as she twisted again, but low this time to knock out his feet.

He fell back with a heavy grunt, half of his body angled over the walkway. A scream tore from him as the heat from the lava singed through his leather glove, which hovered too near the red liquid.

He tipped back onto the pathway, cradling his arm to his chest as Arabessa stepped beside him, flute poised at her lips. She stared down into silver-blue eyes beneath his metal mask. They were full of rage and exhaustion, no doubt a reflection of her own.

In a stopping of time Arabessa wondered who he was, how he had come to be invited, and what made him worthy for the throne as she might be.

But the answers to those thoughts were not for battles. They were for aftermaths, for later, when one would atone for necessary action.

Pushing the needed cold resolve into her spine, Arabessa quieted the whisperings of remorse that had begun to fill her heart.

She prepared to become a monster so she might complete her monstrous act.

With fingers dancing along her flute's keys, she sent a push of her magic to slam into the splayed man at her feet. He did not fight or grip the pathway as he slid from it. He merely kept his gaze pinned to Arabessa's as he whispered, "My king," right before he fell into the river of lava and disappeared.

CHAPTER FORTY-TWO

*A*rabessa was encased in ice, her thoughts numb as she stared at the churning river of fire. She had killed him. She had removed the last contestant, but before she was able to process what that meant, burning script appeared in front of her.

> *Now for your sacrifice*
> *Your final way through*
> *Something must be lost*
> *So very sacred to you*

Heavy dread filled Arabessa, her gaze snapping to her father on his distant throne. What would the crown demand be her sacrifice so she was finally worthy?

Something must be lost so very sacred to you.

Did Dolion know? Could he see what was to come? Though he remained seated, the silver gifts around him crackled and sparked, as though reacting to whatever chaos of emotion filled him.

But Arabessa's attention was pulled away, to a rippling in the air as the throne's magic brought to life a figure on the walkway.

Everything inside Arabessa stopped.

Her heart. Her breaths. Her magic. Frozen.

Zimri stood in front of her. Or a perfect replica of him. Tall, broad, commanding, perfect. He was maskless, his features exposed, his black, smooth skin interrupted only by a scruff of a beard. "My music," he said, hazel eyes pained as they took her in.

"Zimri," she whispered, stepping closer. Her pulse stuttered to life again before it began to race. "You can't be here," she said in a panic.

"But I am," he replied. "I am your last test."

Arabessa shook her head, not accepting his words, not accepting this fate. *No, please, not him. Not him.* "No," she whispered. "No."

Zimri bridged the last gap between them, gentle hand coming to cup her face. Arabessa hadn't been prepared for this phantom's touch to feel so real. Her vision blurred with her tears, her breaths coming out ragged.

Not him. Not him. Not him.

"You do not even know what must be done yet," he said as if sensing her denial, his tone light, amused, like he was not standing before her as sacrifice.

Arabessa did not want to ask what must be done. She wanted to grab his hand and run. Escape before the impending decree of this throne killed her. Killed them.

Despite her understanding this Zimri was a mirage, a figment made from the magic of the throne, it did nothing to lessen how she was being severed into pieces by the warmth of his touch. This Zimri sounded the same: that deep rumble that stroked down her body. This Zimri held his fragrance: caramel and fire and home. This Zimri looked at her with his love, his reverie, his wonder.

How cruel, this final test.

How vicious.

Yes, whispered a voice within her. *It is so you understand what kingdom you are vying to rule: one filled with the wicked, the cruel, the vicious. A monster is needed to kill monsters, just as one is needed to control them.*

"You have been through so much," said Zimri, his voice a gentle wind as his hand lowered from her face. "*We* have been through so much, but now here we are, and you are almost my king."

My king.

"I'm so sorry I could not tell you about this," said Arabessa, throat tightening to keep her sob at bay, "explain to you the reason for me needing time, but I finally had a chance for something of my own. I had to take it, Zimri."

"I am not angry," he said. "I understand dreams are not given; they are worked for. I also know what it is to want a thing." His gaze momentarily fell to her lips. "To burn for it. You taught me that, my music, how to burn brightest for that which you love. Which is why this is for the best." Zimri took a step back.

"What is?" she dared ask, the space between them already growing cold.

"Taking away my memory of ever loving you."

Arabessa was kicked in the chest, every part of her shattering. Nausea raced up her throat. "No," she said, voice hoarse, broken. "*No,* there must be another way."

Something must be lost so very sacred to you.

"This is what must be sacrificed," explained Zimri, expression pitying.

My memory of ever loving you.

"No, please, anything but this!" Arabessa turned in desperation to her king. *Father!* she wanted to yell. *Please, not this, not this, not this!*

But Dolion did not move, did not speak. The only hint that he might be lucid to this moment was his alabaster-gloved hands tightening along his armrests.

You must make personal sacrifices every day. Every grain fall you wear a crown.

Here sat her father wearing his crown, making his daily sacrifice. He watched his daughter suffer and was unable to save her.

A shaky breath escaped Arabessa as she turned back to Zimri.

Alone.

She was utterly alone.

This was *her* test. Her final stone to step upon to make it to the end.

Her end.

Their end.

She and Zimri would forever be over after tonight. No hope of figuring out a new future for them in whatever form their love could be molded.

I am your sacrifice. His words stabbed clean through her heart. She was suffocating, her lungs crushed. Her tears finally streamed unchecked down her cheeks from beneath her mask.

"I . . . don't want to lose you," she said, sob in her voice. No longer was she the warrior who had sent a man soaring into lava. She was a soul desperate for her soul mate.

"I'll still be in your life," said Zimri, tone consoling. "As a brother."

Brother.

Never before had such a name been so cutting, so tormenting.

Arabessa would become like Niya and Larkyra, a sister.

No longer his love, his lover, his music.

An impossible life.

"I don't . . ." The words got caught in her throat as bile rose. "I don't know how to be a sister to you."

Zimri tilted his head but did not respond, the throne's magic reminding her again that this was *her* test, *her* sacrifice to accept or to die rejecting.

Death felt like a mercy in this moment.

Unlike the test where she had watched her sisters die, she knew unequivocally this outcome would be real.

"Tomorrow you would forget everything between us?" Her question came out a whisper.

Zimri nodded.

"You'd be married to another, have your shares in Macabris." She tried to reason her way into her decision even though each word broke her further. But logic and responsibility had always been her compass forward. "I would be your king, and you'd easily be able to serve me," she rambled on. "You wouldn't suffer if we weren't together, if I never became your mistress. Any pain I might have caused you from our past relationship would be erased. With you no longer in love with me, no memories of ever being in love, you'd be free."

Of me.

Arabessa somehow managed not to crumble to the floor, to stay the heavier sobs working their way up. *But I'd never be free of you!* she wanted to scream.

Arabessa would always remember every intimate instant of them together, every stolen kiss and touch and embrace. Each companionable visit, nearness, supportive gaze that had first rooted their love. Their last joining this week was to officially be their last. Arabessa would hold all these memories, these feelings, tangled tight in her heart, always there to recall, to yearn for whenever Zimri was near, but he would be forever free of their meaning. He might love her, but he would never again be in love with her.

She had once believed love made one weak, made one distracted, made one forgetful of their purpose. As she had seen with her father's heartache, as she had once believed of Larkyra and Niya being absent from home.

But Arabessa had come to realize that this same love was what caused people to grow, to become better for those they loved, stronger, to yearn for other dreams, other duties.

"So what shall be your choice?" asked Zimri.

As Arabessa looked into the face of the man who would forever hold her heart, the mysterious boy who had come to hear her play on a night when she hadn't even known she needed company until he appeared, something tugged in her mind at his question.

Choice.

This was *her* choice. Not Zimri's. *Her* choice to take away his memory of being in love with her.

My decisions are mine to make. Not for you to make.

Zimri had accused her of making his choices for him with Macabris, had said that he had wanted to be with her more than to own his parents' club. But she hadn't believed him.

People change; wants change.

She had robbed him of his changing desires, his autonomy for his own life and wants.

And wasn't that all Arabessa had ever wanted for herself? To be able to make her own decisions for her future?

Would she become even more of a hypocrite by taking away his memories?

Like a hot grip, words he had whispered to her as she lay above him flashed through her mind. *The memories of us are forever a part of my soul,* Zimri had said. *They are the only thoughts that have kept my heart beating. I could never forget a single moment with you, Arabessa Bassette.*

Arabessa's heart raced with her realization.

"That is not my sacrifice to make," she said, a tense resolve fortifying her bones.

Zimri watched her curiously. "It isn't?"

"No. I cannot make such a decision on your behalf. That would be *your* something sacred to give up. Your choice, not mine. I will not take away your choice ever again, Zimri."

A flash of silver danced in Zimri's gaze, a reminder that the throne's magic made him up, spoke his words. "A most peculiar way to fail," he said—the magic said—Zimri's voice now lacing with all the thief kings of the past.

"I have not failed," countered Arabessa, ignoring how her gifts tumbled in protest through her blood, sensing the direction of her thoughts. "I will still sacrifice something sacred to me."

"And what is more sacred than the love of the person whom you have always desired?"

There was a precipice where Arabessa was paralyzed with her quick decision, heartbeat a stampeding of beasts, as she knew what she needed to give up. The only thing this throne would consider a worthy alternative to its own asking.

No! screamed her gifts in her blood. *Nononononononono!*

But it was the only way. Her only guarantee to finish this and live. To prove her worth, her dedication, honor the work of her family while not robbing Zimri of his choices.

It would change her life forever, but this would be her great sacrifice for her to claim the throne.

What is more sacred? the throne's ancient magic had asked.

"My magic," answered Arabessa before she bent to the lava churning at the side of her path and held her hands to its fire.

CHAPTER FORTY-THREE

*T*here came a time in everyone's life when the reality of a moment and one's ability to understand it didn't fit together. A breaking in the sands' falling, a tilt where the grains took longer to hit the bottom, instead following the curved surface of the glass.

Zimri was slow to process what had taken place in this throne room as he held Arabessa's trembling body. All he could take in was the overwhelming scent of her pain as he tried desperately to tame her shivers and agonizing screams as chaos swarmed around him. Her torture was his torture as he knelt on the pathway leading to the throne. Niya was somewhere behind him, yelling at the stone guardians in the distance to summon the royal medics. Achak was muttering strange words beneath their breath, their white magic misting around Arabessa as the towering form of the Thief King loomed in Zimri's periphery.

There was a deep, hot flame raging in his heart at his king, standing there. He had allowed this to happen, perhaps even pushed it to, but those emotions were quick to be drowned by every other feeling pouring in: heartache, panic, fear.

Zimri's only reprieve was the threads of Larkyra's song, which touched cool along his arm as her healing voice wrapped gold swaths around Arabessa's hands. The fragrance of sun-soaked meadows attempted to overwhelm the odor of death and destruction. Zimri had a grain fall to marvel at how calm Larkyra's melody could remain under such conditions, especially when he made the mistake of glancing to where she concentrated. Bile rose up his throat as he took in Arabessa's beautiful, graceful hands, now disfigured into a boiling red massacre of muscles and tendons showing through singed slivers of skin. Pieces of her shirtsleeves were melted into her wrists. Fragments of bone visible.

He tried desperately to ignore the added scent of flesh burning, of *her* flesh burning. Arabessa's groans of anguish merely caused him to grip her tighter.

"You're all right." He cradled her close, his pulse a wild, charging horse in his ears. "It will be all right. You will be all right. I am here. We are here."

"Zzimmri," slurred Arabessa, gaze fighting for lucidity. Despite her sisters' ministrations, the pain was obviously too great, for she continued to slip in and out of consciousness.

"I am here, my music. I am here," he assured as he met her blue eyes beneath her mask. They were rimmed with tears, bloodshot, tormented.

His heart exploded in further agony to see her so broken.

"Zimri," she tried again, forcing out his name on a gasp, her body a never-ceasing shiver. The shock of her injuries consuming. "I cccouldn't do it. I couldn't ssssacrifice you."

A knot formed in his throat. "Yes," he said, stroking her damp hair, his own tears now falling. "Yes, I saw everything. I heard everything. I am so very grateful you did not, but this . . ." He couldn't bring himself to say it, to point to what she had sacrificed instead.

Her magic. Her music. Gone.

Despite the power of Larkyra's gifts, whatever ancient prayer Achak muttered to the lost gods or art the medic's healing herbs might achieve, Zimri knew Arabessa's hands would never again be the same. She would never play as she had, pull out her melody so fluidly or conduct her powers with such ease. Her wounds were too great. Too destructive.

She had given up *too* much.

His tears came fast, then, as he began to rock her in his arms.

You know our sister. Niya's words swam forward. *She is sickeningly honorable. Painfully selfless.*

Yes, thought Zimri in anguish, *painfully selfless.*

Tonight only proved this further.

Arabessa had given up one of her greatest gifts instead of robbing him of his choice in loving her.

That would be your *something sacred to give up. Your choice, not mine. I will not take away your choice ever again, Zimri.*

Blast, how was it possible to love her even more? She was a force, her own eclipse. Her sense of responsibility and duty and devotion unrivaled. Misguided at times, but always at the forefront of her actions.

But by the Fade, why was *this* the answer to her sacrifice?

Zimri did not quite understand how much of tonight had come to pass, how Arabessa had come to be vying for the throne, how Dolion was stepping down as king, or how he even could. He especially had not realized that Arabessa had such a desire to fill her father's role. A selfish part of him was hurt and frustrated not to have known, that she had been unable to confide in him, that his king had not. But he also understood the ways of this kingdom. It was a place of secrets, many of which were spelled silent. Zimri had merely been a tortured spectator to the waves of information that crashed into him as he stood on the other side of the observing room's glass. Until it had been too much, even for Niya and Larkyra, as they had watched their sister hold her hands to flames. With their combined gifts surging, they had shattered the partition, running to Arabessa's aid. Bending or breaking rules be damned!

While there was much still to be explained, to atone for and rebuild, he knew right now was not for such answers, such action. Right now was for making sure Arabessa was safe. That she lived. That she would wake up.

She had become still in his arms, her shivering ceasing as Larkyra's spell finally allowed her to drift unconscious.

"We should move her from here before she wakes up," said Dolion.

Zimri blinked up to his white, resplendent form. He was still in his masked headdress, his shadowed gaze peering down, but something about his presence felt different . . . felt lacking. "Take her to my bedchambers," he instructed. There was a crack in his tone, the showing of remorse and pain hidden under years of feigning indifference when ruling. Here stood Arabessa's father, no longer their Thief King.

Zimri pushed away the direction those thoughts were taking him, what that truly meant for the woman in his arms, as he scooped up Arabessa. She was all that mattered.

He hurried to carry her across the long, narrow path where lava churned on either side, gentle so as not to disturb her hands lying on a strip of cloth ripped from Achak's dress. Zimri brought her past the throne, into the private chambers of the Thief King, air bursting with refreshing cool after they had remained so long in the volcanic heat. Niya and Larkyra rushed to help Zimri settle their sister onto their father's bed, while Achak and Dolion spoke to two sightless healers who had arrived. As the medics set to work on Arabessa, forcing Zimri to step back, he found himself doing something he had not done since the night he found out his parents had died: he prayed to the lost gods for strength.

Growing up within the Bassettes' household, Zimri would never have described the family as quiet. Which was why it was more than unnerving as they stood silent sentries around where Arabessa rested.

If they could make light of the events, tease or push sarcasm, it would have put some hope into his heart. But their sober, distraught whispers only held his pulse in a continued panicked rhythm as he stared at Arabessa, who remained unconscious.

Larkyra had helped stop the blistering, the further burning from residual layers of lava feasting on flesh. She had cooled her sister's hands so the medics could set to applying tonics and paste. Arabessa now wore thick bandages, and the healers had given her a heavy sedative upon their leave. They and Larkyra had done as much as they could for the moment. *A bit of time is needed, and then we shall return,* they had said before bowing low to their king and shuffling out.

Only then had Dolion removed his headdress, unclasping the disguise as though he were removing the entire kingdom from his shoulders.

And perhaps he was.

Zimri had not realized how truly exhausted Dolion was in his role until that moment. And now that he knew that he could step down from such responsibility, it was clear how needed it must have been for a new Thief King to fill his place.

A wave of disquiet prickled through Zimri.

Arabessa was to be the next Thief King.

Might already be.

Zimri was wrapped with uncertainty for how he felt in regard to this: he only knew he wanted Arabessa's efforts to not be in vain, for what they had gone through together to not be.

"Did it work?" he turned to ask Dolion, who stood at the end of her bed. His voice was hoarse after not speaking for so long. Zimri had only been doing: fetching clean rags, wiping sweat from Arabessa's brows.

His mentor's tired eyes met his. "If she's alive, it should, yes."

"Wait." Zimri frowned. "What do you mean, if she's alive?"

"There can only ever be one Thief King, my child," explained Achak from where the sister sat in a chair in the corner of the candlelit room.

The meaning of the twin's words slowly gripped him. "She could have *died* claiming the throne?"

The room's collective silence was answer enough.

Hot rage filled Zimri's throat, a protective panic for what could have been. "How could you have let her agree to this?" His seething question was directed at all of them.

"Niya and I only learned of Arabessa's goal this week," Larkyra said from where she and Niya sat along the opposite side of the bed. "Everything was already in motion. And even if it weren't, this was her choice. We would not have kept her from trying to achieve a goal she wanted." Larkyra leaned forward to push back a loose dark curl from Arabessa's forehead. "And she wanted this very badly."

This was her choice.

Zimri was spinning, fuming with ugly, hot ire. In disbelief for what he could have lost. He had known the danger immediately threatening Arabessa in the throne room, but never did he imagine she would have willingly chosen a path that could end with her death.

She wanted this very badly. Larkyra's words surrounded him like ice, solidifying his rage.

And perhaps because he needed a place for his anger to go, a person to blame for why the woman he loved was lying next to him torn and hurt and so very pale, he began to wonder if Arabessa had only decided on this journey because of some misguided sense of duty to her family. That she *had* to follow in her father's footsteps as the eldest. As he himself had thought he needed to with owning Macabris.

I have a duty to the throne to attend to. The words scrawled across the note she had left him shifted with new meaning.

"Did you ask her to do this?" Zimri cut a look to Dolion, his tone the sharpest it had ever been toward the man.

Dolion glanced at Zimri in anguished shock, as though he had stabbed him with a blade.

"Zimri," chided Larkyra in a whisper. "How could you think such a thing?"

Because he's asked you all to do too much too often before.

"You haven't answered my question." Zimri kept his gaze on the man who had taught him everything, who might become his biggest enemy, depending on his reply.

"My daughter's choice in this has been entirely her own," said Dolion. "I may have raised her to lead, but I would *never* force her to rule."

Despite the fervor in his tone, Zimri didn't quite believe him. Even if he had not forced Arabessa outright, all in this room had acted in surprising ways to claim his approval at one time or another—Zimri included. If Arabessa had believed Dolion had wanted this for her, it would have certainly swayed her decision to attempt to become the next Thief King.

"Arabessa knew what could possibly be her fate," continued Dolion, face grave as he stared down at his eldest child. "And though I do not enjoy seeing any of my children hurt, I *am* proud of her. She fought for what she wanted out of life, for *who* she wanted." His eyes rose to meet Zimri's again. "While this throne comes with many burdens, she will make a fine leader because she already was one. Just like her mother."

Dolion's last words snagged in his mind.

Just like her mother.

She will make a fine leader because she already was one. Just like her mother.

Memories from weeks ago rushed forward in Zimri's mind: he and Arabessa embracing within a hidden passage of Macabris. *I learned of something today regarding my mother . . .* , she had said, tone grave, but she had wanted to talk with her sisters first before confiding in him. And then everything else had happened to sever their time alone, to pull forward other tasks, other obstacles. Could Johanna have been Thief King too? Before Dolion?

"Johanna was a . . . leader?" he questioned to the room. He had no doubts that Secret Stealers were at play here, which was why he kept his wording vague.

"Yes," said Achak. The only response needed.

Yes, Johanna was Thief King. Yes, Arabessa's mother sat on the throne before her father, before her.

Zimri took a deep breath in. His final answer for why Arabessa would want to enter into this contest settled like a stone dropped into a pond: a rippling of understanding in his mind. *She wants to continue what her parents have built, what her family has sacrificed for generations to protect.*

How much of that yearning he understood. How much he, too, had suffered to achieve. But where he felt as though he was forcing himself to be as his parents had been, work in a heightened emotional environment that did not agree with his magic's temperament, Arabessa vying for the throne felt obvious. Despite the danger it had put her in, he hated to admit that it *did* feel like fate.

She will make a fine leader because she already was one.

Yes, he thought, *she was.*

This was why she had needed more time, was so adamant about maintaining her focus until after the Star Eclipse.

There is something I must do, complete, before I can allow other distractions. She had been trying to tell him as best she could with her silent oath. And still he had pressed her. Betrayed her.

Zimri's frustration bubbled forward, a hot flash of resentment for the rules and secrecies of this kingdom. They were certainly in place for a reason, but he hated that it had put such a wedge between him and Arabessa. She finally was fighting for something for herself, her own choice of a future, and he hadn't been able to stand beside her in support. In preparation.

You can stand beside her now, a quiet voice reminded him.

Yes, he thought, hands curling into determined fists in his lap. *Always. Forever.*

"She will not be the same after tonight." Dolion's words pulled Zimri's attention back to the room. "What she has sacrificed is a great loss, but Arabessa is much more than her magic, as each of my daughters are." He looked to Niya and Larkyra. "They are Bassettes, and Bassettes have greatness within even without the lost gods' gifts."

Zimri watched Niya and Larkyra slip from their seats to go to their father. They wrapped themselves around his large form. Dolion held them in return, not attempting to wipe free the tears escaping down his cheeks.

Even though Zimri's rage for tonight's events still simmered in his blood, there was a tug in his chest to go to them. He yearned for such an embrace, to be held up by another's strength when his own failed, but this was always where he felt he toed the line between family and orphan come to live with one.

"Brother," said Larkyra, the word a warm touch that spread, its own embrace. Her arm was extended to him. *Come here,* it beckoned.

Zimri's breaths faltered as he stood, but soon he was entangled in the mass that was the Bassettes.

You are family, Niya had said.

In this moment he finally allowed himself to believe it.

In another room the muffled chime of a sandglass turning over echoed into the bedchamber. Midnight.

"It is the eclipse," said Achak, who stood from their corner seat, gliding to the end of Arabessa's bed beside the rest of them. "It is time."

Zimri's heartbeats sprinted awake. *Time for what?* he wanted to ask, but noticing everyone's eyes now pinned to Arabessa's sleeping form, he had a feeling he was about to find out.

As the last chime rang out, there was a sand fall of silence, of nothing, before a hot gust of wind blew through the room. Flames were extinguished, spilling the chamber into blackness. Zimri's pulse jumped as a thick metallic scent of magic filled up the dark. Hundreds of whispers flooded Zimri's mind, voices speaking in languages too old to recognize. They were a mix of old and young, and they were everywhere until they joined together to murmur, *We thank you for your service, our king. We thank you for your sacrifice.*

Bright silver light erupted into the chamber as beside him, Dolion's head was thrown back. Zimri and the rest of the group gave him space as a channel of illumination filtered from his mouth, a matching roar.

It tore endlessly from Dolion until his lips closed with a snap and he bent over to barely catch his weight on his knees.

"Father!" cried Niya and Larkyra as they hurried to support him.

Seeing he was taken care of, Zimri's attention swung to the churning silver cloud of magic hovering in the room above where Arabessa lay. He shielded his gaze from the blaze of it, the crackling and fiery storm in the center.

Our king, the voices proclaimed once again before diving into Arabessa's chest.

Zimri moved forward with a cry, seized with his need to protect her from whatever was about to happen, but a strong grip on his arm stopped him.

Achak held him back, their violet eyes glowing in the dim light as they shook their head no.

He tried to free himself from their grip, but the twins only dug in harder.

"Watch," they instructed.

Still in a panic, he turned to witness Arabessa's eyes snapping open just as the last of the light funneled in. Her gaze glowed bright with silver, with the throne's magic.

Our king, the voices chanted again.

"My kingdom," Arabessa sighed out, her voice mixing with the hundreds of others. Her eyes snapped shut then, white light disappearing as that similar warm wind picked up once more. It spun through the room to reverse what it had put out.

The candelabras and bedside candles flamed back on as the last of the gust disappeared.

No one said a word, tension mounting as Achak glided forward to press a gentle hand to Arabessa's chest.

Zimri felt as though an eternity had passed before the twins glanced over. "It is done," they said, a relieved smile forming. But then they were dropping into a kneel, head lowered toward Arabessa. "My king," they whispered.

Zimri's gifts rushed along with his pulse as the rest of the room followed suit. He watched Dolion bow low, an oddity after so long having witnessed others bowing to him. Niya and Larkyra knelt beside their father. Zimri looked to Arabessa asleep, her features so familiar, so breathtaking, his home. Dolion had said he was proud of Arabessa, and that was exactly the emotion that overtook Zimri in this moment: pride. Here lay a creature who had always commanded his heart, now set to command his kingdom.

Slowly Zimri came to his knee, head bowed. "My king," he whispered.

A small groan from Arabessa caused him to glance up along with the others.

She moaned again, moving slightly.

Zimri was the wind as he came to her side, Achak and his family rushing forward as well.

"Easy, sister," said Larkyra, keeping her from sitting up.

"You are hurt," Niya informed her softly.

"But you will heal," assured Dolion.

"You have done well, child," added Achak.

Arabessa's gazed danced over each of them, brows pinching. "Zimri?" she asked, voice like dry leaves.

"I'm right here." He edged closer.

As her blue eyes met his, an ocean of relief crashed against his rib cage. She was awake, lucid, talking.

"Zimri," she said again.

"Yes, my music?" He leaned forward next to her. "What do you need? What can we get you?" He didn't know where to touch, didn't know where she wouldn't hurt. Her bandaged hands were at her sides, while the rest of her body had suffered its fair share of scrapes and bruises. He settled for stroking back her dark hair, which rippled across her pillow.

She let out a contented sigh at the contact. "I'm alive." She spoke the words in disbelief.

Zimri's other hand gripped the sheets, heartache pinching because it could have been the alternative. "Yes," he assured. "Yes, you are very much alive."

"Is it tomorrow?"

"Just."

"Am I too late?"

"For what?"

"To be with you."

"Oh, my love," he said, hand coming up to cup her cheek. He wanted to pull her into his arms, kiss her, take in her hurt so she could have a reprieve. "You are never too late. You are all the pieces of my heart."

Arabessa smiled then, a radiant, full smile. He was basking in the sun's rays, warm and alive and hopeful.

"I feel . . . different." Her grin shifted quickly, face falling with discomfort as she shifted beneath the sheets. "My gifts, they—" A groan of pain cut off Arabessa's next words, and Zimri was frantic to find the source. "It hurts! My magic, it hurts!"

"It's the transfer," said Dolion from the other side of the bed. "It's weaving into her gifts. It is not pleasant, this part."

"We must help her," said Zimri, panic seeming his forever emotion. "She's already suffered enough."

"Yes," agreed Dolion, his face grave, pale. "My songbird"—he turned to Larkyra—"nothing the medics could give her right now will affect what she's going through. Only magic can help magic."

Larkyra nodded, understanding. "I will ease her," she assured. "She will sleep in peace."

As the room was filled with Larkyra's lullaby, a dusting of calm settled into Zimri's muscles. But even so, he held his breath in waiting as he watched the gold haze of Larkyra's spell cocoon Arabessa. He would not be satisfied until he witnessed the last bit of tension fall from her brow. He would not leave her side until then. He did not want to leave her side at all. But as she let out a soft sigh, her entire body growing relaxed as she slipped to a place where pain could not grip her, he eventually forced himself to stand. Because he had to.

Zimri left Arabessa, preparing the words needed to call off a wedding.

CHAPTER FORTY-FOUR

*H*e found her where he had not expected: at home. Zimri had come to Kattiva's apartments at last after spending more sand falls than he would have liked searching for her whereabouts. It appeared, however, that she had been speaking true on retiring at a reasonable hour despite the heightened revelry thrumming beyond her doors.

The Sky's Return was a masterpiece of color and illumination across their caved kingdom. The closest this world would ever come to experiencing daylight. The residual dusting of fresh magic glittered through the streets and mixed with the drunken revelry. Citizens spilled out of cafés, hollered down from balconies, sang arm in arm as they stepped uneasily thanks to too many spirits. No one needed a party to attend, for the entire kingdom was a celebration.

Zimri must have stuck out like a rotten apple on a ripe tree as he rushed with purpose down the sidewalks, bursting in and out of every haunt he knew Kattiva fancied. He was not glowing with merriment; he was edged with desperate determination.

His and Kattiva's wedding was in only a handful of sand falls when he found himself on her doorstep, pulse a gallop through his blood. Her butler's surprise was evident even beneath his mask at seeing Zimri standing there, so much so that he quickly told Zimri he could not come in. But Zimri charged past the stout man, demanding an audience with his mistress.

Now here he stood, waiting in Kattiva's well-lit sitting room. He had positioned himself by one of the tall windows, tipping back a curtain to stare through his mask at the disheveled crowd streaming by. And somewhere beyond the buildings in front of him was the palace, where deep inside rested the woman he loved.

Am I too late? Arabessa had asked. *To be with you.*

Never, thought Zimri, muscles tensing along his shoulders. *Never.*

The last wall keeping him and Arabessa apart had crumbled. He now knew all she had been carrying, the heavy role she now claimed and what she had been willing to sacrifice for their love to live. Zimri was more than willing to sacrifice something of his own in return. An ambition of his that had changed. He had come to realize that reclaiming Macabris had been his attempt at keeping his parents close rather than any true goal of his own. But his mother and father would always be close, for they made up parts of himself. Every time he looked in the mirror, he saw the eyes of his mother, the nose of his father, each of their smiles.

"It is said to be bad luck to see the bride before the wedding." Kattiva's voice stirred Zimri from his corner by the window. He turned to watch her float in, her rust-colored silk robe swaying. She was not wearing her mask; her burn scar puckered over her cheekbone and across the bridge of her nose. She was always a creature who appeared relaxed, but seeing her as she was now, without painted lips or done-up hair, nothing covering or cinching or pushing up, she seemed serene. This might have been the version of Kattiva Volkov he favored the most.

When he gazed back at her scar, Zimri's chest squeezed, as it reminded him of another woman who had played with fire. The very woman who had driven him here.

"I apologize for calling on you at such an hour," he began, meeting her in the center of the room. "Especially on such a day as today, but we must talk."

Kattiva's expression remained even as she regarded him. "You do not want to get married."

Zimri was robbed of thought. He had not expected that. He didn't know how to respond to such a well-aimed arrow, which was probably why he settled on the truth. "No, I do not."

As soon as he spoke the words, he was hit with a waterfall of both relief and guilt.

"I am so very sorry, Kattiva," he went on. "I thought I wanted this. That I could go through with it, but there is something I will lose if I do. Something much more important than obtaining more shares in my parents' club."

Kattiva studied him for a long while, a honey scent of curiosity lifting from her before she gestured to the two couches facing each other by the fire. As they settled into them, Zimri waited for her mood to flip to wrath, to anger. But each expectation he had of this woman she exceeded. Kattiva merely smiled. "Something or someone?" she asked.

His silence seemed to satisfy her, for she laughed, leaning back. "How delightful, Collector. I had begun to wonder if you were immune."

"Immune?" he inquired.

"To desires," said Kattiva as she stroked a lazy finger along the couch's floral embroidery.

"It is much more than desire," Zimri admitted, finding that he wanted to share this with Kattiva. She had become a strange confidant in the midst of this madness, one he believed he could trust with what was in his heart, if merely a slice. She had certainly trusted him with what was in hers.

"Do I know them?" she asked.

"You met them once."

Her brown eyes shone with understanding.

"My savior," she said. "I knew it!" Kattiva sat up, excitement stirring in the air around her. "How coy you tried to be with that one, but she burns too bright to be ignored or forgotten. I saw much between you in the mere grain fall the three of us were together."

Of course you did, thought Zimri.

Kattiva might not have had the powers to read minds or taste the variants of emotions, but she saw much from a little. Her soul was made from the rock and dirt of this kingdom, a thief to items no one thought could be stolen: desires.

"You are nothing if not an excellent observer," he complimented.

"I tend to agree." She grinned. "So, Collector, will you be marrying her instead?"

Zimri's chest fluttered, hopeful, but he kept his features still. He might feel comfortable telling Kattiva his heart lay with another, but he knew the risk of sharing too much too soon. He settled for more vague truths. "I will be enjoying her in every way I can."

Kattiva laughed again, a floral cloud of her amusement. "I'm sure you will. Dare I say I am jealous?"

"We were never a love match," he reminded her.

"Love has nothing to do with enjoyment." Her features grew devious.

"I suppose not, but it certainly makes experiencing life much more gratifying."

"Does it?" she mused. "Perhaps one day I shall endeavor to find out."

"They will be a lucky group, whoever they turn out to be."

"I appreciate you knowing they will not merely be one."

"With all you have to give, Kattiva," he began, "a single soul could not handle alone."

Kattiva grinned, pleased. "Despite how I detest the confines of marriage, I stand by my earlier words. It would have been a fine life to be married to you, Collector."

Another twist of guilt. "I am sorry," said Zimri. "I don't yet know how to atone for breaking our agreement, but I will make it up to you."

"I'm sure you will." She waved an unconcerned hand. "But for now you've perhaps given me the best wedding gift of all."

He tilted his head, curious. "I have?"

"Mmm." She nodded. "When they learn of our canceled engagement, my parents will hate you more than ever, to be sure, but they will be quite consoling with me. Even pampering, I dare say. They won't mention the idea of marriage again anytime soon, if *ever* again. Oh, yes"—Kattiva smiled wide—"to be a jilted bride is a valuable card, indeed."

"So you are not angry with me?" he pressed, wanting to be sure.

"Not in the least. Quite the opposite, in fact. I could kiss you." She smiled. "What a perfect solution to our problems, Collector. Well, not quite perfect for you." Her expression grew serious. "My father will certainly make every approval within the club more painful after today. And without you having majority ownership . . ."

His life within Macabris would become more painful as well.

"It is a concern that does not weigh on me," Zimri admitted.

He was taking a page from Kattiva's book, doing what he wanted rather than what was expected, despite the consequences. Zhad would always be a thorn in his side; it made no difference to him if he grew to become a barbed bush. Especially not since he had begun to ruminate on a way to prune the man back entirely, a solution that could also pay his debt to Kattiva for ending their agreement. It had been a newly planted thought that had occurred to him only when stepping into Kattiva's house this morning. But he still needed time to work out the details.

"That's good to hear," said Kattiva, bringing his attention back to where she sat in front of him. The warm firelight brought color to her white skin while throwing dark pockets of shadow along her scar. "Though I was hoping to make some alterations to the dipping pools," she explained. "As I recently experienced a wonderful water swing that would be quite fun for patrons and their guests. But I suppose we will have to wait to get that signed off. My father will not take kindly to any suggestion you put forward."

"You could propose the alterations," he explained. "You do hold ten percent of decisions."

Kattiva blinked at him. "Don't be ridiculous. My father has never listened to any recommendations I've made. You're the only one who has ever taken me seriously."

"Perhaps that will change," said Zimri, more certainty unfolding for this idea of his.

"Collector," Kattiva began slowly, "you have scheming in your eyes."

"Do I?" he asked, feigning innocence.

Her grin turned sharp. "I like it."

Zimri let out a laugh, the first in an eternity, and it was like releasing a mountain of weight from his chest. "I'm not certain if you have been a good or bad influence on me, Kattiva Volkov."

"A state of uncertainty in which I aspire to leave all those in my company."

"Then let us solidify your achievement with me. I shall take my leave now to tell your parents about canceling today's events."

"Do not waste your gentlemanly behavior on such a task." She waved a hand. "My mother is set to arrive soon, and I shall tell her then. I'd prefer to witness their reactions myself anyway," said Kattiva, devious delight shining in her gaze. If Zimri hadn't known how horrible the Volkovs were, he would have felt sorry for them.

"Are you sure? I could stay to tell her with you." Though every part of him was desperate to return to Arabessa, to be beside her when she awoke, he would stay if Kattiva needed. It was the least he could do for putting this off until the very morning of their wedding.

"I appreciate the offer, but I will be fine." She stood, causing him to stand too. "Plus, I can play the part of the devastated jilted bride better without you here."

She must have seen the flinch in his expression, for she touched his shoulder reassuringly. "Collector," said Kattiva, "there truly are no hard feelings between us. I hope you can trust me on that."

He nodded, words seeming to fail him in this moment.

"We are a good partnership, you and I," she continued as she walked him to the door. "I look forward to the trouble we can cause, despite today."

Zimri looked down to the woman who appeared wholly different from the girl who had first come to him that night at Macabris, searching for a way to maintain her opulent lifestyle. What she really was desiring was her independence from the expectations of her parents, just as he was, just as Arabessa was. Kattiva wanted her choices to be her own. To build a future of her own.

She was not merely a guest at a gathering but a host. She was capable, intelligent, cunning, a force. So much more than the mask of aloofness and debauchery she wore. Kattiva Volkov was on her way to becoming more than a gossiped-about whisper within this kingdom; she was going to be a name. And Zimri had a way of helping that happen quick.

"I look forward to that trouble as well," he said before lifting the top of her hand to his lips. "Thank you, Kattiva. Your friendship is a gift."

A blush rose to her cheeks, and she swatted his shoulder. "Begone with you," she said. "Or you might finally push me to want to be more than friends."

Zimri shot her a grin before opening the door and diving back into the chaotic streets. As he wove through the crowds, he found himself no longer pulling back his magic. It reached in excitement toward the revelry. For the first time in a very long while, his emotions matched the surrounding joy. With smile stretching, Zimri walked toward where the palace loomed, his steps light, elated. He was as the stars winking bright high above: new.

CHAPTER FORTY-FIVE

*A*rabessa swam in and out of a fog, but in both states there were layered whisperings, hushed voices. She wondered if the Fade held such sound or if whatever drugs she had been given caused these side effects. When she did find the strength to open her eyes, her surroundings were muted, a low glow of candlelight. And though she could sense her arms at her sides as she lay in a bed, Arabessa could feel nothing of her hands.

Which she supposed was a blessing, for she remembered vividly the pain.

Blazing heat, so hot it became ice cold before blazing again. The smell of her own skin burning. Nausea threatening to spill out the contents of her stomach. She remembered the consuming agony and bodily shock as she watched the flesh on her fingers bubble and ooze and melt. She recalled, after her screaming, a silver light climbing into her vision, her entire body filling with a thousand flappings of wings, heartbeats of past kings, layers of their magic fusing with her own. Then more pain, more torture, as if her veins had been filled with fire. Her gifts had howled in her mind, the terror of a child calling for their parent. *Stop the hurt! Stop the suffering!* But Arabessa had been able to do nothing to help. She had merely been a vessel in those moments, a fully feeling body to whatever changes were taking place within her.

Then thankfully, after an eternity, her blood had settled. Her breathing had slowed. Her body had calmed. Her magic was her own again, and yet wasn't. Her gifts now moved differently, thicker, braided with something new and very old. Ancient. History swam in her blood.

Our master, sang her gifts, a layering of new voices. *Our king.*

King.

Arabessa was overcome.

She had done it.

She had claimed her future.

A reality Arabessa was having trouble absorbing. Her veins were full of healers' tonics, causing her emotions to slip quickly away, like water in a sieve.

She merely had bouts of relief, spikes of elation, and if she dug deep enough, she could hold on to a pulse of pride.

Arabessa was the next Thief King. She *was* Thief King. She could continue to build what her family had begun.

Growing whispers grabbed her attention again, the shuffling of bodies leaving the room before a click of a door closing. A wading silence followed before someone's weight settled onto the side of her bed. She turned toward it, eyes still closed as there was a gentle touch to her shoulder, a warm graze to her cheek.

Arabessa wasn't sure if she smiled or merely thought about doing so, but she instantly felt lighter inside, breathing in his familiar fragrance.

Home, she thought.

"Zimri," she whispered, her voice rough and dry.

There was a press of a glass to her lips, cool water a jolt of reprieve down her throat.

Arabessa fluttered her eyes open.

He was in a chair, elbows leaning forward onto her bed. His hazel eyes regarded her as though she were a lost god: reverent, wary, overcome.

"My music," said Zimri, continuing to run his thumb against her cheek. "How are you feeling?"

"Much better, now that you're back."

"I am always with you, even if I'm not by your side."

A kick to her pulse.

"Where is my family?" she asked.

"Just in the other room. I asked them to give me a moment alone with you. Do you want me to call them back in?"

"No. They need a break from watching me sleep, I'm sure."

"Still thinking of what others might need, even when you're the one suffering," said Zimri, a mix of disbelief and awe in his tone.

At the mention of her suffering, of what had led her to lie in this bed with her hands in layers of bandages, she had a rush of worry, a need to explain her behavior as best she could.

"Zimri," she began, "I am so sorry—"

He quickly cut her off. "There is nothing to apologize for."

"But what I have put you through . . . us through. I couldn't tell you—"

"It is behind us now." He hushed her with another stroke to her cheek. "Let us be thankful for what we have in the present. What we can now have in our future."

Each other. The unspoken words filled up the silence between them.

A wave of relief and hope twisted against Arabessa's sluggish heartbeats as she held Zimri's gaze. He had changed from what she remembered him wearing earlier, but perhaps more days had passed than she realized. Time was not linear from where she lay. All she knew was that he was handsome in a fresh high-collared black jacket with deep-purple undercoat. His face was unmasked, his black skin made warm in the nearby candlelight. He was here; he knew everything; no more secrets were wedged between them; and he *understood*. He loved her, *remembered* loving her.

Zimri's brows drew in. "Are you in pain?" he asked. "Should I get Larkyra?"

Arabessa shook her head. "I feel no pain."

"Then why are you crying, my love?" He wiped away one of her tears.

"I am happy."

This had his brows rise. "Are you sure? Your emotions are rather twisted right now."

"They are happy tears," she assured.

"I see." Zimri's shoulders eased slightly. "And what causes such happy tears?"

"We are together," answered Arabessa. "We *can* be together," she finished, though a ripple of unease followed. She wasn't sure if what she had interpreted in her half-delirious state was correct from their last meeting.

Am I too late?

Oh, my love, you are never too late. You are all the pieces of my heart.

Zimri's features shifted beside her, growing serious, determined. "Yes, my music, together we most certainly are."

Despite his assuring words, hearing Zimri call her his music sent a wash of grief through her veins. Arabessa's magic crooning in similar sorrow. *How shall we make music now? How shall we soar?*

She didn't know the answer, but the ancient gifts that twisted up in her blood made her feel as though one day they would. Perhaps not her music but certainly her magic. Her power seemed connected to another door, one that was in the shape of a throne.

Arabessa's attention refocused on Zimri. "So the wedding?"

"Not happening."

Somewhere inside her heart a window was thrown open to let in a gust of selfish relief.

"You talked with Kattiva?" she asked.

"I did."

"Was she mad?"

"She was as unexpected as always," admitted Zimri. "Extremely understanding and, dare I say, amused."

"Amused?"

"Very much so."

"Well . . . that's good?"

"Very good, I would think. There are no hard feelings between us."

"And her parents?"

"I don't care two silver for Zhad and Alyona," said Zimri. "Their daughter is more capable than either of them combined."

"You came to like Kattiva," pointed out Arabessa, feeling something uncomfortable move through her, waiting for his response.

"She is much more than she lets on," he began. "She has become a friend."

A beat of silence stretched, Arabessa letting that thought settle.

"And Macabris? You are certain of letting this opportunity go?"

"Do you regret sacrificing what you have?" he asked. It was a question said not in cruelty but to prove his answer matched hers.

There were no regrets.

There was much still to process from her tests, from her hands becoming something very different from what she had been born to rely on, but there was always more than one way to complete a task, and Arabessa would learn those ways. In time.

Currently, she wanted only to soak in that the Star Eclipse was behind them. She had survived. She had won. Zimri was not to marry another. He was sitting here beside her, stroking her shoulder, surrounding her with his comfort and support and love.

"I do not regret what I have sacrificed," said Arabessa.

"Then we are of the same mind," replied Zimri. "We will build something new from what we have given up. Together."

Together.

Arabessa's chest swelled, a prickle of warmth dancing through her as her new layering of magic sighed with her old.

"I love you," she whispered, wishing she could pull him toward her. Kiss him, taste him, wrap him all around her. But her limbs were presently useless at her sides. She didn't want to glance down at her hands. Didn't want to muddy this moment with worry about tomorrow. Of what she'd find when they were unwrapped.

"And I love you," returned Zimri, wiping away another of her fallen tears.

Despite her wanting to remain like this with him forever, a tug of exhaustion raced through her, the medicine claiming its purpose once more. She yawned wide.

"You should sleep now," said Zimri.

"Sleep with me," she offered.

Zimri held her gaze, a pouring of reverence and fierce devotion. "As my king wishes," he replied, a husky rumble before he slid into bed alongside her.

He was achingly gentle as he tucked her head into the crook of his arm, extremely careful not to disturb her bandaged hands.

"Will it be odd, do you think? For those close to me?" she asked, voice groggy to her own ears.

"What?" he questioned.

"Me ruling this kingdom. Ruling them."

"Not for me," said Zimri before he settled a gentle kiss on her forehead. "You, Arabessa Bassette, have reigned over my heart since the first night I met you."

She smiled at that, edging closer within his arms. She was about to reply in kind, but her words dissolved on her tongue as the fingers of sleep reached forward to pull her under. Yet the bliss found in her dreams was no match for the happiness Arabessa now felt for her future.

When the Sky's Return has grown normal
and a throne has traded owners unseen

CHAPTER FORTY-SIX

*T*he woman was easily manipulated. Zimri had barely caressed her with his gifts before her confession spilled from her lips.

"His name is Dogger," she said, blush in her cheeks as she gazed at him with childish fancy. She did not at all seem to mind that she was bound to a chair in a colorless holding cell.

"And he sold you these Mix-up Markers?" Zimri questioned, his smile warm, flirtatious, as he leaned forward in his seat, resting elbows on knees. *Trust me,* his magic cooed. *Tell me.*

Through his mask he studied the woman, her age visible in her graying hair and crinkled eyes.

"Yes." She nodded. "A ripe sliver of a silver moon too."

"How horrid to pay so much just to lose it," he said empathetically. *I care for you.* His gifts stroked down her back, brushed against her cheek. *Tell me more.* "Where can Dogger be found?"

"Fourth alley of Pickpocket Row," the woman sighed, content. "He is the kid, not the old man. He pays for the other as a front."

"Thank you." Zimri sat back, pleased.

The woman's smile was wide as she took in his own.

"Oh, I'm so sorry," he added. "How rude of me. I didn't catch your name?"

There was a hesitation in the woman's expression, a bit of lucidness that *this* was not meant to be shared, but then Zimri pushed another warm graze along her body. *You want to tell me your name so you can hear it from my lips.*

"Rose," she said. "Rose Willoby."

"Rose," Zimri rumbled. "It's been a pleasure."

Standing, he left the room, the heavy bolted door cutting off his seductive spell. In the next grain fall there was a muffled cry of anguish from behind him, Rose regaining her wits and with them her realization of what she had confessed.

But that was no concern of Zimri's. He had come here to acquire information, and acquire it he had. Striding past the guard who had been waiting on the other side, he traveled down the quiet gray hall of the interrogation wing. His gifts thrummed content in his blood, feeling full with his recent concentrated efforts.

The peace was disrupted, however, as soon as he walked through the next door into the basement brawls.

Shouts, growls, excitement, anger, greed: all frothed at the mouth within this room, attacking his senses with an overwhelming mixture of smells.

Zimri made quick to pass on to the next level, slipping into the hidden passageway that eventually climbed up to the private owner's level. Coming to the intricately carved door, he nodded to the guard beside it, turned the knob, and stepped through.

"You really must start knocking," said Kattiva from where she sat behind her large oak desk. She had stopped wearing a disguise within the kingdom, and her white skin shone luminescent in the candlelight, the scar along her cheekbone only enhancing everything interesting about her. The glass partition that ran the length of the wall behind her framed the ruby gown she wore and gave a view of a crowded Macabris below.

"And you really must start locking the door," he said, coming to splay himself in one of the large armchairs in front of her.

"That is what the guards are for."

"No guards stopped me," Zimri pointed out.

"That is because you are you and they know I allow the Collector's company."

"Then why do I need to knock, again?"

"For *pretense*," she said sharply.

"I have never known you to be a fan of pretense."

Kattiva huffed, a great show of annoyance. "Then out of respect? How about that?"

"Fine." Zimri grinned. "I shall pretend to respect you and knock next time."

Kattiva pursed her lips, but it was more to hold back a grin than from irritation.

She had not changed many of the decorations in his old office, at least not yet. What she had added were great bouquets of flowers, their scent taking up the air in the room.

He knew it was because of him. They did a great job of hiding the fragrance of her emotions. A very clever tactic on her part. Which was why it had been in full confidence when Zimri had offered Kattiva a deal to buy out his shares in his parents' club. He knew there was no one better fit to honor what his mother and father had built. Kattiva *was* Macabris, more so than he ever could have been.

Her power over a room was captivating, her morals perfectly gray, her desires curated to offer up every profitable pleasure, and her gluttony for revelry unparalleled. Kattiva Volkov was a madam any club in the Thief Kingdom would be lucky to have. He certainly felt lucky to have such a friend shepherd the history of his family's creation. Not to mention it had absolutely maddened Zhad and Alyona to find themselves under their daughter's rule.

"What did you collect for me, Collector?" asked Kattiva, opening a ledger resting at her side. She plucked a quill from its holder and looked at him expectantly.

373

"Her name is Rose Willoby," he said, picking off a piece of lint from his black jacket. "A kid named Dogger sold her the gifted Mix-up Markers."

"A kid?" Kattiva stopped her scribbling, the inked wolves on her hands staring at him along with her.

"That's what she said. Rose explained that the kid pays an older man to front as them. Dogger evidently runs his business in the fourth alley of Pickpocket Row."

"How delightful," said Kattiva, hastily writing the information down. "A kid thief is always valuable."

"To be sure," agreed Zimri.

"Will you stay for a drink?" asked Kattiva, setting down her quill and closing her book. "I have just restocked your preferred whiskey."

"Later, perhaps." He stood. "I have another job tonight."

"Always in such high demand." She eyed him with a lascivious grin. "But it is of no surprise."

Since passing Macabris on to her, Zimri had become a hired interrogator, but only for select clientele. Ones who could benefit him in more ways than money. Debts and leverage, these were the priceless items to collect in the kingdom. It had been a seamless transition for Zimri, even an enjoyable one, being able to work with his gifts in an environment that suited. To be a master of his own day-to-day.

He especially didn't miss having to deal with Zhad and Alyona. Another reason Kattiva was better equipped. She had no issue moving those pawns along her board—enjoyed it, in fact.

"You know how to reach me if you need my services." He strode to her door.

"That I certainly do." Kattiva grinned. "As always, it is a pleasure partnering with you, Collector."

He shot her a wink, eliciting her laugh before walking out.

Zimri left Macabris, mind already tumbling forward to where he was meant to be next. To *whom* he was to be with. Zimri was on his way to see his king.

CHAPTER FORTY-SEVEN

eep within the center of the palace, a room stood in waiting. The few figures allowed entry into the private chambers were those spelled silent to the secrets that were held within these walls.

You may come and witness, but never repeat, whispered the flickering candles in candelabras.

Arabessa stood within her dressing room, Larkyra and Niya regarding her from their seats in the corner. Arabessa studied herself in the long mirror as her sightless staff tied and cinched and braided her into a spilling white ensemble of bone, scales, nails, and fur. Precious alabaster beading of diamonds and pearls and moonstone fitted together over her shoulders and torso. Her arms were covered in soft bleached alligator hide.

Arabessa had always wondered what it was like for her father to be placed into this disguise. What thoughts spun as he witnessed his transformation from man to being, father to ruler, person to personification.

Her mind remained one filled with awe.

It had been more than a month since Arabessa had claimed the throne, and still this moment of dressing the part had not grown the least bit ordinary. She hardly recognized herself in the glass with her soot-rimmed eyes, hair twisted back in preparation for her headdress, and wearing a disguise that she had worshipped on another since a child.

But Arabessa supposed that was rather the point. To be unrecognizable.

The costume had been tailored to fit her smaller frame, tapered waist, and flaring hips. No questions had been asked for why the disguise needed alterations. The attendants surrounding her were loyal to the throne and whomever the throne deemed worthy.

Arabessa was worthy.

With the reminder, her chest swelled warm, proud, chin tilting up.

"I am not one to be jealous of your new duty," said Niya from where she sat behind Arabessa, teacup in hand. "But I am envious of how fierce this costume is. I want one for myself."

Arabessa met her sister's blue reflected gaze in the mirror, single brow lifting. "I'm afraid this one cannot be replicated."

"Not even the skulls decorating your shoulders?" protested Niya. "I do love a detailed epaulet."

"I doubt there's room for such adornments on your pirate's ship," suggested Larkyra as she leaned forward to refill her cup from the small tea tray between herself and Niya. "And that's the only place you'll be able to show them off, since you're about to sail with the *Crying Queen* for the better part of this year."

"I'm sure I can find space in Alōs's chambers," reasoned Niya.

"I'd love to hear how that conversation will transpire." Larkyra smiled.

"With me getting my way, I'd imagine." Niya flicked a nonexistent piece of dirt from her trousers. She was already dressed to travel but had come here for a quick visit with her sisters before she set off. Plus, her king had orders to give her captain. One reason Arabessa was currently dressing. She had called an audience with the pirate lord and a few of his trusted crew.

"We must now secure your robe, my king," one of her attendants announced as two others stepped up onto Arabessa's platform. They held up the complicated tapestry.

As they settled her robe into place, Arabessa straightened, carrying the new weight placed onto her shoulders as she had been taught to: effortlessly. The material pooled over her body and behind her back. At the sight, her new, tangled magic curled through her veins, purring in contentment.

"Your gloves, Your Grace," offered another assistant.

Arabessa raised her hands, a sting of anguish racing through her gut.

Just as she had not yet grown used to seeing herself in the Thief King's costume, her injury still tore at her heart. Though her hands were stars and sea better than how they had been during the Sky's Return, they still screamed her sacrifice. Her fingers had, thankfully, been saved, but bending them remained extremely difficult. Her nails were gone, skin up to each wrist a puckering discolored weaving. But Larkyra and the medics had truly worked a miracle in their healing, and Arabessa knew she was lucky to have as much as she did.

Still, understanding she could no longer hold her violin and transport herself away, glide her fingertips easily over her piano to paint the room in purple, broke her heart. Her sacrifice she did not regret, but she did grieve what was lost, and grief took time to heal.

Her attendants were careful with placing on her gloves.

"You know," mumbled Niya, mouth half-full with her bite of short-bread, "I feel a bit left out from you and Larkyra."

Arabessa turned to her with a frown, flexing what she could of her hands. "Whatever for?"

"Well, with Lark missing her finger and now you with your burns, perhaps I shall find a way to join in on these limb injuries during my next voyage."

"You're idiotic," stated Larkyra as she sipped her tea.

"I agree," added Arabessa. "Especially since Lark and I are more than capable of causing injury to you now." She flashed her teeth with her smile.

"Much too generous of you both," said Niya as she quickly came to her feet. She dusted off bits of bread crumbs from her chest. "But I presently have an appointment to see our king. Another time perhaps?" She shot them both a smug grin before hastily making her exit.

"Chicken," muttered Larkyra to her retreating form.

Arabessa let out a low laugh, the feeling warming her earlier somber mood from thinking of her injuries. Since Arabessa had been crowned, Niya and Larkyra had fluidly transitioned into their new lives. Her original fears of ending the Mousai had been properly put to bed. Her sisters were happy. In fact, there was an ease among the trio that hadn't been there before. A sense that their love for one another could finally take precedence over their shared duty. As for the kingdom, well, it noted the Mousai's sudden absence as it did most peculiarities: with a swirl of rumored excitement.

They finally became too difficult to manage. The king had to put them down.

I heard they've been freed to roam Aadilor, wreak havoc for our kingdom.

No, no. That is lunacy. They escaped back to the realm where the king stole them from.

Arabessa welcomed each piece of gossip. It merely buried further the truth. And while she might currently lack the powers of the Mousai to do her bidding as the new Thief King, this kingdom had a tendency to manifest what it needed when needed. Such roles would be filled, and Arabessa was ready to rule whoever desired to occupy them.

"May I do the honors?" A deep, familiar voice had Arabessa glancing over to find her father now in the doorway. He accepted the heavy horned headdress from one of the attendants.

Arabessa's pulse skipped with joy at seeing him. After stepping down, Dolion had been almost exclusively in Jabari or visiting Larkyra in Lachlan. The Thief Kingdom he did not seem eager to return to anytime soon. Understandable after two decades of rule. Still, Arabessa had missed him, most of her time being needed here.

"Father." Larkyra stood to greet him. "How wonderful to see you."

"I was not expecting a visit," said Arabessa, stepping down from her pedestal and striding to his side. She leaned up to kiss him on the cheek.

"I was not expecting me to come today either," he admitted, gaze beneath his mask tentatively sweeping the room. A room that had once been his. "But I thought it time for a visit. Plus, I am rather familiar with this part of the process. I thought I could be of service." He gave Arabessa a soft smile, nodding to the headdress in his hands.

Words were stuck in her throat, her magic swirling warm with the privilege of such a moment. "I would like that very much," she said.

Turning around, Arabessa faced her mirror once more, her glowing white form radiating as Dolion raised the horned disguise. He gently lowered it over Arabessa's head. Her pulse thumped wildly, breaths quickening as she watched a father crown his daughter king.

The heavy touch of the mask was a comfort rather than oppressive, a protection. Her magic swirled with anticipation in her veins as she met Dolion's gaze in the glass, pride clear in his features.

"You are magnificent," he said, resting a supportive hand on her shoulder.

"As you have raised us all to be," replied Arabessa, her smile exposed at the bottom of her mask.

Dolion grinned back.

"They are waiting for you, my king," said an attendant from the threshold of the room.

Taking a deep breath in, Arabessa nodded, leaving her father and sister to make her way to the private entryway of the throne room.

Two figures stood waiting at the threshold. With her approach, Achak and Zimri looked up, but it was Zimri's gaze Arabessa clung to. His hazel eyes beneath his eye mask sparked with his adoration and a glint of desire as he swept the length of her.

"My king." He bowed low.

Here was another view Arabessa could never get used to, get enough of: Zimri's prostrating reverence. It brought forth other memories of him kneeling before her, revering her, worshipping her. Hot liquid pooled low as she thought of their union later tonight.

Zimri's mouth twisted lasciviously as he returned to his full height, no doubt sensing the direction of her emotions. *Soon, my love,* his expression seemed to say.

"Are you ready?" asked Achak, who was presenting as the sister, short silver top matching her flowing skirts.

"Yes." Arabessa nodded as she made her way forward, but before she could follow Achak into the next room, Zimri snagged her to his side.

She let out a hitch of shocked breath as he angled her just so, careful of her opulent adornments as he claimed her mouth in a kiss.

Arabessa's magic purred, a content cat, along with the heat racing down her body. His strong hands gripped her waist through her thick robe.

"Collector," she breathed, pulling away but unable to hide her grin. "You dare kiss your king without first asking?"

"I will suffer any sentence for the offense," he admitted. "The sin is always well worth the punishment."

"Is it now?" She lifted a brow beneath her disguise. "Then I will endeavor to think up a creative one for you to atone with later tonight."

Zimri's gaze was dark longing before it slipped to something else, something devout. "You are historic," he said, a rumble of a whisper. "I am honored to serve you."

Arabessa's chest swelled at the words, her love for him soaring.

"And you both are making me uncomfortable," cut in Achak by the double doors. They apparently had returned to the hall, no doubt wondering what was keeping their king. "Are we ready *now?*" asked the sister, expression dubious.

Arabessa was thankful for her headdress, which hid her blush. Straightening her robe, she gave the twins a nod, watching as Zimri and Achak slipped through the double doors.

They allowed Arabessa to make her grand appearance alone.

She took a few steadying breaths in, a reminding chant filling her heart. *I am worthy; I am more than my music. I am a daughter, a sister, a companion, a lover, a friend, a warrior, a thief.*

A Thief King.

On that last thought she glided forward.

The air switched from cool to heated as she stepped in, the towering black throne room a heady sight that caused anticipation to dust across her skin.

Ours. Her braided magic sang through her blood.

Approaching her throne from the back, Arabessa walked past where Achak and Zimri stood at either side, the king's closest confidants in waiting.

She could feel both their gazes as she ascended the platform, but she kept her attention forward, on her goal: the spot along the walkway where her first audience would gather.

Arabessa lowered herself onto her throne. Upon contact the purple and silver threads of her magic spilled from her skin in a huff. *Our king,* said the multitude of voices through her mind. They filled her with their history, their stories, their wisdom. Arabessa became infinite; she became eternal.

Her body was made weightless, strong as the pulsing cloud that surrounded her. Her hands were made capable, healed for that moment she clutched the skulls on her armrests. Arabessa might no longer be able to produce her elegant music, but her gifts now had another door through which they could be set free: her throne.

With chin held high, the grip of her towering horned headdress secure, she pushed out more of her gifts.

It was a racing of chills down her spine, a cascading of violet and silver pooling from her form.

Disguise, she thought. *Cloud.*

Once cloaked in her gifts, she announced her order, her voice a layering of kings. "Send in the first who await."

Despite the smoke churning in front of her, Arabessa could clearly see the approaching forms who came to kneel at the edge of her dais. She could sense their desires, their fears, and their reverence.

As she held her attention to their bowing heads, her confidence soared, purpose settled. She was ruler to this kingdom, savior to her people, and historic myth who dwelled within a hidden caved world. But it was not her newly won responsibilities or freed gifts that filled her heart with contentment. As she looked forward into her future, it was knowing she had chosen this and that those she loved had chosen as well. Her father had reclaimed a life he had always intended for himself; her sisters, adventures they had battled to hold; and Zimri, a path that he had designed.

As if sensing her emotions tipping toward him, his supportive hand came to rest on her shoulder.

Beneath the layering of souls that made her Thief King, Arabessa's pulse kicked forward.

Zimri was here. He stood by her side.

They were living their lives beyond regret, had fought to make their own choices.

Arabessa chose to sit in her power.

AUTHOR'S NOTE

I come from a lineage of artists. My grandparents were artists, and my parents are artists. I was taught from a young age the importance of opening the mind, of watching and listening for inspiration, as it often can come from the most unlikely places. The Mousai Series is no exception. It started from two things: the echoing of a cane clicking down a long hallway as I sat in an office working late, and a painting my father did titled *Muses*, which was inspired by my sisters and me as well as an interpretation of Botticelli's *Primavera*. Much like this tangling of inspiring seeds that would later grow into an epic world, many of the names and places in my books have been influenced by names and places in our world. Each was chosen for a reason: the feeling it evokes or its meaning or both. In the Mousai Series, every character's and place's name has been crafted or chosen with great care. This is the celebration of a diverse world. Below is an appendix of sorts, providing a background to my naming etymology.

The Mousai: A neologism inspired by the plural word *muses*.

Bassette: A surname. Inspired by the word *bassett* from Old French, which means "someone of humble origins."

Dolion Bassette (Count of Raveet of the second house of Jabari and also the Thief King): The father of Arabessa, Niya, and Larkyra. Husband of Johanna. Thief King and a member of the Jabari Council. Dolion is a neologism derived from the Greek verb *dolioo*, meaning "to lure, to deceive." I chose this for the many masks he must wear and roles he must play, from Jabari to the Thief Kingdom, as well as his most important role: father.

Raveet is influenced by the name Ravneet, which has a few known origins, but I was inspired by the Indian Sanskrit origin, which means "morality like the sun."

Johanna Bassette: The wife of Dolion and mother of the Mousai. Gifted with very ancient and powerful magic. The name Johanna is connected to many cultures: German, Swedish, Danish, and Hebrew, to name a few. The original meanings of its root names are said to be "gift of God" and "gracious," much like Johanna's character.

Mousai + Bassette daughters: I purposefully sought to create names that had tempo and lyricism to them, to connect to their magical gifts of song, dance, and music.

Arabessa Bassette: The eldest sister. Arabessa is a neologism created from the name Bessa, cited in some places to be of Albanian origin, meaning "loyalty."

Niya Bassette: The middle sister. Inspired by the name Nia (Celtic and Swahili origins), meaning "purpose," "radiance," "shine," and "beauty."

Larkyra Bassette: The youngest sister. Larkyra is a neologism created from the base word *lark*, which is a songbird. It is also inspired by the verb *lark*, which means "to behave mischievously" and "to have fun."

Zimri D'Enieu: Zimri is a Hebrew name meaning "my praise" or "my music." D'Enieu is a neologism I created after being inspired by French surnames.

Achak: A Native American (Algonquin) name meaning "spirit." When I learned of this name and meaning, I instantly fell in love and knew it embodied everything Achak was, from their history to how their spirit has lived on in many forms in many realms.

Kattiva Volkov: Derived from the Italian word *cattiva*, which means "naughty" or "wicked," while Volkov is a Russian surname that means "wolf." Kattiva's name can be translated as "the wicked wolf"—very much attuned to her nature and a reason for the wolf tattoos on her hands.

Zhad Volkov: Created from the Russian word *zhadnyy*, meaning "greedy."

Alyona Volkov: Though Alyona isn't the best role model for a parent, I wanted there to be a bit of light in Kattiva's life in the shape of her mother. Alyona is a name of Russian descent and means "bright and shining light."

Charlotte: The Bassette sisters' lady's maid and loyal caregiver. I wanted to choose a *C* name for her, connecting her to my mother, Cynthia.

Aadilor: The realm where everything exists. Aadilor is a neologism inspired by the word *lore*, which means "a body of traditions and knowledge passed from person to person by word of mouth."

Obasi Sea: The only sea in Aadilor. The language of origin for Obasi is Igbo and is said to mean "in honor of the supreme god" or "in honor of God." I loved this meaning and how Obasi flows off the tongue like water. I saw this sea being named this in honor of the lost gods gifting their people such beauty to sail upon.

Jabari: Aadilor's capital city. The Swahili name Jabari, meaning "brave [one]," is derived from the Arabic word *jabbār*, meaning "ruler."

ACKNOWLEDGMENTS

*C*ue the tears. So here we are, at the end of our dear Bassette sisters' adventures. Arabessa, Niya, and Larkyra have changed my life. Grown my writing. Gathered new readers. I was in extremely different places in my life while writing each of their books. Falling in love and getting married for *Song of the Forever Rains*, stuck at home during a pandemic and pregnant for *Dance of a Burning Sea*, and a mother for the first time for *Symphony of a Deadly Throne*. I believe these experiences were serendipitously placed to allow me to channel what was necessary for each character and their story. While these years of cultivating these books have gone fast, the imprint they have had on my life are eternal. Thank you for traveling on this journey with me. Thank you for giving these sisters life beyond the pages in which they are bound. And thank you specifically to those named below for helping make this crazy dream of mine—having make-believe as a career choice—a reality.

To my husband, Christopher, and my son, thank you for being the light in my heart. To my family, my parents, and my three sisters, who inspired these books, you were my first safe space for me to explore my imagination. Thank you for tending its growth.

To my agent, Aimee Ashcraft at Brower Literary, and my editor, Lauren Plude at Montlake, thank you for taking a chance on Larkyra's story and seeing the greatness in sharing the rest of the sisters. You ladies are powerhouses, and I will always be in awe of your brilliance and support.

Thank you to everyone on the Montlake and Amazon Publishing teams who have helped this series soar and shine and dazzle. And a huge shout-out to the legend Micaela Alcaino for blessing these covers with your artistry.

To every book blogger, reviewer, and reader who has supported, promoted, and shared their excitement for this series: I humbly bow to you. Arabessa, Niya, and Larkyra are so very grateful for your love. Well, Niya might be more "of course they love us," but that comes as no surprise. You are the reason I work as hard as I do, why I obsess at crafting perfection. My dream is to forever weave tales we can both crawl into and play in.

TURN THE PAGE TO SEE A
PREVIEW OF E.J. MELLOW'S BOOK,
SONG OF THE FOREVER RAINS!

PROLOGUE

*T*he little girls played in a puddle of blood. They didn't realize it was blood, of course, nor did their nursemaid realize they had slipped from their rooms to find their way into the dungeons hidden under the palace. How would she? This part of the Thief Kingdom was chained and watched by so many doors and spells and beastly stone guardians that the Thief King himself would be hard pressed to enter unannounced. But such obstacles, when it came to curious children, were as easy to avoid as if they were maneuvering through a spider's web—one only needed to be small enough to fly straight through.

So the three girls found their way into the bowels of nightmares, none the wiser of the threats lurking in the walls, peeking through cracks with salivating, toothy grins. Or if they were aware, none felt threatened enough to turn and retreat.

"Here." Niya ran a bloody finger across her younger sister's pale face, setting loose a spiral design around the baby's plump cheeks. "Now you can speak."

Larkyra, recently turned three, giggled.

"*Speeeeak*," encouraged Niya. "Can you say that? *Speeeeaaak*."

"If she could have, she would have," said Arabessa, pressing her rouge palms across her ivory nightgown. She smiled at the new pattern along the bottom of her skirts. At seven, Arabessa was the oldest of the trio, her skin white porcelain against hair that spilled ink down her back.

"Oh, how pretty!" Niya held Larkyra's pudgy little hand as they walked closer to Arabessa. "Do me next."

Finding another ruby pool that seeped from under a locked steel door, Arabessa slapped her hands into the still liquid. The shadow of her reflection rippled away as she coated each finger.

"This color matches your hair," Arabessa said as she drew red flowers onto Niya's gown.

"Let's paint Lark with it so she can match me too."

So enthralled in their game, none of the girls noticed a particular creature who stood watching, unchained, in the shadows of the corridor. A creature with more deadly consequences at their fingertips than any of the beasts locked inside the cursed cells around them, yet the Thief King allowed them to roam free. Perhaps for moments such as these: to watch over those who could not yet watch out for themselves. Because though this being might have been created in darkness, their lives had always bridged one of light.

The little one is rather round, said the brother wordlessly to his sister. It was an easily accomplished feat, given that they were twins who shared one body, wrestling back and forth for space in one mind.

It is a baby. All babies are, replied the sister.

We were not.

That is because we were never a baby.

Well, if we had the chance to be, I can guarantee we would not have been round.

The twins had many names in many different places. But in Aadilor, they were known simply as Achak—ancient ones, the oldest beings this side of the Fade. Here they took on a single human form that shifted from brother to sister faster than crashing waves. Achak was taller than a normal mortal, with skin as black as the deepest part of the sea and violet eyes that spun with galaxies. Their body was beautiful, but like most pretty things in Aadilor, it often masked a fatal touch.

A delighted shriek brought Achak's attention back to the sisters.

The girls stood in the center of a hall in the dungeon, where the path split four ways, leading to endless more complicated corridors. It was a dark, damp place with barely a torch to light the passageways. Which was why a young, joyous laugh in such surroundings might have been more disconcerting than tortured screams.

"How clever, Ara." Niya bounced on her feet. "Lark looks much better painted in spots. What do you think?" She spoke to her younger sister, who sat at their feet, playing with an ash-white stick. "Do you like looking as fierce as a cheetah?"

Bang. Bang. Bang. Larkyra hit the device on the stone floor, her white-blonde locks twinkling in the torchlight as she cooed in pleasure at the sound.

"That's pretty," said Arabessa, finishing up the last circle beside Larkyra's ear. "Keep going, Lark. You can make the song of our painting ceremony."

As if in response to her sister's request, Larkyra continued smacking the stick, the rhythm echoing down the snaking corridors. Only Achak seemed to realize the instrument Larkyra held was in fact a rib bone.

These girls are most peculiar, thought the brother to his sister.

They are Johanna's daughters. Peculiar is only the beginning of what they are.

A wave of sadness entered Achak's chest as they thought of the girls' mother, their dearest friend. But when one grew to be as old as them, such emotions held space and time less and less, and soon the melancholy was dashed away, a slip of a grain through a sandglass.

I like them, thought the brother.

As do I, agreed the sister.

Should we stop their ruckus before they wake the rest of the dungeon and a guardian comes?

I fear it is too late for that.

A putrid stench rushed through the hall, adding a thicker layer to the prison's already-decaying aroma.

"That's disgusting." Arabessa waved her hand in front of her nose. "What dessert did you sneak after dinner, Niya?"

"That wasn't me." Niya tipped her chin back, offended. "I think Larkyra messed her diaper."

The two girls looked down at their smiling little sister, who was still smacking the rib on the floor, before glancing back at one another.

"The last canary to sing gets the broken wing!" they shouted in unison.

"I said it first," Niya was quick to announce. "You change her."

"We said it at the same time."

"If by 'at the same time' you mean I said it slightly quicker than—"

A roar vibrated down the cavern, knocking both sisters off-balance.

"What was that?" Niya turned in a circle, searching the multiple darkened halls.

"Whatever it was, it didn't sound happy." Arabessa crouched down to Larkyra, stilling her youngest sister's hand. "Quiet, Lark. I think playtime is over."

Larkyra turned wide blue eyes up to her sisters. Most children her age were already talking, but not since her scream at birth—which had changed all their lives—had she uttered more than a sound on a rare occasion. The girls had grown used to their younger sister's silence, knowing that though she might not yet talk, she understood a great deal.

Another growl, followed by the slopping thud of a dozen heavy footfalls, echoed toward them; a beast broke through the shadows of a passageway to their left.

As one, the sisters gasped.

The monster was so large that its matted fur scratched along the rocky walls as it approached, its head forced to duck down. The best comparison was to a giant dirt-matted canine, except it had as many eyes as a spider and far more legs than a dog.

Said thick, hairy legs swung forward, ending with octopus-like tentacles. The combination made its movements seem frenzied, a swinging of hungry limbs, and with every step, the feelers suctioned to the corridor's surface, cataloging the smells and flavors of what lay in its path. And if something *did* lie in the monster's path, it was quickly removed with a squeezing pop before being thrown into razor-sharp teeth and swallowed.

A *skylos lak* was merely one of the prison's many nefarious guardians, which bent knee to only one master—who was currently sitting on a throne in a different and faraway part of the palace.

Shall we intercede? asked the brother.

Achak now stood just a few paces from the girls, their body a cloud of smoke hovering between the stone wall and hallway.

Not yet, answered the sister.

The brother shifted uncomfortably, dominating their form for a moment. *But there may not be a later to which that "yet" will apply,* he pointed out.

There is always a later.

For us, perhaps, but for those like them—

Just then the beast seemed to sense the three little intruders, for it made a sound between a growl and a croon of delight as it picked up speed, its tentacles slapping forward in blurring motion.

"It's hideous," said Niya as Arabessa pulled Larkyra to her feet.

"Yes, and it also looks angry. Quick, take out the portal token."

"I don't think it will work down here," said Niya, her eyes glued to the approaching beast.

"Sticks." Arabessa turned in a semicircle. "This way!"

The sisters ran down a corridor, Achak following in the passing shadows as the occupants in the cells moaned and screamed, begging for their own quick deaths.

Though the children were racing for their lives, the *skylos lak* was a great many sizes larger and was quickly on their heels.

The sense of nearing fatality must have touched the girls, for a trail of orange began to seep from Niya's hurried form, giving a metallic sting to the air.

Magic, thought Achak.

"Ara!" screamed Niya, chancing a look behind them as a drop of something wet from the beast's tentacle hit her legs.

"I know! I know!" Arabessa pulled Larkyra forward. The child glanced back, getting a full view of what chased them, but did not cry or scream. She merely watched, with curious eyes, the monster that followed. "Sticks!" Arabessa cursed again, skidding to a halt before a large onyx wall—a dead end. "I thought this was the way we came."

"It must have changed." Niya swiveled. "What of our powers?"

"Yes, yes! Quickly!" shouted Arabessa as she began to bang on the walls, the sound echoing waves of purple magic that burst from her fists.

"I cannot get my flames to work!" growled Niya, flailing her hands in frantic circles as the beast tumbled closer.

There is still much they have to learn, thought the sister.

Indeed, replied the brother. *But they need to be alive for such lessons. Would you say it is "yet" yet?*

It is, said the sister.

But Achak had barely edged their feet forward when a high-pitched sound pierced the tunnel.

Larkyra had wiggled from behind her sisters to stand between them and the beast, sending a single world-shattering note from her mouth straight at the oncoming monster.

Both Niya and Arabessa crouched together, covering up their ears as honey-yellow tendrils of magic soared from Larkyra's tiny lips, smacking against the guardian.

The *skylos lak* howled in agony, trying to back away, its sides ripping against the grating walls.

She was a sight to behold, such a tiny thing: innocent in a white gown, standing in this dark hall, forcing back the hulking monster. But Larkyra did not look at all doubtful in her abilities as her note kept streaming from her lips, higher in pitch until even the powerful Achak had to plug their ears as well.

The sound was simple but held a storybook of meaning. It was laced with despair, loss, and anger. Its essence was a sharp energy, a powerfully uncontained one. Achak could hardly imagine the pain one might feel if the sound were directed solely at them.

But they didn't have to wonder for long, for in the next beat, the hall filled with sweat-dripping heat as the corridor shook and the beast roared its last; Larkyra's hot yellow magic was cooking it from the inside out. The *skylos lak* exploded with a sickening splash, coating the walls and floor in black blood and guts. A severed tentacle landed with a plop in front of Niya and Arabessa. The girls jumped back, glancing from the limb to their baby sister.

Larkyra held her tiny hands in fists at her sides, her breath coming heavy and fast, as she stared at the space where the *skylos lak* had once been.

"Larkyra?" Arabessa cautiously stood. "That was—"

"Incredible!" Niya hopped over the tentacle to hug her sister. "Oh, I just *knew* you had magic in you. I kept telling Ara you must, didn't I, Ara?"

"Are you hurt, Lark?" asked Arabessa, ignoring Niya.

"No," came a melodious reply.

Arabessa and Niya both blinked.

"Did you just speak?" Niya twisted Larkyra to face her.

"Yes," answered Larkyra.

"Oh!" Niya hugged her sister once more. "How wonderful!"

"Yes, wonderful . . . ," said Arabessa, watching a string of intestines fall from the wall to the floor. "Why don't we find our way home to celebrate?"

As they discussed which way might best lead them to their destination, Larkyra adding in one-word responses, to her sisters' continuous delight, they once again failed to take note of the slight shift in energy along the far wall, where Achak had spun themselves invisible.

Children should not be here. A deep voice laden with a thousand others filled the ancient ones' minds.

We know, my king.

Remove them. The Thief King's order held no room for mistakes, especially when blackness began to block out Achak's vision in a suffocating warning. The twins' soul shivered.

Yes, my king.

He was merely a grain of an apparition from where he still sat on his throne, but Achak could sense the king's energy shift to watch the three girls, holding longest on the youngest.

Her gift completes the trio, they offered.

The king's power churned in response. *Let us hope some good will come of it.*

Then, as silently and quickly as his presence had filled Achak's mind, he vanished, snapping the prison back into focus.

Achak took a deep breath.

Shall I? asked the brother.

Let me, said the sister, forcing herself to solidify their form as they finally stepped from the wall. Achak now stood barefoot in a deep-purple velvet gown, her head shaved, with delicate silver bracelets snaking up her arms.

"Who are you?" asked Niya, spotting Achak first.

"We are Achak, and we are here to take you home."

"'We'?" asked Arabessa.

"We," replied Achak.

The brother quickly shifted forward, expanding his sister's jewelry and dress to fit his muscular arms and revealing a thick beard.

All three girls blinked.

"Are you the same one or two different?" asked Arabessa after a moment.

"Both."

Arabessa paused, considering this, before adding, "And were you a prisoner here who escaped?"

"Would my answer have you trust us more?"

"No."

"Then don't ask useless questions."

"Oh, I like them," said Niya.

"Hush." Arabessa glared at her. "I'm trying to decide if they are worse than the thing that just chased us."

"Oh, my darlings, we are *much* worse."

Niya grinned. "Now I *really* like them."

Larkyra pulled her hand from Niya's.

"Careful," warned Arabessa as the child approached Achak before stopping by the brother's feet.

Larkyra seemed unconcerned by the possible threat; her blue eyes were transfixed by Achak's shimmering dress. "Pretty," she said as her tiny hand brushed against the rich material.

Achak raised an impressed brow. "You have good taste, little one."

"Mine?" Larkyra tugged on the fabric.

Achak surprised them all by laughing, the sound both deep and light. "If you choose wisely, my darling." Achak bent to pick up the child. "One day you could have many pretty things such as these."

"Could I as well?" Niya stepped forward. "I like pretty things."

"As do I," chimed Arabessa.

Achak glanced between the three girls, all so different, yet each uniquely the same. They were an odd trio, each two years apart but all with births on the same day. Achak began to wonder if such a quirk had something to do with their gifts. A thread that tied them together. For their powers promised greatness. But in devastation or salvation? The question remained.

They will be trouble, thought the sister to her brother.

Thank the lost gods for that, he silently replied.

"Most things in this world are obtainable, my sweets," said Achak, turning to place a hand against the onyx wall beside them, Larkyra perched on his hip. "And those that aren't . . . need only to be found through a door that will take you to another." As he spoke, a large glowing circle was cut against the black stone. It burned blindingly white before he lifted his hand, revealing the stretch of a new tunnel. A pinprick of light sat at the end. "Now, shall we walk you home?"

The girls nodded in unison, delighted by their new friend's tricks. With a suppressed grin, Achak showed them the way, traveling past the muffled moans of prisoners and leaving behind the memory of blood, guts, and terrible things. Instead they filled the sisters' heads with stories that sparkled with adventures and promised dark, delicious dreams. They told them a tale of their future, one that had begun the moment the youngest had opened her mouth to sing.